KYNSHIP

The Way of Thorn & Thunder

Book One

Daniel Heath Justice

Kegedonce Press
Cape Croker Reserve
R.R. 5 Wiarton, Ontario
Canada N0H 2T0

Kynship

First edition
Book design: Rock Paper Scissors Design & Print
Cover & inside images: Steve Sanderson
Original Sketches: Daniel Heath Justice

Published by Kegedonce Press
Cape Croker Reserve, R. R. 5 Wiarton, ON Canada N0H 2T0
Website: www.kegedonce.com

Editor: Kateri Akiwenzie-Damm

Library and Archives Canada Cataloguing in Publication

Justice, Daniel Heath, 1975-
     Kynship / Daniel Heath Justice.

Contents: v. 1. The way of thorn and thunder.
ISBN 0-9731396-6-8 (v. 1)
I. Title. II. Title: Kynship.
PS8619.U84K95 2005   C813'.6
C2005-903324-X

Kegedonce Press gratefully
acknowledges the support of
the Canada Council for the
Arts and the Ontario Arts Council

 The Canada Council for the Arts
Le Conseil des Arts du Canada

 ONTARIO ARTS COUNCIL
CONSEIL DES ARTS DE L'ONTARIO

Distributed by Lit-Distco
100 Armstrong Avenue
Georgetown, Ontario Canada L7G 5S4
Tel: 1.800.591.6250 Fax: 1.800.591.6251
Email: orders@litdistco.ca

Member of Cancopy

Printed in Canada – 100% recycled – Ecobook 55lb.

Acknowledgements

I was twelve years old when I first starting writing about Tarsa and Tobhi. We've all changed quite a bit since then, and though the journey from cramped scribbles in a green-tinted notebook to a published novel has been a long one, it's also been a distinctly joyful experience. Many people have traveled this path with us, and I'd like to acknowledge their contributions in bringing these characters and this story to life.

First, to my parents, Kathy and Jim Justice, I owe a deep and loving debt of gratitude. Mom is a dreamer, too, and has eagerly followed these Folk since the beginning, always offering both thoughtful critique and unstinting encouragement. She was the first person who shared my love of the Everland and its peoples, and she remains my most faithful fan and most challenging reader. Dad is a mountain pragmatist who prefers Westerns to fantasy novels, but he's always given me room to follow these dreams and fancies, never belittling or dismissing those interests of mine that were different from his own. Their generosity of spirit provided me with the spiritual and emotional sustenance to follow my dreams without hesitation. It's been a loving gift, and one for which I thank them with all my heart.

A number of people read the book, and their responses helped me to better understand the characters, their motivations, and their relationships. Many thanks go to Lydia Allain, Colin Kennedy Donovan, and Qwo-Li Driskill for their thoughtful comments on the early manuscript. Sky Youngblood provided pages of detailed revision suggestions that tightened the prose, made sense of awkward plot lines, and gave further dimension to the characters. Matthew Peros drew a wonderful early map of the Reach and Everland that enabled me to better conceptualize the geography of both lands.

Kateri Akiwenzie-Damm and Renee Abram of Kegedonce Press have been energetic advocates of this book from the beginning. Their vision for the book has taken mine far beyond anything I could have imagined, and I constantly count myself very blessed by their dedication to the project. It's been both a privilege and a delight to be part of the Kegedonce family and to work with such talented professionals. Wado!

The remarkable Sophie Mayer–poet, scholar, editor, and Buffyverse aficionado extraordinaire–deserves a particular note of appreciation for her insight as a reader, her fabulous proofreading skills, and her friendship. She's read and commented on more drafts of this book than almost everyone, and each time she's helped me to find the truth behind the characters and their story.

Many people have contributed to the realization of this dream, but none so much as Jeremy Patrick. It's no exaggeration to say that this book wouldn't exist without his support. He's read every page of every draft multiple times with great care and enthusiasm. He's endured untold hours of my monologues about the minutiae of the tale–from characters and plot points to background information, textual philosophies, and publishing issues–and always without complaint. Above all, his firm belief in the worth of this project and my storytelling has given me the strength to push through all the struggles and frustrations of the writer's craft to bring this world to life. For all these things, and for his unyielding friendship, I am grateful beyond measure.

DEDICATION

To Jeremy, for believing.

CYCLE ONE
Aspenglow

I want to tell a story.

This story has many beginnings, like the great Wildwater that runs in a roaring rush through the narrow canyons and high peaks of the old Everland, its voice loud with the knowing ways of uncountable years. Some of these beginnings are swift and wild, with unseen dangers, pockets and shadows, while others are slow and gentle, a lover's tender touch over the land, giving a spirit some time to ponder the deep, restless ways of the water. It's sometimes hard to tell which of these beginnings give it life. Maybe it isn't one way at all. Maybe it's all of them, each giving a true and necessary part to the whole.

The memory of the world is short, and death rides hard in the forgetting, so I hold these teachings and share them, mindful that only the stories weave our past into our future. The memories of those days are clear, though the pain sometimes gives shape to the joy. But I suppose that all the important stories are like that, if they're told truthfully. Everything that endures seems so much more precious when you've suffered thorn and thunder to keep it.

So I hold to these teachings, and I tell these stories, with the hope that they'll stay true to what we fought for, and what so many died for. This isn't my story alone, but this is my knowing of the story, and this is my understanding of its beginnings.

CHAPTER 1
Stone and Spear

Wears-Stones-For-Skin stalked with an easy grace through the canyon toward Red Cedar Town. His was the steady walk of one to whom fear was barely the itch of a memory. He was in no hurry; time was his own. Only the rumbling in his stomach, like two river-rocks grinding against each other, gave any indication of his purpose, for he hungered this day as he always hungered. He knew that he would feed well at his destination, even if the Kyn fled at his approach. He would sniff out all their hiding places, from the forest canopy to the root-tangled caves; his untiring pace was more dependable than their panic. They would run, they would tire, and then they would die.

He stopped and looked with some satisfaction at the stinking elk skin he pulled along behind him, piled high with rotting Kyn bodies in a fly-swarmed mass. He bent and tore a large bite from a leg severed roughly at the hip, the bone gleaming in the leaf-shadowed sunlight. A thick stream of blood and saliva slid down his cobbled chin, but he ignored it. His thoughts wandered elsewhere. Old meat was tasty, but it was empty of spirit; he much preferred his food warm and screaming.

Three towns were behind him—Nine Oaks, Downbriar, and High Marching—and perhaps two dozen more lay ahead in the deep clefts and wooded valleys of this end of the Kraagen Mountains. Wears-Stones-For-Skin had fed well in the weeks since he fled his own rocky ridge up north. While Kyn were not his favourite meat—he particularly enjoyed the rare and savory deep-rock Gvaergs, as their struggles were most desperate and delicious—he could hardly remember a time when he was so well fed. Of course, the Kyn had fought back valiantly with all manner of weapons: stone and copper blades, stout wood and bright fire, even pitfalls and more ingenious traps. But he was a Feaster, one of the Eaters of old, and his thick gray skin was dense with thousands of jagged stones that protected him from most wounds. Those wisdom-keepers who had once challenged him and his kind were rare these days, driven from these lowlands by their own people, and their teachings now lay hidden in dark, secret places, leaving his ravenous path clear.

His chewing slowed slightly. No, it wasn't just those wise ones of the elder times who could have driven him away. Now there were others– bright-eyed, hairy creatures with sharp iron and a hunger almost as great as his own, and it was their unyielding persistence that had sent him fleeing from his beloved high-mountain cave to these ancient wooded valleys in the southlands. Those pain-bringers made him an exile, and he hated them even more than he hated the blazing light of the sister suns, now mercifully shrouded by the thickly-crowded pines lining the canyon.

He pulled a resistant tendon from his teeth and tossed it into the ferny undergrowth, and his pebbled brows narrowed in memory of his desperate escape. There were some who could hurt him. Their cruel shining weapons burned through stony flesh, and the wounds festered and ached for days. But there was no smell of Humans in these valleys. Those creatures were far away, and he was safe. Nothing worried him here.

Wears-Stones-For-Skin grunted and moved forward again, carelessly dragging the skin behind. His path led up a steep slope, along a dry riverbed that cut a deep gorge through the mountain. The pathway was littered with river stones and larger rocks, but there was a manageable trail to follow.

As he shifted his massive frame between two smooth boulders, he lifted his nose to smell the air. A broad grin split his knobby gray head. His fat lips parted to reveal dozens of broken brown teeth, and he inhaled again, deeper this time: he-Kyn waited for him on the walls of the canyon above. Wears-Stones-For-Skin slowly swung his head back and forth, catching the different scents, each lingering for a moment on his tongue as he counted the distinctive odors of eleven warriors with freshly-uprooted stones ready to toss down; he tasted the soil's sharp tang on the air, mingled with the softer sweetness of fear. His smile grew larger. The feeding was always better when he could play a bit.

Pretending to be unaware of their presence, Wears-Stones-For-Skin moved forward again, his heart beating faster in anticipation. The canyon narrowed. Despite his massive bulk—twenty feet high, and at least half that wide—he passed smoothly through the gap, walking with the ease of a two-legged panther, the slow certainty of a patient hunter. The smells of the he-Kyn were stronger now, and Wears-Stones-For-Skin could barely conceal the deep chuckle that rattled in his belly as he continued up the slope to a level path ahead.

The Feaster sniffed at the air for a moment and nodded with satisfaction. The he-Kyn were at the upper rim of the gorge, only about fifty strides ahead. He would let them throw down their rocks for a while; he might even pretend to be crippled by their attack. He liked games, and this was one of his favourites. When these proud warriors were sure of their success and curious about their 'wounded' quarry, he would stop playing and begin the feast.

As he rounded another large boulder in the path, Wears-Stones-For-Skin stopped suddenly. His watery yellow eyes narrowed. Not far ahead, a lone she-Kyn stood in the path to block his way. She was small but solid, not much taller than five feet, but there were powerful muscles under the green flesh, and she promised to fight with far more enthusiasm than was demonstrated by the spindly oldsters and squalling fat babies of the former towns. Her pupilless turquoise eyes were hard with cold anger.

As odd as it was for him to see a Redthorn she-warrior among the fighters, Wears-Stones-For-Skin was more intrigued than worried. Though the Redthorns were skilled opponents, they were rare—the Feaster had seen none of their kind in the earlier towns he'd raided, and very few in the ages before that. They, like the wisdom-bearing Wielders, belonged more to memory than to the living age. Like most Kyn, this Redthorn was solid, her body's curves round and full, her arms and legs tightly-muscled but not bulky. She held only one weapon in her three-fingered hands: a long, black-bladed spear. It was an inconsequential defense.

The Feaster let his mocking laughter fly free, and the harsh sound shook the canyon walls. Though the solitary she-Kyn stood firm, Wears-Stones-For-Skin could feel the fear roll off of the he-Kyn on the canyon wall. It was as it should be. He was an elemental power who had existed since the elder times–he'd always fed on the Folk of the Everland, and they would continue to amuse and nourish him well in the limitless ages to come. He relished their fear. These quivering creatures were little more than gristle and bone; they would soon come to understand how inconsequential they truly were. With a gleeful roar, he loped forward in slavering anticipation.

The she-Kyn stood pale but unwavering, her spear held ready. Her stance was firm, even as the wave of corpse stench boiled over her, even as the massive monster rushed on, his jagged claws clenching in anticipation. She stood in his path, waiting.

Wears-Stones-For-Skin opened his mouth to bellow again in murderous triumph, but he suddenly slid to a stop, sending a spray of gravel flying. Something was wrong. It wasn't the Redthorn's determined stance that unnerved him. It was something else that fluttered moth-like around his thoughts, elusive but vital.

Then he knew, and his blood became ice: he'd never smelled her.

He smelled the fear and anticipation of the he-Kyn above, perceived each individual's salty tang as clearly as he could sense his own gnarled gray hand before him. He smelled the stones at his feet, the chickadees and ravens nesting in the thick, scrubby pines, the deer and squirrels and bobcats in the forest undergrowth. He even smelled the Kyn in the town beyond and those he'd left dead, wounded, and grieving in the ravaged towns, but he couldn't smell *her*.

Now he knew why, and for the first time since leaving his dank cave, he was frightened. He knew terror here, and the freezing sensation rolled off his body like river water.

Without another glance at the she-Kyn, Wears-Stones-For-Skin swung around to flee back down the gorge, but he recoiled in disbelief as six other she-Kyn closed the gap he'd just walked through. Two wore Redthorn leggings and loincloths, with wooden breastplates and copper bracers. The other four wore simple woven skirts, blouses, and short boots. And all were in their moon-time, like the solitary figure who now stood at his back. Unlike the four town matrons who also walked toward the cringing Feaster, the Redthorn warriors were fully trained in blood and battle. But this cyclical power made *all* the she-Kyn doubly powerful. Wears-Stones-For-Skin's ancient might, the bindings that kept his spirit whole, were scattered on the wind by their strength. He was death's shadow–they burned with life's fire.

It was all they needed to unmake him.

He stumbled backward. As deadly and strong as this ancient predator had been during his ageless life, the she-Kyn were stronger still. Their blood-time was power beyond bearing for a creature of death, and he was more terrified now than he'd ever been, even when the iron blades and thundering fire-sticks of Men bit through his stony flesh. He moved to flee, but the strength dropped from his legs like a falling tree, and he crashed against the dry riverbed with the squeals of a suckling cub. The seven she-Kyn moved forward. The lone warrior stopped near the Feaster, spear held firmly in her hands.

Unable to bear the torment of their presence, Wears-Stones-For-Skin thrashed onto his back, vomiting a rolling black plume of slime into the air. Stones burned and cracked where the inky fluid struck earth. The creature writhed and screamed, and the six other she-Kyn stopped beyond his reach.

Then, rocks fell from above. The he-Kyn had moved up from their earlier position; they were far better prepared than the ancient one had thought. Boulders and smaller stones, some no bigger than a Kyn's fist, others larger than the Feaster's head, clattered down the walls of the cleft, each smashing into the invader's body with furious precision. Wears-

Stones-For-Skin screamed louder, the noise growing to a wordless howl as bones shattered beneath cracking gray skin, as his weakened body snapped and sagged like a stick-pierced waterskin. He was helpless. He'd never known such pain in his life, or such fear.

As quickly as the assault had begun, the rocks stopped falling, and all was quiet except for the rasping groans of the creature on the canyon floor. The spear-wielding Redthorn moved toward him again. Wears-Stones-For-Skin lay on his back, his split and battered face pointed toward the pine-rimmed sky. One milky yellow eye watched her movements with wild terror; the other lay crushed in its socket.

She stood above the once-terrible Feaster, her face impassive as she looked at him. Her presence alone filled him with ripping agony, but he couldn't escape. He could only twitch helplessly before this small, green-skinned creature, his throbbing heart a death-drum in his chest.

Hope was his only comfort now. *If only she would go away. If they would all leave me, I could heal—I could survive. Maybe they think me already dead.*

He was wrong. As though sensing his desperate thoughts, the she-Kyn lifted her weapon, and Wears-Stones-For-Skin realized in sudden horror that the spear's shaft was of wyrwood, blood-bane to the Eaters and their kind. Like spring lightning from the Upper Place, the obsidian blade flashed in the sunlight and drove down into the Feaster's chest, past the fragments of his rock-lined flesh, deeper through soft, creamy tissues into his bursting heart. The she-Kyn plunged the spear into the creature with such force that the weapon shattered in two. The other warriors rushed forward and rammed long wyrwood spikes into his belly and throat, pinning him to the riverbed, sending his burning blood spattering into the air.

Wears-Stones-For-Skin screamed again, this time with a torment so great that the ground trembled. The Kyn fell to their knees and covered their oak-leaf ears in pain. Not even the bindings on their sensory stalks could muffle the creature's death agonies, and a few of them collapsed from the sudden shock. The sound rang through the rocky canyon, ripping through the air, driving birds and beasts from their rest, sending younglings in Red Cedar Town wailing to their mothers and aunties. The sound shredded the gorge and travelled back again, a twisting whirlwind that rose louder and louder, drowning out all thought, all feeling but pain.

Then the screams ended, and the world was quiet again.

Wears-Stones-For-Skin lay unmoving in a steaming pool of his own blood. Faces pale and drawn, the she-Kyn looked at one another and back to the creature's body. Their attention moved upward as a trill of victory erupted from the he-Kyn warriors on the gorge's rim, who scrambled hurriedly down to the riverbed.

The spear-bearer felt her knees buckle, and she sagged, shaking, to the earth. Her heart throbbed wildly and her eyes were bright with tears of relief and delayed fear. "We did it," she whispered as Oda'hea, the eldest she-Kyn warrior of the group, knelt down beside her.

"Yes, young 'thorn," Oda'hea smiled. "Red Cedar Town is safe. We'll send a runner to tell the others, and then we'll burn this murderous filth."

The younger Redthorn stood shakily and looked at the body. "Where did he come from?"

One of the unarmed she-Kyn matrons shook her head. "We've never had a Stoneskin down this far before. I've only ever heard of them in the upper mountains, where the snows linger through the seasons."

"Another bad sign. Well, whatever his reasons for being here may have been," Oda'hea growled as she drove more wyrwood spikes into the creature's broken flesh, "he won't be going back."

<hr/>

A runner sprinted through the forest toward Red Cedar Town, and the battle party, eighteen in all, gathered together to burn the body of the Stoneskin before his poisonous blood corrupted the path. The he-Kyn stood apart from the moon-time females and praised their bravery from a safe distance, and all talked with joy and relief about the event. The spear-bearer shared their mood, but the emotions of the experience still sent her head and heart pounding. Aside from a few raids against Human squatters, this was her first great excursion as a fully-trained Redthorn warrior. She'd faced a powerful foe and she still lived. She even had a new name now, one given to her by her fellow Redthorns: Tarsa'deshae–She-Breaks-the-Spear. It was the honoured name of a warrior, of the battle-strengthened she-Kyn who was no longer the youngling Namshéké.

Tarsa still held the broken spear shaft. She looked at it from time to time in amazement, and she often had to remind herself that she was still alive–it seemed somehow unreal, as though she stood halfway between the waking world and a dream. But she stood tall beside the other she-Kyn, her body sore with tension and training, her heart only now slowing from the surge of excitement and fear. Her thick gold-brown hair, the colour of old honey, was swept away from her forehead and oak-leaf ears by a plain copper headband, and it was woven into a single tight braid. Her serpentine sensory stalks, two on each temple, were now unwrapped and moved gently in the open air, free from the bindings that protected them from harm and dulled their sensitivity to the emotions and pain of battle. Fresh honour marks scored her cheeks, joining the other simple blue tattoos that tracked the green skin of her face, arms, and legs. The blouse, leggings, supple boots and breechcloth she wore had been chosen for comfort, not protection, for there was no armour in Red Cedar Town that could have withstood the fury of the Stoneskin's claws.

Tarsa's stomach clenched at the thought, but her rising nervousness was broken as the zhe-Kyn, pox-scarred Fa'alik, stepped toward the Stoneskin's body with a burning cedar branch. The zhe-Kyn straddled the male and female worlds in all things, garbed in blouse and skirt, head tattooed and shaven but for a braided topknot, moving between the blood of war and the blood of the moon without fear. Fa'alik drew the group together and, singing a song of healing and reconciliation, drove the flames into the monster's chest.

The Stoneskin's blood caught fire instantly, and within moments the body was ablaze, the sweet scent of cedar wafting through the air, the smoke cleansing their thoughts of death and destruction while easing the creature's journey into the Spirit World. Each group went separately to a nearby creek to wash the blood from their bodies and purge the death-taint from their spirits with the help of bitter herbs, prayers, and cold water. When they were finished, Fa'alik gathered them together and shared stories from the time of the Ancestrals, when it was told that a Stoneskin, though brutal and bloodthirsty, was also one of the wise ones of long ago, and that with his death came great knowledge. But there were none here who knew what that knowledge would be, as none of them, even the eldest of the Redthorns, had ever challenged a Feaster and lived. Those who might have once been able to tell them no longer lived in Red Cedar Town, where the Redthorns and Fa'alik were the last followers of the old ways of the Deep Green.

Tarsa stood away from the burning body. She felt strangely distanced from the events around her. Her head still pounded, but it was like a deep beating drum, a rhythm that moved in cadence with her heart. The smoke swirled in time with the beat to envelop her, turning gray, sometimes fire-light-red, as it drifted into the star-strewn sky. And as she watched the Stoneskin's body crumble into gritty ash, she felt a voice singing to the drum inside her head and heart. It was the voice of the Stoneskin, but there was no rage, no pain or hunger. It was an ancient song that twisted into her blood, diving deep, calling down to sing into being the secrets that pulsed there. The drums beat faster, the voice rose higher, the flames filled her vision and pulled her into the burning rhythm.

Tarsa stumbled dizzily out of the circle. She couldn't breathe, couldn't think beyond the pounding surge that filled her consciousness. The world slipped away–the dark sky and red soil shifted places and spun in wild confusion. The earth was no longer beneath her feet–she barely felt her body pitch forward, towards the Stoneskin's smoking remains. She struck the ground with a cry, and a shroud of darkness fell across her mind.

CHAPTER 2
RED CEDAR TOWN

Like the warming months of spring, Unahi came slowly to the inner valleys of the ice-mantled mountains, and the old Wielder's arrival was as certain as that of the blossom-bearing season. She usually waited until the first leaves budded on the aspens before leaving the deep shadows of Thistlewood on her spring rounds, travelling to most of the towns and isolated settlements within a two-week walk of the cluttered but comfortable cabin that she had called home for many years. She had little rest until the aspen leaves turned a brilliant gold at the first bitter touch of winter. By that time, the gray-green Wielder would have assisted in a few dozen births, numerous marriages and love-bondings, the removal of a handful of minor curses and harmful medicine chants from meddling gossips and vindictive conjurors, the proper observation of a wide range of rituals and ceremonies to ensure good harvests and harmonious relationships with neighbouring towns and, sadly, in recent years, far too many funerals.

The old Wielder was bent and wrinkled like a wind-worn cypress, and though she walked with the strength of a warrior, her spirit carried a heavy burden. Only that morning she'd finished the lengthy rites of mourning and purification at Downbriar Town, which had been ravaged by a Stoneskin a few days before. Unahi's fourth day of isolation was over; the death-taint of the bodies would no longer follow her. She was relieved that the creature had been stopped before it reached Red Cedar Town, yet it grieved her that such an aged spirit was now lost to the world. It was unusual for those Feasters to leave their rocky homes in the high mountains. Many things were changing these days, and few for the better.

Unahi stopped to lean against her wyrwood staff, her callused fingers absently tapping the red-veined chunk of amber embedded in the smooth golden wood. She'd walked this trail many times in her youth, more years past than she cared to remember. She knew the placement of every bearded pine, each sheltered hollow, the brush-hidden game trails and the clear, cold creeks that tumbled down hidden pathways through the tangled mountains. It wasn't just the voices of the *wyr* that gave the Wielder this knowledge, although at this time of her life it was sometimes difficult to tell where that spirit-language ended and her own understandings began. Her memory was still strong, her flowing head-stalks still sensitive to the pulse of green life around her, her wyrweave boots still thin enough to let her feet feel the heartbeat of the soil. In other days, these things would have been enough to sweep the shadows from her mind.

Unahi breathed deeply, taking in the earthy spice of the pine and aspen slopes around her. There was even the slightest sweet hint of willow from the streambed below. But there was also pain in the air. It was nothing like the pain of Downbriar or High Marching Towns, which had a tangible source and a clear reason for their ache. The Kyn of those towns had already been sorely wounded by the latest wave of wasting fever that came with last year's snows. The cold months had cost them much that they had treasured, particularly their younglings and elders. Now, after the Stoneskin's bloody visit, only a handful of younglings remained, and two of them would never walk again. Unahi hadn't yet been to Nine Oaks, but she feared that its survivors would share similar stories.

No, the pain that Unahi felt now was something different. She could sense it all the way up the valley, a gnawing pain deep in the bones, scattering across the world like crows in a tempest. She couldn't fully identify the feeling yet, but she knew where it came from, and that was now her destination. The Kyn of Red Cedar Town were not as friendly to Wielders these days as they had once been. Her Branchfolk would be bound by kinship and still-strong traditions of hospitality to give her a pallet and a meal during her visit, but that would be the most she could expect. Besides, even though she would have sought the source of the pain on her own, curiosity and duty compelling her forward, she'd received a soft summons from someone in the town just a two nights before, a blue clay bead delivered deep in the night by a skittish bat who longed to be elsewhere. Blue was the colour of the north, a portent of despair and fear. She could hardly ignore that call.

The Wielder moved forward again, and, although her heart was heavy, she continued on with weathered determination. She would almost rather face the Stoneskin herself than what waited for her in Red Cedar Town.

Her sisters had long and unforgiving memories.

"Sit down, Unahi, but let's not pretend that you're welcome here," Ivida scowled at the Wielder as she handed out steaming wooden bowls of pumpkin soup. Unahi nodded silently as she accepted the bowl and leaned back against the wall, her staff beside her, a long-stemmed clay pipe jutting from her lips.

The five sisters sat on the floor together in a small, octagonal cabin, the four she-Kyn of the town eyeing their long-absent sister with wary hostility. Unahi was silent as she sipped the spiced soup and looked around. The cabin was well-built and insulated, a testament to the high status of the Cedar Branch-mothers. A fire-pit in the centre sent playful shadows skipping around the seated figures, oblivious to the tension that hung heavy in the air with the pine smoke. The walls were coated with a thick clay glaze and adorned with dull blue and gray images, generally meek sky and star scenes. Aside from these designs and the fire-pit, the rest of the cabin was sparse and bare, a far cry from her long-ago youngling days, when the Kyn of Red Cedar Town had celebrated the *wyr*-rich world around them with bright and complex tapestries of colour. Every dwelling, no matter how humble, would have been boldly painted, with ribbons, baskets, wyrweave banners, bits of bright rock, and chunks of river-worn driftwood in strange and pleasing shapes scattered everywhere. Even her own little cabin in Thistlewood, a worn assemblage of log, stone, and living pine that dozed comfortably against the base of a rocky outcropping, was warm and pleasing to the eyes. Her sisters' Branch-house was a symbol above all else, and not a welcoming one; it was far from being a home.

Vansaaya, the eldest of the sisters, placed her bowl beside her crossed legs and leaned forward. Her hair was silver like that of the Wielder, and it shimmered in the firelight. "Why are you here, Unahi? Red Cedar Town has long been Celestial."

The others exchanged smug smiles as the real business of their meeting began.

The Wielder followed Vansaaya's movements and spoke. "I haven't forgotten, and for twenty-six years I've avoided this valley as you demanded. In spite of my vow to Lan'delar, and even after Kiyda died, I stayed away from here, no matter how much my heart ached to share the burden of my family's grief. But something has happened; someone has called me here." She held out her hand to reveal the blue bead to her sisters, and locked her gaze with Vansaaya's own. "And I mean to find out why."

"Witchery!" Ivida hissed through clenched teeth. With Lan'delar long dead, Ivida was the youngest, and she enjoyed the freedom that role provided, even now that she was six times a grandmother and her black-green hair was streaking gray. "You don't belong here! Your ways will bring nothing but pain and suffering to us again, to the entire town. Look at yourself, Unahi. Your back is bent, your face worn by age and marred by those wicked symbols on your skin. You're a ragged ghost of what you could have been. And you'll determine conditions for us?" She snorted scornfully.

Unahi shook her head. "No, sister. As I told you those long years past, I have no intention of challenging your decision, no matter how wrong-headed or foolish it might be." Ivida's face darkened, but the Wielder continued, her eyes narrowing to hard slits as she spoke. "I'm not here to stay. I am here, however, to find out why I was called here to help. I was summoned for a reason."

The others looked to Vansaaya, whose expression remained mild and disinterested. Geth, the oldest aside from Unahi and Vansaaya, ladled more soup into her sisters' bowls, her left hand shaking, fingers knobby and curled from pain that had burned into her joints for years. Her eyes glanced quickly at the Wielder and scanned the others, as if in silent debate. All was silent except for the gentle slosh of the steaming pot. With the barest intake of breath, she mumbled, "No more, sisters...please. I sent for her."

The others turned on her. Sathi'in, a recent widow who generally preferred to follow Vansaaya's lead, spat, "Be silent! You'll only make it worse!"

Geth shook her head with weary resignation. "How? We can't help the sapling, and Luran knows we've tried. Not even the Shield knows what's wrong. Maybe Unahi can help. If we just stand back, if we don't try something, Tarsa might die.'

"Better that," Ivida said, her voice dripping with malice, "than be corrupted by a Wild One."

"Enough!" Vansaaya stood abruptly. Though older than Unahi, her body was straight and proud, unbent by the passing of the years. She turned toward Ivida. "Whatever else we may be, kith-killers is not among them. We do not cut healthy fruit from our Branch if we can avoid doing so. She is our niece, the only surviving child of our youngest sister. We are obliged to help her by whatever means are available." She cast a dark glance at Unahi. "No matter how distasteful those means might be."

The others stood up, although Geth wavered a bit as she tried to stand without putting pressure on her left arm. Vansaaya turned to her. "As you brought her here, she is your responsibility. Take her to the youngling." Her lips tightened. "We will speak about this later." She walked out the door without another glance at the Wielder, followed silently by the dutiful Ivida and Sathi'in.

Geth's eyes filled with tears and she rushed to embrace Unahi, who held her gently, careful not to jar her sister's curled hand. "I knew you'd come,"

Geth whispered as they walked together out of the Branch-house. "I knew you wouldn't forget your promise."

As she looked around at the site of her birth and of much of her life, Unahi noted that Red Cedar Town hadn't changed as much as she'd feared it might in the past twenty-six years. The cabins were much like her own, and they still stood scattered in roughly circular rows around the central clearing. They were short and widely round, like oversized mushroom caps, with mud-and-thatch or wood-tiled roofs, and solid stone chimneys rising from the centre of each structure to send plumes of smoke and shimmering sparks into the night sky. Warm light filtered through thick wyrweave curtains in the circular windows. Small, unfenced gardens surrounded each house, and rich reddish soil lay piled in mounds around wooden stakes driven deep into the ground. Two- and three-story drying houses stood on stilts throughout the town. Beneath them were the underground storehouses that preserved the dried corn, squash, beans, nuts, herbs, and other foodstuffs.

Beyond the central settlement, just outside the protective log palisade, were the community growing fields, which mirrored the home gardens but on a larger scale. The watch-pillars–tall, bare tree trunks with rough seats that stood at various locations throughout the fields to enable sharp-eyed scouts to see anyone approaching–could still be seen in the moonlight beyond the palisade. From time to time Unahi would see other Kyn walking past on errands of their own. It was dark, and the shadows obscured her tattoos, so that none seemed to know that a Wielder was in their midst. They smiled at Geth and tipped their chins pleasantly to Unahi as they continued on their way. She recognized some of the eldest among them, and homesickness washed over her.

But as she and her sister moved closer to the central ceremonial clearing, the changes from the years gradually grew more apparent, and nostalgia gave way to sad resignation. Even here Time held sway, the embracing circle giving way to the unyielding line. The houses, once adorned with beautiful carvings of plant- and beast-people, or of the hidden spirit creatures who shared the Everland along with the Kyn and their Folk kith, were now dull and lifeless. There were no guardian masks hanging on the doors, no shell or copper chimes hanging from the eaves, no double-woven splint baskets piled high with drying herbs dangling from the roof beams. She was shocked to see haunches of deer and various dead birds and fish strung up on tall poles leaned against the cabin walls. In earlier days, the soil had provided all the necessary food without one of their animal neighbours paying a blood price for the meal. Hunting was only practiced against creatures who threatened the towns and their fields, and even that action required the Kyn sensory stalks to be bound against the death-pains of the hunted.

Even the little gardens, so promising in the distance, were now revealed to be strictly separated from one another with ruthless precision. The sisters stopped at one for a moment. Unahi reached into the mound and closed her eyes, drawing on the *wyr* that permeated the soil. Unlike her own garden and those of other Greenwalking Kyn, the gardens of the Celestial Kyn were segregated—only one type of bean grew in this mound, unnourished by the rich possibilities of many different seeds sharing their *wyr* with one another. This food might provide health for the body, but it would never provide true nourishment for spirit, not like those foods that were planted together to help one another grow strong. A solitary seed was vulnerable and weak. A flash of fear went through her thoughts as she reflected on the reality of her own isolation, but it was only a passing worry. True, she lived alone, but she was part of a larger community that extended far beyond the little cabin in Thistlewood. It was an understanding of communal duty that her sisters would never be able to comprehend in their safe Branch-house at the top of the valley.

Unahi shook her head and stood up. She'd never expected to return to Red Cedar Town, and if she didn't look too closely, she could almost feel like she belonged here again with her sisters and Branch-kith. Any lingering hope of connection crumbled, however, when she turned toward the clearing.

She'd known it would happen when she left—they told her as much as she was driven down the valley that long-ago morning—but the physical reality of the change still shook the heartwood of her being. Tsijehu, the tall, lush cedar who once stood rooted so solidly in the centre of Red Cedar Town, his bristling branches bedecked with bright wyrweave ribbons and fragrant beeswax candle lanterns, was now gone. Even his roots were absent, torn up and burned away years before. Only the memory of that great tree remained, and even that was fading. There was no one here to mourn his passing. Now, instead of the green-headed uncle who had been old even when the Kyn had first built their cabins around his sheltering branches, there stood an arch of white stone, hard and cold in the moonlight. Geth looked around nervously but followed Unahi, who walked heavily to the arch for a closer look.

The arch stood nearly twenty feet high and stretched fifteen feet wide. The stones were polished to an unforgiving white shine, and each segment was joined to the others by thick bands of reddening iron, which the Wielder had felt at a distance. Iron was mortal poison to the Kyn and many other Folk, and yet here, in the heart of a Kyn town, were two dozen or more coils of the toxic metal as wide around as her fist. She turned to Geth, who placed her finger over her lips.

Unahi's eyes scanned the rest of the arch. Along its entire length, strange markings had been cut, all sharp angles and deep gouges, along with the requisite symbols of the stars, the sister suns, and the moon. The night sky was cold through the open arch. It was a Celestial shrine, raised here to remind everyone in Red Cedar Town that the Greenwalker ways had been crushed and forgotten. Zhaia, the Tree-Mother of the Kyn, was overthrown, and Luran, the Moon-Maiden, stood in her place, a cold, pale substitute more suited to the world of Men than the Everland. Those who disagreed, like Unahi, were given a simple choice: leave this place, or die.

For some, it had been no choice at all, and their bones could still be found in shallow graves scattered throughout the mountains. Though scarred in body and in dreams, Unahi was one of the lucky ones.

Geth tugged at the Wielder's shawl, leading her toward the tree-lined shadows to the north of the clearing. "You didn't need to look at that," she whispered.

"Of course I did," Unahi said in a normal tone, unwilling to keep her voice low. "I had to see what happened after I left. I just didn't expect it to be so... final." She kept her face fixed forward, hoping that the fluttering ache in her chest wouldn't force her back in search of old Tsijehu's ghost.

Geth was silent as they moved into the woods. They were surrounded once again by pines and aspens, immersed in a fragrant hush of heavy green wood. The trees teased the sisters' senses and drew them up the slope. But beneath the whispering welcome of the shaggy old forest, Unahi could feel an unease caressing her thoughts. Her sensory stalks grew tense in warning. She stopped and looked quizzically at her sister.

The younger she-Kyn lowered her eyes. "It's been this way since the troubles started. Everyone can feel it, even the Shield. They try to explain it away. But I didn't forget the old teachings, Unahi. I always remembered. I shared the stories with her all her life. That's why she became a Redthorn. That's why she faced down that creature. And that...that's why we brought her here." She pointed to a thin, nearly overgrown trail that disappeared up the slope into the deeper darkness of the trees, barely discernable in the moonlight.

"But what's–?" The Wielder stopped, understanding at last. The memories flooded back, and with them came a nearly blinding rage. She grabbed her sister's good arm and hissed, "What have you done?"

Geth stumbled away. "We didn't have any choice, Unahi," she whispered, her eyes filled with hurt. "She was mad with pain. Things were happening, awful things. One of the warriors who brought her back was almost torn apart by thorns that grew out of her skin, long and sharp like knives. He nearly died. Tarsa couldn't help herself–she didn't know what was happening. It was like she was witched. Every time someone came near to help, she'd unleash some new monstrosity. It was either this, or...." She went silent, but the meaning was clear. An Awakening was agonizing even in the best of circumstances, but the young she-Kyn–once a bright-eyed youngling named Namshéké, now called by her warrior's name of Tarsa'deshae–had Awakened alone and unguided. Tarsa was older than most who'd had the benefits of a Wielder to lead them safely through the storm. Given the lingering hostility of the Purging that had decimated the ranks of the Wielders not so many years past, Unahi was surprised that the young Redthorn warrior was given even this reprieve.

It was likely due to the very fact that Tarsa was a member of that honoured company that she still survived. Redthorns were the only traditionalist Kyn who still remained generally unmolested by the Celestials and their followers, more out of a need for the Redthorns' unrivalled skills in defense and warfare than from any sentimental attachment to kinship with Greenwalkers.

But even this knowledge wouldn't be enough to help Tarsa unless they reached her soon; the young warrior was strong, but only death would ease the pain without an experienced Wielder's guidance. Unahi pushed through the pine boughs, ignoring the bite of their needles on her skin and Geth's rasping breath as the latter tried to keep up. The aspen leaves whispered frantically at their passing. The evening chill disappeared as they moved through the underbrush, thin moonlight turning the slight path to deep-night silver. They had to hurry.

There were dangers in the Burning Mouth that no degree of Redthorn courage could overcome.

A Redthorn warrior stands strong.

Tarsa could feel the fire in her blood. Each muscle, each span of her flesh ached from within. She desperately wanted release, but there was none. If she could have detached her spirit from flesh, she would have seen herself curled into a corner of the pit, hair matted with blood, mud, and filth, skin bruised and torn. She would have seen that body thrash and become a creature possessed, then contract again into a tense, quivering ball. But she was trapped inside herself, and there was no escape, no freedom of detached observation.

And the pain. It was nearly beyond bearing.

A Redthorn warrior is a stranger to pain.

The Stoneskin's bloodsong rose up again. It pushed at the limits of her skin, drawing the *wyr* through her body, pushing her body to the dull edge of sanity and then, sensing the pulsing iron veins that stretched like spiderwebs across the walls and floor of the pit, fell back again. But each crest of the *wyr* reached higher than the next. There would soon be a flood, and her spirit would rush away forever, leaving the body to rot in the stinking darkness.

It hadn't always been this way. Once, not so long ago, when she was still Namshéké, she'd been powerfully alive, certain in her strength and courage. The memory of the night she'd passed the Redthorn blooding ceremony and joined the ranks of that honoured fellowship was etched deeper in her spirit than the Stoneskin's song could reach, and it was the calm centre to which she desperately clung. The Greatmoon had been bright and full, and the light from his scarred, smiling face painted the trees and mountains a shimmering silver-gray. After months of trials that tested her body's limits and her spirit's endurance, she'd come that night with Oda'hea and the others to the ceremonial grounds, where they painted her skin red and black, and shaved the sides of her head. When they'd finished, Fa'alik emerged from the whispering aspens and evergreens with a basket of long thorns and leaf-covered shells. Zhe sang an honour song as zhe etched her flesh with pigments of bright blue and dull black from the shells, until Namshéké's face, shoulders, arms, and thighs were slick with blood, paint, and sweat.

She'd known pain that night, but it had been fleeting, and she hadn't been alone–the Redthorns had been with her, and she'd understood that they'd each shared the same emotions, the same fears, the same exhilaration as Fa'alik smiled broadly, helped her stand, and presented her to the group as one of their own. It was the first time that she'd ever felt like she belonged somewhere. There her presence had been not just welcome but essential; her strength, courage, and cunning made the Redthorns more than they'd been before, and they recognized the qualities she brought to them. Their numbers were few and fading, but with such gifts as she possessed, they had a chance against a world that was increasingly turning against their long-guarded skills and wisdom. Every moment of that night–from the body marking, the songs and dances, and the feasts, to the tender love-making with Fa'alik that followed–was woven through her spirit like the graceful patterns on the zhe-Kyn's chanting sash, and every moment had been a reminder of all that was perfect and beautiful and balanced in the world. They'd all known who they were and where they belonged, and she was one of them–they were Redthorn Kyn, and they were born of these tree-covered mountains. That night had been warm, the Redthorns had rejoiced, and she'd been fully, vibrantly, alive.

But now Tarsa'deshae was dying, and she was utterly alone. The loneliness made the rising pain so much harder to resist. Not even facing the Stoneskin had been this frightening.

Yet, amazingly, something new now tugged at the burning tide in her body, and Tarsa responded instantly, every fibre of her agonized consciousness reaching out to any chance of hope. She didn't recognize the sensation, but it had a hint of familiarity, like a lingering taste on the tongue of something she'd once known and treasured. She drifted on the pain, no longer submerged within it, but lingering in the middle place between consciousness and oblivion. There was a voice, one she might recognize if she could calm the crashing of the waves around her. With what little strength remained to her, she pushed her thoughts forward, drawing her spirit up through the jagged slice of the bloodsong, back to the cold wetness of the pit, back to the heavy ache of her battered body.

"Tarsa, youngling, hurry!" It was Geth's voice, but it sounded strange–there was a rush to her words, an energy that Tarsa had never heard from this meek shadow of an aunt. The stench of her own waste swept over her when she tried to move her head. *How long have I been here?* she wondered thickly. Her temples and sensory stalks throbbed violently, and she slid back into the mud, her body convulsing with nausea and sudden shame.

Through the haze of her sickness, Tarsa heard another voice, and her heart raced wildly. She hadn't heard the voice in ages, and it was only through the thickest fog of memory that she could feel its ties to her spirit.

"Tarsa, listen to me." The voice was strong, firmly rooted in the green growing world. The Redthorn's pain diminished slightly as the bloodsong grew muted. She sobbed with relief, then with rising fear, for she could feel another wave boiling inside.

The voice continued. "You must listen to my words very carefully, Tarsa. We can't come down there–the iron is too strong. We've thrown a rope near you. All you have to do is wrap the loop around yourself, and we'll pull you up. You must be strong, and you must hurry."

The Redthorn warrior tried to speak, but her throat was raw from days and nights of frenzied screaming. Shaking her head, she pushed herself toward the rope, but the effort was too much. Her hands slipped in the mud, and she collapsed again with a groan.

"What are we going to do?" Geth wept.

Unahi moved to the edge of the pit but backed away, her face pale. It wasn't very deep, only about three times her height, and a stout wooden ladder rested beside the hole–it should have been easy. But the powerful natural iron that coursed through these stones was almost as toxic as forge-strengthened ore. "There's nothing I can do from here. The wild *wyr* is the only thing keeping her alive. If I try to go in there, I'll be almost as sick as she is."

"Interesting." A shape materialized out of the darkness behind them. Vansaaya. She walked toward her sisters with a small wrapped bundle in her hands. Looking impassively into the pit, she said, "There was a time, Unahi, that I would have welcomed that knowledge."

The Wielder's eyes never left the hole. "It shouldn't be a surprise. You were here when I was in her place."

"Yes. I was here." Vansaaya turned to Unahi and, for the first time in many years, the Wielder saw sorrow in her sister's eyes. "I remember your Awakening, Unahi, and your agony. I said then that I would have gladly taken your place. But you were the one who had been chosen. There was nothing I could do, nothing anyone here could do to help you. And after we sent for one of the few remaining Wielders to still your blood and draw you back from your pain, I knew that you were lost to us forever."

Vansaaya's face grew hard again. "For all these years, you have walked the Way of Deep Green, turning your eyes from the immortal heavens towards the dying wilds of this twice-cursed world. And when you were held in the Burning Mouth, finally given the choice to surrender to something greater than yourself, to join the Shields in readying the world for the Realignment, to turn from the darkness of our past and seek the possibilities of illumination, you chose to remain in the mud with the rest of your backward kind. You shamed our family, a blight of honour that I have spent my life working to erase. And now you are here again, drawn back from the wilderness, a proud and tattered old carrion bird still certain of your choice, still clinging to the world of the Ancestrals that is destined to perish." Her voice suddenly broke in aching frustration. "And yet you are the only hope that this youngling has."

She dropped the bundle at her sister's feet. Unahi bent and unwrapped the cloth, her hands struggling for a moment with the cord, to find inside a heavy stone necklace. It was a chunky, unwieldy thing, slate gray, with thin, interlocking chains of wood interspersed between the dull stones that seemed to absorb the moonlight.

Vansaaya answered her sister's unspoken question. "An iron-ward. Our Shield uses it when he trades with Humans, to avoid the possibility of deceit should they slip some of the metal into his presence. This will help you–both of you."

Unahi nodded. She slid the clinking stones over her head and let them rest heavily on her chest. Without hesitation, she and Geth maneuvered the wide-bottomed ladder to the pit's edge as Vansaaya stood to the side. After testing the ladder's stability, the Wielder descended swiftly into darkness.

Vansaaya and Geth stood waiting with ill-disguised impatience and listened for sounds in the pit. There was nothing. The air was heavy and still. Even the whispers of the aspens were silent. The only movement in the sky was a stream of clouds that slid noiselessly across the greater moon, Pearl-in-Darkness, and his two shattered brothers, who gleamed like silver dust among the stars.

Geth turned to speak to her elder sister, but Vansaaya held up her hand. A noise drifted up from the darkness of the Burning Mouth. They watched as Unahi pulled herself up the ladder and back over the edge of the pit, one end of the rope she'd tied around Tarsa firmly in hand. Vansaaya stepped up and grabbed the rope, tugging it hard around a stout aspen trunk for leverage, and she and the Wielder pulled steadily on the long fiber braid as Geth guided the rope with her good arm. A ragged tangle of dark, mud-caked hair soon appeared over the side of the pit, and Tarsa lay on the grass, her body heaving with sobs.

Eyes warm with worry, Geth moved toward her weeping niece. Unahi grabbed her sister's shoulder. "Let her be."

Vansaaya opened her mouth to protest, but Tarsa's body, now freed from the toxic effects of the iron-lined pit, began to thrash wildly. A violent wind rushed through the clearing. Dust and debris swept against the sisters, blinding them with its sudden ferocity. The Redthorn's back arched, her hands clawed desperately into the earth, and her eyes rolled back in agony. A low howl erupted from her throat.

"Get back!" Unahi gasped through the choking wind. Geth stepped away from her niece, but not quickly enough to avoid the thick green vines that burst from the soil and whipped around her legs. They curled and twisted, climbing higher with each of the convulsing warrior's screams.

A tendril wrapped around Geth's crippled arm. She screamed in pain and fell heavily to her knees. Dozens of vines burst upwards, slithering with impossible speed and determination, pulling her against the earth. Small, sharp thorns erupted along the edge of each tendril and tore into her flesh. Geth, too terrified to scream, simply gaped at the twisting shapes that roiled along the ground around her. She tried to turn, to look behind her, but there was no escape. The vines were everywhere. A dagger-like thorn, growing long and wickedly sharp before her eyes, slashed into the soft flesh of her cheek, sending a gleaming spray of blood into the moonlight. Geth covered her face with her right arm and finally found her voice. Her desperate screams echoed Tarsa's own.

And then, as quickly as it had arisen, the wind was gone. Geth heard the gentle rustle of leaves and pine boughs, and felt the burning tightness of the vines around her body begin to loosen. She opened her eyes, distracted for a moment by the dull amber glow that pulsed from Unahi's staff, which stood upright at the end of the clearing, its base driven deeply into the earth.

Unahi knelt over Tarsa. The old Wielder was covered in mud and fresh cuts. Her clenched left hand moved back and forth over the young warrior, while her other hand traced the woven threads of the ragged sash she wore around her waist. She muttered low and rhythmically, as she reached into a pocket of her dress and removed seven white beads. These she dropped on the ground in a circle around Tarsa's unconscious body. The beads quivered for a moment as they darkened, shifting from white to pink, red, purple, and finally black. Unahi waited only a few heartbeats before she gathered them up again and tossed them into the Burning Mouth.

Tarsa lay still, her chest rising and falling steadily in sleep. Geth stood, shaking and pale, while Vansaaya wiped blood away from a series of thin gashes on her legs and watched the last of the tendrils slide back into the ground. Nothing remained of the thorny plants but hundreds of small dark holes in the red soil.

Unahi pulled her shawl from her shoulders and draped it across Tarsa's sleeping form. She then removed the iron-ward and handed it back to Vansaaya. The elder sister nodded once, her eyes cold, and turned wordlessly back down the trail that led to Red Cedar Town. When she had passed into the shadows, the mountain slope seemed to find its balance again, and the aspens took up a whispering chorus on the rising breeze.

Geth, though hesitant at first, knelt beside her niece and softly brushed the matted hair away from Tarsa's face, tracing the recent tattoos that celebrated the young warrior's victory over the Stoneskin. "We won't see her again, will we?"

Unahi sighed and turned her gaze back toward Red Cedar Town. It was lost beyond the trees, but she could smell its familiar hearth-fires burning. The deep spice of pine was heavy in the air. She was a stranger here, or would be again in the morning. It was still spring in the mountains, and, though she hadn't noticed it before, she could now feel the coldness wrap around her old body. "We should bathe her, and gather some of her things for the journey. We'll leave before sunrise. There will be fewer questions that way. " Geth nodded, her fingers still softly caressing the Redthorn's hair.

Unahi draped a strong hand over her sister's shoulder. "I don't know if she'll be back, Geth; that's out of my knowing. But I swear that I'll look after her as best I can. I can promise that, at least." Geth reached up and grasped Unahi's hand, but she kept her soft gaze lingering on Tarsa's sleeping face, so gentle now in the moonlight. They remained by the young warrior's side in the cold darkness, watching over her sleep. It was a long goodbye.

CHAPTER 3

UPROOTED

An excerpt from Chapter 12 of the classic Reach-wide Journeyer's Gazetteer, written by the Learnèd Doctor Abrosian Dellarius of the People's Academy of Alchaemical and Mechanical Arts in Chalimor, titled "On the Matter of the Forever-land":

The fertile and untamed territory, known to its aboriginal inhabitants by the roughly translated "Forever-land," remains the last great enclave of lawlessness and chaos in the Reach. The goodly justice of the Reachwarden's authority does not extend into those dark forests and jagged mountains, wherein bandit, robber, thief, and all manner of outlaw find refuge among the feral remnants of the once-proud Unhuman tribes. Traders and explorers who have braved the interior of this "Forever-land" tell of savagery run rampant, of Human decency given way to Unhuman license and ignorance. Yet they tell, too, of great bounty, for there is a fierce beauty in these lands: woods that promise both timber of magnificent quality and great tame herds of deer not unlike those that once roamed the Allied Wilderlands; blue-cold rivers teeming with strange but succulent fishes; and skies darkened with the passage of bright-plumaged birds as appealing on the lady's cap as in the stew-pot. . . .

There can be no remaining doubt that there will be much virtue in bringing this "Forever-land" fully under the authority of the Assembly of Reach-States. Law, order, and civil society must always stand firmly against the corrosive chaos of barbarism. Provincial and territorial administrators have repeatedly called upon

the Reachwarden to cultivate this weed-choked garden, to girdle rank trees and fill miasmic marshes for the benefit of all Men of the Reach and their descendants, a call that is increasingly heard in the marbled halls of Chalimor. It is the destiny of all lands to be tamed by Men of virtue and strength, without fear of the difficulties of such an undertaking. The plowshares and mercantile virtues of Human civilization will endure long and bring credit to their cultivators. Not so the fragile trees and hunted beasts of the wilderness of the much-diminished Unhumans, whose wanderings are moving ever-swiftly toward sunset, where they will inhabit hearthside stories and memories of our great nation's heroic days of old.

<hr/>

Unahi and Tarsa passed their first day out of Red Cedar Town without speaking. The second morning dawned with a cold drizzle, a steady drenching that drained the walking warmth from their bodies and pulled their spirits mudward. Even the thickly-clustered pines and firs seemed bedraggled and gloomy. Still weak from her imprisonment, Tarsa leaned on Unahi's staff and silently mourned her sudden banishment, while the elder Wielder's thoughts often lingered on a past she'd thought safely buried.

They returned back down the stream-fed valley that the elder Kyn had travelled just two days before, a path largely ignored by most Folk who sought Red Cedar Town. Only root-gatherers and hunters spent much time on this trail, and both she-Kyn were relieved that the rain kept questioning eyes away. Tarsa noticed that a raging downpour slammed down on them at the few times they encountered another traveller–forcing everyone to hurry forward, heads bowed, with nothing more than polite chin-nods of acknowledgement–then faded away to a lighter misty patter once the strangers had passed. Immediately afterward, Unahi would untie the colourful sash from around her waist and sprinkle a few pinches of cedar shavings over it before wrapping it back again, her mouth moving with a noiseless prayer, and continue on as though nothing was amiss. Tarsa eyed the bent old she-Kyn warily but said nothing.

Her misery was complete. Fewer than five days past, she'd been the most honoured warrior in Red Cedar Town, and her new name reflected that status. Then it all changed, and the same warriors who'd stood by her side over the Stoneskin's body had carried her to the Burning Mouth, terror in their eyes, as the wild *wyr* drove her toward madness. No one knew what had happened to her, but there was nothing they could do beyond abandoning her in this ghostly hole at the margins of the town. There was no expectation of a healing; she'd been left to die. If not for Unahi...

Tarsa swallowed the lump that rose up in her throat. It was too much to think about now. She was an exile, driven from her home, sent into the wild forest far from Red Cedar Town with a Wielder she'd only heard about in furtive whispers and scornful asides. She'd been raised with Geth's stories of the Old Ways, even experienced them as a youngling, and she'd always treated them with respect, but for most of her family these philosophies were nothing more than unwanted history. Her other aunts were firm Celestials, and their dictates gave the greater form and substance to her world. Even when she'd joined the traditionalist Redthorns, she'd found it hard to reconcile the two ways.

Now that uneasy balance was gone, hidden in the mountains behind her, and it was Unahi, ragged and aloof, who walked beside her.

Midday came but brought no warmth, just a brief rest under the wide-spreading boughs of a giant spruce and a meal of dried apples and fried dough that Geth had given them for their journey. Unahi passed a small water-skin to her niece, who accepted it wordlessly before walking to the trailside stream to refill it. They gathered their goods together again, Unahi carrying much of Tarsa's share for a while, and continued on in silence.

The rain lasted into the late afternoon of their second day of travel, and by that time they'd emerged from the sharp alpine valley into the heavy scrub oak and willow of the higher hill country. Red Cedar Town was the first settlement of twenty or so that crept up the sheer canyons into the soaring heights of the Kraagen Mountains. The she-Kyn were still in the embrace of the mountains–the peaks rose over the land for days to the east and west, and for the full length of the Everland to the north and south–but the tall hills they were approaching lost their snowy crowns as the summer grew near, whereas the higher summits of the Kraagens never knew the warmth of the sun. Here, tall jumbles of red sandstone stood scattered across the landscape, some reaching up hundreds of feet in strange flowing shapes, looping into bridged arches or stony spears jutting skyward. The valley beneath the hills was blanketed with a spread of thick green growth, a bewildering mix of scrubby oaks and pines on the dry sandstone ridges and dense willows in the boggy stretches.

Tarsa had never been so far down the western valley; most of her travels were to the east, where trade and conflict were more common. This was a lovely sight, but she was too miserable in flesh and spirit to appreciate the landscape. Unahi rested for a while, allowing the younger she-Kyn to stretch out her tired muscles and to breathe in the refreshing air, and motioned to a particularly large outcropping to the northwest. "We'll stay there tonight. We'll find some dry overhangs at the top of the ridge where we can rest without more drenching. These old bones need a fire, and I'm sure your young ones do, too."

The Redthorn nodded. Her head had been pounding since early afternoon, and every muscle in her body seemed to have twisted itself into knots during the night. Her moon-time had passed, but she hurt too much everywhere else to be pleased at the loss of those pains. Until now, she'd pushed most thoughts of Red Cedar Town away, concentrating instead on keeping one foot following the other down the seemingly endless valley trail. A few times, she'd felt the terrifying tension in her blood begin again, but Unahi, sensing her rising panic, had rested a callused hand on her back each time the heat rose, and the tightness faded back to the endless dull throb in her muscles.

The trail narrowed as they drew closer to the thick scrub. They moved down the slope toward the marshy bottoms, and all they could see were slender gray-gold willows crowded in upon one another, a tangle of leaf and bough so dense that little of the fading light could be seen through their shaggy branches. The violet hush of twilight would soon fall, but there was little chance that they would see it in the unending drizzle. They hadn't seen the sister suns all day, and it was hardly likely they would see the Greatmoon or the farther spheres and stars tonight.

Unahi stopped at a small tussock at the base of a massive old willow and motioned for Tarsa to kneel in the wet grass beside her. "The Awakening shocks the body out of its understanding of itself, and there's much left to be done for a healing. You've survived much of the worst of it already. It's past time for survival. Now you've got to understand what your survival means." Unahi smiled. "You've been given a powerful gift, niece."

Tarsa flushed. "It's no gift to me," she corrected. "It's a curse. I don't want it."

"Want it or not, it's yours, and you have to decide what to do with it. You can either let it destroy you, or you can learn to understand it."

"I'm not interested in witchery."

The old Wielder's eyes narrowed. "You're a Wielder now, Tarsa, and it ill-serves a Wielder to be a fool." Her voice hardened. "There's no going back to who and what you were before."

Tarsa knelt in pale and stony silence and stared off into the distance. Unahi lowered her palms to the damp ground, and a heavy hush descended on the night. The Redthorn's heart began pounding hard, a deep rhythm that seemed to echo in the circle of willow branches that rose up and reached towards them. She felt a sudden surge of fear, but Unahi reached out to calm her. Tarsa stiffened at the touch, but she didn't move away.

Heartbeat. The trees moved with her heart's rhythm—it was

mesmerizing. All of the world seemed to flow toward them, each movement drifting on the throbbing drum in her chest. In spite of her fear, Tarsa felt herself slide back into the bloodsong, down into the steady scarlet rush beneath the skin, deeper than the terror that clung, sharp and clear, to the back of her thoughts. She heard the Shield of Red Cedar Town rail against the Deep Green, but his voice was thin and weak. His words were like mist, more fear than truth. With every liquid beat, with every slow and steady rumble of that inner drum, she felt the green world open up to her again, heard the Stoneskin's song draw the rhythm from her blood. She drifted down into the warmth of her belly, then to her knees and two-toed feet, into the very earth itself, no longer cold, wet, and ragged with pain and hunger, no longer terrified of the steady song that flowed within, nor ashamed of that fear.

Opening her eyes, she saw the curtain between her world and the Spirit World pull away. Her eyes grew wide, body rooted in the soil, sensory stalks tense in the moist air, and she watched through a green-blue haze as the fog in her thoughts dissolved to reveal the pale, curious faces of the willow-spirits in the tree. Their gaze was ageless and deep, utterly alien to her mind but warmly familiar through the understanding of the *wyr* that coursed through her. They reached towards her, their spirit-fingers stretching like long and slender willow branches.

It was too much. Tarsa cried out and cupped her face in her hands, silencing the bloodsong. When she looked up again, the curtain between worlds had dropped across her perception, and the spirits were gone; the tree's quivering branches were the only evidence that they'd even been there. Her awareness of the chill drizzle returned slowly. For a moment her body trembled, but Unahi stood and pulled the Redthorn firmly to her feet.

"Come now. We'd better get these clothes to drying by a fire. We're in for quite a rain tonight, I think." Leaning alternately on the old Wielder and the wyrwood staff, Tarsa followed Unahi's guidance as they moved into the dense twilight of the hill country willows.

They found a sizeable supply of dry firewood in the back corner of the overhang, which the elder Wielder stacked in the firepit, while Tarsa spread their wet clothes on the ground. The rocks were streaked with soot from unknown numbers of past visitors. On clear days, the view of the steep valley and mountains must have been remarkable, but all they saw was darkness, and the occasional burst of lightning in the rainy night.

Flames rose up crackling through the wood in the fire-pit, but Tarsa's thoughts were elsewhere. Unahi watched the young warrior with interest, thinking about her conversation with Geth as Tarsa had slept on their last night in Red Cedar Town. The old Wielder was only now realizing how much a stranger she was to her niece; Tarsa had already experienced a whole lifetime of joys and pains before Unahi arrived. The elder she-Kyn had rarely seen Redthorns of such a young age before, but the tight muscles and proud silence of her niece gave hints as to why the young one had accomplished so much so quickly, and why the Wielder had failed to sense her Wielding potential earlier.

There had been inklings, surely, when Tarsa was a strong-willed seedling named Namshéké: Storm-in-Her-Eyes. Unahi had even spoken to Lan'delar about the possibility. And in those days, even though the Purging was still going strong, her youngest sister was pleased to hear the news. Wielders tended to run in families, and it was a great honour among those who followed the Deep Green to say that one who walked the Wild Path was in one's Branch.

But then came the feverish pox, and the blisters that boiled through the skin, and Lan'delar was dead. Unahi could do nothing to help her sister; this sickness came from outside the Everland, from the beyonder lands where Men fed upon each other and the land cried in unceasing pain. She'd hoped to have another opportunity to see her infant niece then, but the Shields followed the fever, whipping terror of the unknown plague into hatred of the Wielders, and Unahi found no welcome in Red Cedar Town.

For all these years, Tarsa grew up in a world where the *wyr* was something to be scorned and cast out, where the many spirit people of the forests and mountains were enemies to be overcome rather than wisdom-bearers to be understood. Geth had shared her own lingering loyalty to the Old Ways with the youngling, but it was a thin memory generously mixed with romantic nostalgia that was as distant from the heart of the Deep Green as were the lies spread by the Shields. Geth was thus utterly unprepared when the young Namshéké fell into dazed states for whole days, emerging to tell her aunt about the voices she heard and the spirits she saw—sounds and sights shared by no one else around her. This was nothing like her stories of gentle forest spirits helping lost younglings find their way back to home or hearth, or the noble mountain ghosts who gave riches and glory to beautiful and virtuous she-Kyn maidens. The unnerving reality was far closer to the menacing stories of the Shields than to her own sentimental imaginings, and the terrified old she-Kyn did the only thing she could think of to help the youngling: she thrashed her niece into fearful silence.

This was another new gift of the Celestials.

So Namshéké hid her growing awareness of strange voices that spoke in her sleep. For a while it seemed that those hidden voices had given way to the more immediate surprises of the body, especially after she reached her first moon-time and was initiated into adulthood by the elder aunts of Cedar Branch. The voices faded as she became more aware of a different kind of fever that followed a run with the young he-Kyn of the town, or when she escaped her lessons and splashed in a hidden mountain pool with a few shapely she-Kyn. They all intrigued her, and she quickly learned from both what delightful mysteries could be found in the flesh.

These new understandings drowned out the subtle but ever-present drumbeat in Namshéké's blood. These things she understood: the thrill of rushing through the mountains, sweat hot on the skin, in pursuit of a greedy bear who thought to make an easy meal of their crops; the release of smashing the traplines of Human trespassers in the Everland and driving them back to their own blasted lands; or the fiery joy of sliding

beneath a doeskin blanket and feeling the moist lips of a lover or two on
her soft green flesh. These things she knew. They were all she wanted.

Then the Stoneskin came to the valley. And now the young warrior
named Tarsa didn't understand anything anymore.

Unahi nodded slightly to herself as she chewed on a freshly roasted
acorn, its bitter tang lifting a bit of the night's gloom. She was old, but she
still remembered her own Awakening and how swiftly it had thrown her
world into turmoil. Tarsa still stared off into the darkness. Lightning
illuminated the tattoos on the Redthorn's face–a good sign. Shields and
their followers never tattooed themselves anymore; only those who were
given to the Deep Green continued those traditions. The Redthorn way was
one enduring holdout in the few but growing Celestial towns, and Unahi
was glad of their endurance. She'd known a couple of younglings who'd
Awakened into Kyn families that were unflinchingly Celestial, and
although she'd eventually spirited them away from the brutal punishments
of the Shields, to whom their gift was a sign of shame and corruption, she
was never able to fully guide them into the Deep Green, and they were
ultimately consumed by the wyr-fire within. Such happenings were
fortunately rare. There were still enough Wild families within the
Branches to give guidance to those who were yet to Awaken.

She noticed Tarsa's shining turquoise eyes on her. It was time for truths
to be told. "Things will be different for you now. If you ever return to Red
Cedar Town, don't expect to find the friends you once knew. You might
find the necessities of Branch hospitality, but nothing else."

The Redthorn shrugged. "There's nothing for me in Red Cedar Town."

Unahi sighed. Tarsa had lost many things in her short life–her mother,
friends, lovers, and now the only place she'd ever known as home. Grief
still hung heavily on the young she-Kyn's shoulders; it was likely that this
helped to start her Awakening, as great emotion sometimes opened a
sensitive spirit to the *wyr* in unexplained ways. She'd been so strong for
such a long time. Yet as strong and stubborn as the Redthorn was, if she
continued to reject the Deep Green, she'd eventually lose this battle.

Unahi felt the gloom settle on her own shoulders, and she fell again into troubled silence.

The night passed slowly. Warm now, they sat by the red embers and stared off into the darkness. Tarsa hesitated to speak; she didn't know how to say what she was thinking, but the silence was too oppressive. She couldn't go back to Red Cedar Town, not after revealing herself as a Wielder. Her family had already demonstrated that their fear of her overwhelmed any sense of kinship. And although she was no longer alone, one question in her mind was a wall that separated her from this strange old she-Kyn.

Tarsa generally felt comfortable around Unahi. It was a surprise for her, especially considering Unahi's curt manner. She rarely felt at ease among others, and those who'd once shared comfort with her were far away now, back in Red Cedar Town. Her few friends and lovers had once ignored her strangeness and loved her in spite of it, but that was before the Stoneskin came to the valley. Everything changed then. She could still see their fear-maddened faces as they joined her family in driving her to the Burning Mouth. For a moment her chest tightened, but she didn't cry–those memories belonged to another life. It was Namshéké's life, not hers. Namshéké was gone. Through blood, death, and fire she'd become Tarsa'deshae, and she'd now have to build a different understanding of herself. Unahi was the only one who could help her with that task.

But one thing still kept her from embracing the old Wielder's presence and guidance. She took a deep breath. "Did you kill my mother?"

Unahi's mouth dropped open in shock. "Why would you ask such a thing?"

"Ivida told me once, when I was very young. She said that you were jealous of my mother, so you made her sick and then refused to heal her." Tarsa's eyes shimmered, but her full lips were drawn in a tight line of defiance.

She looks just like Lan'delar, Unahi thought sadly. "Not all elders are wise, Tarsa, remember that. A mean spirit sometimes just gets stronger with age, not smarter." The Wielder chose her words with care. "No. I never harmed your mother, except maybe in a youngling game of tag-the-tree. But then, she usually hit me back twice as hard."

Tarsa smiled nervously, and Unahi continued. "I loved Lan'delar. We all did. She was the youngest, a little sprout in a grove of tall saplings. No one thought our mother would be able to have any more younglings; she'd suffered greatly when Ivida was born, and two seedlings were lost before your mother joined us. But though we all adored her, I was her favourite, and she was mine."

Unahi stood and walked to the edge of the firelight, rummaging around in her pack for a small cloth bag that she brought back to the fire with her. Her three fingers drew a handful of leaves and twigs from the bag and tossed them into the fire. The air grew rich with the earthy scent of juniper that cleared the mind and the eyes. She returned to her seat and looked back at her niece.

"The pox was a sudden one. I'd heard of it, of course; in those days, you usually heard about these sicknesses from traders and refugees, before death suddenly appeared in the town, usually in a sucking youngling or a weak old burl who couldn't leave his pallet. And this one was no different in that way. It struck the old and young without mercy. It ran like fire through dry leaves, burning all that it touched to ashes."

Her voice grew hoarse. "I was one of the first of Red Cedar Town who fell to the fever. All my understanding of the *wyr* was useless. This pestilence came from outside the Everland, like so many of our woes. I thought I would die alone. That's usually what happened when the blistering sickness hit a town; all who could leave did so, as quickly as they could, and they generally scattered, sometimes carrying the plague with them to other towns. So I lingered in a fever for I don't know how many days. And when I emerged, I saw your mother. She'd stayed with me through the worst of it, bathed my wounds, kept me from scarring too terribly." Unahi drew a mottled hand across her gray eyes. "She stayed with me until I recovered, but by then she'd already started to suffer herself. So

I stayed by her side and cared for her as best as I could in my weakened state, but it wasn't enough."

Tarsa hugged her knees to her chest as she listened. The lightning had ceased, but the rain was heavy again. Occasionally, the eyes of small beast-people glinted in the darkness beyond, their curiosity aroused by the two figures who sat on either side of the crackling fire.

The old Wielder cleared her throat. "When everyone returned, the Shield blamed me for the deaths. What defense did I have? No one was there to see what had happened; Lan'delar gave you into Geth's keeping before coming back to look after me, and in the end it was just the two of us in Red Cedar Town. I was the only survivor; I should have been dead too, but instead, it was Lan'delar who was gone. My sisters went mad with grief. Your mother's last words were for you, Tarsa, and I begged the others to let me share them with you, but they believed the Shield and drove me away. Even Geth refused to listen. Most had turned away from the Deep Green when two of our brothers–Greenwalkers to the heart, and Redthorns themselves, like you–fell to an ambush by a Human raiding party. My sisters believed the Shield when he said that the Old Ways were useless, that the only peace our brothers would have was in the arms of Luran. And they believed him when he said that I had brought Lan'delar to her death through jealousy and witchery. So I was beaten and sent from the only home I'd ever known, and I'd never returned until two nights ago, when I saw you for the first time since you were a swaddled sprout."

Unahi smiled softly at the younger she-Kyn, but it did nothing to mask the sorrow in her eyes. Tarsa rocked in place for a while, listening to the rain fall off the rock shelf above them, and to the steam of the nuts roasting in the coals of the fire, watching as sparks popped and flew on smoke into the night. A nightbird cried mournfully in the distance. His shrill voice railed against the rain that would leave him drenched and hungry this night.

"Geth did believe you," Tarsa said at length, still staring off into the darkness. "She told me that it wasn't your fault. She told me a lot of things, but there was a lot she didn't know. We stood at the arch with the others, but we weren't Celestial, not in our hearts. She never wanted to leave the Deep Green." She turned to her aunt. "Will you teach me?"

Unahi nodded. Tarsa remained silent for a moment more, then said, "My mother—you said her last words were for me?"

"Yes," the Wielder nodded, draping her still-damp shawl on the rocks beside the fire.

"What did she say?"

Unahi's eyes were warm. "Tell her to tend to her roots."

CHAPTER 4

VISITATIONS

Although Jitani generally thought that cattle were rank and disgusting creatures, she reserved some measure of admiration for oxen, if for no other reason than the slow and steady strength that they showed in dragging their heavy carts over such a long distance. That admiration extended to the Human teamsters of the trading train, for there was a strange gentleness in their regard for the hulking beasts under their care. A well-trained pair of oxen rarely required the whip, for they were eager to follow their Human guides if reared and treated with kindness, and they'd patiently pull even the heaviest loads over these many miles of rough and rocky trade roads. It was only an incompetent teamster who lashed his charges in temper; as her employer had little patience for the lazy, foolish, or inept, such Men disappeared from the train in short order, to everyone's relief.

Of all of her jobs over the past ten years, this was one of the best, even though the bronze-skinned she-Kyn generally didn't like to work too closely among Humans—she'd had too many unpleasant experiences to trust them completely. But Sylas Gwydd had paid her well for her blade skills on each of these trading trips, and his many years of life and business in the Everland had brought him a reputation as an honest merchant who regarded the Folk as friends, not just customers or trade targets. It didn't hurt his reputation that he'd had a long and happy marriage to an Apple Branch she-Kyn, nor that their children were among the most promising young Kyn traders in Sheynadwiin. The name of Gwydd was one of esteem in the Kyn capital, and Sylas defended that regard with utmost care.

The recent attacks on his mercantile trains were thus more than a business loss—they were a personal affront to his character. Two trains had been seized by Eromar authorities under the most absurd bureaucratic justifications, while another had simply been plundered and burned by Human bandits. Silas's eldest son had barely survived that attack. Traders in the past had generally been able to pass through Eromar from eastern Béashaad and the Allied Wilderlands to the south without much difficulty, but the newest agitations by Lojar Vald, the prefect of Eromar, boded ill for the future, as they were becoming increasingly aggressive, and often without any pretense of legality. Gwydd's business interests weren't the only ones suffering from seizure and destruction, but his high status among the small group of intermarried Humans made his own troubles very public. Now, at last, they were getting as worried as their Folk neighbours had been for some time.

Jitani's mood turned ugly at these thoughts, and she grimaced as she spurred her pony forward towards the head of the train. Like most Kyn, she disliked binding animals to her service, and though she'd long since trained herself to tolerate the sensory backwash of the pony's bridle pain and saddle-sores, it was an experience that she was eager to finish with when they reached their destination. She was tired of the incessant squealing of the wagon axles, tired now of the stinking, trundling oxen and their hunched and bearded keepers. And she wasn't the only one: most of the Folk kept to themselves at the back of the wagon train, rarely mingling among the Men. They all wanted to see green trees and blue sky, not the ass-end of Humanity and their cud-chewing beasts.

Trust Men to wait until their own selfish interests are endangered before they look around and see the suffering of others. Folk had been dying in Human raids for months now, ever since Vald declared his intention to extend the political authority of Eromar over the Everland, but it was only when their own fortunes were threatened that Gwydd and the other Human merchants had started to pay attention and add their voices to the growing protest. Vald's proposal of levying a hefty tax on all Humans in the Everland who refused to declare their loyalty to Eromar certainly added to their new-found defiance.

No matter how annoyed she might be, Jitani still had a job to do, and right now it was to protect Sylas Gwydd's shipment of housewares and bolts of fine cloth all the way to its destination. They'd had a bit of trouble in Eromar just after the wagons were loaded, but they'd been out of the province's boundaries for nearly a week already and were well inside the Eldarvian Woods. Still, a tension in the air had followed them from Eromar City, and none of the sixteen Folk or twelve Men would feel completely secure until they reached Dardath Vale and the protective palisade around Sheynadwiin.

The she-Kyn heard some of the teamsters call out from the front of the train, bringing the wagons to a halt. She kicked the pony into a trot. When she reached the lead wagon, Sylas was already off his horse and deep in conversation with Ryn, an old Tetawi scout. Seeing the green-haired warrior ride up, Sylas waved her forward.

"Problems ahead," he said in the Folk trade-tongue. He was a stout Man, but with more muscle than fat. His bristling cheeks and forehead were always flushed, though they'd turned an angry red at Ryn's report. "Damn Vald and his drag-tailed lackeys! A toll-gate here, so close to Sheynadwiin?"

"A toll-gate?" She looked at the Tetawa.

"It's recent," the Tetawa said, nodding. "Probably no more than a six-day at best. They have a rough cabin there too, and a few horses–I counted five, but there could be more in the trees. They have logs blocking the road at three points: one at the gate, and two just beyond."

Jitani nodded. "How many Men?"

"Four at the gate. I don't know how many in the cabin." Ryn frowned. "They've got steel swords, and muskets, too."

Sylas' cheeks paled slightly, though his nose and forehead remained bright pink. "Do they know we're coming?"

Jitani turned to look at the ten creaking wagons and twenty grunting oxen. "They probably knew we were coming ten miles back." She shrugged and turned to Sylas. "Well, we can't turn around. Go to the middle of the train and spread everyone throughout the wagons, from the front to the back. Most of the Folk are keeping to themselves at the back. Have them come up to the front where they can keep a better eye on things, and tell them to have their weapons handy in case we need them. Ryn, go into the trees, and make sure that nobody's out there waiting to surprise us from behind. We'll keep going forward, and we'll see what happens when...."

A flintlock explosion and scream from the back of the train cut off her plans. Cursing herself for allowing the more keen-eyed Folk scouts and hunters to linger too much together at the rear of the train when they were so close to home, Jitani threw Sylas to the ground and dragged him under the head wagon as her pony whickered shrilly and galloped back down the road. Ryn lunged for cover in the underbrush, but a Man in soiled leathers stepped out of the trees in front of him and brought a well-used blade down hard and fast on the scout's neck. The Tetawa's head rolled wide-eyed into the rutted road, his body following with a sickening thump.

Ignoring the screams of Men and the rising panic of the oxen, and thankful that she kept her remaining stalks tightly bound against unexpected sensory trauma, Jitani drew her own sword from its scabbard and rolled out from under the wagon. The blade she held was a rare weapon, shaped from the heartwood of an ancient wyrwood tree, and given strength and keenness by a Wielder's patient skill. She'd hoped that she wouldn't need to use it on this trip; she'd grown tired of death and killing. But she had a duty, and now she had even more of a reason to fight, one that had nothing to do with protecting Sylas Gwydd's trinkets from destruction. It had everything to do with avenging the Folk who were watching their land disappear piece by piece, who were dying all around her. It had to do with keeping her attacker's blade from spilling her own heart's blood, and with avenging the brave Tetawa scout whose grandchildren would weep at the news of his murder.

This wasn't the first time she'd felt the cold threat of a steel blade, but she was no longer a frightened youngling. She could defend herself now.

Jitani raised her voice in a war-song as she rushed forward, and the wyrwood sword tasted hot blood again.

The destruction of Nine Oaks Town was worse than either Unahi or Tarsa had expected. It was a smaller town than Red Cedar, but it was older and infinitely more defensible, with a wider range of protections, including rockfalls, hidden alcoves in the stone wall that provided cover for ambushes, and sheer cliffs without handholds. It sat in a jagged bowl of stout red rock, and could only be reached through a handful of tight clefts in the steep walls. Kyn scouts and warriors used arrows and spears to keep enemies at a distance, and if danger came too close, there were always obsidian-spiked war clubs and wyrwood blades to help seal up the gap. But these defenses were only useful against conventional attackers, and the Stoneskin had been anything but that.

Unahi would have preferred that Tarsa not experience this side of a Wielder's duty so soon, especially as the young she-Kyn was still largely a stranger to the necessary teachings. The last few days had made painfully clear that most of Tarsa's early education about the Old Ways was actually a mishmash of romantic youngling tales, naïve fantasies, and superficial suppositions that had nothing to do with the long, often lonely work and painful transformations that the Way of Deep Green would demand of her. The Awakening was only the first great change she'd experience. Ordinarily, Unahi would have been rather discouraged by the young warrior's ignorance. But Tarsa had had wiser teachers than her meek aunt Geth–the Redthorn war-leader Oda'hea and the zhe-Kyn ceremony leader Fa'alik–and they'd started her toward a deeper understanding of the Way of Deep Green, their training interrupted only by her Awakening. Tarsa, to her credit, was a quick study; what she lacked in experience, she made up for in a willingness to learn. And it was fortunate that she was so accommodating, because they couldn't delay with the purification rituals at Nine Oaks–Tarsa would just have to follow along, pay attention, and do the best she could. Neither she-Kyn imagined that it would be an easy task.

Tarsa shivered as they climbed the narrow path that led to the larger of the passes into the bowl, though the sister suns had long ago emerged from behind the morning clouds. No wagon could make it through this pass, so anything that entered into Nine Oaks came by foot or on pack-animal. At least, that had been before the Stoneskin came. Now, the gap stood wide enough for three Kyn to walk abreast through it. Huge chunks of rubble lay scattered as far as they could see. The normalcy of the scene unnerved the Redthorn warrior: the quiet whisper of a breeze through the pine needles, the warmth and brightness of sunlight as they neared what both knew to be a site of slaughter. The sides of the cleft were scored by claw marks. Blood stained the stones and rust-coloured gravel that little black-feathered sparrows hopped and twittered through in search of seeds and small insects.

Unahi stopped, her breathing laboured. It was a steep climb up the ridge, and these last few days had given her little rest. Her gray eyes scanned the narrow gorge facing them. She was old; she'd been old even when Tarsa was born, although she would never have admitted it in those days. As the only Wielder remaining to serve and protect the Folk in Thistlewood and its surrounding hills, Unahi had spent much of her life cleaning up after conflicts and accidents. She knew too well the sticky flow of blood over her callused hands; she'd bound innumerable wounds with those same six fingers. Sometimes she awoke in the night to an endless chorus of screams, the cries of all the pain she'd watched and experienced. Sometimes she wondered if there would come a time when she would get used to the horrors of mortality, but she doubted it. If anything, her sensory stalks were increasingly sensitive to the emotions of those around her. It wasn't always a bad thing. It was likely the reason she felt Tarsa's anguish from her own warm cabin far away in the woods. But it was more exhausting all the time, and there were far too many nights without sleep.

Unahi turned to the Redthorn warrior. "Do you want to wait here? There's no reason that you should have to deal with this right now."

"No, I'll go with you." Tarsa cleared her throat and stood proudly. "After all, I'm the one who killed the monster." She didn't add that the empty silence of the world outside the rock ring held far more fear for her than anything within it.

"Monster?" Unahi frowned. "That he was. But he also belonged to the days of the Ancestrals, a spirit of the mountains given flesh and blood long before we came to this world. He knew the voices of the stones and snowy heights, sang the songs that travelled on thunder from the far reaches of the world. For that alone he deserves respect."

Tarsa stared at her aunt in sudden disgust. "Respect? He would have slaughtered everyone in Red Cedar Town if we hadn't stopped him. Look there." She pointed at the blood-stained rubble on either side of the rocky cleft. "I can't respect that." The warrior's stalks quivered with agitation.

Unahi grunted slightly as she started up the slope again. She leaned heavily on her staff for support, having retrieved it from Tarsa when the warrior was strong enough to walk on her own. The old Wielder reached the wall without much difficulty and slid her hand across the claw marks in the stone. The gouges were thick, each as wide as her two large fingers together. The Stoneskin had ripped through the rock in a frenzy. His emotions still clung to the red stone around her; she could feel his elation, his eager joy to tear through the wall and feast on the town beyond. His weren't the only emotions here. So, too, were those of the handful of Kyn who were surprised on their watch; their death pain nearly drowned out all other sensations. The Wielder's fingers drifted farther across the stone. There had been five who died here. Four were he-Kyn. The fifth was a young she-Kyn, the sister of one of the warriors, there to visit and share a laugh with her brother and one of his handsome friends. She was the last of the five to die. Unahi's stomach tightened.

"No, Redthorn, I can't respect that either," she said. "His cruelty was well repaid. But he's still connected to us; he's still a voice in the song. Things are rarely as simple as we want them to be. Vengeance for its own sake, without concern for balance, is destructive in its way, too." She reached into one of the many small pouches around her waist and pulled out a handful of long cloth strips, handing a few to Tarsa. "Tie up your stalks. You're already sensing too much, and there's going to be much more pain

and ugliness in a moment." Without another glance at the younger
she-Kyn, Unahi slipped into the shadows of the cleft.

Tobhi tried to stretch the numbness from his legs, but it was tough to do
so from the back of an irritable deer. Whoever thought that deer were
sweet and docile forest creatures had never met Smudge, a black-nosed,
long-eared little brute with sharp teeth and even sharper antlers. Rather
than risk another nasty bite, the Tetawa pulled on the reins and
dismounted.

They were later getting to Nine Oaks than he liked, as night was
approaching all too swiftly, and the stories he'd recently heard about the
area didn't make him eager to camp in the open air. But Smudge had
nearly reached the end of his brown-eyed patience with all this business.
The deer shook himself vigorously. Without Tobhi's weight, the saddle and
blanket slipped easily to the ground. Turning an exasperated eye toward
the Tetawa, who stood stretching against a tree, Smudge tore huge clumps
of spring grass from the roadside and munched on them in noisy spite.

Tobhi grinned and flopped to the ground, the tingle now gone from his
limbs. "Not a bad idea. It's best not to show up with a grousin' belly; who
knows if they even got anythin' good to eat." He reached over and grabbed
the nearest fallen saddlebag, rummaged through it and pulled out a bag of
crumbling corn cakes.

Smudge ignored him.

It had been too long since Tobhi was last in the mountains. There was
really nothing quite as wondrous as the sunset over blue peaks in the
distance, unless it was sitting right in the middle of them when the last
scarlet gold of day slid down over the shining edge of their crowns. He
hadn't been in this area since he was nearing his age-naming, probably
twelve years past or better. He was pleasantly surprised that he still
remembered the shortcut through the pass. Jekobi would be proud of him.

"Wonder where Pepa would be right about now," Tobhi muttered softly to himself, a habit developed over the last few years of travel since he left home.

"Prob'ly nappin', if I know him. He's likely teasin' Mam, pretendin' to sleep instead of huskin' sweet corn for supper." He looked at the bag in his hands and sighed. "I 'magine she's cookin' somethin' a sight better than gritty travel bread tonight."

He stood up and stretched again. The last leg of the day's journey was always the longest, and though he'd been travelling for weeks and should be used to the pace, it seemed that every day dragged out longer than the one before. His eyes spotted a thick trail of smoke from the centre of the rocky ring below. It wasn't quite as far away as he'd expected. "Maybe they got enough for us down there; it can't be no worse than what we got up here." Tobhi picked up the saddle and stepped toward Smudge, but the deer's glare stopped him.

"Now, now, Smudge," Tobhi cooed, moving forward slowly, his round brown face sending what he hoped was a look of benevolent brotherhood. "Ye know I en't tryin' to hurt ye none. We're almost there. Just a little farther, and I'll give ye all the grain ye can eat. Maybe I'll even give ye a shiny green crabapple. I got one in m' pack, just for you. Ye'd like that, wouldn't ye?" The deer stood staring; the only muscles that moved were the ones still working through a particularly large mouthful of grass.

Tobhi inched closer and reached out a hand to stroke the deer's back. Smudge bounded quickly to the side and trotted into the trees on the opposite side of the trail. The Tetawa, now unbalanced, fell heavily to the ground, his shapeless brown hat slipping over his eyes.

"Ye stinkin', mean-eyed drum skin!" Tobhi shouted. He pulled the hat up and glared at the deer, who now stood contentedly chewing in the trees about fifteen feet away, with what Tobhi was certain was a look of smug superiority. Another strategy was clearly necessary. With a dramatic flourish, Tobhi stood and wiped the dirt and pine needles from his green leggings, hefted the saddlebags over his shoulders, and walked toward the trail. "Well," he called behind him, "I guess I'll be eatin' that feast by m'self tonight. Sure will be sad, though, to throw all that good food away, 'cause there'll be more than I can eat by m' lonesome. 'Specially that apple. Ah, well. At least *I'll* get plenty to eat." With that, he strolled down the trail toward the red stone ring.

Smudge remained where he was, still chewing and watching the path that Tobhi had taken. Suddenly Tobhi raced back up the hill with lips puckered. "Ye'r more jackass than deer, ye know that?" He charged after his mount, who skipped just out of reach and turned to face the Tetawa. They squared off for a moment before Tobhi rushed again. This time, however, Smudge stood his ground, taking Tobhi off his guard and his feet by planting his antlered head into the thick leather vest over the Tetawa's belly and flinging him backward into the grass. Tobhi landed with a grunt but stood up again with a smile, a little breathless but unhurt. The deer shook himself and lowered his head again.

"All right, ye want to play that way, do ye?" Tobhi grinned and crouched. "Well, then, let's go—ye'r about three steps away from deer stew anyways." Smudge snorted and moved toward the little Tetawa, but stopped as a large shadow moved over them. They looked up to see a scowling figure astride a stout horse.

«By Luran's grace, what are you doing?» The newcomer's voice dripped with exasperation and scorn.

Tobhi shrugged and grabbed one of Smudge's antlers with a grin. «Nothin' to worry yerself about,» he said, following the visitor's lead by speaking in the Reach-tongue of Men. «We're just havin' ourselves a bit of fun.» With his other hand, Tobhi swung the saddle across the deer's back and cinched it tight, noting with some satisfaction that Smudge was more subdued—even dignified—in the presence of the mare. That knowledge made the cinching even more entertaining, as one particularly hard pull of the belt across the deer's belly brought forth a simultaneous grunt of displeasure and a loud blast of gas from Smudge's hindquarters. Tobhi chuckled and swung himself into the saddle, pretending that he couldn't see the deer's reproachful glare.

«I hardly think this is a time for levity. We have an important duty to fulfill, and the sooner we accomplish that, the sooner we will be able to get out of this wretched wilderness.» The figure shook his head wearily and spurred his horse toward Nine Oaks town. Smudge and his grinning companion trotted close behind.

CHAPTER 5

A CLEANSING FIRE

Night was the flock's favourite time to travel; the deeper shadows of the alpine forest were soothing to the creatures' nerves in this strange world. Even the thin light of the Greatmoon was painful to their senses–born as they were of the wrappings of shade and darkness, light gave form to the creatures but no comfort. The hidden springs and deep, fragrant hollows of mushroom and moss in the timeless forest were welcoming more for their night-time murk than for the rush of life that flourished there. These things held not even passing interest; something much more compelling drew the creatures on.

The air was pensive, as if all the hidden spirits of the forest readied themselves to flee from an approaching storm. The creatures felt the tension and flapped their black wings in annoyance, but they were used to such a response, for they knew too well that they didn't belong here. Wherever the shadow-creatures had been, whatever their origins, the purpose of their belonging was lost far behind them, like a dying breath in the night. The past was gone; they had a different purpose now, one that had been delayed by unexpected frustrations. Occasionally, they squawked and gibbered their tangled fury on the wind. They'd never been thwarted like this before, and while the creatures had little idea of their age or history–little tangible memory of anything but hunger, and the unnamed compulsion that pushed them forward–they knew that they'd been on the hunt many times before this, and nothing so far had escaped their patient pursuit. The most maddening thing was that the hunters were certain that their quarry was unaware of the seeking shadows, yet it remained so elusive. Those who knew they were stalked tended to make stupid and ultimately fatal mistakes; this particular prey had no such weakness.

The shadow-creatures had first followed the scent into the deep forest, but the lichen-covered cabin was empty when they arrived. The hunters descended on the cabin like a sudden tempest, tearing at the logs and stones of the structure, smashing clay jars and shredding baskets and thick quilts, but it was useless: their frustration was vented, but they had lost very valuable time. The shadows rushed from that shattered forest cabin over marshes and hills and narrow canyon walls–sending wood-spirits and water-folk scrambling in mad desperation to avoid the unnatural otherness–up to the edge of a small settlement that stood proudly on a flat mountain ridge. Even as they crowded around and sniffed the palisade wall, the creatures knew that their quarry was gone again, but they couldn't sense the best direction to follow. Daylight was fast approaching, so the shadows glided up the hillside and found a dank pit on the edge of the settlement to lair in until darkness returned. The hole hummed with pain and fear, and this made it a surprisingly comfortable place to rest, in spite of its stink of iron. The metal irritated the creatures' senses but caused no lasting harm; not born of the *wyr*, they possessed none of the weaknesses that came with such an inheritance. The shadows spent two days there gathering strength and enjoying the residue of hurt that clung to the rocky walls, a memory that was strong enough to taste–and to nourish.

Now, after slipping again through mist, rain, mud, and forest, the creatures knew that the end of the hunt was growing near. Although the prey was still some distance away, the unwitting quarry had stopped again. This brief hesitation would be its last.

✦

Choking clouds of ash and smoke billowed from the bonfire, and Tarsa wiped sweat from her forehead as she threw another armful of wood into the flames. It had been an achingly long day, and night promised to be even longer. As they'd walked in from afar, nothing looked amiss. Nine Oaks was a tiered town built into a hollow bowl against the eastern edge of a large sandstone butte, one of the many natural stone towers scattered through the hill country. A central meeting-house, round and squat like that of Red Cedar Town, stood at the base of the stone wall, while the individual Branch-houses clung to the sides of the stone like brightly-painted mushrooms growing from fissures in the rock. A series of tall wooden poles, each draped with bright cloth banners and topped with the roughly carved image of one of the seven Kyn Branches—Oak, Willow, Thorn, Pine, Cedar, Ash, and Apple—surrounded the meeting-house. The town fields were still only half-planted; abandoned wooden hoes and planting sticks were the first sign of wrongness.

It was only as they approached that the devastation became evident. Every dwelling was damaged in some way, mostly around the doors, which looked as if a massive boulder had smashed through the narrow entrances. Darkened splatters of blood were everywhere—even, to Tarsa's horror, high atop the Branch-poles.

They were surprised to find that the bodies had already been wrapped and placed atop thirty makeshift scaffolds of various sizes. Kyn were generally buried after a season or more of exposure to the elements: during this period, their flesh would feed the four-legged, crawling, and winged people who shared the land with them, and their spirits would have enough time to surrender their attachments to this place and travel to the ghostlands in the Lower Place, where they would return fully to the endless voices of the *wyr*. But these rough scaffolds might remain untouched by Kyn for years, thus leaving incomplete the necessary rituals that would bring peace to those who had died.

This would be the legacy of Nine Oaks town. Both she-Kyn wept at the thought, and at the sight of so many younglings among the dead. Tarsa had expected to see carnage beyond belief, bodies savaged and torn apart, but all she saw was a mournful emptiness, and this absence, the cold erasure, was so much worse. The very presence of living Kyn had gone with the survivors, likely to another town where they had Branch-kith to take them in. Before leaving, the survivors had fulfilled as many of their duties to the dead as they could. But it wouldn't be enough. The spirits would remain in this place for ages to come, until their bones were dust scattered on the wind or until they were at last buried deep in rich, red soil, to give strength to the growing world and the deep-rooted people again.

Tarsa didn't realize how much was left undone until she removed her stalk-wrappings late in the day to cool her head in the pine-scented breeze. A sudden wave of anguish knocked her to the ground, where she rolled gasping in pain and shock. Dozens of screaming and weeping voices battered her mind, to be swallowed up in the Stoneskin's gurgling laugh. The bloodsong took control again, so fast that she had no chance to fear its approach, and she released it into the world again, the unheard voices of the *wyr* flowing through the ground and up into the charred branches of the slender pines around her. The first wave passed; as Unahi had taught her that day, she forced herself to push the burning song from her surface thoughts to drift back to muted currents. Tarsa lay sprawled on the ground for a few moments, chest heaving as she caught her breath and tried to push back the gnawing ache that burrowed again deep into her muscles.

She lifted her eyes to an unexpected and terrible sight: the pines were now twisted and malformed, contorted into nightmarish, tormented shapes. The branches of one tree curled like strangling ivy into those of the next, pulling them together into a pained and inescapable embrace. The thick bark gaped in places to reveal tender heartwood, now bleeding sweet red sap in the fruitless attempt to heal the sudden, deadly wounds. Tarsa watched, bile rising in her throat, as the needles turned brown before her eyes, and her stomach clenched violently.

Unahi stood beneath the trees and coolly regarded her niece. Tarsa dropped her head. After Tarsa was able to stand again, the elder Wielder curtly directed her to gather up whatever still remained in the dwellings—from furniture and clothing to corn-husk brooms and youngling gourd dolls—and set them ablaze in the meeting-house's fire-pit. They couldn't leave these remnants to linger on with the taint of death.

Neither looked at the tortured pines again that day.

Unahi stepped to Tarsa's side and threw a stout stool into the flames. Her eyes watered from the ashes and the acrid stink of hair that burned along with various clothes, brushes, and hide-rugs. "That's the last of it. We should eat a bit," she said, pointing to a stout log near the firepit, where a clay pot bubbled with a thick stew that Unahi had put together from gatherings of their journey. After washing the grime from her skin and performing a brief prayer that Unahi had taught her to cleanse away some of the death-taint, Tarsa sat down and stared into the fire. The flames were the only comfort she had in this ruined town. Even after all their work, the place looked no less ghastly. Directly opposite she could see, through the flames, the misshapen forms of the pines she'd wyr-twisted. And beyond the trees, barely visible in the firelight, stood row after row of death-scaffolds. The possessions of the dead were now crumbling to clean ash, free of the lingering effects of their deaths; their spirits wouldn't be hindered in their journey by the material desires of life.

"This town was built by nine members of Oak Branch, from Dropwater," Unahi said, filling two pitted wooden bowls with the stew. "They came here during the Purging, in the hope that they could keep the Deep Green alive until later generations would appreciate those ways. And they'd succeeded quite well–for a while, anyway. Kith from the other Branches, including ours, came to live here too. I was always welcome here." She frowned and shook her head.

They continued eating. Unahi watched the flames dance in the night air, but Tarsa was now restless. She didn't want to be here. She didn't want to keep feeling all the emptiness and pain, or to know that, no matter how hard they worked this day, Nine Oaks Town would be a haunted place for years. Her eyes drifted back to the pines; she couldn't have avoided looking at them if she tried, and even though she had rewrapped her stalks immediately after regaining her strength, she could still almost hear their tortured screams.

"The *wyr* is the heart-fire of the Folk," Unahi said, interrupting Tarsa's uncomfortable reverie. The elder she-Kyn pulled out her pipe and filled the shallow bowl. "It's the language of creation, the voiced embodiment of the Ancestrals and their spirits. The words belong to another time and another world, but we continue to speak them, because they continually renew our world. Without the *wyr*, the Folk are rootless."

As the pipe-smoke mingled with that from the fire-pit, Tarsa clenched her fists. "I don't understand them...the voices. When I hear them, everything comes at me in a rush, and the words tumble all together in my head. It's maddening. Every time I feel the words rise up, it's all I can do to keep from losing myself in them. And when everything clears away..." She glanced back toward the trees and flushed with shame.

"Only those who walk in the Spirit World speak the *wyr* with full grace," Unahi said, patting Tarsa's arm awkwardly. "The rest of us just have to try to keep up. It will come, with time. But you must be careful, youngling, because words are very powerful, especially these words. They can hide or reveal truth with equal ease, and many people have Wielded the spirit-tongues without respect, and come to terrible grief because of it." She pointed at the long woven cloth wrapped around her own waist. "We'll make you a chanting sash in the next few days; it'll root you better, help you focus your mind. You have a powerful tie to the *wyr*, Tarsa, but it'll demand much..."

A noise from the shadows caught their attention. Two figures stepped out of the darkness beyond the flames. Tarsa jumped to her feet with a burning brand in the right hand; her left strayed to a throwing knife hidden in the back of her belt. She might have had very little confidence in her wyr-Wielding abilities, but she had no such hesitation about her Redthorn training.

When the shapes emerged into the light, Tarsa watched them closely, for both were unexpected in this grim place. The first was a stately he-Kyn leading a tall brown horse. He wore a high-collared gray coat with thick brass buttons that glinted like solid flame in the firelight. Beneath the knee-length coat she could see a dull red vest and white shirt with a flowery neck wrapping, each trimmed with golden thread. His breeches and high trade-leather boots, like the rest of his clothing, were clearly of fine quality and well cared-for, though red with dust from his travels. Around his neck hung a heavy, slate-grey medallion, which Tarsa recognized as an iron-ward not much different from that of the Shield of Red Cedar Town.

But the most surprising thing about him was his face: although she'd seen many Kyn with blue skin and red hair, she was a stranger to one whose flesh was free of tattoos and honour-marks, whose oak leaf ears were unsplit and free of rings and other piercings. Even the most dedicated followers of the Celestial path in Red Cedar Town had at least some facial markings. She didn't know how to respond–he looked more than naked to her.

She was glad to turn her attention to the young Tetawa who stood beside the he-Kyn. While not often seen in the mountains, the Tetawi were occasional visitors, and this one looked very much like the others she'd seen. He stood only about half her height, well-formed, solid but not stout, with brown skin the colour of ripe acorns and shining black hair that trailed to his waist in a single braid. Two small black eyes twinkled pleasantly, and two parallel trails of small black tattooed circles crossed his wide cheeks and nose to mark his own people's adulthood rites. He had a floppy brown hat on his head, with bright feathers woven into a red hatband at the base of the brim; the hat may have once had a peak, but that, like the brim, dropped lazily to the side. The Tetawa's vest was mostly red, but green, black, and yellow beaded swirls danced like snakes across the heavy fabric. In one hand, as a walking stick, the Tetawa held a long-handled hatchet with a dark stone blade; in his other hand, he tugged on the reins to a small mule deer who glared at the world with undisguised contempt.

The Tetawa walked to the elder she-Kyn and jerked his chin upward once in greeting. Unahi returned the gesture. The old Wielder still smoked her pipe as she sat on the downed tree, seemingly unsurprised by the new arrivals, but Tarsa stood with her branch held slightly toward them. The he-Kyn watched her warily.

"*Hanahé*," the Tetawa greeted them in the high-mountain Kyn-tongue. "What happened here?" His tone was friendlier than his suspicion-filled eyes. Tarsa suddenly realized how strange she and Unahi must look. Here were two she-Kyn, calmly eating and smoking together in the middle of a scene of carnage. She listened while Unahi briefly recounted the story of the Stoneskin's raid and eventual demise. The Tetawa nodded and let out a low whistle of awe as he looked around at the devastation, casting an appreciative glance toward Tarsa when Unahi came to the story of the creature's death. He turned back to the he-Kyn, and they walked away to speak.

Unahi sat unperturbed, but Tarsa clasped the brand tightly. They both watched, in the dim edge of firelight, as the Tetawa drew something from a pouch on his belt. His hands gyrated slowly in a wide arc before him. The air tingled slightly, a tensing of the *wyr* around them. It was a Wielding, but one with a different feel than those Tarsa had experienced—it was tentative, a gentle probing of the *wyr*, a soft, slow questioning. The Redthorn's eyes widened, but Unahi shook her head. The moment passed, and the Tetawa turned with a smile. "*Hanahé*," he said again, this time without hesitation.

The elder Wielder smiled, motioning for him to sit beside her. He slipped the bridle from the deer's head, letting the creature roam freely through the town, and settled himself onto the log. "*Tsodoka*."

"You're welcome," Unahi said. Her eyes strayed to the deer. "You ride him all the way here?"

"Yes, as much as he'd let me," he laughed and pulled up his left sleeve to show a nasty bruise on his forearm. "He en't been none too happy 'bout it, neither. This en't the only one I got, but it's the only one I can show without turnin' four shy shades of red!"

Unahi laughed and Tarsa smiled hesitantly. The Tetawa seemed pleasant enough, but the he-Kyn's strangeness troubled her. Still, she felt she should at least be polite until she learned more about him. "Have you eaten?" she asked.

The he-Kyn turned to the Tetawa with a quizzical look. The little deer-rider replied in a strange tongue, and the he-Kyn nodded curtly. Turning to Tarsa, the Tetawa said in Kyn, "He en't interested, but I'd be willin' to take somethin', if ye'r offerin'." Noting her glance at the he-Kyn, the Tetawa added, "He don't know the old Kyn-speech of the high country, but I'd be glad to tell him what ye want to say."

Unahi turned to Tarsa. "There are extra bowls in my pack. Bring them here, would you?" Her voice was gentle, but Tarsa could sense the tension in it. A Kyn who couldn't speak the People's tongue? He was more alien than she'd guessed. Nodding once, Tarsa dropped the brand back into the fire and turned to the pack. Unahi and the Tetawa continued chatting, engaging in the customary introductory conversation that preceded formal discussion. When Tarsa returned, Unahi filled both bowls and handed them to each of the visitors. The Tetawa took his with a smile. "*Tsodoka.*" The he-Kyn bowed stiffly but remained standing at the fire's edge. With an exasperated sigh, the Tetawa turned and said something sharply in another language, which Tarsa recognized with shock–it was a Mannish dialect, similar to that used by a couple of Human traders who'd married into Ash Branch in Red Cedar Town. With obvious discomfort, the he-Kyn accepted the bowl from Unahi's outstretched hand.

"Sorry 'bout him," the Tetawa muttered between mouthfuls of stew. "He en't the most sociable fellow I ever travelled with, nor none too polite 'bout it. But he don't mean no harm; he just don't know any better."

He suddenly stopped and put his bowl down with a shake of his head. "Here I'm criticizin' his manners when I don't use m' own." He extended his hand palm up, which Unahi touched lightly in welcome. "I'm Tobhi Burrows, Badger Clan from Bristlecone Hollow, 'bout a tenday ride north of here. It's a pleasure."

"I'm Unahi Sam'sheyda, Cedar Branch from Thistlewood, and this is my niece, the Redthorn warrior Tarsa'deshae, of Red Cedar Town." Both she-Kyn nodded at the Tetawa and turned their eyes to the other visitor. Tobhi smiled at the he-Kyn and then turned back to Unahi. "This is Leith Fynon. He's a messenger from the Sevenfold Council, and I guess ye'r the last one we been lookin' for."

Neranda Ak'Shaar stood at the rostrum, her shimmering white cloak and gown flowing in pleated waves around her feet, and waited with dignified patience for the tumult to die down. It took some time. She calmly scanned the vast Gallery of Song where the other Lawmakers continued their heated debate. More Assembly members were listening to her than ever had before; she and her allies were still in the minority, but their righteous position had greater momentum now. The discussion had been going on for weeks; tempers were fraying on both sides, yet no one could deny the calming influence of the white-cloaked she-Kyn at the central dais—not even the Governor, who had bitterly denounced her in his private rooms that very morning. His words might have burned when she was younger, but a few years in the Assembly had taught her much, and she'd come to realize that opinion and conviction were often two very different things. Neranda could trust in her own convictions; his opinions were weak without similar certainty.

She was a powerful Lawmaker from a long line of respected political figures in the Nation, a fitting image of what the Kyn could become—a stately Shield in both body and spirit. When many of the old Branch elders had surrendered the autonomy of their individual towns for a unified government that they believed to be better suited to face the threat of Human encroachment, her father's immediate Branch-kith—the Ak'Shaar family, in particular—found themselves in a fortunate position. They were concerned less with Branch customs and the expectations of their extended families than with the fortunes of their direct line. To their mind, the Branches belonged to the past; the more immediate concerns of the Ak'Shaar family belonged to the future of Man's growing influence over

70

their world. And the Ak'Shaars led the way. They'd long studied the ways of Humanity–even sent some of their sons and daughters, like Neranda, to be educated in the cities of Men and to learn the foundations of the Celestial Path from benevolent Human proselytors–and were well prepared to advise the Assembly of Law and the Governor, who now led the combined Kyn Nation.

For the past three generations, at least one Ak'Shaar was groomed to guide the Nation toward what the family believed to be a more reasonable relationship with their Human neighbours, in spite of the unending intransigence of the traditional Wielders and their mountain-bred supporters. But as Neranda often noted, those old Wild ways were dwindling as surely as the Branches, and soon the Celestials would find their path to a dignified state of grace that would be free of barbarity and the blind chains of the past. The days of the Greenwalkers were gone, no matter how much the Wielders wanted it to be otherwise. They must now find a way to exist in the world of Men.

Neranda, though by tradition of her mother's line, embraced the new ways of her father's folk, becoming the first member of his Ak'Shaar family to seek election, the others being content to lead from behind the Assembly's curtains, where influence was hidden and all the more powerful because of it. There were dangers to public life, to be sure, but Neranda knew that hidden influence depended entirely on having trustworthy allies to put your suggestions into practice, those confident enough in their beliefs to stand against unpopular opinion. Such allies were, unfortunately, entirely too rare, so Neranda took it upon herself to be the example of such virtue in the Assembly. If one strong voice was raised toward Truth, others would follow.

She became that voice.

When the shouting had diminished, she struck the brass tip of the speaker's staff against the granite circle in the dais, sending a sharp ring through the chamber to signal the conclusion of her speech. "Benevolent Lawmakers, friends and family, do not allow your fears to outweigh your good judgment. Do not let your uncertainty obscure your duty. This offer is more than generous, and shadows lengthen on the horizon. Will we continue to deny the inevitable, and thus leave our people to chaos and ruin in the coming storm? Will we abandon our responsibilities to lead our Nation into the future, even though we know too well how few of our unfortunate brethren truly understand the complexities we face? My kith, we were elected not as followers of public opinion but as leaders of the Kyn Nation. If we fulfill our duty, future generations will look upon us with both respect and love, as we will have been the steadfast champions who made an unhappy choice in dark times for the good of all. But if we fail to change, if we surrender to our fears and blind nostalgia, there will be no future reflection on us, for there will be no future for us or our descendants."

The hood of her cloak slid away to reveal a cascade of burnished copper hair that fell in shining streams down her back. Hers was a cold beauty, but it seemed to glow with warm righteousness as she lifted the staff in the air. "We have two choices: resistance, or life." Her violet eyes flashed in the everlights that illuminated the chamber. "I choose life!" With that, she brought the speaker's staff down again, and its thundering peal was drowned in the overwhelming roar of applause that erupted from the Assembly. Voices cried out "Life!" in response. Any voices in opposition were lost in the chaos.

The Lawmaker bowed to the Assembly and stepped from the dais into a wave of enthusiastic well-wishers. It was the finest moment of her career, but it was only the first step of a difficult journey. She looked to the tall chair at the far end of the chamber, where the Governor sat in his massive seat carved from wyrwood and precious stones into the shape of a butterfly in flight. His silver head was bowed. Neranda's elation faded, and her throat tightened in momentary sorrow: Garyn Mendiir, the great warrior and politician who had bravely led the Kyn for half her life, sat alone in the shadows, and she stood tall in the light.

Neranda's sadness vanished. All things changed—it was the way of the

Melded world. The wisdom of those Wild ages no longer served in this time. It was inevitable, and she would be the one to show her people the new way—a stronger, wiser way.

All was as it should be. She smiled and returned her attention to her allies in the Assembly. The Governor's grief was quickly forgotten.

CHAPTER 6

SHADOW AND STORY

Tobhi translated Leith's words again. "The leaders of the seven Folk Nations are worried 'bout the raids and growin' pride of the Eromar Humans, so they've called a gatherin' to meet soon. The Kyn Assembly will host the Sevenfold Council in Sheynadwiin."

Unahi stared into the fire. When no questions were forthcoming from the elder she-Kyn, Tarsa asked one herself. "Why have you been looking for my aunt? She's no Assembly member." She knew a little about the Assembly, as every Kyn town had a representative in Sheynadwiin to be their voice in National affairs, but beyond that the concerns of the Kyn capital had had little visible impact on Red Cedar Town. Sheynadwiin was a place shrouded by stories and rumors; it hardly seemed real enough to require travelling messengers to look for Unahi.

The he-Kyn waited for Tobhi to translate, but the latter replied directly to Tarsa's question. "She's a Wielder, and they're the most important part of the whole thing, 'cause they understand the Old Ways better than anyone. There's more to this mess than just politickin'. The Wielders is the only ones who can bring the Folk back to a sensible understandin' of things—the world is all out of balance right now. Them Kyn Shields is gettin' completely out of hand. They're even talkin' 'bout givin' up the Everland and movin' away to some forsaken place in the lands of Men. I'd say it was a joke, but there en't nothin' funny 'bout it. They're deadly serious."

Surrender the Everland? Tarsa wanted to laugh, too, but Tobhi's grim face silenced her. It was an absurd notion. Who would want to abandon their homeland? It was one of the few Thresholds of the Eld Green that had survived the Melding, when Men had shattered the barrier between the worlds and brought their world and that of the Folk together in catastrophe. Many of the 'Holds were destroyed then, and much had been slowly stolen and fragmented in the thousand years since that devastating betrayal, but the Everland remained strong and resilient. Within its fertile borders, the Folk were truly alive; the *wyr* coursed unhindered through all that lived there. The innumerable spirits of creation—from the leaf-headed standing people and the lichen-spotted stone people, to the furred four-leggeds and the feathered ones who danced on wind and breeze—were woven together in this world, and they belonged to the land as much as the land belonged to them.

Leave the Everland? It was barely imaginable. Yet she believed him.

Unahi turned back to Tobhi and Leith. "Are other Wielders going to the Council?"

Tobhi interpreted, and Leith responded to him. "Yes. He's already talked with a few of 'em, and there's other messengers headin' throughout the Everland to show 'em the Governor's seal." Leith reached into an inner pocket of his coat and handed a flat clay disk to the Wielder. Tarsa saw the image of a butterfly on the disk, each wing a different colour: red, black, blue, and white. Beneath it was a symbol she didn't recognize, an angled half-moon or bear's claw, with a small azure circle to its right, but Unahi seemed satisfied and handed it back to the messenger.

Tarsa watched Leith closely. "Why doesn't he speak to us himself?"

The Tetawa shrugged. "He's on the One Moon Path, with his learnin' taken from Men most of his life, and he never learned to speak the Kyn Tongue. Why they sent him is beyond me, but with all the fightin' goin' on in the Assembly, he's prob'ly the only one who'd go, honour and glory and all that. There's lots of them types in Sheynadwiin these days. When the Council sent him out on this errand, m' Clan mothers asked me to help out as best I could, since I been speakin' both tongues, and a few others, all my life; my pepa's tradin' days among the Kyn have been comin' in useful. I been wantin' to come this way for a while, anyway—to remember over old times, ye know—so I saddled up this bow-legged deer, grabbed m' hat, and headed for the hills. Leith and I en't had too much to chat about, to be sure, but as he don't bother me much, we generally been gettin' along just fine."

He bent over and scooped another steaming batch of stew into his bowl. The old Wielder was quiet, her gray eyes again lingering thoughtfully over the dancing flames.

"We'll come," Unahi said at last. "My niece is a Wielder as well, although still very young and unsteady in her knowledge." Her eyes flickered to the twisted pines, and Tarsa's face went hot with shame. "She would need to meet with the Wielders' Circle before finishing her training, anyway."

Tobhi repeated the elder she-Kyn's words to Leith, who smiled broadly and turned to secure his saddle. "That's all he needed to hear," Tobhi said, but made no move to follow.

As the he-Kyn finished his preparations to leave, Unahi's head-tendrils twitched in agitation, and she lifted her head. There was something strange in the air, but she was weary in flesh and spirit, and she couldn't quite identify the sensation. It unnerved her. She walked over to Leith and rested a wrinkled hand on his arm.

"Wait until dawn," she said softly, her eyes slightly glazed from sending her thoughts into the distance. "There's no real hurry."

The he-Kyn looked at her quizzically and turned to Tobhi, who translated. Leith smiled and shook his head proudly, pulling a hand-musket from a bag on his horse's saddle as a sign of his preparedness. Unahi stumbled away from the sudden taint of cold iron, and Tarsa jumped up to catch her.

The he-Kyn hurriedly returned the firearm to its case and said a few words to the Tetawa as he swung himself into the saddle.

"He en't worried," Tobhi said, clearly unconvinced. "Besides, he says he can't get no rest here, not with all this death around."

Without another glance at the trio, Leith spurred his horse toward the shadows, and soon the only sounds left were the crackling logs of the fire and the cawing of ravens in the dark night.

The dolls were often a mystery, even to Quill, who had known the craft of their creation since before her granny passed over to the ghostlands when she was still a cub. The dolls and the secrets of their creation passed down through Spider Clan from granny or mam to daughter, along with the soft tongue that would help the cub understand them. She learned much before and after Granny Pearl's death, but there was still much about the dolls that remained maddeningly outside her comprehension. She half suspected that the little apple-headed figures preferred it that way—they were every bit as cranky and mischievous as their squinting, wrinkled features indicated. They were also her closest family now, and she cared for them with as much kindness as her own mam had given her.

Quill loved the dolls deeply, but that didn't stop the frustration, especially at this time, when she really needed them to share what they knew. Many Tetawi came to her squat little cabin on the family acreage she shared with her maternal uncle and cousins, and each visitor hoped that the dolls could give wise counsel or offer hope for a problem or healing for a wound. Yet tonight it wasn't a love-medicinal for a pining young *fahr* that took Quill's attention, nor a soothing treatment for an elder's dull aches and unspoken loneliness. This was an entirely different, and desperately urgent, situation. Yet the dolls remained stubbornly silent.

The four cubs had disappeared the day before, and there had been no sign of them since then. Even the settlement's hunting hounds couldn't catch a trace of them. Bird and his sisters were not likely to run away; ever since their oldest brother had been kidnapped by slaving Men, they were much too skittish to wander past the ravine that separated the mound-house cabins of Spindletop from the Edgewood. Everyone was trying to pretend that the cubs were just teasing, that they were crouched giggling in their mother's pantry, that they were anywhere in the Tetawi settlement and not Out There. But such imaginings didn't bring the cubs back.

The room was quiet in spite of the dozens of Tetawi who sat on cushions, benches, and thick braided rugs, or who stood, tense and grim-faced, when they couldn't find any room to sit down. Quill sat in her doll-making chair, a high-backed seat of smoothed tree roots that her uncle had carved for her when she reached her age-name birthday. It was here that she fashioned the dolls from dried crabapples, corncobs and corn husks, beads, feathers, shells, bits of colourful cloth, and other scavenged or crafted accessories, each element combining to create another wizened figure who looked into the world's mysteries with polished-pebble eyes and sometimes came back with wisdom. Quill could often understand their speech, but just as often the dolls chattered away in a language that was completely their own, unintelligible to others, or they just kept quiet, unable or unwilling to share what was going on behind their shining eyes. To non-Dolltenders, the dolls simply sat, stiff and silent, on their shelves. Whatever it was that Quill saw and heard, it belonged to her alone.

The Tetawa's shoulders slumped and she let out a long, ragged breath. Her tawny face, recently adorned with the three-claw mark of adulthood under her left eye, was pinched with exhaustion. She'd already tried to speak with six of the dolls, but they shared nothing. It wasn't that they were ignorant of the situation—far from it. The Moth Clan cubs were well known to both Quill and the dolls, largely because of the youngest, Chadda, who insisted on stopping in every time she was passing Quill's home to squeal with delight in anticipation of the dolls' patient conversation, to which the cub was already sensitive, even at her young age. The Dolltender had reminded the dolls of Chadda's loving ways, but even that sentimental appeal was useless. They stared at her without emotion in their dark eyes. She'd never known them to be so unyielding. Perhaps her granny could have moved past that barrier to wrest away the dolls' secrets, but Quill wasn't her granny, as she had to acknowledge once again. She was lost.

"Anything yet?" It was Meerda, the cubs' mother. She'd been beautiful once, with full round cheeks and luxurious dark hair, but the loss of her eldest son and his uncle—her dearest brother, who left to find the kidnapped cub and disappeared along with him—had ravaged her. And now this. A thick knot swelled in Quill's throat, and she shook her head as she reached for another doll.

Someone bumped into the table beside her tree-root seat, shifting the doll that she wanted out of her reach, and her brown fingers closed on another one. She looked up. It was Hickory. The doll was an old one, but he wasn't one of her favourites. His face had dried into an unpleasant grimace, in spite of all her efforts to mold it into something a little less gruesome, and she'd never quite gotten used to his scowl and beady, narrow eyes. A stiff shock of white thistledown stood up on his head, adding to his unpleasant strangeness. Quill had never destroyed one of her dolls—it was almost unthinkable to do so—but if any of the sixty or more dolls were to be the first, Hickory would be the one to burn. Still, he was the nearest to her, so she pulled the frowning doll from the table and spoke to him.

She wasn't at all surprised that he was as silent as the rest; she'd expected nothing more from him—he'd never once spoken to her. His wizened face seemed to twist into an almost spiteful grimace, and his eyes rolled around to take in the gathered Tetawi. He watched them sit, hands clenched in fear and anticipation, some clinging tightly to one another in the suddenly cold room, hope swallowed by a growing fear.

And then Hickory laughed.

It was a thin, piercing giggle that ripped through the terrified gathering. Even the other Tetawi heard the awful sound, and many cried out. The world seemed to darken, like a cold blanket dropped across their eyes. Quill gasped and tried to release the doll, but Hickory's twine and twig arms wrapped tightly around her hands, digging hard into the flesh. The puckered apple mouth rose and fell maliciously as the cackle grew louder, more biting. The air went frigid as a shadow filled the room. The Dolltender heard the others cry out, but their voices were distant, as if they were calling to her from another place. She wasn't with them anymore. All that she could see was the doll in her bleeding hands, his contorted face growing more malevolent with each shrieking laugh. Her gaze fell into his burning eyes, shiny black stones no longer. She was drawn into their endlessness.

Then she saw the cubs, and she shouted to them. They couldn't hear her. They clung desperately to one another, eyes shut in terror, as a tall shadow slid through the trees towards them. Quill was sharing the shadow's view, could hear its gurgling laugh echoed by the doll in her hands. The children were torn and bloody, Bird most of all. He pushed his sisters and brother behind him when the shadow drew near. Quill watched helplessly as two clawed white hands rose into view and slashed downwards with uncanny speed. Bird threw his hand up to protect himself, pulling it away to stare at the bloody stump that was once his arm. Slowly, the cub turned his eyes to the gaping hole in his chest and the heart that pumped, steaming still, in the pale talons.

Quill's own screams rang louder than those of the cubs, and the shadow slid forwards over Bird's still-warm body. She could almost feel its glee as it reached out again. A sudden rage filled her, and she felt her body become her own again, if only for a moment. In that brief flash, Quill threw herself into the table of dolls, knocking it over to spill its contents over her body and the floor. She slid back into that grim half-world, but this time noted with satisfaction that the shadow had stopped. The air was filled with a new sound that drowned out the weeping of the cubs and the hissing laughter of the shadow. *Shakka-shakka-shakka, shakka-shakka-shakka.* Dozens of small figures emerged from the darkness in the trees, their corn-husk garments crackling softly, and surrounded the children. *Shakka-shakka-shakka.* Beady stone eyes stared at the shadow. *Shakka-shakka-shakka.* The laughter ended abruptly. *Shakka-shakka-shakka-shakka.* The dolls brought their circle closer around the cubs and withdrew with a soft shuffling whisper into the trees. *Shakka-shakka-shakka. Shakka-shakka-shakka.*

The tension in her hands loosened, and Quill opened her eyes to see Hickory's broken body crumbling into pieces in her fingers. The apple head was distorted into an expression of feral rage, the brows knotted in frustration, but at least he was silent now. She took a deep breath. A couple of Tetawi helped her get shakily to her feet. The room was warm again, and it was in shambles. Many of her neighbours had fled, although a few still remained, including Meerda, who lay sobbing on the wooden floor. Whatever Quill had seen, all those present had shared the grisly experience.

Quill draped her arms around Meerda's shoulders and held the grieving *firra* tightly to her, as a few of the remaining Tetawi picked up the scattered furniture and tried to give some order to the room. Most of her dolls were gone, but they would be back with the surviving cubs, and she would prepare the dolls' meal of cedar and tobacco and thank them with the proper words. And after that, the Tetawi of Spindletop would prepare for Bird's funeral.

She turned her attention to the remains of old Hickory, now broken and impotent on the worn wooden floor. Quill walked to the corner beside the fireplace and drew out a broom and thin-edged copper shovel. She was careful to gather all of the pieces, leaving not even the smallest shred of cornhusk or chunk of apple behind, and when she was finished, Quill strode to the fireplace and drove the entire head of the shovel deep into the still-smouldering ashes. There was a rush of air and a crackle, followed by a blast of flame that flew up the chimney. She stepped back. The sweet smell of burnt apple filled the room… and something else with it, a bitterness that gathered in the back of her throat. When she was sure that Hickory had been reduced to ashes, Quill washed her hands in a basin beside the fireplace, turned toward the door, and waited for her dolls to come home.

❦

Leith wanted to escape quickly from the ruins of Nine Oaks Town, but the horse stubbornly refused to match his desired pace; instead, she pulled back, snorting and shaking her head, her hooves digging deep trenches in the hard red soil. The he-Kyn snapped the reins and shouted at her, and she finally moved forward, but slowly, grunting and quivering with each hesitant step.

This mission was meant to be the first glorious step in a great career. He'd actively pursued the assignment when he overheard one of his mother's Assembly friends mention that a Sevenfold Council had been called. He was one of the finest riders of Sheynadwiin's Celestial families, widely admired for his grace in the saddle and his casual mastery of the temperamental beasts. When the call came for messengers, he was first in the queue, and he was the first to receive the Governor's seal and his instructions. He'd been more than a little disappointed that his guide would be a back-country Brownie scribbler, but Leith was eager for the adventure, and he was confident that the journey would be a success in spite of its rather mundane beginning.

The journey was anything but the romantic adventure he'd anticipated. In fact, it was an experience in humiliation all the way. He didn't understand the Kyn of the Wild lands, either their customs or their language, and he found out quite quickly how unprepared he was for the rigours of the mission. He'd expected to ride along well-maintained roads, only to find that they generally took rough and rocky trails that left him battered and sore. Sleep was no better, as his bedroll was inadequate for the mix of terrain he slept on. His fine clothing was too thin for the cold nights; he'd forgotten an oil wrap, so rain often left him damp and sniffling for days.

And this was before he even encountered any of the Folk he was meant to speak with. Far from being the mysterious figures out of winter-time stories that he'd expected, the Wielders turned out to be rather ordinary and uninspiring. Leith seemed to always cause offense when encountering them; he didn't know when to speak or be silent, when to eat or not eat, which direction to walk around the town fires, what he should or shouldn't offer as a gift. Tobhi told him to simply pay attention and follow his example, but the Brownie seemed to insist on indulging every superstition and backwards custom they encountered, and whenever Leith tried to intervene with good Celestial teachings, he'd find his guide looking at him with lips pursed and eyebrow raised, as though the he-Kyn was an ignorant youngling. So Leith simply stood back, aloof, and waited with ever-growing impatience for the time when he could return home and finally get away from this strange world. He just didn't belong here. He was lonely, and frightened. Tobhi had seen it, and even though the Brownie had never used it against him, there was some small part of the he-Kyn that hated him for it.

And now the old Wielder and her niece had seen his fear, too. It was more than he could bear. He had to get away from them all, and quickly.

Full of rage now, he finally slammed his heels into the mare's side, piercing her flesh with the spurs. She rose up with a bubbling grunt and at last jerked forward down the road, just as a black shape streaked out of the darkness and swept past Leith's head. He barely had time to duck as a second shadow rushed toward him. His hand went to the flintlock at his side, but the mare twisted wildly, and the weapon fell, unfired, to the ground. The air was suddenly thick, and Leith gagged as the acrid stench surrounded him, burning his eyes and throat. He covered his mouth with his arm, but the oily foulness permeated everything.

The mare reared back again, her eyes rolling wide in stark terror. The he-Kyn cursed the beast and drove his spurs hard against her, heedless of her pain and his own stalks' sympathetic throb. Weaponless, and unwilling to return in frightened shame to Tobhi and the she-Kyn, Leith saw only one reasonable option: to ride far and fast.

Leith's mother had begged him to withdraw from this mission for the Sevenfold Council and its Speaker; she'd never approved of Garyn's sympathetic coddling of the Greenwalkers and their backward ways, and she certainly didn't approve of Leith's restless interest in the Wild lands beyond Sheynadwiin's walls. But she was as indulgent of her eldest son as Garyn was of the Wielders, so in spite of her disapproving frowns, she nodded her reluctant assent when Leith kissed her forehead before he departed, his saddlebags slung carelessly across his back.

«*You worry too much, mother,*» he'd laughed then, as if this journey would be nothing more than a brisk canter through the city's centre green. «*I have my musket, and I have a guide who is quite knowledgeable of the area. Do not worry about me–the most troubling events I am likely to encounter will be rain or saddle sores.*»

«*You might get fever from the rain, or skin-blight from the sores...*» Leith had laughed again at her final appeal, waving farewell as he spurred the horse onward, not even bothering to look back as he called out to her, «*I will return in glory, mother.*»

The words returned now, unbidden and unwelcome. They pierced his thoughts with their mocking irony. His mother was always wringing her hands in fear and worry, and always without good cause–so why should this night be any different? Why should she now be right, when she'd so often been wrong?

The answers never came. Blots of darkness streamed out of the forest, and Leith gasped in an agony too deep for screams as a talon raked across the surface of one of his sensory stalks. The stalk thrashed wildly, like a worm skewered on a fishhook. He couldn't breathe. He hurt too much even to be afraid. He didn't notice that his nerveless fingers had loosened their hold on the reins, or that the mare's frantic movements had tossed him from the saddle to writhe blindly on the rock-strewn earth.

Maddened by pain, Leith never saw the shadows darken in the trees above him, nor did he hear the sniggering mass of sharp-toothed figures descend in eager anticipation. He only became aware of their presence when they began to feed.

❦❦❦❦❦❦❦

Tobhi found what remained of Leith's mangled body the next morning, just outside the wall of Nine Oaks Town. The he-Kyn's horse was gone, but the musket lay broken in two on the ground next to his blood-stained iron-ward. Tobhi searched for tracks, but other than signs of the horse's frantic escape, there was nothing more than a handful of foul-smelling black feathers. None of them spoke about the night before, or the reason for the savage attack. It clearly wasn't random; the Governor's seal was conspicuously missing.

They carried what remained of Leith back to Nine Oaks Town, wrapped and prayed over his body and added it to the others on the scaffolds, and followed the ceremony with a cold purifying bath. They didn't have the luxury of four days in purifying isolation–yet another breach of etiquette and ritual that grieved Unahi. Gathering up their own few belongings, the travellers left the shadows of Nine Oaks behind.

Of the three, Unahi was the most familiar with the hill country, so, after brief consultation with Tobhi, who'd spent much of his childhood on the trade routes in the area, she decided to go east to the banks of the Wildwater, which would lead them north for a few weeks through the lower Eldarvian Woods, and then on to the city of Sheynadwiin within Dardath Vale. There were faster and more direct ways to Sheynadwiin, but the she-Kyn and Tetawa hesitated to travel in the view of too many interested eyes, just in case whatever had killed Leith was waiting for those Wielders who had actually received his missive.

They finished out the night beyond the rock ring that enclosed Nine Oaks, and then, with dawn and another frigid creek bath, headed out again. Unahi estimated about ten days to the Wildwater, if they stuck to a steady pace and didn't encounter any unexpected delays. Though never mentioned by name, Leith was often in their thoughts.

It grieved the old Wielder to be taking Tarsa away from Thistlewood, where the younger she-Kyn could have received a full understanding of the *wyr* and its teachings in a calmer place that still sang with ancient spirits. But the People needed them at the Council, and that was the higher duty now. Perhaps, when the gathering was over, they would return to the deep forest, and Tarsa's training could expand in peace. In the meantime,

Unahi would just have to do her best on the road and hope that the young warrior's emotions and frustration could be directed towards more productive channels.

The Kraagen Mountains stood high and strong along the eastern horizon. Travel across the mighty, snow-peaked range was difficult at the best of times, unless one knew of the few passes that cut through the peaks. Tarsa was an utter stranger to this place; the wall of gray and white that loomed in the distance filled her with curiosity and–though she would have been too proud to acknowledge it–more than a little hesitation.

The Wildwater would be their first significant destination. The valley stretches that spanned either side of the raging river were some of the easier routes for travel in this rocky expanse. Few of the more communal Folk knew or cared about the inner valleys, as they tended to prefer the more temperate slopes that stretched, lush and green, on either side of the mountains; what happened in the middle of the cold and brutal Kraagens was of little interest. The life-giving Wildwater was much beloved in the lowlands to the south of the Kraagens, as most of the river's fury had already been spent by the time it reached these gentle regions, and that broad, muddy stretch was the form in which the great water was best known to most of the Folk. Yet there were hearty Folk–relatively few in number, but not entirely rare–who treasured the fierce, mid-mountain river and the fertile grasslands that flanked it. Mineral-rich waters descended from the tall peaks, first in thin rivulets, then in thick streams that cascaded down five-thousand-foot cliffs, finally drawing together into a boiling flood of frigid whiteness that crashed and smashed through the mountains, and fast on its way past Tangletop Forest at the southeastern edge of the Everland, where it disappeared between worlds, never reaching the lands of Men. Most who knew the river at its greatest strength were solitary wanderers, like the Stoneskin who ravaged the Kyn towns, but rock-spirits were everywhere, and some small communities of Gvaergs, Ubbetuk, Tetawi, and Feral beast-folk called the valleys home. Some of these were cautious but friendly with strangers; others preferred to kill interlopers as a matter of expedient principle, especially in these unsettled times.

The first full day's travel was slow and generally quiet, as both Tarsa and Unahi were exhausted from their earlier journey and their unpleasant labour in Nine Oaks Town. It was a pleasant day, though, that combined the crispness of spring with the bright clarity of the approaching summer, and the gentle mood helped to lift the gloom of Nine Oaks. Tobhi was thankful for the silence. He hadn't known Leith too well or even liked him much, but the brutality of the he-Kyn's death still pained him.

They walked at an easy pace when possible, but the eastern side of the hill country was littered with steep, blocky cliffs that required careful planning to maneuver around. Just when they were sure that they'd reached the end of the mesas, they'd find themselves on another one and spend much of their time searching for the faint game trails that led to the scrubby base of the bluff. They'd occasionally see a flight of great firebirds wheeling in the far distance, the creatures' multicoloured plumage iridescent in the two suns' light, or encounter giant elk grazing calmly in the peace of rustling aspen groves, grumbling bears who lumbered past with no more than a glance of cursory interest at Smudge's panicked snorts, and once even an antlered greatwyrm sunning itself on a vast flat slab of red stone just a few miles away. They kept close to the bluffs to avoid agitating this latter creature but returned to their planned course when the pearly silver of a mid-air stormdrake glinted in the late afternoon, sending the greatwyrm slithering swiftly back into its lair.

They camped in a pine grove at the base of a tall, chunky mound of streaked sandstone, one of many that dotted the rising hills to the east, choosing the site largely because of a little spring-fed creek that wound its way down the slope. Tobhi took Smudge into the trees and returned with a few thick bundles of firewood lashed to the deer's back, while Tarsa swept a gravelly area free of pine needles and other debris and dug a fire-pit, lining it with a dozen of the large stones that littered the area. Unahi searched through the Tetawa's saddlebags and found some dried marsh rice that she added to some of the root vegetables that she carried in her own travelling pack. These she placed in a clay pot of water that she nestled inside the ashes. The Wielder then mixed a few handfuls of ground nut flour with water and formed a sticky dough to bake on the rocks.

Unahi ate quickly and excused herself early that night. After so much pain and death over the past few days, she was exhausted, and this was as safe a place as any in the Everland these days. She spoke briefly to a few of the pines, who agreed to shrug off some of their listlessness to watch over the travellers that night. Tobhi and Tarsa remained awake and began an unspoken contest to see who could eat the most food. Though just a little over half the she-Kyn's height, Tobhi maintained a respectable pace.

While working on her third bowl of stew, Tarsa's glance fell on the thick pouch that the Tetawa kept tightly fastened next to his belly. "What were you looking at last night when you first talked with Leith?" she asked.

Tobhi's hand went defensively to his belt. "Did ye see it?" he mumbled through a mouthful of stew.

"No," she said, breaking off another piece of bread. "You were turned away from us, but I definitely felt something. Are you a Wielder?"

He chuckled. "A Wielder? Nah. Our Wielders en't often as easy to spot as yours; Tetawi Wielders are healers and shape-shifters, medicine-makers and spies. They're filled with animal spirit; sometimes they even become like their Clan animals, more spirit than flesh, I reckon. No, I en't one of them wisdom-bearers; I'm just a Leafspeaker."

The she-Kyn gave him a questioning glance. The Tetawa smiled. "Ye en't never heard of a Leafspeaker afore? Well, then, ye gotta see for ye'self." He finished his stew and glanced at the last bit remaining in the cooking pot, then sighed and slipped the pouch off of his belt. It was a beautifully-crafted bag of hand-tooled leather, with a front pocket cunningly designed to look like the head of a badger, the symbol of Tobhi's maternal Clan. He lifted the badger's snout and pulled a bundle wrapped in red cloth from the pouch. Tarsa set her bowl aside and moved closer.

Tobhi's nimble fingers quickly unwrapped the cloth to reveal a stack of

Tobhi

broad leaves of various shapes and colours, each at least half the size of the Tetawa's hand. "They're lore-leaves," he grinned, proud to be sharing his talent with someone so clearly interested. He lifted a single leaf into the air to reveal a dark sigil carved delicately into its surface. "Every leaf's got a different story to tell, and together they can tell ye pretty much any story ye might want to hear. The leaves sorta talk to me, ye see. Stories 'bout the past, or stories 'bout what's comin' down the road."

"You can see the future with them?" Tarsa asked, her eyes bright. Her stalks, now unwrapped and pulsing slightly in the cool air, curled softly against her cheeks.

Tobhi shook his head. "Depends. Sometimes I can get a sense of what's comin', but the future's a tricky thing, and it's hard to get the full understandin' of the story. It's too easy to read what ye want to read instead of what the true story is. So I try to avoid lookin' at them stories. They bring too much grief and misunderstandin'. I prefer to read the stories that brought us here, the stories that help us know where we come from and who we are. Them stories is generally more helpful for guidin' the future than tryin' to look ahead and seein' what's on the way. It's a knowin' circle, tellin' us that what's come afore can help us with what's comin' now."

He lifted the leaf into the air and pulled his hand away. The leaf remained in mid-air, floating as if pinned to an invisible wall. He followed with other leaves–oaks, birches, aspens, maples, and others that Tarsa couldn't identify–each large and marked with its own distinctive symbol. Soon there were twenty leaves, then thirty-two, then forty, each hanging in the air, combining together in a series of vertical spirals. Finally, satisfied with the number, Tobhi folded the remaining leaves into the cloth and returned them to the pouch.

His attention firmly fixed on the leaves, Tobhi said softly, "This en't a common gift among my people; I think m' pepa learned somethin' like it when he lived with the Kyn at Thornholt afore I was born, then put it to Tetawi uses, so ye might say it's a Kyn-gifted talent. Now, think 'bout somethin' ye want to know more 'bout, somethin' that's important, some-thin' that might help ye with decisions in yer life." He shifted the location of some of the leaves but they maintained the same complex pattern of intersecting spirals.

Tarsa thought for a few moments. There were so many things that she wanted to know—too many, and most of them were about the future. She was at the start of a new life, and it was a frightening beginning. Yet it was also one that brought a strange sort of anticipation and excitement. Her world had been completely remade in just a few days. Transformation and change—that was the story for this night. Suddenly, she knew the story she wanted to hear.

"Tell me about the Melding, Tobhi. Tell me what's in the leaves." She had heard the story many times, and by masterful Kyn storytellers, but Tobhi's gift promised to reveal something new.

The Tetawa nodded, his face grave. "I'll tell ye the truth as I know it, but there's lots of other stories that have the truth, too. I still en't that far past a cub m'self, so there's lots I don't know in the story. But the leaves tell me a little more each time, so I've got to listen to the stories over and over to really understand 'em. It en't a happy tale, that's certain, but it's an important one. All right now." He lifted his hands into the air and closed his eyes.

The light of the Greatmoon and his shattered sky-brothers was brighter tonight; it was still some time before the greater sphere would be full, but the glow of the moon and the shimmering band of silver that cut across the night sky dimmed the stars and illuminated the little lore-keeper's outstretched hands. The sigils on each leaf suddenly flared into a reddish-gold light. For a moment, Tarsa thought the fragile leaves would burst into flame, but their brightness only illuminated the shadows around them. Forty strange symbols flashed into life against the night. Tobhi's hands began to move, and the leaves followed the motion. The glowing shapes spun and wove together as they circled around in a rhythmic pattern that slipped from ages past to the present and back again. They moved so quickly that Tarsa lost track of the individual signs and soon saw only golden trails of twisting, dancing light. Tobhi's dark eyes tracked their movements, and he began to speak, his voice low and hollow, his attention fully focused on the swirling flashes of green, gold, and red in the darkness.

"This is the truth as I know it. This world en't always been what it is today, ye know. Our world was once our own–it was all the Eld Green. There wasn't any 'Holds, no Darkenin's, no Decay or Otherness. Everythin' was the *wyr*, and we was part of it. The hills spoke to us, told us stories, as did the trees, the rivers, the hollows and the swamps. The beasts had themselves councils in them days, and we all respected 'em as equals. The Tetawi still do, ye know, but we're the only ones, I think, 'cept for them other Folk who follow the Old Ways.

"There was no time back then, nothin' like there is now. Sure, there was death, but it was different. It weren't somethin' to be feared like it is today. It came to us when our time was done, after a long, full life, and our passin' was a cause for celebration of a life lived, not mournin' for a life lost. But now things is different, and too often the flower is cut down afore it blooms.

"In them days, we had all we needed for livin', and we made things of great beauty, things that spoke to our joys and our happiness. In them days, any grievances we had with one another were settled peaceable; if we couldn't do that, we talked in council with Granny Turtle, Ol' Jenna, first of my people and mother of all the beasts and the birds. Granny Turtle would listen and then decide what was best, as was her duty as first Clan mother, and we'd generally live just fine together. If we couldn't, well–even in them days we fought with one another, truth to tell, but it was always somethin' we could handle, and it was for survival, not for conquerin' and power.

"Now, Granny Turtle had herself a few sisters. There was Zhaia, the True Tree, the mother of yer folk. There was Shobbok, the Winter Witch, who brought all kind of sufferin' and critters out of the stone and ice of the north country. There was Avialle, the river-mother, who gave life to all them swimmers and mud-divers. There was others, too, and some brothers among 'em, but the sisters was the first to come about, so they're the ones in this story.

"It was gentle, trustin' Avialle who first met up with the Man called Kaantor. He was a bad sort, but nobody could've known that at the time, 'cause they'd never seen themselves a Human afore. He was a tall, fine-lookin' Man, with long hair and a short bit of beard. He didn't come across the Canopy Veil by accident; he was sent here by some of his own kind who'd come across the Veil in their greedy reachin' for knowledge that twisted on itself, becomin' witchery and the like. He came across and saw green bounty and happiness like nothin' he'd ever seen afore. He saw trees so heavy with sweet fruit that their branches nearly dragged the ground. He saw the Folk, the tree-born and the river-born, Folk of air and mountain, hill and swampy-land, Folk of rocks and deep places, too, all livin' peaceable most of the time, side by side, and he wanted to be part of it. After a while, he forgot them that sent him.

"Our way is to trust folks 'til they give us reason not to, so there was no way of knowin' what was to come. The first one to meet up with this Man Kaantor was sweet Avialle, who soon fell in love with him. I suppose he fell in love with her, too, in his own manner of doin' things. So for a time they was pretty happy. They spent most of their time rollin' in the furs—natural, of course, but somethin' them Humans seem to have all kinds of trouble with, gettin' it wrapped up with shame and guilt and meanness and such. Avialle didn't know any of them ways, so she was happy, and she gave of herself freely. But Kaantor never intended to stay and be satisfied with what he had. He wanted more, and he'd betray the one that loved him as well as them that called 'emselves his masters.

"It didn't help matters none that Shobbok, that tricky ol' thing, had a bit of meanness in her heart for Avialle, too. Winter ain't a kind season to rivers, ye know, even now, freezin' 'em solid, cuttin' 'em into pieces even when the warmin' months come along. But even them big ice glaciers in the Waste of Sleet can't stop the rivers from flowin' through 'em, so I guess Avialle gives as good as she gets, eh? Anyway, Shobbok knew what was bubblin' up in that Man's heart, so she whispers to him that there's treasures across the Canopy Veil, and all he has to do is cut it open with his iron sword to find 'em, 'cause that's the only thing that'll do it.

"Now, I don't know what was goin' on in that ol' spirit's head to put such an idea out there; I en't entirely sure that she knew what she was doin', neither, but all Kaantor's greed and selfishness couldn't be held back, no matter how much Avialle loved him, so one mornin', while she was sleepin', he took up his iron sword and walked up to the Veil between the worlds. Avialle woke up sudden-like to find him missin' and a deep, groanin' ache in the world, a pain so deep and raw that all life in the Eld Green cried out. She rushed to the Canopy Veil only to find Kaantor standin' there, sword piercin' the curtain, his flesh withered and worn like a dried-up apple. The Veil had kept all that age and dyin' and Decay out of the land, but since he cut it up with poison iron, Decay flowed in like a poisoned river, reachin' its dry claws out to claim everythin' it had been denied. I reckon even ol' Shobbok didn't expect that.

"So there stood that dung-hearted Kaantor, now an old man made mad by greed and lust, and when he sees Avialle come up to him, he turns his iron sword on her, sayin' that she tricked him, that she denied him what was by rights his, that she was hidin' all the treasures that should'a gone to him. He said that she'd seduced him, that she was nothin' but a ruttin' whore, that she'd cursed him with her feminine ways. And then he attacked. Poor, gentle Avialle. She never knew that her love-mate would turn out this-a-way. It's an old story, sad to say. She had no way of knowin' how her trust would be repaid, but she was no weak flower–she had sharp thorns. She fought back. She called on all the *wyr* she could reach to drive Kaantor and his new master, Decay, back through the Veil. And even then, the *wyr* was stronger than Decay, at least in the Eld Green. All the spirits of the Eld Green came to help her out, and soon Kaantor and Decay fell together into shadow. But Kaantor wasn't done yet. As he slid toward the Veil, Decay's burnin' hand clutchin' and witherin' his legs, the treacherous Man drove his sword into the Veil again, piercin' it from the inside, mixing the sword's poison with the last bit of bile his spirit could muster. And as he fell dead into the Darkenin' between the worlds, the Canopy Veil split completely, and the two worlds crashed together, destroyin' much of both and givin' Decay another chance at us.

"Never afore, and certain never since, was there such a terrible time as the Meldin'. It was a lot like two balls of soft mud smashed together—entire lands destroyed, their spirits lost in the shatterin'. Some parts of both worlds was only lightly touched, while others was broken and scattered like a seed pod in a storm. Mountains rose up from oceans, deserts took the place of ancient forests, rivers flowed into new cracks in the land that disappeared into nothin'ness, and everywhere there was death and devastation. The Greatmoon, ol' Pearl-in-Darkness, watched as his two brothers were shattered into shinin' dust, and he still bears the scars of the Meldin' on his round face and weeps for his lost family. Some entire lands was pushed into shadows, becomin' Darkenin' pockets where the spirits still go on, neither dead nor livin', always hungerin' for the warmth of the life they once had. Doors opened up into other worlds unknown to either the Folk or Men, bringin' monstrosities into the Melded world, and with 'em pain, sufferin', and unendin' turmoil. Them was bad days for everyone, but the Meldin' was worst for the Folk, as we was driven on and on into fragments of the world we once knew, brought down by diseases as much as by the Men who hungered for the wyr-rich 'Hold-lands we call home.

"So now, all these many years later, our world is different. This broken world en't just ours no more. Many of our 'Holds are strong, but them Humans is never satisfied, and they want more and more of what little we got left. They never suffered like we did, but still they want more, and they begrudge us them things that's always been ours anyway. But we keep fightin', hopin' one day that they'll listen to all their own high talk about goodness and justice and fairness and peace, and not keep trying to take all of ours away. And maybe they will, one day."

Tobhi lowered his hands. The bright lights faded away, leaving only dark marks on the leaves. He pulled the lore leaves from the air, wrapped them up, and placed the bundle back into his pouch. He and Tarsa finished their meal, and the rest of the night passed quietly, the Greatmoon's scarred and mournful light blanketing the world around them.

CHAPTER 7
DETERMINATION

"Come in."

The sturdy oak door swung open slowly, as though hesitant to admit the visitor. Neranda looked up from her desk, laying her quill and paper to one side and rubbing the exhaustion from her eyes. The room was illuminated by everlights, adding softness to the bright moonlight streaming in through the great windows that overlooked the Sheynadwiin falls. The Lawmaker generally disliked anything more than the gentlest lighting in her chambers at night, as this was the best aid for deep reflection and undistracted thought. But there was simply too much work to be done these days, and such time, once inviolate, was all too scarce now.

Her maidservant Iseya entered and bowed. "Forgive the interruption, my lady, but Desha'al Myyrd, second to Captain Pradu Styke, has arrived."

Neranda smiled. "Of course, Iseya. Please show him in. And please bring us some wine. Ask Mandra to be at hand—you deserve a bit of rest. It has been a very long day for us all." Iseya returned the smile and dropped for an instant to one knee before leaving the room.

The Lawmaker stood. She was still dressed for visitors, although she would much rather have been retired for the night and in her silken sleeping gown. She wore a violet dress that draped far past her slippered feet. It had been dyed specifically to match the hue of her striking eyes, all the more heightened by the stark white collar and ruffled sleeves of the dress. The only accessories that she wore were a small silver Celestial medallion of the Greatmoon in crescent hanging from a chain around her neck, and a slender silver diadem that held her thick copper locks from her face. Blue face powdered white; nails modestly painted and trimmed to a respectably fashionable length; only the most subtle silver embroidery along the hem of her dress. Neranda turned to the polished silver mirror mounted on the opposite wall and quickly scrutinized her appearance.

Neither too ornate nor too simplistic–it would be suitable for tonight's business. Satisfied with the result, she returned to her desk. It was essential to be prepared, to find a balance of grace and strength, as this would not be a pleasant visit.

The door opened again to admit Myyrd, his thin face haughty but pleasant enough. In spite of herself, Neranda felt her face flush with stirrings of anger. Yet it took only a well-trained heartbeat for her to shift the rage into the necessary energy to accomplish her task. She held her hand out, palm up, and Myyrd lightly touched her fingers in greeting.

"Lawmaker Ak'Shaar. I was most pleased to receive your invitation. It is, I trust, in response to my own brief query, which I promised to expand upon in this meeting?"

Of course. No delay–the matter at hand immediately. There were few things Neranda missed about the old social etiquette, but one of them was the slow, considerate entrance into diplomatic discussions. In the old days, such a meeting would never have begun until each member of the gathering had engaged in conversation with the others. The process would sometimes take days, even weeks, but it was time well spent, as the representatives of all perspectives would come to know and respect one another's lives, strengths, and weaknesses. Any conflicts were minimized by the intimacy of familiarity; the alliances and agreements that emerged were strengthened by everyone's mutual regard for one another. Such basic courtesies were a lost art these days, among Kyn as much as anyone.

The councillor was taller than the Lawmaker, but his slight stoop made him seem her shadow. His sensory stalks were drawn severely back and tied, along with his thin hair, into a simple topknot. He wore the standard brown cloak and golden vest of Assembly councillor, but they were threadbare and worn, conspicuous details in spite of the dim lighting in the room. Desperation clung to the shabby he-Kyn like a rancid second skin.

She nodded and motioned him to a seat opposite her desk. "Why else would I invite you here? Please sit down." Iseya entered and handed the

Lawmaker a small tray bearing a cut-glass decanter of jeng wine–a rare delicacy from the Human lands of Pei-Tai-Pesh, drawn from her family's private stock–and two unadorned silver goblets. The housemaid slid out of the room, drawing the door closed behind her. Myyrd flashed Neranda what he surely thought was a charming smile, and she returned the gesture, even though her stomach tightened with the first risings of bile. She handed him a goblet, filled one for herself, and returned to her seat at the desk. "How may I help you, Councillor Myyrd? Your letter was most…intriguing."

He sipped his wine slowly, savoring it, watching her with heavy-lidded brown eyes. When an awkward silence settled over the room, Myyrd drained the goblet and said, "I come on behalf of your old friend, Captain Styke, to remind you of an offer he made, a number of months past, that he believes would be of great service to you."

"And what would that be? Remind me."

"The Captain is, at this very moment, heavily engaged with protecting the trading routes on the western border, but he has, to date, received very little Assembly support or compensation for his defensive activities. It is regard to this matter that he urgently requests your immediate attention."

Neranda lowered her goblet. "I see. What, Councillor, does Captain Styke believe to be a reasonable demonstration of support?"

He smirked. "One of your fellow Lawmakers, Braek the Younger, has introduced a Writ of Commerce into the Assembly Rolls that would, among other things, provide additional financial resources and a small stretch of land–almost insignificant–on the northern side of the road, to ensure the safe travel and responsible transport of trade goods to Eromar. We feel certain that the passage of this Oath would eliminate the unfortunate delays of the trading trains and would, in fact, provide the western centre for safe commerce that Sheynadwiin so clearly requires, especially in these unsettled times. Such passage would increase not only the ability of Captain Styke to expand trade opportunities to the west, but it would also expand the influence of those families, like your own, that have strong familiarity with such commerce. It's entirely a winning proposition, for the Nation as well as for those families who most quickly take advantage of its possibilities." His smile stretched wider.

Neranda returned his smile as she pulled a detailed wyrwood bark map from her desk drawer. It showed the lands in question, and the Lawmaker scrutinized it closely. "A declaration like this would violate our most ancient laws on the distribution and possession of land, would it not? It would seem to give the good Captain a rather strategic stretch of land into his private keeping, land that is not under the full authority of the Kyn Nation. How might the Tetawi and Ferals of that area respond to such a law, given the fact that those particular lands are shared hunting and gathering grounds for various Folk, not for Kyn alone?"

Myyrd shrugged, clearly unconcerned with the conflict. "It's been Kyn blood that has kept the road open; they can hardly begrudge their protectors this tiny bit of land."

"Protector, I think you mean," Neranda said, her voice even. "And what do you make of the fact that, by law, no Kyn can be the sole master of any territory in all the Everland? These lands are held in common, not owned by one alone. This custom has kept our domain from being fragmented by petty rivalries and alienated by personal desires for enrichment."

The he-Kyn leaned forward and smiled again. "Yes, but as you've so often pointed out, the world as we know it is changing, and our laws and customs can and should change with it. The only way we'll ever be able to compete with Men is by understanding our lands as power. And power in the world of Men comes from ownership. This could be the beginning of a great new era for our people."

"With Captain Styke leading the way, it would seem. Do you think, Councillor, that my support of this Writ will significantly assist its passage?" She stood again and refilled their goblets, then returned to her seat. "I am, as you well realize, of a minority in the Assembly."

"Yes, but even your opposition has nothing but the greatest respect for you, Lawmaker. You are well-regarded as a voice for reason and for…

honesty. These are qualities that could well decide the entire fate of the Writ." He leaned forward eagerly.

Neranda stood by the window, looking at the Greatmoon beyond. "Yes, I suppose your assessment is correct in that regard. I have long prided myself on serving the truth and abiding by the laws of our Nation, no matter the consequences to myself. Sometimes we must suffer much to keep the truth and our honour unblemished. Is that not correct, Councillor?" She turned her strange gaze toward him, and the air grew thick. Myyrd blinked twice and gurgled, as his windpipe tightened and squeezed shut. Neranda's eyes were as bright and cold as the moon.

The Lawmaker stood and walked over to the Councillor, who leaned back in the chair, wheezing in terror and pain. He was frozen, the air slowly, teasingly drawn from his burning lungs, as panic whipped through his body like fire. Neranda reached down and grabbed the goblet from his nerveless fingers before it dropped to the floor and stained the carpet.

She leaned down. "You will not die, Councillor—not this day, and not here. But you will travel to Captain Styke, and you will share a message with him: Neranda Ak'Shaar cannot be bought. I will not bring dishonour to my name or to that of the Kyn Nation. You may also tell him that, as a result of this treachery, I will personally see to it that the Writ is crushed in the Assembly, and that your maggot-bound hides are delivered to the most undesirable, beast-infested outpost in the Blackfly Fen, where you will spend the remainder of your serviceable days subsisting on bogworms and keeping a detailed log of the rates and consistency of the filth that the Eromar Humans are so fond of dumping in the swamp."

Myyrd slid to the floor, sobbing as the air returned to his spasming lungs. He lay face down on the carpet, a stream of spittle pooling beneath his mouth. Neranda knelt beside him. "One more thing, Councillor, before my servants escort you from my home: your days as traitor and bribe-seeker are over. Prepare for a significant change of occupation—and pray that you find bogworm to your liking." A tinkling bell rang in the distance, and two well-muscled young he-Kyn, both dressed in high-collared white shirts and black vests, entered the room to drag the half-conscious councillor away.

Mandra, the younger maidservant, entered after, her eyes filled with concern. "My lady, are you…"

"No, do not concern yourself." Neranda gently patted Mandra's arm. "All is well. It is one of the inevitable but intolerable aspects of my position. There are many who believe themselves entitled to any number of privileges, generally because they are experienced thieves and bullies who have never been denied anything in their lives. Not one of them has a jot of self-respect or self-restraint, and each believes himself to be untouchable by the law." She returned to her desk. Mandra gathered the goblets onto the tray and left the room.

"But they are always wrong," the Shield continued to herself. "There are laws of the earth and laws of the heavens, and there are many ways to be a lawmaker." She smoothed the wrinkles from her dress and sat down, taking up her quill again as though the interruption had never occurred.

***

The old garden should never have been this warm. The trailing end of the winter cold still lingered at night. Spring was a reluctant visitor to Eromar City, hampered by the city's high steppe elevation and its proximity to the ice-shrouded lands of the Lawless to the north. The garden, untended for a generation or more, lay at the farthest western edge of Gorthac Hall's rambling grounds. Skeletal trees jutted like pale spears into the air, while all around their trunks, wrapped in a shroud of sooty snow, were the withered remnants of the garden's brief bounty. It stood open to the frigid night, the stars and slivered moon bright in what should have been chill air, but the binding and reaving of Fey-spirits shifted the surrounding reality, invoking the conditions of the spirits' Elsewhere home. The Dreydmaster had just as often suffered through crackling electric storms and shrieking blizzards as blistering heat waves.

Yet, as with all things, he knew that this necessary stage, while disconcerting, would last only a moment. It would pass.

The reaving of spirits from their Otherworldly existence was a treacherous and often deadly business, and it was thus a profession suited either to those without regard for their own lives or those with a will and mind honed sharp with merciless determination. Lojar Vald was of the latter persuasion. His many years as a hard-eyed jurist had taught him about the depths of depravity to which both Humans and Unhumans could descend; he had learned too well that the only worthy aim of any dignified people was the reasoned application of consistent and unyielding law. It was the law of Men that had moved him up through the ranks of the judiciary and into the political arena, where survival required him to understand his enemies better than they understood themselves. And it was the greater law of the hidden Dreyd–those Human alchaemists who had long ago overthrown the Old Immortals of Men during the cataclysmic Great Ascension–that had shown him possibilities beyond the mortal realm. The only way that his name and deeds would live beyond his death would be to reshape the world of Men, to guide it towards the principles of the Dreyd and their followers, by linking the profane and the sacred, the temporal and the eternal. He became a Dreydmaster, and the mandates of the Dreyd became the guiding laws of Eromar. Lojar Vald closed the shackles on the chaos of Men, and law ruled supreme.

The dangers of his new life didn't end with the reaving of Fey-spirits. Any entity drawn from afar and entrapped by a Binder–the second rank of the Dreydcaste and those who brought the spirits into the Reaver's control–would always hold unmitigated hatred for the Reaver who had drawn it into slavery. Reaving required one's thoughts to be as unyielding as forge-hardened iron. A Fey-spirit might be fickle or furious, but it would always be dangerous, and it was only through brutal control that it surrendered to the Reaver's will, often being torn apart in the struggle, and never lasting long even if it acquiesced. If the Binder's skill faltered, or if the alchaemical bindings themselves ever weakened, every spirit who was released would seek out not only the Binder but also the Reaver, even if decades had passed since the summoning-spell. And their vengeance was always bloody.

Yet Reavers were needed by the Binders, for each served a purpose. So, too, did Reavers and Binders need the Seekers, who roamed the Reach of Men in patient search for those Human witches and Unhuman Fey-Folk who possessed spirit-given powers that could be used by the Binders. That none of these sorcerous creatures had any interest in sharing their powers was of little concern to the Seekers; there were many ways of ensuring cooperation, most rather painful.

It was all in a delicate balance: the Seekers found witches with particular talents, the Binders drew the captives' spirits and wrapped enchantments and magical chains around them, and Reavers bent the spirits to their will. All ranks of the Dreydcaste served and supported one another, each performing the tasks that others could not.

The Binders of Eromar City were devoted to the Dreydmaster and his law; even now they were putting their thoughts firmly towards Vald's most ambitious goal, one that even the other Dreydmasters scattered across the Reach could barely imagine. Other people saw only that Vald had devoted years to returning Eromar to its former national glory, which was now eclipsed by the upstart petty politicians who pranced through the Reach's bloated, gilt-edged capital, Chalimor. Eromar was now one of the most powerful of the allied nations of the Reach, a position that it claimed as much through aggressive expansion as through cunning political maneuvering. While not yet in any position to challenge the authority of Chalimor directly, Eromar would not be a subject state for much longer–through an iron fist and an unwielding will, Vald was fashioning a new order of things.

Yet that was only the surface of his plans. Mortal law was weak; it crumbled with time and the inevitable frailty of misdirected sympathies that undermined the convictions of Men. Vald's goal now was far greater, and it would be rooted in eternity. The will of the Dreyd, and thus that of

Lojar Vald, would endure forever. This night's ceremony was yet one more step down the road to perpetual glory.

The sweltering heat had slowly drained away, like the easy ebb of a leaking wineskin. The Crafting was complete. The trio of Binders beside the Dreydmaster moved backwards, their eyes wide and bodies shaking in sudden terror, as they beheld what they had helped to create. Each held a massive, leather-bound book in one hand, which was shackled to a chain that led from a bony wrist to a book's spine. These were the snaring-tomes, the Binders' source of power–and their curse, for their own souls were wrapped within the mystical Craftings placed on the books. They spent their lives in service to the Reavers, unable to escape, for the snaring-tomes hungered for Fey-spirits or the souls of Men, and the Binders had no choice but to let their tomes feed. If they denied the snaring-tomes for too long, the books would begin to feed on them, and such deaths were gruesome and painful beyond imagining. Theirs was a brutal existence, but such sacrifice gave worthwhile glory to the Dreyd.

Vald's dark brows lifted slightly as he looked upon the result of the evening's ceremonies, while the other Men in the garden swallowed in discomfort. In form as well as manner, the Dreydmaster was an imposing figure. He stood over six feet tall and rigidly straight, all sharp lines and angles. His iron-gray hair rose away from his forehead in a sharp widow's peak; thick brows met over dark, narrow eyes that absorbed the light but never reflected it. He wore the dark coat and maroon waistcoat of his office as jurist, with a stark white neck cloth knotted and pulled tight against his pale throat. The wide cuffs of his coat exposed just the slightest hint of white linen shirt sleeves, and his buckled black boots were polished bright from toe to knee. He was a Man on whom happiness looked unhealthy, even wrong. And yet, as he surveyed his Crafting, a thin smile crept across his tight lips.

Where once had stood a dead, weed-choked fountain, there was now a shimmering crack in the air, as though the Dreydmaster gazed upon a darkened window with a single streak of flashing light shining through.

The shape stretched at first nearly seven feet high, sometimes expanding to a greater height, sometimes shifting and shrinking to three feet or less, but the longer Vald watched, the more stable the opening became. An iridescent glow oozed out of the gap, pulsing with an erratic beat that strengthened and became a regular throb as the edges of the portal solidified.

It wasn't the first gate he'd opened in this garden; there had been another, one he'd used not long before to summon the hunters he sent to the Everland. The creatures were spreading further across the land every day–they were his eyes, ears, and claws far beyond the reach of his official authority. He now knew the Everland and its defenses better than did most of its inhabitants. Soon, very soon, he would put that knowledge to use. Tonight's Crafting was one more move toward that goal.

Dreydmaster Vald stood motionless, his sharp gaze taking in every edge of the portal, each snow-bound weed beneath it, even the bright stars in the sky above, until he was certain that everything was as it should be. He stepped to a leafless sapling that quivered beside the portal and tied a small silver bell to one of its stouter branches with a yellow ribbon. After flicking the bell and listening to its shrill chime echo through the garden, he turned to the six militiamen who stood at the doorway leading into the Hall.

«Captain,» the Dreydmaster said, his deep voice harsh in the crisp air, «you know your duty. Send for me at once when the messenger arrives. You should have adequate time to find me. There will be no unpleasant surprises if you follow my orders exactly.»

Vald turned to one of the Binders, a pale-faced youth who seemed more unnerved by the Crafting than did his companions. He'd stumbled over a few of the words during the ritual, and, although his companions made up for his mistakes, the risks were anything but minimal. Any weakness, even now, could make the gate unstable. It was entirely unacceptable. The boy would have to be reminded of his responsibilities to the Dreydcaste–and to his Dreydmaster.

Vald

«What is your name?»

Fear rolled off the boy, but he licked his chapped lips and said, «Mmm…Merrimyn Hurlbuck, Authority.»

Vald's eyes held no pity or warmth. «Come with me, Merrimyn Hurlbuck. We shall discuss your incompetence this evening. Be warned: I am not in a generous mood.» He walked away, and the young Binder reluctantly followed behind.

From the darkness of a window that overlooked the garden, green eyes watched the Reaver and the Binder disappear into the shadows of Gorthac Hall.

"How many survivors?"

Averyn wrapped a worn gray cloak around hir shoulders and rushed from the bedchamber to grab a heavy satchel from the woven-reed trunk by the parlor door. The magpie swept through the house behind the healer, cawing in response, and Averyn stopped short, hir eyes wide.

"So few?" The bird descended to a table and bobbed her head in affirmation. Averyn swallowed. Such a small number spoke of desperation, ferocity, or both; the injuries would be grievous, and likely beyond the zhe-Kyn's strength to heal; hir gifts belonged more to the mending of the spirit. Although zhe could set broken bones, heal burns, and bind the common injuries of hearth and home, Averyn's greatest skills were with aching hearts and wounded minds. There would be plenty of such work with the survivors in the days to come, but that was a later consideration; what mattered most now was simple survival, and there were others in Sheynadwiin who were far better equipped for this task.

Averyn swung the bag across hir back and opened the door. "Find the Tetawa named Jynni Thistledown of Bristlecone Hollow. She's staying in the east quarter of the Tetawi settlement. Tell her what you've told me. I'll meet her at the gathering ground in front of the main gate." Zhe took a deep breath. "Tell her to hurry–Jitani was a guard on that train."

The magpie let out a deep croak and shook her glossy feathers, but Averyn was already running up the red cobbled road towards the city gate by the time the bird took flight.

The destruction was terrible indeed. Averyn tried to blot out the smells of hot blood and putrefaction and the cries of the wounded and grieving, but even with hir sensory stalks tightly wrapped, the sharp tang of trauma bled through, and in a very short time zhe was dizzy with nausea. Of the twenty-eight Folk and Men who'd left Sheynadwiin on this trading journey two months previously, only five now survived: the merchant Sylas Gwydd, a young Human teamster, two he-Kyn hunters and, to Averyn's great relief, the sell-sword Jitani. Thanks almost entirely to Jitani's fighting skill, Gwydd would survive with little more than bruises and nightmares; the teamster and one of the hunters, on the other hand, would likely die in the night. Jitani had been hurt in the raid, but aside from a few ugly scars, she'd fully recover.

Averyn didn't know Jitani very well, but zhe was quite familiar with the she-Kyn's brother Sinovian, an angry and vocal Greenwalker warrior who despised the presence of Humans in Sheynadwiin–anywhere in the Everland, in fact. Had Jitani died in Gwydd's service, nothing could have quenched Sinovian's fury, and every allied Human would have been targeted, even those adopted into a Branch and accepted as kith. The bonds of kinship were vulnerable these days, and not only through the actions of the Shields and their Man-ways.

But Jitani had survived, so that confrontation wouldn't happen–not yet, anyway. The allied Humans still had a place among the Folk, albeit a tenuous one. Averyn looked at Gwydd, whose leg was being bathed and wrapped by one of Jynni's daughters, while silver-haired Jynni herself cared for the more grievously wounded. It didn't take an empathic Wielding to tell Averyn what was in Gwydd's heart. The Man's gaze was hollow. His financial loss was great, but he'd lost something far more precious than trade goods in the attack. Sylas Gwydd had finally experienced for himself the carnage that the Folk dealt with every day, and all his Human rank and privilege hadn't protected him or his money. He'd been just a sword's-thrust from death; never again would he have the illusion of safety.

Good, thought Averyn in a sudden rush of bitterness. *Let him know what it's like to feel afraid in your own home, to be expendable to all the world. If he wants to live like one of us, let him know our fear.* They were uncharacteristic thoughts for the kindly Kyn, but these were unhappy days, and Averyn had already seen more pain than hir gentle spirit could absorb in one day.

Zhe turned away from the Man and moved towards Jitani, who sat beside a blanketed pallet, her sword in its belted scabbard lying nearby. The body beneath the blood-stained shroud was small and clearly mutilated, for the head wasn't where it belonged–it lolled to one side at a strange angle. This was one of the few bodies that had been recovered in the quick retreat; the others were still in the woods, unprotected and exposed to scavengers and the elements. There would be no burial rites. Until and unless they were recovered, they might be lost forever. Averyn felt hir sensory stalks grow tense, and bitter bile rose up in hir throat.

Jitani looked up as the zhe-Kyn approached. "*Hanahé,*" Averyn whispered thickly, lifting hir chin in greeting.

The mercenary returned the gesture, but anger clouded the welcome in her eyes. "You'd better sit down before you fall down, healer."

"Yes," Averyn said, kneeling beside Jitani on the grass. "I knew it would be bad, but not like this." Zhe took a few deep breaths and closed hir eyes until an unsteady calm drifted over hir thoughts. Zhe opened hir eyes, gave Jitani a weak smile, and pulled a bundle of thin linen strips from hir satchel, along with a lidded clay pot. "How deep are your wounds?"

"Not bad. I've had worse."

Averyn cast a furtive glance at the warrior's head. Jitani's hair was shaved along the sides in the old warrior's style, leaving a long green mane that stretched from brow to waist. This was unremarkable. What drew

Averyn's attention were Jitani's temples, where the withered remnants of two sensory stalks jutted outward like rotting stumps in a fallow field. The other two stalks were well-wrapped, but the damaged ones remained stark and exposed in the late-day sunlight. Yes, indeed, Jitani had suffered worse injuries than these new cuts on her face and arms. The loss of a stalk through accident was a rare but devastating event that, more often than not, drove its bearer mad with both pain and the sudden deprivation of the sensory world. Averyn had heard it described as a heavy muffling of the world, where the most precious tenderness of touch and connection was forever stripped away.

An accidental loss was one thing. But Jitani's injury had been far from the natural way of things. A Man with a steel sword had taken the two brow stalks years before. It was the sort of brutality that was becoming almost commonplace as Men grew bolder and celebrated their attacks on Kyn with the desire for a memento, or for evidence to ensure a lucrative bounty. Jitani hadn't been the first to lose her sensory stalks to such attacks, but she was the only one Averyn knew who'd survived it and remained sane.

Well, largely so, anyway. There was a coldness to the mercenary that signaled a deep wounding far beyond the skill of any healing *wyr* that Averyn could draw upon.

Suddenly aware that zhe was staring rudely at Jitani's old injury, the zhe-Kyn opened the jar and dipped the linen strips inside, coating them with a sweet-smelling paste. "This will hasten the healing, though you'll likely still be scarred. They'll harden soon in the fresh air; in a few days they'll come loose, and you can go on as usual."

"*Tsodoka*." Jitani's golden eyes turned to the remnants of the single wagon she'd managed to salvage after the attack, where weeping relatives of the slain and injured had gathered. Some of the Kyn were in Celestial mourning robes, and there was as much anger as grief in their faces.

Averyn followed her gaze. "It's going to get worse for us again."

Jitani nodded. "Just one more arrow for the Shields to feather us with.

Each death adds to their strength. They'll play with these bodies like buzzards, and with less grace."

"But what about the traders? Surely they'll stand with us?"

The warrior gave a bitter bark of a laugh. "Not likely, now that they're targets. No, healer, Gwydd and his family have little to gain from supporting us, and much to lose. Their gain won't come through loyalty to the Folk." Her face darkened. "They're established in the Everland now. They know the trade-ways and hunting paths. They know how the planting and harvesting seasons differ here than from the Reach; they know what will grow and what will wither in our soils. These Men and their families have valuable knowledge about the Everland. But they can't use it as long as there's chaos. They're going to push for peace at all costs—it's in their best interests to do so."

Averyn felt hir skin tingle with dread as zhe finished wrapping the last of the bandages around Jitani's sword arm. "How can you be so sure?"

The mercenary stood and pointed her chin toward Gwydd, who stared with empty eyes at the ravaged wagon. "Look at him, healer." Her voice was low and stone-hard. "Everything about him says it. He's a broken Man now, and he's terrified." She grabbed her scabbard-belt and buckled it around her waist, where it hung snug and low on her hips. "I've spent enough time around Men to know one fundamental truth about them: when Men are scared, that's when they're most dangerous."

Nodding once more to the zhe-Kyn, Jitani walked stiffly away, leaving Averyn to sit alone beside the body of the Tetawi scout. It was a long time before the healer returned home to share the day's events with hir mate, as was each day's custom. Zhe generally tried to bring good news to hir beloved, to lessen his burdens with the mundane pleasures and simple joys of the people who depended upon his strength and wisdom, but Averyn couldn't keep these unpleasant tidings from Garyn—they were already spreading like pestilence through the city. The Governor would need to be prepared when the grief-maddened families came to his door.

Of all his remarkable qualities, it was Garyn's strength that Averyn loved most of all, but each day's news brought new weight to the Governor's already bent shoulders, and even the strongest tree couldn't stand forever under blistering winds. Garyn, Averyn, and their Greenwalker allies put much hope for the future in the Sevenfold Council and the Wielders, who could remind the Folk of their own strength again.

But the Shields were finding more support with every new death, and far fewer of the Wielders had responded to Garyn's appeal than they'd expected. The fragile dream of Kyn unity was unraveling, and Averyn didn't know how much longer it could survive.

CYCLE TWO
The Eternity Tree

This is a story of the First Days, and the beginning of the Kyn.
This is a teaching.

In a birthing storm that made the Three Worlds tremble, the Seven Branches emerged from the loins of their deep-green mother, Zhaia, the True Tree: Oak, Pine, Willow, Thorn, Cedar, Apple, and Ash. Born of leafy-haired Zhaia and her green-skinned lover, Drohodu, Grandfather of the Mosses, the first Kyn danced to life in their new world, and they gave joy to their Mother and Father and to their world. Their roots drank deeply from the endless Eld Green, and they flowered in the sunshine and bounty of the unending heavens. The Kyn grew strong and flourished, and each family Branch brought different gifts to all the People.

Those Kyn of Oak Branch were the chieftains of the deep forests, the voices of leadership and reason, orators and philosophers of old. Those of Pine Branch called the high mountains home. They were teachers, wisdom-bearers, the mystics of the People, and in their dreams sought the future and the knowledge of the past. Willow Branch was dedicated to the way of the wanderers, and Willow Kyn travelled the rivers and great waters, becoming great diplomats and traders, friends of other Folk in lands far away. Within rocky hills and brush-hidden caves lived the Thorn Kyn, and they were honoured for their war-teachings and courage. They were the weapon-makers, the strength-finders, the warriors who rose against all enemies and led the People to victory. Cedar Branch was the line of the artists, singers, storytellers, and history-keepers of the Kyn. They wove the teachings into their songs and baskets, and it was in their paints and clay statues that the Old Ways endured. Among the Apple Kyn were the earth-bearers, the planters and ground-watchers, those who brought great bounty forth from the dark soil. They understood and honoured the ways of the plant-people, who in return gave sustenance to all the Folk. It was left to the Ash Kyn to bring comfort to the People when death and pain brought down the green tree. They were the healers, the spirit-tenders and guides to the ghostlands, where the People would endure in another form and return again, as the lightning-struck tree falls to earth and becomes new seedlings with the care of fresh rain and warm sunshine.

When all was in balance, the Branches grew strong and wise, and the People flourished. But there came a time when some of the restless ones–those who watched the stars and turned from the green world–lingered too long in the heavens and forgot about their deep roots. Their hold on the old earth began to wither and die, and they drifted, seeing nothing but the sky, even as they hungered, their mouths filling with cinders. They forgot the ancient language that all Creation shared; they forgot that the trees have long-reaching voices, that the clouds sing to heron and goshawk alike, that the river whispers to the swimming otter, the minnow, and the little water beetle. The balance unravelled, the soil weakened and crumbled away, and even those who held to the soil found themselves falling, washed away by the rain, scattered sunward by the blistering wind. Some of the People dug deeply in the earth and turned away from the sky, thinking to return to the balance, but they forgot the sunshine. Their leaves became dust, and their roots starved.

Those treading firmly on the Celestial Path called themselves Shields, for they saw themselves as guardians of a new way of being in the world, and they scorned the flesh and its joys and pains. Those holding fast to the Way of Deep Green were the Greenwalking Wielders, and they drew on the lifeblood language of the Eld Green, the wyr, and ignored the gathering storm that, even then, threatened to uproot them without mercy. So it came to be that the Shields fell upon the Wielders, seeking to purge *the People of the trees in their blood and the moss in their skin. And though many Wielders survived, many died, their blood running like floodwaters through the Lower World. And the People suffered.*

This is a teaching.

It is a reminder, and a remembrance.

CHAPTER 8

WRATH

Even though the birds and other beast-folk of the forest had gone eerily silent, the attack came as a surprise, as the travellers had become careless in the gentle warmth of the afternoon. The first blast shattered a branch above Tarsa's head. Splintered wood and sap exploded in the air, and she dove headfirst into the underbrush, dragging Unahi behind her. Tobhi frantically rushed Smudge to the road's edge and hurled himself on the deer's neck, pulling the squalling beast to the ground. They were all hidden by thick brambles and bushes, but the cover was neither effective nor comforting.

Tarsa tried to gauge where the attackers were hiding, but something blocked her senses. She shook her head dizzily. Her connection to the *wyr* was confused again, and now so were her thoughts. The small inklings of understanding that she'd developed from her aunt's teachings over the past few days scattered aimlessly. Her thoughts wrapped back into themselves. Her skin turned cold.

"They have a wyr-ward," Unahi whispered to her niece. While iron-wards protected the Folk from the toxic taint of that cold metal, the wyr-wards of Men blocked the Folk from their most fundamental connection to the world. Crafted by Human witchery from the ensorcelled blood and pain of captive Folk, these implements were rare abominations suitable only for murder and torment. Both the elder and younger she-Kyn found their Wielding disoriented by the wyr-stifling instrument, though the effect was more wearing on Tarsa, whose skills and defenses drawn from the Old Ways were less developed.

They were now in the High Timber, a region of mostly brown grass and gray sage among gnarled pines, spruces, and cedars, with only smallish thickets of aspens and willows to break the gray-green blanket surrounding them. They'd made good time in their last eight days of travelling together, far better than expected. Their route took them along one of the better dirt paths northward, and they occasionally encountered other travellers along the way, stopping once or twice to share meals at homesteads near the path. They were always made welcome, and Tarsa had her first full taste of Tetawi hospitality, which was as warm and respectfully curious as Tobhi had promised it would be.

Only two weeks or so remained until they would reach Sheynadwiin, the valley home of the Kyn Nation. Earlier that morning, they'd crossed over a high, long slope, and, aside from this tree-strewn knob, the next few days on the road would take them on an even draw between gentle brown hillocks. Yet here the trees weren't as thick as they'd been during their first day in the Timber, and the travelers were far more vulnerable as a result. Their hiding place was a temporary respite at best; it wouldn't be defensible for long.

"Men, ten or more of 'em," Tobhi announced, after a quick scan of the area. The invaders were clearly unconcerned about being seen. "Why're they so far in the 'Hold?" None of them liked the possibilities. Human traders weren't uncommon in the Everland, but they were generally integrated into specific Folk communities, and they rarely had the freedom to wander without an escort; they were safe from harm only if interwoven into the social web of kinship responsibilities and rights as defined by a particular Kyn Branch, Tetawi or Feral Clan, or Gvaerg House. The Men facing the travellers were different. Beyonder raiders on the periphery of the 'Hold were increasingly common these days, but neither Tobhi nor the she-Kyn had ever heard of Men bold enough to find their way so deeply into the Everland's interior. Bold indeed, and foolish.

But here they were, and as objectionable as their presence was, they held the advantage.

Another explosion shook the air. Pine needles and small branches rained down on the she-Kyn and Tetawa. In the distance, bird-people cried out in panic at the unfamiliar sound.

"They have muskets." Unahi had seen a few of the weapons before the encounter with Leith. The Kyn of Far-Meadows Town, near the upper fork of the Panther River to the west of her home in Thistlewood, had long maintained uneasy relations with Humans travelling upriver, a relationship that turned hostile when the Kyn discovered a large cache of strange weapons after driving a group of Human squatter families from the area. They'd found mostly swords and crossbows, all laced with cold iron, but there were some strange thundering smoke-sticks as well. The Wielder was summoned to help those who'd been wounded in the attack and saw first-hand the terrible damage caused by the weapons. "One of the he-Kyn I tended was struck by musket-fire," she whispered to Tarsa. "A hole in his belly the size of my fist; he didn't last the night." She puckered her lips. "I thought they were very rare."

"Not rare enough," Tarsa said, her voice thin and strained, and the air crackled with tension. Unahi looked at her in alarm. The wyr-ward was sapping the Redthorn's strength far more than it should have been. Either the artifact was more powerful than most of its kind, which the old Wielder doubted, or Tarsa's hard-fought defenses against the rising bloodsong were weakening under the wyr-ward's influence. Either way, something unpleasant was building, and there was little Unahi could do as long as they remained trapped.

The Men weren't moving any closer, but they weren't retreating, either. Unahi's own quick glance confirmed Tobhi's estimate: there were at least ten invaders, males of varying heights and appearances, but all wearing dirty knee-high boots, flared breeches, and thick linen shirts cinched around the waist with belts or twisted rope. A pile of canvas bags rested on the ground between them, and all the Men were armed—most had shovels and picks, but the silver-haired she-Kyn could see at least one firearm, held high and at the ready by a slack-jawed stripling.

"They're waiting for us to move," she hissed. Their bit of underbrush wasn't very big, and, with the Men on the upward slope, there was little chance that the Folk would be able to get to a more defensible spot without exposing themselves to danger.

Tarsa groaned and slid face-down into the dirt. Her resistance was dangerously low. Smudge jerked slightly as the air grew suddenly thicker, as though a heavy, unseen cloud had descended on them. Though his own eyes were filled with growing concern, Tobhi kept pressure on the deer, smoothing the terrified animal's neck with gentle strokes. "They're well-armed for squatters, don't ye think?" he whispered, his words muted in the strange air.

A couple of the Men shouted down the hill, and the others laughed gratingly. Unahi's face flushed with anger; she could understand some of their mocking speech, and their audacity annoyed her beyond her fear. Her temples and stalks burned. The chortling ended, and the world went unnaturally quiet again. She and Tobhi exchanged puzzled glances.

Tarsa's breathing went suddenly shallow–she'd been trying to draw on the *wyr*, and the exertion of pushing past the Men's addling iron instrument was almost beyond her abilities. She felt the world grow hazy and distant. Without thinking, she reached out and grabbed her aunt's hand for support. Unahi's sensory stalks were rigid in response, both to the effect of the wyr-ward and to the Redthorn's burning touch, and in that moment a heated rush of *wyr* flowed from her, unhindered by will or flesh. Unahi collapsed, too surprised to cry out, in too much pain to scream. For an instant, she saw Tobhi straining to see past the undergrowth while keeping his poor shuddering deer from bolting, and then the world went suddenly dark.

The earth erupted under the Men, and a hulking mass of tendrils, stones, leaves, and soil smashed into the screaming knot of flesh. Shovels and picks were useless against this heaving aggregation of root, dirt, and mulch. Two Men disappeared into the earthy maw, their shrieks silenced by its grinding force. The musket-bearer and a few others fled, but some, knowing nothing else to do, lifted their weapons and drove against the onrushing heap. Great arms of compacted soil burst out and struck the Men where they stood, pulling them screaming into the depths of the wyr-shaped monstrosity.

Earth Awakens

Unahi's vision cleared, and her breath returned with a gasp. For a moment, she couldn't understand what was happening. As she coughed and fought to orient herself to the raging turmoil, she dimly perceived a wyr-strengthened Tarsa bursting from their hiding place towards the writhing mass of earth. Smudge had bolted when the hill exploded, and now Tobhi, too, rushed from the undergrowth, though he followed after Tarsa, seemingly in pursuit of the young she-Kyn. Unahi was alone on the hill. Dust and gunpowder smoke filled the air, and, even in their wrappings, her stalks were burning from the agonies of the wounded and dying Men.

The *wyr*-ward was gone, swallowed up by the great elemental force that still writhed on the hillock. Unahi's muscles trembled from Tarsa's unwitting wyr-drain, but the old Wielder forced herself to stand. Her staff was gone, still in Tarsa's hand, so it took Unahi a few false starts to find her footing and walk back up to the road.

All was devastation. One of the great canvas bags lay split wide, its contents broken and spread across the area: brown and yellow Kyn skulls, dragged from their burial rest by fortune-seeking grave-robbers. Screams of pain roared in old Kyn's ears and the agony of the injured Men filled her stalks and mind. Her head pounded and her chest tightened, and a red-black curtain of pain dropped swiftly over her eyes. Unahi staggered and stumbled into the dirt as the roiling earth rose above her like a cresting wave ready to crash down.

She looked up, and her gray eyes flashed dangerously. "ENOUGH!" she cried, and the heavens split apart. A driving blast of wind slammed against the surging earth and sent a tremor of confusion through its newly-awakened consciousness.

She would have to be quick–the words and their order had to be chosen carefully for their desired effect, as though her intention had already come to pass. "*You have returned to your deep roots–you are sleeping again, as you were meant to do!*" the old Wielder shouted, her voice straining over the howling winds and bursts of thunder. One hand traced the patterns on her chanting-sash; the other was raised in a tight fist. Lightning crackled in blinding streaks all across the hill, and sudden rain fell hard and fast, turning the hard soil to thick, boiling mud.

The earth-form shuddered in slow understanding as spirit-tongues of sky-fire, wind, and water bore down hard against it. It tried to resist the Wielder's will, but her words created an irresistible reality, and the force of the other elemental voices were too strong to deny. A low, deep groan of surrender rumbled across the hill, and the wyr-summoned aberration collapsed in upon itself.

The storm broke at that moment, and the soft glow of dusk returned to the road. The few surviving Men crouched quivering in lightning-formed holes along the muddy slope. The only things still standing on the hill were dozens of freshly torn and ravaged tree trunks, and a bent old she-Kyn spreading a thin dusting of cedar shavings and tobacco before each squelching step, her eyes hollow with exhaustion…and fear.

❦

Tarsa didn't remember standing up or rushing after the Man with the musket. All she knew, when her mind cleared, was that she was still a Redthorn warrior, trained to challenge any threat to her people, no matter how chaotic the circumstances. She called out a high-pitched trill and rushed forward, Unahi's wyrwood staff suddenly in her hands as though it had been crafted to belong there. Though the Man was badly injured, desperation carried him quickly down the dirt trail. He didn't make it far enough to miss the howl that flew from the Redthorn's throat as she bore down on him. He turned to level his musket at her, but he'd underestimated her speed, and she spun like a whirlwind, the amber-topped staff smashing hard into his weapon, sending the barrel sidewards. It roared in blinding smoke and fire, but Tarsa was too far into this strange, sudden battle-rage to be distracted by the noise. The Man recoiled as the staff swung down again. This time it caught the musket's stock and sent it flying down the path, bent almost double and now useless.

The Man screamed and turned to flee, but his injured leg twisted beneath him and he fell. Tarsa drove the end of the staff into the earth and howled in near-mad anguish. She still didn't know what the *wyr*-voices sang in the hot depths of her blood, and she didn't care–all she knew was that the voices were now free to live in the world, carried on the force of her rage. The staff twisted, its surface bubbling, as piercing thorns jutted out to shine in the orange light of the lowering suns.

She lifted the staff high above her head. "Defiler!" she hissed through clenched teeth. The grasses beneath the Man tangled themselves into scores of fibrous ropes and lashed across his limbs to pin him to the earth. He opened his mouth to scream, and a clump of vegetation crept across his lower face. Soon, only his terrified eyes remained free of the creeping plants that writhed beneath him, helpless to deny the she-Kyn's bidding.

Tarsa's body shook. In the brief moment between the shattering of the earth beneath the Men and her emergence from the roadside, she'd seen the freshly-dug skulls roll free from one of the sacks, matted grave-dirt still clinging to the bone. She'd barely suppressed the bloodsong after the pain and helplessness of Nine Oaks Town–this terrible sight sent her strength past the weak barriers of her waking consciousness.

"*Grave-robber! Murderer!*" The words rose free, tangled with grief and blinding rage. The spirits of the dead were now cursed to wander until returned to the green earth, but even if these bones were reburied, it was likely that the disturbance had been too great to allow the spirits to make their way in peace to the ghostlands.

The enormity of the violation was too much. Tarsa brought the staff down on the Man's struggling body. He screamed, but it was the satisfying crack of bone and the meaty splut of pulverized muscle that burst through the raging haze in her mind. She looked down. The thorns glistened red and green; the remnants of the flailing grasses that bound the Man writhed in his blood. Pain pulsed through the green world, and she could feel the plant people and their roots aching to get away from her. She stared at the dripping thorns, and the white-hot fire across her eyes faded as she looked at the gasping creature and the crimson stain that spread across his upper body.

She returned the end of the staff to the earth. The thorns were the first to recede, then the grass tendrils and other vegetation unwound themselves from around the Man. He curled into a tight ball, in too much pain and far too frightened to try to escape.

The crackle of leaves caught Tarsa's attention, and she turned as a heavy fist smashed into the side of her face. She stumbled backwards over the Man on the ground and rolled into the dirt. A hob-nailed boot caught her in the ribs. She cried out and spun helplessly into the coarse trunk of a bristlecone pine. Another foot lashed out, but this time she saw it coming. Though barely able to breathe, she jerked to the right, threw her arms outward and grabbed the iron-shod boot, heedless of the cold burn that raced through her blistering hands.

It was another invader, a massive bear of a Man, whose hairy face was twisted and scarred. Using his weight against him, she lunged to the right. His balance was off. As she twisted back to the left, he bellowed and plummeted hard to the ground. Such a fall would have stunned an ordinary Man, but this one seemed to be more angry than hurt, though his face was scraped bloody.

Tarsa's chest ached from the blows. The rage had disappeared, and now pain pulsed all around her, unchecked by other emotions. But she knew that to abandon herself to this churning sensory world would be her death. The second Man was regaining his feet, and the other might soon join him. In this weakened state, she was clearly vulnerable.

Tetawi, however, had no sensory stalks to bind them to the world's pain—Tobhi was now beside the Redthorn warrior. He dropped Unahi's staff at her feet and spun his own hatchet menacingly into the air, its sharpened stone blade flashing in the failing light.

The first Man wouldn't be a problem now—he lay screaming on the ground as Smudge pawed the earth and lunged at him, antlers dagger-sharp, dirt flying in thick clouds. The performance was harmless, but it heightened the little deer's suddenly demented appearance.

The second Man howled and charged toward the swirling brown shape, but Tobhi was ready. The Tetawa twirled around, a diminutive and deadly dancer. He darted under the rushing Man, smashing the flat end of his hatchet into the Man's kneecap as he slid past. A splintering crunch split the air, and the Man shrieked and collapsed. Tobhi stood and turned, ready to face his opponent again, but the hulking shape lay shuddering on the ground.

Tobhi rushed over to Tarsa. She was weak now and leaned heavily on the staff, but her eyes were clear. "What about the others?" she asked wearily.

"They're mostly dead or wounded; these was the only ones to get away. That wyr-ward disappeared into the ground first thing, so I s'pose yer aunt was able to keep 'em out of the way." He took her free hand in his and frowned. "We'd best get ye looked at, or the iron sickness could set in on ye." She nodded. They walked up to Smudge, who seemed to be thoroughly enjoying himself by repeatedly bumping the younger Man with his antlers.

"Enough of that," Tobhi muttered and pulled the deer away as thunder crashed upslope. They looked up to see a mass of black clouds and lightning suddenly rage on the hill. They heard a booming voice roll through the storm, and fear clutched at their hearts. "Unahi…" Tarsa began, but a blast of debris-choked wind enveloped them, and they clung to one another, coughing and gasping for breath.

As swiftly as it had struck, the storm was over, and calm returned to the hillside. They wiped the dirt and rain from their faces and, ignoring the injured Men, hurried back up the slope toward the old she-Kyn, who stood stark on the hill against the day's last light.

"What happened?" Tarsa asked. "What attacked the Men?"

Tobhi glanced up at her in surprise. "Ye don't know?" he said, one eyebrow creased in suspicion.

"No..." She looked up to see Unahi picking through the wreckage on the slope, gathering up all the scattered Kyn bones and fragments that she could find. It was a delicate task, for many of the bones had been shattered beyond salvaging in the melée, and there were great pools of mud and dirty water everywhere.

The handful of surviving Men clustered together in a terrified mass at the base of the slope. Their weapons were missing, swallowed up by the now-still earth. They'd be set free–the Folk were in too big a hurry to keep the Men as prisoners for the next few weeks–but, without weapons for defense, the grave-robbers wouldn't likely last very long in the Everland, especially when word spread of their plundering. Scores of small trees had been uprooted or shattered in the frenzy, and the Redthorn could feel their death-pain trickle toward her as they drew nearer. All was silent, save for the groans of some of the injured Men and the soft call of a raven nearby.

She looked down at the Tetawa by her side, a cold awareness flowing over her. "I did this." Unahi looked wearily toward her niece and the surrounding destruction before returning to her search in the uprooted soil.

Tarsa's knees buckled. "I didn't know, Tobhi," she whispered. "I swear I didn't know."

Merrimyn lifted his sleep-addled head from the splintered bench, eyes wide in alarm, but the darkness was complete, and he saw nothing but the now-familiar flashing shadows that danced across his straining vision. The cell stank of death and excrement, and the terror of solitude returned like a crashing surge, swamping him, pulling him under until he crouched against the wall, his breath thin and laboured. He listened intently. There. He heard it again–a soft metallic scraping at the door. It wasn't the sound of a key, so it couldn't be the Dreydmaster or his Questioners. The Binder didn't know how much time had passed since he had been brought here, but he was long past hunger, so it didn't seem likely that food was on its way. He'd given up hope some time ago, when, in the darkness, his fumbling fingers out the shape of a wet Human skull in a pile of rotting fabric. After that, all was despair.

For a moment, he thought the noise might be a rat, or something worse. Unseen creatures had slipped past his limbs as he struggled to sleep, and not all had resembled rodents. He'd long ago screamed himself hoarse, so his only defense was to retreat to the farthest corner and hide from whatever was creeping along by the door.

A light click echoed in the room, and the iron door swung open on screaming hinges. The Binder covered his head with his left arm, the noise and sudden light burning into his senses. It was a while before he heard a voice at his shoulder urging him to his feet. He opened his eyes, squinting tightly, and saw a dark silhouette against the lantern light that streamed from the hall.

«Hurry, Man,» the figure hissed, shaking him roughly. «If you want to live, you must come with me!»

Merrimyn wanted to ask a thousand questions, to learn what was happening, but the demands of survival took control and he lurched to his feet, stumbling out of the cell as the stranger pulled the iron door shut with a shudder. The pulse in the Binder's right wrist began to beat harder, and the snaring-tome on his right arm trembled with hunger. He stared at his rescuer with the shock of recognition.

«You…an Unhuman!» he gasped, his voice little more than a croaking whisper.

The figure turned. It was one of the Snake-heads–"kiin" in their own strange tongue–the most dangerous of the Unhuman races, mockingly dressed in the manner of civilized Men. Somehow, the unnatural contrast wasn't entirely unpleasant; although the creature had two writhing tendrils draping from the sides of its head, waist-long black hair woven into dozens of thin braids, dark tattoos on its yellow cheeks and chin, and split-lobed ears with trade-silver rings, its gray velvet cassock and lacy sleeves, high-wrapped neck scarf, long breeches, and high, buckled boots gave it a comfortingly Human appearance. The Binder supposed the creature to be a male of its race, but it was hard to tell. Those strange eyes–deep green, without pupil or whites, and lit with the inner fire of a polished gem–filled him with new fear, for it was in those eyes that Merrimyn saw the creature's Unhumanity. Even its rhythmic use of the Mannish tongue wasn't enough to drive away the fear that pulsed through the young Binder's veins.

Merrimyn might have flung open his snaring-tome at that moment, but Vald had ordered an iron band to be wrapped around the book when he'd been locked away, so he was denied even this defense. Untrained in the ways of battle, weakened with fear and exhaustion, and unable to protect himself with the only weapon he knew, Merrimyn was helpless before the creature. He almost preferred being locked away in the cell. Almost.

The Unhuman stared at him. «Well, why are you waiting?»

Merrimyn blinked. «What? I don't….»

«You're free, fool. Now go, before Vald discovers what I've done. It's both our lives if you're caught.»

«But where do I go?» Merrimyn looked around. The tunnel stretched into yawning darkness in both directions; the only light he could see was the small, quivering lantern in the Unhuman's three-fingered hand.

The creature sighed, turning its strange gaze on the Binder. «Follow me–for now. I'll help you to the stables; after that, you go on alone.»

Casting a nervous look down the hall, the Unhuman shuttered the lantern until nothing but a thin stream of light guided their way, and they hurried into the gloom. The Binder was weak, and he often stumbled, but the Unhuman slipped a strong arm around the young Man's waist, and it was enough to help Merrimyn get his footing. Every little while they came to another tunnel, and Merrimyn's strange guide looked around at the dirt, as though he'd lost something. After a few minutes, he moved forward again, sometimes turning into the new tunnel, sometimes continuing down the old one. Eventually they came to a rough stone stairway that stretched upwards until it disappeared beyond the limit of the lantern's light.

«Up there,» the creature whispered. «Those stairs lead to the back of the Hall. When you reach the top, go left, and you'll find your way to the stables.» It began to move away, but Merrimyn caught its arm.

«Wait a moment, please!»

The Unhuman turned and looked at him again with those unnerving eyes. «What is it?»

The young Man swallowed in fear, but he had to know. «Why did you do this?»

An expression, something like sympathy, passed over the creature's face. «My people don't believe in cages, Merrimyn, and I've seen far too many of both our peoples disappear into the darkness beneath Gorthac Hall.»

The lantern light suddenly vanished. Merrimyn felt a pressure on his arm and heard a crack. As the sliver of light returned, he looked down to see the iron lock on the snaring-tome fall to the ground. The book began to throb with sudden hunger, but Merrimyn held it in check–his will was still strong enough to deny it, for now. The Unhuman handed the lantern to the Binder and disappeared into the darkened tunnels.

Merrimyn was nearly at the stables when he wondered how the Unhuman knew his name.

CHAPTER 9

OWL AND DRAGONFLY

"What's happening to me, Auntie?"

They were gathered on the mossy bank of a small spring, a lengthy walk from the battle but still well within sight of the now-treeless hilltop. It was deep night now. Tobhi sat at a respectful distance from the Wielders, combing the brambles from Smudge's smooth coat, his battle-tainted clothes freshly washed and drying on a flat rock beside the fire. Tarsa had been grim and largely unresponsive since the incident, and, though she'd helped Tobhi and Unahi bury all the Kyn remains that they could find, even leading a prayer before their individual purifications to ease the spirits' pain and passing, she'd since fallen into a dark mood.

The Leafspeaker was worried about her. She had a good heart and a fiery spirit, two traits much honoured by his people. Her wyr-rooted talents, however, were quickly becoming a crippling burden to her and a danger to everyone else, and Tobhi was afraid that she'd soon be overwhelmed by them. It was different with Tetawi wyr-workers–their strengths came from their connections to the beast-people, not from the voices of the elements themselves. The thoughts of the beast-people weren't all that different from those of Tetawi, so the understanding was easier; of all the Folk, Kyn suffered the most from their particular link to the *wyr*, because of the nearly-alien minds of the spirits in wood, sky, and stream, and the deeper connection that they had to those entities through their mysterious sensory stalks. He didn't much mind that Tarsa had used the *wyr* against the Men, but he could tell from Unahi's reaction that there was terrible danger in the Redthorn's actions. He thought about reading the lore-leaves, but decided against it, at least for now. It wasn't his place to interfere. Not yet, anyway.

It was all very depressing.

Unahi sat away from the water. They'd washed the mud and blood from their skin and clothing, and had eaten a bland meal of trailbread, nuts, and dried fruit. The elder Wielder turned stiffly to her niece. The young she-Kyn beside her was nothing like the wyr-maddened creature who'd drawn on Unahi's own life-spirit and created an abomination to wreak brutal vengeance on her enemies. Tarsa was on the edge of a precipice now, and Unahi wasn't sure whether the warrior would be able to step away before the fall. "Come here, seedling," she beckoned awkwardly, and Tarsa leaned into her aunt's arms, insensitive to the old she-Kyn's discomfort.

"I don't know what to do." The Redthorn's voice cracked. "What am I becoming? I used to know who I was, but now…nothing makes sense anymore." Her voice fell to a near-whisper. "I've never been so afraid."

The old Wielder held her niece tightly, rocking her gently but saying nothing. There were no words of comfort that she could share this time: Unahi was frightened, too, more so than she'd been in a very long time. Tarsa's Awakening had come late in life; she'd already survived more trauma than most Kyn who were similarly delayed in coming to their own awareness. They were most often like falling stars, blazing briefly and then disappearing into darkness.

And Tarsa's power—Unahi had rarely seen such unbidden strength. It even rose up against the ensorcelled iron wyr-ward, which should have limited Tarsa's connection as it did her own. Unahi had trained other Wielders in her long life, but none possessed so much possibility, or so much potential for catastrophe, as the young she-Kyn warrior who was curled crying in her arms.

Unahi looked down at Tarsa. For a moment she saw Lan'delar in the near-youngling's face. The resemblance did nothing to ease the pain. But it did remind the Wielder of something.

"To be truthful, brown-hair, I don't know the full measure of what's happening to you. You're travelling a rocky path that's very different from the one I walked so long ago." Tarsa's sobs increased in intensity. "Hush, now. Just because our paths are different doesn't mean I can't help you understand your own. Do you remember your mother's last words for you? 'Tell her to tend to her roots.' What do you think she meant by that?"

Tarsa didn't look up, but her crying softened. "I don't know anymore."

"That's a bit too easy, isn't it?"

Tarsa's lips tightened. "My roots–the Old Ways, the Deep Green. But I'm already following those ways."

"Are you?" Unahi's pointed back down the trail, back to the battle site and beyond. "Doesn't look like it from here. You can draw on the *wyr*, that's certain, but what are you doing with it?"

The Redthorn pulled away. "I saved our lives, didn't I?"

"But at what cost?" Unahi grabbed her staff and held it under Tarsa's flushed face. The shard of amber was now lined with cracks, and the wood was stained with blood and pocked with the remnants of broken thorns. "A Wielder will often have to call upon the *wyr* to protect herself, but she never *forces* it to do anything. That's where you've crossed over, seedling. The *wyr* is the spirit-language of kinship, a part of you, of all the Folk and our land, and that means we have to respect it and give it care, to honour its strengths and also its weaknesses. Words give shape to the world and our relationships, but they can poison as readily as they can heal. We must listen to what those voices tell us, not drown them out with our own wants."

Her voice hardened. "Through you, the language of the *wyr* has become twisted; you turn it against itself, against the green world that would gladly help you in its own way when your heart and mind are balanced. You're not there yet, not by any means. You've destroyed many tree-people, warped their spirits out of all recognition. You uprooted the little green ones, tangled them together into weapons, fed them with the poison of Man-blood. Forcing spirits to your will is Mannish witchery, Tarsa, not the way of a Wielder."

Tarsa stood up, but she didn't walk away. Her hands were clenched so tightly that the nails dug into her palms. Tobhi, seeing her anguish, turned back to Smudge. Unahi's expression shared the Tetawa's sorrow, yet it was mingled with anger as well.

"Until you stop fighting the bloodsong and give honour to the *wyr* that flows through you and through all the Eld Folk," said the old Wielder sharply, "you will always be a stranger to the Deep Green."

Tarsa looked at her aunt, eyes brimming with tears, and fled into the darkness. Unahi sat for a while and stared at the bubbling spring. When she finally stood, her old joints creaking, she carried her bedroll to a thick blanket of pine needles at the flat base of an old wind-twisted pine and settled down for a troubled sleep. Tobhi waited until the Wielder's breathing became soft and even, slid a feedbag over Smudge' snout and tied the deer to a neighbouring tree, then slipped into the shadows.

The grave-mounds were easy enough to find, for they radiated stark pain. Tarsa followed the dull throb, pulsing like a rotten tooth, into an old, hoary stand of stunted pines on the windswept side of a low ridge. The first mound was actually outside the trees, just barely distinguishable from the broken brown grass that carpeted the meadowlands of the High Timber. The soil was uprooted, gouged outward to leave a gaping blackness behind, and the heavy remnant tang of iron hung in the air. Chunks of rocks lay scattered all around, each oozing hurt from its shattered sides.

Tarsa stepped gingerly around the hole and looked in. Yellowed shards of bone lay scattered in the dirt, pieces too small to be of interest to the looters. She cupped her hands and refilled the hole as best she could but left her six digits deep in the soil. Closing her eyes, she pushed her thoughts into the dry brown ground, searching for the voices that lingered there, voices she felt but couldn't yet hear. There was no response at first; it seemed like nothing more than empty earth. But soon a furtive emotion reached out, and she recoiled in bitter understanding.

The spirits were afraid of her.

Shame, guilt, and anger twisted around her heart, but Unahi's words returned. She was a Redthorn warrior in name, but the society's guiding principles had slipped away since her Awakening. The *wyr*, once a gentle throb of life that constantly caressed her stalks, had become an overwhelming chorus of voices that nearly drove her mad, and she'd forgotten her duty to the Old Ways, to the Way of Deep Green. She could play-act at Greenwalking all she wanted, but it wouldn't give her peace or help her understand what she'd become, and it wouldn't keep those around her safe.

I don't want any of this. How many times since the Stoneskin's death had she repeated those words to herself? Was she being punished? Unahi said it wasn't a curse, but if it was truly a gift, it was a terrible one. She wanted to be a Redthorn forever, to be a brave warrior and fight with spear, knife, and throwing axe until death-chants were sung in her memory. That was the life she'd planned to have. It was the life she *should* have had.

But that life was lost to her now. Now she had a very simple choice: she'd be a Wielder, or she'd die. She could show true Redthorn strength and take hold of her unwanted gift, or she could end up raving and broken. There were no other choices.

Tarsa pushed her thoughts away and opened herself to the *wyr* as it was given, not as she wanted it to be. She could almost hear the spirits now, timid and uncertain but still present. Faintly, at first, they answered her soft query, sliding against her fingers and her thoughts. When satisfied and certain of her intent, the voices wrapped themselves around her flesh, their words weaving into her senses and her mind, drawing on her strength as she drew on their pain. They remained together for a long time, spirit on spirit and thoughts joined as one, until she felt the pain grow muted. It didn't disappear—it might never fully fade, as its echo was too firmly rooted in the earth around the violated mound—but the hurt no longer drowned out the voices.

Tarsa felt as though she'd stood up too quickly. Her muscles were weak, her head dizzy. The link had taken more concentration than she'd realized. Heaving a deep sigh, she pushed the hair away from her face to see Tobhi strolling through the meadow toward her. The thin glow of the Greatmoon danced on the Tetawa's shapeless brown hat, sometimes catching the reflective surface of the beaded band or his small black eyes that gleamed in the pale light.

"*Hanahé*," he said when he reached her, his face grim as he surveyed the ravaged grave. "What a hard-hearted mess."

The Redthorn nodded, her voice weak. "I haven't been to the other mounds yet; I'm not sure that I want to." She took his outstretched hand and stood up, brushing dirt and loose grasses from her leggings. "Why would they do something like this?"

"I couldn't begin to understand the ways of Men," the Tetawa shrugged. "They just don't make no sense at all. M' mam travelled a lot afore she and m' pepa married, and she went to Harudin Holt once, out by the western ocean. Lovely place, by her reckonin', but colder than she'd expected, and there was orphaned cubs ever'where—she couldn't turn 'round without seein' hungry younglin's reachin' out for a crumb or a smile. Anyways, she told me that she was troubled for a while by a well-to-do Man who wouldn't leave her alone over what he said was 'a most important business matter.' Said he was willin' to pay well for anythin' he could get ahold of that belonged to dead Folk, 'specially bones and burial gifts. Mam was pure unnerved by him, and he just wouldn't let it go, but he weren't the only one like that—apparently there's a fairly flourishin' business in Human circles for all things that can make 'em believe that we're long dead and forgotten. I even heard once that some of their more learned types measure the bumps and dips of the skulls they dig up to tell how smart we are. Trust Men to come up with somethin' like that. Ye can figure we never rank too high 'gainst Humans by them standards. It's all just another way of provin' that Humans is better than everybody else. Ye'd think, with all the energy that they's always puttin' into these tests and laws and such things, they wouldn't be so worried all the time 'bout us havin' a little somethin' of our own, but I guess they just won't be satisfied 'til everythin' comes out the way they want it to." He pulled a thin shoot of grass from the ground and chewed thoughtfully on one end.

They walked together to the trees, where they found more than twenty recently-looted graves. Shards and splinters of bone littered the ground, as did the remnants of those grave-goods that the Men didn't think had immediate value, including the fragments of an unadorned brown clay bowl, some decomposing drinking gourds, and a few torn shreds of cloth. It was a gruesome and sobering sight. Even without sensory stalks, Tobhi could feel the wounded pall that ebbed through the soil, trees, and air in the grove.

"I'm too weak to do it again," Tarsa whispered. "I wish I could do more."

The Tetawa nodded turned back toward the moon-lit meadow. "Ye did what ye could. No one's askin' ye to do no more."

The young Wielder's brows narrowed. "Unahi is. She never said anything about what I did right—the only thing she talked about was what I did wrong." Her proud chin quivered slightly. Turning away, her voice thick, she continued. "I know I'm a danger to you both…to everyone. I'm trying to learn how to control it. But it's so hard. It's all I can do to hold it back when nothing is happening, but when things get dangerous I can't seem to stop myself. It just flows through me. I become part of the storm—or it becomes part of me. I don't know what to do." Her last words were soft, but they cut through the night. "No one can help me. I can't even help myself."

Tobhi looked at Tarsa again. She was so alone. Whatever family she'd once known was now far away. Without sisters or brothers to look after her, she'd drifted in isolation, and, though Unahi was kind in her way, the older Wielder was often distant and impatient. Tarsa needed a friend. More than that, she needed to feel like she belonged somewhere. She needed deep roots to keep from blowing away in this rising storm.

The pain in the grove was heavier now with their intrusion, so they left the darkness of the trees and moved into the open air again, where they looked up to admire the world around them. Nowhere had the sky ever been so endlessly clear as it was this night, with stars and distant worlds shining like burning jewels on night's dark mantle. Pearl-in-Darkness seemed to understand the burdens of their day, for the silver softness of his light brought a calming peace to their spirits. The air was crisp–not enough to chill the body, but enough to charge the skin and clear the senses.

Morning was still some time away. They walked away from the graves and lay down on the ridge, where they watched the heavens and tried to forget the day's traumas. Occasionally, an owl or other night wanderer would call out, and they both shuddered, for among many of the Folk the owl was a traveller between the worlds, and its knowledge of the Spirit World gave it wisdom in all things, as well as the unmistakable taint of death and Decay.

Tobhi took off his hat and smoothed a small shell comb through his long hair. There were a few tangles, so he gently teased them out with the narrow edge. Tarsa lay on her back, arms crossed behind her head, and stared at the stars, her thoughts as distant as the sky.

The owl-song brought something to Tobhi's mind. "Have ye ever heard the story of Dragonfly and Owl?"

Tarsa rolled toward him and shook her head. "No. Is it a good one?"

He glowered in mock outrage. "'It's one of mine, en't it?!"

"Well, in that case, tell it," she laughed. "Will you use your lore-leaves again?" She was fascinated by the ways of the leaves, and she wanted to see them dance again in story.

He shook his head. "No, I only use 'em for special occasions, when I'm learnin' somethin' new, or when I'm addin' to the stories they tell. This one I can tell without 'em." Seeing the flash of disappointment on her face, he added, "But don't ye worry–I'll be sharin' lots more stories with ye."

"Anyway," he said, leaning back against the grass, "this story comes from the days of the Eld Green, when all the People could talk to one another. It weren't like today, ye know, where most folks don't know how to share words without losin' their understandin' of each other. In them days, Dragonfly—we call her Akjaadit, the Hummin'bird's granddaughter—was a small, almost insignificant nothin'. Well, she saw herself that way, anyways. She really weren't much to look at, to be truthful. In them days, she didn't have no pretty blue nor green nor gold on her wings. In fact, she didn't have no wings at all—she was just a pale little wormy thing. There weren't no place for her in the way of things. After all, there was already worms around, and so she weren't much good for that job neither.

"So one day she decides that she's goin' to find ol' Strivix the Unseen, the first and most ancient Owl in the world, and ask that ol' night-seeker to just end her days and make a quick meal of her. At least that-a-way she could provide some nourishment and be of some use to somebody. Now Strivix, she weren't too set on doin' such things. She en't trusted by a lot of us, sometime for good reasons, but at heart she really en't so bad; she's just been painted by the fact that she knows more than she oughta 'bout the end of things, 'specially life, and she en't too welcome when she comes to let us know 'bout it.

"Anyways, Strivix sees this poor ol' worm-thing weepin' all over her feathered claws, and she says, 'Now, listen here, Akjaadit, don't ye know nothin'? Ye en't a worm at all. Ye'r a Dragonfly.' Of course, there was no way Akjaadit could'a known that, as there'd never been no Dragonfly afore, but it sounded interestin'. So Akjaadit says to Strivix, 'I don't know how to be a Dragonfly,' and Strivix says, 'All ye got to do is tell yer people's story, and ye'll figure it out.' "

Tarsa's brows narrowed. "What story? How could she know a story about something that didn't exist before?"

Tobhi smiled and scratched his nose, nodding. "Well, to be perfectly truthful, there weren't no story to tell at all—at least as far as that ol' Owl was concerned. Strivix just said the first thing that came into her ol' feathered head. But she didn't let on none. She just kept sayin', 'Tell yer story.' So li'l ol' wormy Akjaadit crawls back home, and all the way there she's sayin' to herself, 'What's our story?' And as she's movin' and thinkin' 'bout her story, she starts to think back to her mam and the rest of the family, and the way they was always tellin' her how smart she was, how beautiful she was, how she was gonna be the prideful joy of the family, how with her speed and quick wits she and her kith was gonna find their way in the world and make it a sweeter place. So she's walkin'–well, since she's a worm, I s'pose she's crawlin' along–and she feels this itchin' on her back, so she turns and sees these pretty green and blue wings just a-shinin' in the sunlight. Then she looks down and sees that she's got herself six delicate li'l legs and a long, shimmerin' tail swishin' 'round behind her. It don't take her too long to figure out what them wings is for, and soon she's flyin' around her family and tellin' 'em all what happened. They laugh when they hear her, 'cause her story is theirs, too, and pretty soon they's all flyin' around, pretty as can be, dartin' here and there all over the world, tellin' everybody their story. And when they tell ol' Strivix, she just nods to herself with a wise look on her face, like she was expectin' that all along. And maybe she was."

"So," Tarsa said with a smile, "is this story supposed to be a teaching?"

The Tetawa shrugged his shoulders. "'En't they all? Maybe it'll ease yer mind, and maybe it'll just rattle around in yer thoughts for a while 'til ye find what ye'r lookin' for. It could even just be an interestin' story 'bout how Dragonfly learnt to tell the story of her people to all the world." He stood up and stretched. "And maybe it was just a way to distract ye, to get you sleepy and relaxed so's I'd beat ye back to camp." Grinning, he sprinted down the hillside.

Tarsa laughed and jumped up to race across the meadow after him.

<hr />

Vergis Thane nearly always worked alone; he preferred solitude. He trusted himself and his own abilities, but he didn't have any control over the others he travelled with. They were weak, easily turned from the seriousness of their mission toward frivolities that wasted time and tested his patience. He'd begrudgingly accepted this charge with the knowledge that, for a while at least, he'd be part of a larger group. He wouldn't make that mistake again. Fortunately, this part of the journey was almost over. He'd be on his own again at dawn, and then he wouldn't have to deal with their timid minds and weaker characters any longer.

While his name was hated in certain circles, and fearfully admired in others, he wasn't a large or physically imposing man; in fact, those who didn't know him nearly always underestimated him, inevitably to their deep regret. He was a few inches under six feet in height, with thinning brown and gray hair, a ragged goatee, and long, bristling mustaches that he twisted when in deep thought. One eye was covered with a dirty black patch, the lasting reminder of the one and only time he'd misjudged an opponent; the other eye, shocking blue, shone brightly under a bushy brow. He held no bitterness over the loss of the eye. He'd accepted it as a lesson that had kept him alive through many situations that should have ended in his death.

Thane's clothing was as unimpressive as his physique: a wide-brimmed, water-stained leather hat and thick cloak, durable leather boots, drab breeches and tunic, and an open-sleeved traveller's coat. He looked like any one of a thousand Human wanderers, except for the frigid blue eye and the long knife and short sword that hung in matching scabbards from his belt. They weren't particularly special weapons—no alchaemical formulas had been read over them to ensure a keen edge or unbreakable strength—but they served their purpose, and Thane cared for them well.

He lit his pipe—one of the few purely hedonistic pleasures he allowed himself—and settled back against the tree to watch the other Men slip deeper into alcoholic imbecility. The Seeker had little use for drunkards at the best of times, and none at all when working, but he saw no reason to intervene; the others already hated him, and even a Man as well-trained to survive a solitary life found it desirable to avoid agitating others when possible. The shattering of a wine jug on a rock near him, however, made it clear that he wouldn't be able to avoid it tonight.

Thane looked up. A pale-lipped young Man, thin and sickly-looking, teetered unsteadily on the other side of the fire, his eyes boring into Thane with the arrogance of an angry inebriate. A couple of the Man's more sensible friends pulled at his arms, trying to drag him away, but he jerked out of their grasping hands and stumbled toward the Seeker. Thane drew easily on the stem of his pipe, his gaze never wavering.

The Man stopped just out of reach and leaned down, head bobbing awkwardly. «Why don't you have a drink with ush?» he slobbered.

Thane didn't move. «I don't drink.»

«You heard that, didn't you?» the young Man sneered, turning back to his friends. «He shaid he don't drink. Know what that meansh? Meansh he don't drink with ussssh.» The word hissed through his teeth like steam from a kettle. «Ish that what you're shaying, you ugly bashtard?»

«I said, I don't drink. Go back to your friends.»

«What did you just shay t' me?» He wobbled beside the fire and crouched down. The stink of cheap whiskey and brown teeth wafted through the pipe smoke toward the Seeker, but Thane showed no sign of his disgust.

«I shaid, what did you shay? Are you ordering me around? Jusssht who do you think you are? You're jusssht shome dirt-shniffing vagabond who don't show proper reshpect for hissh betterssh. Maybe I'll teach you a lesshon, how 'bout that?» He lurched forward again, now with a glowing brand from the fire in his hand, and shrugged off the restraining hands of his more sober friends.

«You won't get another warning. You either walk back to your friends now, or they'll be burying you at dawn.» Thane blew a smoke ring into the air.

«We'll sshe who'sh gonna be buried,» the Man bellowed, rushing at the Seeker. He never reached his target. Thane's leg shot out to catch the Man in the crotch and lift him forward in one fluid movement. There was a bright crimson flash, and the Man slid to his knees, staring in drunken disbelief at the long, neat gash across his belly that slowly opened to let his intestines slip steaming to the bloody ground. Thane, still smoking his pipe, drew a clean white cloth from an inner pocket of his jacket and wiped the long knife's blade, then tapped the Man's forehead with his boot. The body slumped limply into the dirt.

No one made a noise. When he'd finished cleaning his knife, Thane stood and walked away from the fire toward his hammock, which hung between two large standing stones some distance from the others. He never looked back, but he could hear the whispers begin.

Good. They'd leave him alone now.

He swung himself into the hammock and pulled his hat down over his face. It had been a long day, and it didn't look too likely that tomorrow would be much better. Still, it was a nice enough place to spend the night. The smell of burning cedar and pine was a comforting one, as it had been a common mixture in the firepits of the hill country of his youth in southern Duruk. That particular smell brought back good memories. He was always amazed at the little joys that popped up unexpectedly on even the most routine mission.

Thane pulled the hat away from his eye and looked around again. The standing stones had been part of a large arch just half a day before. Each etched pillar was polished white and bound with rings of iron, which surprised the Seeker, given the natural aversion that most of the Snake-heads felt for the ore. The keystone of the arch, carved with symbols apparently meant to represent various heavenly bodies, had been one of the first things loaded into a cart. Those females who hadn't died in the initial attack, from squalling babe to crooked-armed crone, were chained and loaded into one of the iron-barred wagons; they would bring a good price, spoiled or not, at the market in the Dreyd-hold city of Chimiak in southern Eromar. Unless they were children, the surviving males were killed outright, as they wouldn't bring much gold in that slaving square.

He reached under his coat and pulled out the chunky stone necklace he'd taken that morning. It was clearly a primitive ward against witchcraft—even these creatures feared the witches in their midst—and so precious to the Unhuman priest who held it that Thane had to kill him for it. A waste of a life, but the crazy creature wouldn't let go of the necklace. Although he'd skewered that babbling old fool, Thane refrained from joining the brigands as they swept through the village; he had no stomach for useless torment and slaughter. Besides, his quarry wasn't there.

But Thane was on the right path, and he was patient. He'd find Fey-witches in these mountains. He had fortune's favour. Even as skilled a Seeker as he was, Thane believed in the reality of luck as much as he believed in the importance of a sharp mind and well-honed fighting skills. When the other Men were finished here, they'd return to Chimiak with their cargo, and Thane would take the new-found treasure with him into the mountains. It might be useful.

He slid the necklace back into his coat, pulled his hat back over his face, and slipped into a dreamless sleep, the smoke of the ravaged remnants of Red Cedar Town wafting over him, reminding him of home.

CHAPTER 10
SHEYNADWIIN

If any place could be fairly considered the centre of the Everland, it would be the venerable peace-city of Sheynadwiin, a populous settlement hidden deep within Dardath Vale, the ferny green home of the Kyn Nation. The valley lay nestled in a region of sheer, vine-streaming cliffs, turbid rivers that crashed with abandon down mountainsides and rocky precipices, shadowed grottoes that had never known sunlight or starshine, and ancient emerald trees stretching hundreds of leafy feet into the air, moss-covered sentinels whose deep-rooted memories travelled back to times far outside the understandings of the walking world.

And if any place within the great valley could be considered the heart of the Everland, the living essence of all it was to be woven into the *wyr* and the world, it would be the Eternity Tree, the pulsing heartwood of the *wyr*, which grew deep within the verdant arms of the valley, guarded by high-walled Sheynadwiin itself. The Tree was the covenant between the Folk and the land, the law of reciprocity that both sides had honoured in good faith since time immemorial. This was the home of antiquity, of ancestral memory and song.

Alone of all the remnant 'Holds, the Everland grew green and wild; many believed that this was due to the Eternity Tree, held by the Kyn as the living embodiment of Zhaia, the forest mother of their kind, from whose leafy body the seven Branches of the People had long ago emerged into an endless golden summer. Time held little power here. While other 'Holds fell to the grasping hand of Humanity, the Everland stood proud against the onslaught, and, although it grew no larger in the Melded world, it surrendered nothing, and it continued on as it always had, its wyr-fed currents nourishing the old growth and protecting the new. Those Folk who called the Everland home were known throughout the Reach of Men as implacable foes who gave no quarter in defense of their lands;

trespassers never escaped unscathed, and most who came with iron blade or burning brand were never seen again, as a warning to others who would dare intrude upon the Folk. Though wars of power and plunder carved a bloody swath through the lands of Humanity, the Everland had long remained untouched. Men had enough to worry about without risking the wrath of the Folk.

But those wars were largely over now–the Reachwarden of great Chalimor ruled supreme in the Reach, in name if not entirely in fact–and the eyes of Men turned once again to the deep forests and mist-shrouded mountains, eyes that saw only downed timber, gleaming gold, fine furs, meat, and slaves for the market. And so they came, a few at first, but soon Men and Women began to build on the outskirts of the Everland in ever-greater numbers, pushing farther inward, driving Folk deeper into the interior, a rising stream that threatened to become an overwhelming flood.

Much had already been lost. Word came to Sheynadwiin on the wings of bird, bat, and butterfly, on the swift cloven hooves of doe and the steady pads of bobcat and coyote, that the customs of Men ruled in places where once only the voices of Folk and their kith had echoed free. Kyn towns were burning to the south; Gvaerg-havens in the north echoed with the fresh ache of mourning songs; Tetawi moundhouses to the west lay in ruins, abandoned to scavengers on four feet and two. Beast-folk fled from warren, canopy, and copse, unable to withstand cold iron or hot flame. Even the implacably urbane Ubbetuk, called Goblins by Men, were surrendering their great learning-houses to the onrush of Humanity, taking to the safety of their distant sky-cities.

Yes, much had been lost, but not all. As messages came into Sheynadwiin, other messages went out. For only the fourth time in a thousand years, since the Melding that had forever severed the way to the Eld Green, a Sevenfold Council had been called. Representatives of the Seven Sisters, the first seven Folk of the Everland–Kyn, Tetawi, Gvaergs, and Ubbetuk, as well as the Wyrnach spider-people, the beast-folk, and the eldest of the half-animal Ferals, the Harpies—were asked to travel at great haste to Sheynadwiin, where together, it was hoped, they would discover a way to ensure the continued survival of the Everland.

For one thing was clear to all who called the Everland home: a great storm crouched on the borders of their home, and it wouldn't pass harmlessly over them.

***

"En't it a pretty sight?" Tobhi asked. Both she-Kyn nodded in awestruck silence, neither having seen anything quite as beautiful as the great green valley. Thin streams of mist rose here and there over the verdant expanse, and on each side of the vale rose tall cliffs of gray, red, and green, their heights lost in the low-settled clouds. The trio stood on a packed-soil road that moved northward through the Vale toward their destination: Sheynadwiin, the gathering place of the Sevenfold Council. Day would soon fade to night, but they wanted to linger here, to try to absorb the vast reach of life that surrounded them.

Tarsa suddenly felt very small and uncertain. This was a world entirely different from the one she had known in Red Cedar Town. Here great minds gathered to debate issues that would affect all the Folk throughout the Everland; it was no bickering town council chamber where, more often than not, petty jealousies and long-held grudges were the greatest concerns of the community leaders. Sheynadwiin was a place of heroes, of powerful speakers and war-leaders who knew the ways of their own world and of those beyond the misty edges of the Everland.

Tarsa wiped a layer away from her dirt-caked clothes and tried fruitlessly to untangle her matted hair. Unahi had given her an old, threadbare cloak to wear against cold in the deeper mountains, and it looked far worse now, with roughly-sewn gray and brown patches scattered randomly across the dull green fabric. Her copper armbands no longer shone in the sunlight, and cracks now snaked across her wooden bracers where once had gleamed richly-oiled wood. The journey had been fairly uneventful after the battle with the grave-robbing Men, but even with easy travel and baths every sunrise, she still looked bedraggled and unkempt; a quick glance at her similarly-disheveled companions merely deepened her depression. *Why would anyone listen to us?* she thought grimly.

Neither Tobhi nor Unahi seemed to share her discomfort, so Tarsa kept her thoughts to herself and tried to absorb the new experience, pushing the shadows to the back of her mind. As Tobhi had said, it was a truly magnificent sight. Dardath Vale itself stretched for many miles to the east and west, fewer to the north and south, and was lined at the mountains' base, from edge to edge, with massive wyrwood trees. Wyrwood was native to the Everland but alien to the Human lands beyond; it was the most important of the standing-people to the Kyn, and precious to other Folk. Weapons made with the proper Wieldings and entreaties to both Zhaia and the tree-spirits were not only equal in strength and sharpness to Human steel, but they could also draw on the *wyr* to enhance the already considerable powers of those who carried them. Wyrwood armour and wyrweave clothing crafted from the naturally-shed outer bark were largely impervious to the elements and could often be used to hide the wearer from unfriendly eyes; indeed, the power of wyrweave cloaks was enough to protect the sun-fearing he-Gvaergs from turning to stone in the daylight. Free-fall branches or deadwood could become walking sticks, furniture, even canoe hulls; seedpod beads and leaves made their way into jewelry and delicate works of art. Even the sweet golden sap that the Kyn tapped from the reddish trunks in the fall was used for medicinals and to give great nourishment to a wide range of foods. Wyrwood clothed, nourished, protected, and healed the Kyn, and there was no question why that was the case: the great Eternity Tree was the first wyrwood tree, and each of its descendants carried on the covenant between Zhaia and her descendants.

The Redthorn warrior had never seen so many wyrwood trees in one place, nor any so imposing: even the smaller trees were as big around as a Kyn council-house. The few wyrwoods remaining in the southern stretches of the Everland were deeply treasured by all of the Folk who lived nearby and were treated with utmost care. Tarsa's wyrwood bracers had been given to her at her marking when she'd passed the trials to join the ranks of the Redthorns, and Oda'hea, her mentor and friend, made all too clear just how difficult those gifts had been to obtain. Yet everywhere around the young warrior walked Folk bearing all manner of wyrwood decoration with an almost casual disregard. It was as common here along the road to Sheynadwiin as the knobby old pines in the hills around Nine Oaks Town. The only Folk unadorned with wyrwood were those wanderers like themselves from other areas far from Dardath Vale, and the Celestial Kyn who walked in tight groups, their chins high, silver jewelry jingling, eyes never straying from the path ahead of them.

Unahi waved her hand across the horizon. "Where will the Council meet?" she asked Tobhi.

The Tetawa pointed ahead. "Ye'll be meetin' in the Gallery of Song, where the Kyn Nation's been debatin' for a long while 'bout the proposal to leave the Everland. Ye can't see the Gallery yet, but it won't be too long 'til we can look down on the city and see everythin'." Smudge trotted along, pulling at his bridle with the knowledge that he'd soon be back to enjoying life in a well-stocked stable along with other Tetawi riding companions: deer, goats, burros, even large dogs and the occasional stout wolf. This more congenial attitude pleased Tobhi enormously, as Smudge had grown more and more irritable on the journey until, in a fit of temper, he'd charged into Tarsa and had nearly been skewered by her quick knife. Since that incident, the deer had remained quite docile, although he refused to come anywhere near the Redthorn warrior again.

As Tobhi had promised, the road soon crested on the high edge of a hill, and the travellers looked down on the city of Sheynadwiin itself. Unahi gasped with long-awaited joy at the sight, but Tarsa's throat was too thick with emotion; all she could do was stare with brimming eyes.

Built inside a massive, river-swollen grotto at the jagged feet of the great Kraagen Mountains, the city seemed to shimmer in the rainbow light of sunset that gleamed through the river spray. The air was alive with light and laughter. Twisted into beautiful arches and swirling waves by the erosion of the river water, great stone towers stood tall and proud throughout the city, the sharp, angular images of leaves, trees, and animals carved into their sides until each looked to be formed more by mindful intent than by the water-worn effort of ages. Bridges of stone, vine, wood, and rope spanned the city to link with dozens of stout wyrwood trees that each stretched at least five hundred feet into the sky. Brightly-painted Kyn houses, taller than those of the south but still comfortably familiar, crowded both the ground below and the bustling canopy above, lining well-maintained streets that bustled with activity. Not unlike tall gourds with thatched and tiled roofs, some houses were multi-leveled like the city itself, with gardens growing untamed on each level. Their round doors and windows had few shutters against the clean air and the warm sun. Grocers, traders, merchants, singers, cane-flute players, storytellers, and others sold their wares to or shared their skills with appreciative passers-by; from time to time a flock of birds with brilliant plumage would skim like winged arrows of fire through the treetops and dart among the people above and below. And there were the smells–sweet baking spices mingled delicately with the rich earthy musk of the forest–rising up in the air to welcome the new arrivals.

Tobhi pointed to a massive amphitheatre at the far northwest edge of the grotto. Though it was largely open to the sky, a wide half-dome extended outward beyond it, like the leading edge of a rolled sea-shell. "That's the Gallery. They sometimes draw that roof over the top of it, but most folks like to see the sky when they're debatin' with one another. Can't say as I blame 'em–there's nothin' quite like the stars above Sheynadwiin." Even in the last light of the fading day, Tarsa could tell that the night sky would be spectacular, as Pearl-in-Darkness and the various astral spheres were already bright. The great ring that circled the world–remnants of the

Greatmoon's shattered brothers–gleamed like a silver band in the sky, which seemed deeper here, more distinctly otherworldly. You could look into the heavens and see something new every time. Here the dense green world opened up into endlessness above.

On a low stone ridge to the northeast of the amphitheatre stood a massive stone-and-lashed-timber longhouse, four times as long as its fifty-foot height. Various designs resembling beaded knot-weavings were painted onto large squares of colour on the sides. At the apex of the front eave stood a massive carving of a bull elk's head, its wooden knot eyes turned eastward towards the rising suns. Well-tended vines wrapped themselves into the antlers and extended down the sides of the lodge to the ground. It was a sacred space, where ceremony adhered to the Old Ways, safe from winter snows and summer storms.

Yet here, perhaps more than anyplace else, Tarsa could see the impact of the Shields and the Celestial Path, for dozens of large stone-carved arches, like the one that stood over the memory of the old cedar in Red Cedar Town, had been erected in proud defiance throughout the city. Three of the arches crowded together around the lodge, as though to hem in its influence, to force Kyn through their stony embrace before they gained the freedom of the lodge. And yet here the arches seemed almost insignificant, a futile attempt to confine the laughing wind. The Deep Green still endured.

Tobhi led them down the road toward the city. They stopped at a rising series of four guarded walls, some built of ruddy stone and mortar, others formed from the living trees and earth by the still-strong Wielding of generations before. The warders looked at both Unahi and Tarsa without hostility, as Greenwalkers were not strangers to Sheynadwiin. After passing the fourth wall, the travellers headed toward the large city centre, a grassy gathering place from which the red-stone cobbled roadways extended up and down throughout the grotto. Kyn and other Folk gathered in the area, many purchasing provisions and goods from the various merchants wandering around, others locked in intense conversation.

Though the earlier sense of peace hadn't faded completely, the mood among the People was not as calm as the newcomers had assumed from afar. Here the very air seemed to ache. Some passers-by cast dark looks at the Wielders while ignoring Tobhi. The Tetawa was surprised to see weapons hanging in plain view from belts and bandoliers, rather than being secured in the weapons-house by the gate militia before permission was granted to enter the peace-city, as was the long-standing tradition. Kyn warriors–both Greenwalker in dusty wyrweave garments and Celestial in pristine white and blue silks–walked through the crowd with lips pursed and eyes darting around in search of trouble; some seemed a bit too eager to find it. The few Human merchants in the city were given wide berth, even though most of them had long since demonstrated their loyalty to the Folk, and many were married into Folk families. Although the two she-Kyn Wielders couldn't understand all of the speech around them, it was clear that life was changing in Sheynadwiin. It was not a comforting realization.

Darkness had, by this time, fallen in the valley, but when twilight deepened toward night the air erupted with the soft glow of everlights hanging on trees and atop tall wooden posts on the ground and in the canopy of trees. The lanterns were wrought to resemble pine cones and apples, acorns, willow baskets, and other shapes in honour of the seven Kyn Branches. Their lights were soft, not so brilliant as to drive away the gentle hush of night, but bright enough to give shape to the shadows.

They stopped here to rest. Tobhi walked up to the wagon of an old Tetawa baker and chatted with him for a moment, then returned with a warm armful of plump pumpkin cakes and a steaming clay jar of apple cider to share. Hands sticky from the meal, the three gathered at the base of a good-sized wyrwood sapling on the edge of the green.

"Well, niece, we've finally found our way here," said Unahi, sipping from the cider jug. Tarsa nodded silently, her mouth too full with cake to speak. The elder Wielder turned to Tobhi. "What's next for you, Leafspeaker?"

He held a pumpkin cake out to Smudge, who nibbled contentedly at the snack, and shrugged. "I en't too sure, really. M' aunties might want me to take notes at the Council and add 'em to m' lore-leaves; they're really interested in gettin' a good understandin' of the proceedin's for future reflectin'. Until then, though, I s'pose I'm pretty well free to do whatever I like."

Unahi nodded. "And you, niece?"

"I'm going with you." Tarsa hesitated. "Aren't I?"

"Eventually, yes. But first I must meet with the other elder Wielders. We rarely meet in large numbers—not since the Purging—and we'll have plenty to talk about with one another for the next couple of weeks until the Council is fully underway. After we've cleared a path for the upcoming discussions, you and the other young Wielders will join us."

Seeing Tarsa's face drop in disappointment, Unahi reached out and gently patted the young she-Kyn's hand. This time there was no hesitation in her touch. "This has nothing to do with your Wielding, niece. Your strength and bravery are very much needed at this grim time. But for now, rest and let your heart be light; you've had far too many burdens on your strong, young shoulders lately, and I haven't been able to give you the kind of attention you deserve. I want you to see the city, to meet people, to understand all the many different ways it is to be Kyn, to know our other kith among the Folk." She smiled wearily, not adding that she hoped this brief respite would extend a calming influence over Tarsa's spirit as well. "This is the heart-home of our Nation, Tarsa, and one of us must be familiar with both the city and with the many peoples who are here; that one must be you. I'm a stranger here too, and I'll need you to be my eyes and ears outside the Wielders' Circle, to help me understand what's happening out there, to know who our friends are and who opposes us, to know fully what's at stake. Will you do that for me?"

Tarsa nodded and breathed easier. It had been a long time since she'd felt truly needed—a lifetime ago, since she'd killed the Stoneskin. And, in truth, she did want to see more of Sheynadwiin, to immerse herself in the noise and energy of the city, which was so very different from anything she'd experienced before. So many different peoples were gathered together in this place as they'd done for countless ages; the deep and abiding spirit of Sheynadwiin was so clear to her senses that she could almost see it. If she could satisfy her rising curiosity and still be of help to Unahi and the other Wielders, she'd be content. For the first time since her banishment, her heart didn't ache for the familiar comforts of Red Cedar Town.

Tobhi's face erupted into a broad grin. "Ye know, if ye'r gonna be wanderin' all over the city, ye'll need y'self a guide." He winced. "This time, though, I en't takin' along that tail-bitin' beast with me—I'm so bruised that I en't likely to sit down comfortable for at least a tenday!" Tarsa laughed, but Smudge ignored them and continued chewing on a pumpkin cake.

News of Tobhi's arrival spread quickly, and, between his daily explorations of the city with Tarsa, his aunties soon had him busy running errands between Tetawi Clans throughout Sheynadwiin. Unahi and Tarsa took up quarters with one of the elder she-Kyn's friends, an enormous Gvaerg Wielder named Biggiabba. Tarsa had seen a few Gvaergs in her patrols as a Redthorn warrior, but never so closely. Even bent low in a perpetual stoop, Biggiabba stood well over twice the she-Kyn's height. Her thick gray skin was mottled and creased like the bark of an old spruce, and her dull green hair fell down in thick cords around her broad, sloping brow. The old Gvaerg wore a coarse brown robe that covered her vitals without constricting her movement; it was free of adornment, as Biggiabba had little use for vanity. The two she-Kyn slept in hammocks strung from the upper timbers of her open, two-storied roundhouse, while the kindly old Gvaerg snored peacefully on a thick wyrweave mat on the floor below them.

Like Tobhi, they too soon had frequent visitors, and it was these first few days that gave Tarsa a clear sense of Unahi's true work. The handful of Wielders who called Sheynadwiin home had for some time been overwhelmed by the number of Folk seeking assistance during these dark days, so they were thrilled to be able to send the overflow to the various visiting Wielders throughout the city. Tarsa soon discovered that both Unahi and Biggiabba had good reputations that extended far from their respective home grounds, and every day brought with it a steady stream of Folk looking for guidance or comfort. Tarsa had a fast education as a result, learning a wide range of medicinal and counter-witching formulas from Unahi, while from Biggiabba she learned to identify dozens of different kinds of rocks and minerals and their surprisingly diverse uses. She helped both of the elder Wielders in setting broken bones, delivering younglings, counselling the bereaved, guarding the fertility of crops, driving out minor menacing spirits and curses, and performing other duties of greater and lesser significance. Tarsa learned from her aunt many of the Kyn ways of the *wyr*, and from Biggiabba she learned those teachings that were most appropriate for non-Gvaergs. Gvaerg Wielders zealously guarded their deeper knowledge from riijik—"unbelievers"—for the Gvaergs were a deeply devout people, and they took few into their confidence.

Those weeks were a revelation. While in Red Cedar Town, Tarsa had always thought of Wielders as being strange and romantically menacing, appearing in times of great peril with powers out of legend, then disappearing again to their mysterious fog-guarded hollows. Her own Awakening had shattered that fanciful illusion while heightening her fear, yet it wasn't until she encountered Unahi's daily work that she lost much of that discomfort. Yes, the *wyr* demanded much, and she wasn't entirely sure that she was up to the task of being a Wielder, but she saw that Unahi filled a need in the lives of the Folk, and, while most of the work was rather mundane, its value was no less important in the lives of the Folk than Tarsa's own Redthorn war-craft. The Folk who visited were generally quite pleasant and grateful for the help. Some were clearly far more comfortable with the idea of Wielder wisdom than others, whose reluctance and occasional fear spoke to both their own desperation and the growing power of the Shields in the city. Yet no matter what their motivations or misgivings, each visitor brought a gift of food or cloth or other practical item for respectful exchange, and the house became so packed with these gifts that Unahi soon had Tobhi and a few of his cousins making regular distribution runs to the refugees who were arriving in the city in ever-growing numbers.

And each night, after the last visitor had gone home with a kind word and gentle touch, Tarsa would prepare the evening meal while Unahi and Biggiabba went through the day's teachings with her, encouraging questions and giving thoughtful answers that seemed to bind themselves firmly to the young she-Kyn's memory. She learned quickly, and she learned well. Unahi's gruffness hadn't vanished entirely, but Tarsa saw far more of her aunt's gentle spirit than in all the weeks before, and she treasured the gift.

Those lessons slowed down after the first few weeks, as the members of the Wielders' Circle began their own discussions in their great longhouse beside the Gallery of Song, and the older Wielders spent more time among their colleagues, leaving Tarsa more often in Tobhi's good company. She was increasingly restless, even during the most intensive teachings, but neither Unahi nor Biggiabba ever mentioned her distraction, even though their shared glances made clear that they noticed the change. Her walks with Tobhi through the city helped her to clear her thoughts, if only for a while. She felt as though something called to her at a great distance. Its voice was too soft to hear, and, as much as she tried, she couldn't make out the words.

She learned much from Tobhi, too. Of all the Folk, the Tetawi were the closest to the Kyn. Both peoples preferred to live in deep woods and wild places. They organized their communities on a similar structure that passed through the female line–Clans for the Tetawi, Branches for the

Kyn–and both Folk were deeply committed to both their immediate and extended families. Yet the Tetawi were far more sociable with others than were the Kyn. Many Tetawi travelled throughout the Everland and beyond as traders, writers, musicians, and performers, or as archers and scouts. Tobhi was far from unusual in his familiarity with other tongues and peoples, although his leaf-reading was certainly a rare gift.

Tetawi settlements tended to be rather large and spread out; the one in Sheynadwiin was very small and compact by comparison. Their little moundhouses–stocky timbered cabins with carved entry posts and arched roofs–were clustered in Clan groups and built around the base of a great earthen mound at the centre of the settlement. They buried their dead inside the mound and performed ceremonies atop it. Every few years they hauled more dirt to the top and built it up higher; the central mounds of older settlements were truly massive. The mound in the centre of the Sheynadwiin settlement was goodly sized, speaking to a lengthy presence in the city.

Perhaps the most striking difference between the Kyn and Tetawi was in their connection to the *wyr*. Both peoples loved and honoured their wild world, and Tarsa found deep comfort in that. Whereas the Kyn found their greatest love for and connection to the green growing things of the world, the Tetawi followed the guidance of the beasts of the earth and of the air, from Tobhi's own Badger Clan to others that honoured Spider, Nuthatch, Lizard, Moth, Marmot, and more. Kyn Wielding linked to the spirits of the elements, but Tetawi Wielding linked minds with those creatures closest to the Wielder's Clan animal or, if a healer, with any creature in need.

"Some of us," Tobhi mentioned to her one day, "can even take the shape of their Clan animal–it seems to give 'em a deeper understandin' of the ways of beasts, but it en't common at all, and we don't often talk 'bout it. It's a more intimate connection than most things we do, and so it en't much of a topic for heedless mouth-rattlin'." He continued with a story about the shadow-side of that connection, the cannibal Skeegers, those Tetawi shape-shifters who had been cast out of their Clans due to unspeakable crimes, and who now wandered through the world and lingered on the outskirts of Tetawi settlements in search of warm-blooded prey.

"And then there's the Owl Clan," he began. "Nobody is born into that Clan of death; ye gotta be called to it… " It was still early afternoon, but a sudden chill in the air gave the Tetawa pause, and he quickly diverted their conversation to more benign issues. Their mood brightened when some of Tobhi's cousins arrived to play a vigorous game of Groundhog's keep-away, which involved a round clearing, a double-woven basket, a round ball of tanned bearskin, and stout wooden cudgels that smashed into toes and shins with surprising frequency. Tarsa watched the enthusiastic aggression for a while from the clearing's edge before joining in and receiving a few bruises of her own.

Skeegers and Owls were a distant menace. Most Tetawi were like Tobhi: open and generous, with a respectful curiosity that inquired but never demanded. Many spoke with Tobhi's same deep-woods bluntness, while others were more refined in their speech, but all were friendly. Tarsa ate well as Tobhi's friend and guest–huge feasts of thick-grained breads, rich gravies, corn, beans, squashes of varied flavors and forms, and a wide array of fruit, including a rich fermented strawberry drink that eased the body's tensions and gave comfort to her increasingly-unsettled spirit. Out of respect to her own traditions, the Tetawi refrained from placing meat on the table, although they generally had no hesitation to eat animals that had fallen on the hunt. There were few visible tensions between Clans, although Tarsa noticed a great deal of good-natured rivalry among groups, notably between those who followed Buborru the Keeper, the old Badger-father of Tobhi's Clan, and those of Boar Clan, who honoured Mother Malluk as the protector of their family. It was a bit different from her own upbringing in Red Cedar Town, where the Willow Branch Kyn often clashed, sometimes violently, with Ash Branch.

She learned other things, too, more personal stories about Tobhi's family, his parents in the far-distant Edgewood, his older sister, and extended kin. And she learned about Tobhi's love of a sweet young she-Tetawa, a firra, who lived a few days from his birth-Clan's settlement. The story transformed him. His stories about his sandy-haired beloved burned with an honest fire that stripped away the shadows of those dark days. He planned to talk to her family when he returned from Sheynadwiin, for he had his own family's blessings for the marriage. Once the Sevenfold Council had finished its business, he'd head back to Spindletop with gifts and a wedding belt, and there begin the next great stage of his life. Such deep feeling filled Tarsa's own heart with longing.

Tobhi caught her pained expression. "Are ye all right, Tarsa? D'ye have someone of ye'r own back in Red Cedar Town waitin' for ye?"

"No, not anymore," she said quietly. "They always seemed to want something more than I could ever really give them. That sounds ridiculous, doesn't it? But it's true. I guess I always knew that there was something dangerous inside me, something wrong." She smiled, but the pain bled through. "And I was right. With everything now–it's probably good that no one is waiting for me." They didn't talk much for the rest of that day, nor did Tobhi return to the subject.

✶✶✶✶✶✶

Tarsa enjoyed her visits with Tobhi's folk, but she couldn't always be with him, so she sometimes explored the city on her own. She'd linger at the centre green and peruse the traders' stalls, or measure the difference in training styles between the city's Greenwalker and Celestial guardians. Sometimes she'd help with the building of temporary arbors for the refugees. Most often, though, she'd simply walk among the great wyrwood trees and feel their stable rootedness ease the day's tension from her thoughts. The bloodsong was calmest in these moments, but the respite was only temporary. When her wanderings were over, she inevitably found her way back to the house Tobhi shared with his aunt Jynni and a few cousins, and there she'd stay until late in the night, listening and watching as they ate and laughed together, quietly experiencing the kindly joys of Tetawi kinship. It was so different from the cold dignity of her socially-conscious aunts in Red Cedar Town, for whom any public frivolity was a danger to the Cedar Branch position. This new freedom—and acceptance—was wholly unexpected, and not at all unpleasant.

One afternoon, while Tobhi was busy writing a letter for his aunts, Tarsa decided to explore the northern part of the city on her own. The Tetawi settlement and most of the trading centre was in the southern half of the grotto, closer to the trees of the Eldarvian Woods than to the great Kraagen Mountains, so she'd seen very little of this area, and she was drawn to the misty ridges of the high northern quarter. Unahi and Biggiabba had been in council for three full days and nights, leaving her alone in the Gvaerg's roundhouse, and that time had weighed heavily on her restless spirit. When she felt the pull toward the upper city, she didn't even try to resist. The call was too strong; she hungered for something she couldn't name.

A great waterfall rushed down the vine-choked northern cliff, plummeting hundreds of feet into a deep, roaring pool below. White spray turned to thick silver mist at the base of the falls, absorbing the greater part of the noise. The effect was surprisingly soothing, as though the river's enthusiasm for life could ease the minds of those who heard him. The water glowed with a soft light of its own that wasn't lost in the brightness of the early afternoon.

A dozen spray-splashed stone benches sat around the pool, and Tarsa walked to one. It was a place to sit and listen to the river's voice, to watch the play of light through mist and deep water. Each bench was carved with odd faces of spirit-creatures, some rather comical, others grotesque and unpleasant. But they were silent, and she gave herself to the sounds of the water. Her thoughts drifted away. She was safer in this place than she'd been in a very long time. There was no tension in her blood, no pain, no fear of herself or her rage. She didn't know what brought such sudden peace to her mind and spirit, but her heart swelled with love of it.

An odd scraping noise caught her attention, and she turned to see a tall, russet-skinned he-Kyn approaching a bench not far from her. He was old but unbent, with a full head of bright silver hair that cascaded down to the middle of his back, matched by a silver moustache that draped past his chin. His gray eyes were large and heavy, but he smiled at her in friendly greeting. In one hand he held a slender walking stick that was smoothed and polished a deep red-brown.

"My apologies," he said gently. "I did not mean to frighten you." His voice had a pleasant roughness, like the creak of old oak.

She shook her head. "You didn't. I was just looking at the water."

"There are few places more suitable. May I join you?"

Tarsa dipped her chin. He sat on a nearby bench and watched the waterfall. She returned her own gaze to the pool, while at the same time casting furtive glances at the he-Kyn near her. He looked like a Strangeling, the child of a Human female and a he-Kyn, born without Branch identity and thus something other than Kyn. His ancestry seemed clear from the dullness of his ear tines and sensory stalks, his height, and the thickness of his chest. Most of the Strangelings that she knew in Red Cedar Town were firm Celestials, occasionally even called upon to be the ceremonial Shields. In some ways he reminded her of the messenger Leith: his clothing was similar to the Celestial fashions she'd seen since coming to Sheynadwiin, complete with chin-high white cravat, layered jacket and forest green breeches, knee-high boots, and a dove-gray cloak of fine satin. Yet he had none of Leith's aloofness. She stared off into the water again, but turned to the newcomer in sudden surprise.

"You speak the Old Tongue!"

He smiled at her. "Yes. It is my language, too."

"Oh." She looked away. "I'm sorry to be rude. It's just that I haven't been able to speak with any of your kind since I've been here." Even the most Man-friendly Celestials in Red Cedar Town had spoken the old Kyn language, but here in Sheynadwiin, a number of Celestials—and nearly every Greenwalking Strangeling who'd visited Biggiabba's house—spoke nothing but Mannish.

"'Your kind'?" he asked with an eyebrow raised.

She shook her head again. They'd just met, and this was already going badly. "It's just…I didn't mean to offend you. You are a Strangeling, aren't you?"

"Ah." He smiled. "No, I am Pine Branch Kyn. True, my father was Human, but I am no Branchless Strangeling–my mother was Kyn. I belong to her people, and I wear my honour markings with pride." He lifted the hair away from his neck to reveal a series of intricate spiral- and cone-shaped tattoos that disappeared beneath his collar.

Tarsa cringed. She should have known the distinction–the Strangelings in Red Cedar Town were all born to Human Women, not to she-Kyn. The few younglings born to she-Kyn and Human sires in that community were Kyn, no matter their appearance, and belonged there as much as any of the other Branch-born. "Please, forgive me. I'm quite new here, and I'm still learning a great deal. I shouldn't have assumed anything."

The he-Kyn held up his hand. "You did not offend me. Pray, do not concern yourself about it any longer. As so much has lately changed in Sheynadwiin, you were not entirely wrong in your assessment; many born of two bloods follow the unbending Celestial Path. But not all two-bloods follow the ways of Men, nor do all Strangelings follow the guidance of the Shields. Many here who speak Mannish or walk among Men are still dedicated Greenwalkers." He smiled. "I must admit that it is something of a pleasant surprise to be able to speak with one who knows of these things, especially considering your youth."

Tarsa's green skin darkened. "My elders have taught me well."

The he-Kyn held his hands up in mock surrender and laughed. "Now it is I who ask forgiveness. I did not intend offense. Indeed, age is no better a sign of one's path than is one's outer raiment, be it flesh or cloth." Tarsa nodded and smiled in spite of her embarrassment.

"Who is your family?" the he-Kyn asked.

"I am a daughter of Cedar Branch, Red Cedar Town, to the far south.

My mother was Lan'delar Last-Born, my father Setharian Kills-Two-Men of Oak Branch. My mother named me Namshéké, but the name I share is my warrior-name, Tarsa'deshae, which I earned through blood and battle." Her voice trembled a bit towards the end, but she held her chin high as she claimed her Redthorn name.

The stranger nodded appreciatively. "Indeed, you were taught well. I am of Pine Branch, Thornholt town, six days southwest of Sheynadwiin. My mother was Kei'shaad Mendiir, my father a Human merchant named Ramyd Thalsson. My mother named me Garyn, and that is the name I share with you." He held his hand out to Tarsa, palm upward, and she briefly rested her three digits on his own five-fingered Man's hand.

"I have heard of you before this," Garyn said. "You came here with Unahi, the Wielder of Thistlewood, and the Tetawa Leafspeaker." Tarsa nodded. "Then indeed, this is a rare and wonderful privilege. There are few Redthorn warriors in these lands, and none within memory who can tell of facing down a Stoneskin and surviving. Most impressive. Most impressive, indeed."

Garyn stood up. He favoured his left leg, and Tarsa realized that the scraping she heard earlier was the he-Kyn's right foot, which curled inwards slightly.

"I will not trouble you any longer, Tarsa'deshae. I have stayed away from my duties much too long as it is. I thank you for your conversation; you do not know how much you have lifted my spirits." He smiled as he bowed in farewell, but his gaze seemed to pass beyond her to take in the whole of Sheynadwiin. "Perhaps we will have a longer opportunity to talk of the Old Ways again. In the meantime, I must say farewell."

She stood and nodded to him, watching him go with a mingled sense of relief and curiosity. Before he disappeared up the stairs that led away from the pool, Garyn turned to her again. "Follow the path behind the waterfall if you would see the Eternity Tree. You will find it well worth the visit, I assure you. *Hanahé.*" He moved up the stairs and vanished into the mist.

Tarsa looked back to the waterfall. A small but well-worn path hugged the wet cliff face and disappeared behind the rushing water. She tried to look past the waterfall to see what lay beyond. For a moment, all that she could see was the silver-blue water curtain, but as her eyes became more accustomed to the movement, she could see a bright spot in the darkness. It was the same light, the same soothing blue that flowed through the pool, and her spirit sang with sudden recognition as a deep peace washed over her body. She forgot about the he-Kyn stranger, her worries, her fears. All she saw and sensed lay beyond the river's roar. It called to her.

Tarsa didn't hesitate in answering. She hurried across the leftward path, slipping slightly on the slick stones but never falling, and disappeared behind the waterfall.

CHAPTER 11

BECOMING

The roar of the falls faded in the distance as Garyn limped slowly through the grotto. His eyes, gray as old slate, held a heavy distance in their depths, as if his spirit looked out through a drizzling veil. He stopped on a high patch of ground that overlooked much of Sheynadwiin and took in the mid-day sunlight and crisp air. Here in the mountains even summer carried a bite. The ache in his leg was easier to bear on days like this, but he still mourned the old trail injury. The city was as beautiful now as it had been when he'd first stepped through the vine-wrapped gates as a Speaker to the Gathering, the ancient council-meet of Kyn town representatives from throughout the Everland. Those days were long past, but he could still remember the happy arrogance of youth, the mingled fear and heady anticipation that had accompanied him on his first truly adult task. He'd served his town wisely and well–so well, in fact, that his Branch-mothers had sent him back to the Gathering the next year, and the year after, eventually gaining support from other Branches to choose him as the Firstkyn of Thornhold. The Gathering had slowly given way to the Assembly, and still he'd spoken for Thornhold. Twenty years later, after the unification of the autonomous towns into the Kyn Nation, the town elders chose Garyn as Governor and Voice of the Nation. For all these many years, he'd served his people as wisely and courageously as he could, and the Nation had flourished.

Politics were less Garyn's pleasure than his duty, but he held no resentment; he was honoured to have been chosen, time and time again, to speak for his peoples' interests and for their concerns. But he no longer burned with the fire of youth. The full, fresh lips that had once turned up in a winning grin now rarely found joy enough to smile. He was still dignified, still a powerful figure with a commanding voice and compelling gaze, but his heart had somewhere lost its lightness.

The city that had once known only the joy of eternal summer now trembled under autumn's shadow. It was a time he'd never thought to see. Though his people went about their lives much as they always had, fear dogged their steps and darkened every task. Younglings no longer ran laughing together through the streets, dodging merchant wagons and their aunties' grasping hands. Now they sat, together or alone, and watched with too-old eyes as their elders trembled with each day's news.

And every day his own fear grew that he would have the grim honour of being the last leader of the Kyn. The thought was like cold iron in his blood. He bowed his head and squeezed his eyes tight, but he pushed aside the desire to wish the new times away. Such wishes were fleeting solace at best; he could change nothing by ignoring the world. He looked up again. The cobbled streets were still clean; the windows remained open to the wind. Wyrweave flags and banners still fluttered atop the thatched and tiled houses, river-cane flutes and gourd-bodied fiddles still rang up from the mossy trunks of the lower tree-city, and from the branches above the Shields still sang their songs of penance with each new day's light. Life would continue much as it had for all time; normalcy was their greatest comfort. Sometimes the crouching fawn fell under the cougar's claws, but sometimes death passed it by.

Sometimes.

Garyn listened to the melancholy music that danced down through the canopy. It was a fitting companion to his mood. He turned to walk down the road to the centre green of the city but stopped to wait for an approaching figure dressed in deep vermillion who strode with purposeful ease up the wide street, a golden shawl wrapped tightly around her shoulders to keep out the chill. His mood soured further, but he didn't walk away.

"Health and long happiness, my Governor," Neranda said with a respectful nod, slightly winded from the climb.

"Hanahé," Garyn replied.

The Lawmaker looked at him with one eyebrow raised at the old greeting. "You were not in your rooms when I came to speak with you."

"No. I wanted some peace; it is far too difficult to find it at the Gallery House. Too many voices, too much noise. I have much on my mind."

Neranda looked at the fog-shrouded path behind the Governor that led toward the waterfall. "It is not wise to linger in the past, Garyn."

"Perhaps not," he sighed, "but it may have more to teach us than you think. Why have you come here, Neranda?"

Thick strands of her dark red hair fluttered on the breeze, pulled free of the heavy silken mesh that draped backward from a silver circlet on her forehead. She pulled the shawl closer. "I know too well the burden that rests on your shoulders, Garyn, because that burden rests heavily on my own. Why must you insist on carrying that weight alone? It need not be so."

The Governor shook his head. It was a familiar and tiresome argument, and he was in no mood to continue it this day. "The same song, Neranda, if a different tune. Our burdens are not the same, although well they could be." He pointed to the city below. "Look at them. Listen. This is their home—our home. We cannot forsake them."

The first hint of emotion flashed in her violet eyes. "Forsake them? I suffer with them, as much as you do, if not more, as I can actually see the full measure of darkness that hovers on the horizon. Our people are stronger than you suppose, Garyn. They can make a life elsewhere… anywhere. You can make them see this. The People trust you as they trust no one else. They can rebuild, better and stronger, in a land that will always be ours, far from the grasping hand of Humanity."

"There is no such place."

She smiled. "There is. The offer is most generous. We would never have to deal with Men again unless we wanted to. In the new land, we could become a power unlike anything we are now. We could throw off the old shackles," she cast a glance toward the waterfall, "and the old superstitions. We could learn the best things that Men have to offer and, one day, become stronger even than they are. This is the legacy that we are offered,

Garyn. Our names will be remembered for all time. We will be the ones to bridge the transformation from the dark past to the bright future. It is more than a great opportunity–it is a great obligation." Her powdered blue face fairly glowed with sincerity. Garyn had no doubt that she believed every word that she spoke, and her certainty chilled his marrow more than her words.

Garyn gestured towards the heart of the city. "And what of their decision to remain? Would you dismiss it so readily?"

Neranda shrugged. "They do not understand all that is at stake. They are still held by barbarism's allure. The Celestial Path is a difficult and demanding way, and too many who applaud its virtues in public still dance with the Tree in their hearts. If they cannot be taught–and I am afraid that too many of our wayward kindred have proven themselves uneducable–it is our responsibility to make these choices for their own best benefit, much as a caring uncle forces a sick but obstinate youngling to eat the bitter healing root. This is why we were chosen to lead. Some must follow."

"I place more trust in the good judgment of our people than you do, Neranda. We have survived well for untold ages trusting in the Deep Green. Besides, I do not have your faith in the good word of Men. They have proven themselves treacherous and faithless too often. Why should we trust them now?"

"Look around you, Garyn. We have no choice. This is the twilight of our kind. Men will never stop until they have claimed all that is ours. We can either remain here with our eyes turned inward and fall to their unending numbers, or we can accept the inevitable and start again."

She reached out and placed a hand on his arm. They had been close once, not so long ago. That bond was strained, but it still endured.

"Garyn," she said softly, "we cannot stay here much longer. The longer we remain, the worse our fate shall be. The Dreydmaster's terms, while by no means generous, are satisfactory. Yet he is not a patient man. If we delay…well, you know the result as well as I."

The Governor looked at the shimmering valley in the far distance. "What terms, Neranda, are worth our homeland? If you will not look at the city, look at the world around us. It is not just land: it is our lifeblood. Zhaia gave birth to us in this valley. She resides here still, giving us strength, weaving us into the pulse of life that beats through the Everland. We have kept faith with Her, and She has kept faith with us—this is the Law that we have always honoured. We belong to this place; it is our source, everything we are. Many Humans understand this. For generations, we have signed pacts and oaths with Reachwardens and Assemblies of the Reach, each acknowledging, again and again, that this is our land by birthright and by right of existence, as is manifest in the Tree. What could Vald possibly offer us that would be worth sacrificing all that we are and all that we hold dear?"

"Our lives, dear uncle," she replied. She pulled away from him and walked towards the Gallery. Garyn watched her depart, his heart heavy, and walked slowly to the city's centre green.

The Dreydmaster's expression was mild when Daladir entered the icy room. Other than a couple of hard, high-backed benches and an inadequate fire that crackled weakly in the gaping fireplace, the only furniture in the tiled room was a small table, upon which sat a long wooden board with triangular ends, riddled with scores of small holes and multicoloured pegs. The soot-streaked drapes were pulled away from the windows, but drizzling clouds outside blanketed any sight of the afternoon sky. The he-Kyn was trembling, in spite of every ounce of inner strength he tried to muster. If Vald noticed, he didn't acknowledge it. Instead, the Man stood up and waved a hand to one of the seats, taking off his overcoat as he did so. Daladir nodded and sat down.

Vald's cold eyes swept over the he-Kyn, but his face seemed placid, almost pleasant. He pulled three smooth bone dice from his vest pocket and placed them on the table. Daladir removed his own ragged-edged coat, folded it over the back of his chair, and leaned forward to examine the board. The pegs were unmoved since the night before. He wasn't surprised; Vald had never once cheated in the many games they'd played since Daladir first arrived with the other diplomats from the Everland. And, although the he-Kyn rarely won a game, he knew that his failures came from his own slow skill with the pegs and dice, not from any dishonesty on the Dreydmaster's part.

Over those long late winter and early spring months, the ranks of the diplomats had slowly thinned, one by one, and each night Vald summoned Daladir to this room in the deep bowels of the many-gabled Hall, where they would play trump-the-peg for a few hours and engage in genial conversation. And even after all this time, Daladir was no closer to understanding the Man than he had been when he first arrived. This, more than the disappearances and deaths, filled the he-Kyn with a waking terror, which he revisited every night when he scribbled in his daybook by tallow candlelight, chronicling his danger, trying to make sense of the shifting shadows, hoping to find courage in the scrawled words that left no room for doubt or uncertain memory. It was the way that he kept sane.

His mind was his only sanctuary in this cold place, but even that was beginning to break down. Trump-the-peg wasn't the only game being played in Gorthac Hall, and Daladir was painfully aware that he was losing at all of them.

They took up again where they'd ended the evening before. Daladir rolled the dice: three, one, four. His green eyes scanned the holes on the board–eighty-seven holes divided unevenly between six rows–and then at the coloured pegs scattered across them. His pegs were blue; those of the Dreydmaster were red. Finally, he chose the third row and moved one of the pegs four spaces. He had other choices within the dice numbers, but this seemed a safe choice.

Vald stroked his muttonchops thoughtfully as he watched the he-Kyn's move. «What were we discussing last night before our game was interrupted?» he asked, his voice a rumbling growl.

Daladir's jaw clenched. The "interruption" of the previous night had been a steward's hurried announcement that a member of the Kyn delegation, Fear-Takes-The-Fire, had been crushed against a wall by a raging stallion in the stables. When Daladir found the battered body of his friend, he found no evidence of a horse, but plenty of indications that the younger he-Kyn had been beaten to death somewhere else and his body dumped in the stable, just steps away from the door that the young Binder had fled through a few nights earlier. This was the most blatant message thus far that Merrimyn's disappearance hadn't gone unnoticed.

Now only three members of the Kyn delegation remained.

Swallowing his anger and fear, Daladir responded in mannered Mannish, «Your philosophy on trade, sir.»

«Of course.» The Dreydmaster rolled the dice–six, six, and five–and surveyed the board. Doubles weren't good; he'd have to sacrifice one of the rolls. «It is always a pleasure to share these thoughts with one who pays close attention to the world around him. You are quite observant, Daladir; I respect that. I am observant too.» The he-Kyn's heart skipped, but Vald continued smoothly. «Trade, you see, is but one stream in the lifeblood of a nation, yet it is vital to every nation's continued health. A people can be virtuous, but if they are limited in their access to wealth, such virtue crumbles, and chaos erupts. The only solution is to lower those impediments to a nation's success, and the swiftest course is to start with the foundation of all wealth: land. At the heart of all is land. All Men must have land of their own, to use it as best they see fit. What else will a Man fight and die for if not for the soil under his feet, his measure of immortality. Otherwise, what can be the impetus for improvement? It is my understanding that the Fey-nations have no such belief?»

«Although I can't speak for all of the Folk, my own people don't believe that the land is something to be used as such, no. She belongs to us, just as we belong to Her. We owe our lives to the green world; we honour Her as kith, as family. Whatever She gives us belongs to all the People, not just to a few with rank and title to enjoy it.»

Vald pursed his lips thoughtfully as he surrendered his turn, unable to move his chosen row further. «Yes, but then what is the motivation for advancement?»

Daladir rolled. Two, three, four–a good roll. When the numbers came in a row like this, a player could choose any row and move a maximum of six pegs forward to the highest number on the dice. He went with the third row and moved the pegs into place. «We don't generally measure success as Men do, Dreydmaster. We are linked to one another, and to the rest of the world, by bonds of kinship and history. To follow my own desires at the unthinking expense of others would be an act of gradual suicide, for those actions would always come back again to me. It's a philosophy of responsibility to all things, not just unfettered freedom for oneself.»

«Interesting,» Vald purred. «So it is not so very different from our laws of accountability: all Men must be held responsible for their actions. If you blind your neighbour, you must lose your eye; if your tongue speaks untruths, it must be cut away to purify your mouth.» His voice took on a subtle edge. «If you steal from your host, you must lose something you treasure as well.»

Daladir felt a trickle of fear creep down his spine, but a long-smouldering rush of anger moved against it. «The comparison isn't entirely apt, sir. One must always think of the higher good and balance, as in all things. The sightless life of the first Man is in no way improved by the blinding of a second, nor is the harm of falsehood ended by tormenting the liar. Instead, the wrongdoer in both cases should give of his service to those he's harmed, until such time as the measured harm is repaid.»

Vald's gaze never left the board as he rolled the dice, but Daladir could feel the room grow colder. «And what of the thief?»

«In this case, we must look to see if the property belongs to the one who claims it. Perhaps it didn't belong to him at all. Perhaps the one called a thief is doing nothing worse than avenging an earlier theft.»

The dice bounced on the board: one, five, six. The Man moved five of the pegs in the first row forward six spaces, bringing the first to the single hole at the triangular end of the board. Another win for the Dreydmaster.

«There is a great deal of supposition in that hypothesis, Ambassador. We cannot look too far into the past, can we? If we did so, would anyone emerge untainted by guilt? No. The only true justice is swift, certain, and unclouded by irrelevant complications. We cannot look to ghosts for justice.» He pulled the pegs out, one by one, and returned them to the other end of the board. «Shall we play another, or would you like to end this game?»

Daladir smiled grimly. «Let's play.»

<hr />

The first thing that Tarsa noticed when she crossed the curtain of water was the sudden, overwhelming silence. She looked back. The water still crashed down in boiling waves, but the only sounds that the young Wielder could hear were the slow and steady drip of water down the cavern's walls and the echo of her own ragged breath. The air nearly crackled with wyr-fed vitality.

Tarsa examined her strange surroundings. She stood in a wide tunnel that stretched into the distance, its end unseen in the bright blue phosphorescence radiating towards her. Down the centre of the cavern's floor, reaching far back into the tunnel, snaked a deep stream of the glowing water. The walls and roof were etched with strange sigils and shapes of curled, vine-like tendrils and sharp-angled symbols, but the floor on either side of the tunnel was undecorated and worn smooth from ages of traffic. The flickering sunlight through the waterfall flashed like silver scales across the walls of the cavern, dazzling her eyes and making her slightly dizzy.

She thought of turning back for a moment, but the light beckoned her away from the silver-white radiance of the waterfall. There was nothing menacing here, of that she was absolutely certain, but fear still gnawed at her chest. Whatever lay beyond the end of the tunnel existed outside of anything she understood. There was a rising anticipation in the air that sang in chorus with the bloodsong throbbing again beneath her skin.

If she continued now, there would be no turning back; she would never be free of the touch of the *wyr*, not even in death.

This was the threshold. The Stoneskin's song had laid bare her spirit, but she'd never fully chosen this path, not when she followed Unahi and Tobhi into the mountains, not even when she'd slipped into the *wyr* currents and drawn herself into the Spirit World and its ways. Unahi's teachings over the last few weeks had helped Tarsa learn to still the bloodsong enough so that it wouldn't completely overwhelm her; the Redthorn had nearly finished her chanting sash, which further stilled her blood. The ancient patterns of the wide woven band held stories and songs of great power, and when she recounted them in her mind, they shifted her consciousness away from herself to the voices of the world around her. They gave strength to her spirit.

She now had what she needed to survive, if not to thrive. She could always step away and return to the warrior's ways she knew and loved, the ways that had long been her refuge and her only dependable strength. If she continued on this path, the life she'd known would become something else entirely.

Tend to your roots. Tarsa stood at the mouth of the tunnel. She remembered very little of her mother, more feelings than images. Even the stories that Geth and her other aunts had told her throughout her youngling days were indistinct, the trailing edge of memory rather than any tangible remembrance. But when Unahi had spoken those four words and shared her own memories of Lan'delar, Tarsa's heart had warmed with recognition, with the touch of light and laughter. Her mother hadn't abandoned her through death. Those roots ran far deeper than she'd thought.

This is my choice now. It isn't given by force or someone's idea of destiny. What I become is freely chosen. Her thoughts returned to the sight of her life-long community as they threw her into the Burning Mouth during her Awakening, visceral fear stark on their faces as the next wave of desperate power flowed through her writhing body. It hadn't mattered whether they were kith who'd watched her grow from shy seedling to strong warrior, or lovers who'd shared moist, warm pleasure with her in the darkness. To them, she was now a monster out of unwanted stories, and they'd never see her in the same way again. As Unahi had explained not so long ago, there would never again be a welcome for Tarsa'deshae in Red Cedar Town, for, with her Awakening, the youngling Namshéké had gone forever.

Tarsa cast one glance back at the waterfall, then at the azure star-shine beyond. For a moment longer she hesitated, but it was only for the space of a heartbeat.

"Yes, Mother–I go rootward." She stepped boldly down the tunnel.

<hr />

She walked on the left side of the swift stream, where the footing was firm and dry. The azure light bounced off the water and walls to break into a thousand glimmering shards, but by this time her eyes had adjusted, and she could see the tunnel's features more clearly. The symbols on the walls continued on like a stone tapestry. Tarsa recognized a few of the more common images, mostly those double-woven geometrical designs that were often beaded onto or etched into ceremonial regalia, but most of the symbols were strange to her. On occasion, a shape would emerge that resembled a living creature–an odd combination of snake, stag, eagle, and panther, or other strange hybrid beast–but most of the designs remained distinctly stylised, although always rhythmically organic. The stream cut a deep swath through the stone, the natural result of an ageless flow. She stopped once to peer into the water but stepped away with a start when she could see no bottom through the clear depths.

As she neared the end of the tunnel, Tarsa heard a soft, low rustling in the distance, a gentle pulse on the air that sent tremors through her sensory stalks from the sudden wave after wave of pure, unbound *wyr*. She stopped and clutched at the damp stone wall, gasping from the intensity. It wasn't unpleasant, but its sensual charge throbbed through her body, trailing down through every hair and length of flesh. Her entire body trembled with awareness, and she let the feeling wash over her for a long time, until her body grew accustomed to the rhythmic sensation. Tarsa had never known such a wholly energizing power, not even in the depths of her bloodsong frenzy. It cleansed the body and unravelled the tension that coiled in the back of her mind.

The light beckoned her on. Tarsa stepped into the blazing blue. She couldn't see beyond it. All she could see and feel lay beyond that brilliance, now azure, now cobalt, flowing into hues as bright as the daytime sky, as deep as midnight's mantle. She moved forward, eyes streaming, and felt a voice in her mind, low and rich, untouched by the heat of life.

"None may look upon the Tree without a true face."

The light dimmed. Tarsa blinked and squinted. Her eyes slowly adjusted to see two worn and moss-thick standing stones, each looming tall above her and carved with the rough representation of a scowling Kyn face, flanking a brown path that disappeared into shadows. The stones glowed with a soft light of their own, but all else was darkness. Between the stones stood a short, bowlegged creature less than half the warrior's height. Its limbs were thin and lanky, shining red-brown like polished cherry wood. Tarsa couldn't tell anything about the creature's face, for it wore a thick wooden mask that somewhat resembled the wide-mouthed images on the standing stones. The mask was painted brightly in red, black, blue, and white, with strips of animal fur glued onto the surface to resemble facial hair and eyebrows. The creature's bright eyes gleamed in the light of the stones. Its green hair was unkempt and flowed wildly down its back and over the edges of the mask. In its right hand, it held a thin stick topped with a rattling gourd and various small bird skulls, feathers, talons, and pierced fragments of polished turtle shell strung together with rough twine.

The creature pointed its stick at the she-Kyn and rattled it. Tarsa felt the voice again. *"None may look upon the Tree without a true face."*

"I don't understand," she said. "This is the only face I have." Her voice sounded muted and hollow in this shadowed place.

"You must have a true face. You must be honest in your choice."

Tarsa looked around. The tunnel gaped dark and empty behind her, but she gave no thought to going back.

"How do I choose my face?"

The figure shook the stick in a wide arc. The rhythm of the rattling gourds followed Tarsa's heartbeat. *Shukka-shukka. Shukka-shuk. Shukka-shukka. Shukka-shuk.* The creature turned around and around, lifting its feet high and bringing them down hard to the ground again, spinning slowly, moving faster and faster still, until it jammed the end of the stick hard into the ground. Tarsa cried out as thousands of glowing faces burst from the darkness, like a horde of hungry ghosts. She stumbled back towards the tunnel, but she stopped as her outstretched hands moved toward the dark opening. The tunnel was still there; she still had the choice to leave. She looked back to the standing stones and saw that the shapes weren't ghostly faces at all, but masks of all kinds. Some were crafted of thin sheets of gold and silver, others of heavy clay, still others of rough wood, hornets' nests, beaten copper, thick cloth, leaves, or wild feathers. Everywhere she looked the masks stared at her, an arching curtain of empty faces watching from the darkness.

"To see the true Tree you must wear your true face."

The young Wielder's head swam. There were so many. How was she supposed to choose the right one among them all? How would she know which one was hers? She turned to the creature, but it offered nothing else as it stood looking at her with dark, shining eyes.

Tarsa looked back at the curtain of masks floating in the shadows. She would never be able to decide—not this way. She thought for a moment.

"The eyes deceive when the will overwhelms thought," she whispered, remembering Oda'hea's advice during her early days of Redthorn training. The older warrior had said these words after Tarsa's fifth failed attempt to hit a water-filled sack target that swung from a tree branch during a spear-hurling lesson. The younger she-Kyn's impatience had lost her both the lesson and Oda'hea's praise, but only until she'd returned the next day with firmer resolve and determination to defeat the other hopeful initiates and even Oda'hea herself, much to the warrior's pleasure.

Tarsa closed her eyes. One of her hands rose into the darkness; the fingers of the other traced along the knotted pattern of her chanting sash. She felt her spirit grow lighter in the space between that touch and the bloodsong it guided, and she drew her thoughts away from herself and into the medicine songs that were wrapped in the fabric. The stories within those songs came free, and the young Wielder felt a sudden rush of mingled fear and peace flow across her body. She felt herself fading for a moment into something greater, and the thought both thrilled and frightened her. The only barriers to the *wyr* in this place were stubborn flesh and spirit. She pulled those walls aside and let the *wyr* course unchecked through her consciousness, again feeling that wondrous tingling flow through her flesh, hearing the spirit-voices whisper beyond sound to the very core of her being. The voices throbbed with her blood, riding deep in crimson currents, drifting with unbidden ease from heart to hands and beyond.

The sound of a soft gourd rattle threaded its way into her awareness, and she felt herself returning from the wyr-flow to her tender flesh. Her skin tingled still. She held something in her outstretched hand.

"You hold your true face. Wear it now, and you will see the Tree as it is, as it was meant to be."

Without opening her eyes, Tarsa lifted the mask to her face. It was light and made of wood, with a soil-deep spice to it, but it felt unadorned and unmarked, little more than a rough strip of wood with holes for eyes and mouth. She didn't hesitate. As the mask touched her skin, a tremor went through her body. Something opened up and flowed free inside her.

The rattling stopped. Tarsa opened her eyes and touched her face. The mask was gone. Her skin was different; her forehead and cheeks felt strange, almost numb.

A sudden shift in the light drew the Wielder's attention away from the sensation, and she turned again to the standing stones. They were as before, but the little creature with the gourd rattle was gone. The path was clear, bathed now in a soft green light, like sunshine through a leafy curtain.

The path back to the waterfall was open as well, but she gave it no thought. She wouldn't leave now, not until she had done what she came to do. She walked between the great mossy stones.

Although she'd entered the hollow cliff face and stood now in a tunnel, she could see no sign of being underground. Above, beneath, and all around her was night sky unlike any she'd ever seen. There were thousands of brilliant stars in a firmament as deep as midnight. Dozens of blue, purple, red, golden, and silver moons and planets hung like jewels in the darkness. Comets blazed both far above and below the Wielder, their streaming tails shimmering into stardust as they passed. There was no end to the heavens on any side of her. Tarsa looked into endlessness yet felt no fear or hesitation. The trail beneath her feet was soft moss and wildflowers floating in the night, the air rich with the light, earthy fragrance of spring rain.

Standing tall and ageless before her, growing green from the centre of a gleaming blue lake, stood the Eternity Tree.

Ever after, when her thoughts would return to her first visit to the Tree, Tarsa would never be able to fully describe the sight. But then, no mortals ever were. The Tree didn't fully belong to the ways of the Melded world; it was a remnant and reminder of the Elder Days, a living symbol of the bonds between the Folk and the land from ages past, when all the Eld Green grew wild and whole, when life stretched past forever. What she saw was the Eternity Tree at its closest point to the Folk between the present and the past. It was larger than it seemed at first, or else it changed its size according to whim or purpose, with wide-spreading silver branches that disappeared into the heavens, boughs reaching past sight above and beyond her. She didn't know whether she'd walked to the Tree or whether the Tree had found her. All she'd later remember would be that one moment she stood at the stones, and the next she stood by the shining waters floating in eternal night.

Tarsa felt again as she had when she reached for the mask. There was no room for what she knew as Tarsa'deshae or even Namshéké here; everything she was, everything she took such pride in, faded to nothingness in the Tree's presence–she was small, insignificant, fleeting. Her fire was doomed to fade, but the Tree would continue. Her mind pulled back, but her body no longer responded to her will, and, before she realized what she was doing, she stepped forward into the water and felt it caress her body. Her clothing dissolved; there was no barrier between her flesh and the rippling touch of the water. The pool was deep and warm, and she was a good swimmer, so she dove down and let the waters embrace her worn and battered body, bruised in flesh and spirit, the pain now eased beyond any expectation or even hope. She opened her eyes and saw undulating flashes of silver light shimmer through the waves. Rushing upward, she surfaced with a joyful shout. The air was afire with energy, like a new-birthed storm, but she felt no more fear or shame. She swam easily toward the Tree, cutting through the water like an otter, and there looked upon it with awe.

The Wielder couldn't identify the colour of the Tree's bark–there didn't seem to be a word to describe it. It was neither silver-blue, nor gray, nor green, but a shifting marriage of the three, sometimes distinct, sometimes blending together as one. The bark itself didn't remain constant either, but changed from the craggy roughness of spruce, with streaks of blue light shining through, to the smooth and silver silk of aspen or wyrwood red-gold. Every time her eyes seemed to fix the Tree, to define it in some way, the image changed, swirled, and twisted out of known description to become something else entirely, to tempt her away from expectation. It rose far above her, its branches stretching out wide over the horizon; only the brightest stars shone through the canopy.

The leaves, too, defied Tarsa's mind, but she turned her thoughts from grasping the Tree and instead sought only to observe, to allow the Eternity Tree to exist beyond the limits that her mind would impose. The leaves were of all seasons and none. The burning red, brown, and orange of autumn flared amidst the young green of spring-born morning, and these mingled with ageless silver, copper, brass, and gold. The Tree was of all species, all forms, but each image was unique in its way, and each leaf grew large and lush, wild beyond living memory, as tendrils of endless generations of ivy wrapped themselves around the great trunk and branches, dipping deep into the waters that lapped against the wide and reaching roots.

Tarsa's head spun from the heavy scent of earth and wild undergrowth, the deep embrace of rooted life. The stars could just as easily have dangled from the branches as from the sky, for the leafy canopy glimmered with the light of thousands. Blue and green fire danced on the leaves, across the branches, down the trunk, but no smoke rose into the sky, no char remained after its passing. The flames slid across the water and Tarsa's skin and hair, and, though it gave no heat, her flesh thrilled at the touch. This was *wyr* as it was meant to be. It burned with the rushing brightness of life.

A soft wind rustled through the leaves, sending its whispers in unknown tongues through the world, to bring precious pain to those whose hearts could still know longing. The whisper wound its way around the Wielder, lifting her soaking hair around her trembling shoulders, and she wept to hear the sound, for in that gentle rustle sang the voices of the Ancestrals, all the Folk who'd gone before her, heroes and traitors, friends and family, the loved and the forgotten. Tarsa floated in the warm water's embrace and heard, at last, her mother's honour song among the chorus. These voices were the heartwood of the Eternity Tree, and of all the Everland:

their memoried story was life incarnate, the abiding currents of green beneath skin and soil.

This flame burned within all that was of the Everland, within the Folk and all that they honoured and guarded. The Kyn were more than just the children of Zhaia, the seedlings of the Eternity Tree: they were the living embodiment of the Tree itself. Only through them did the Tree blossom fresh and fertile; only through them could it give life to the Everland and to the memory of elder days. Tarsa wasn't insignificant—she was part of something far greater than she'd ever imagined. The sacred word-fire—the wyr—burned brightest here. And in that endless night, in the healing waters of the Eternity Tree, far from the memory of Men and the shadows that crouched on the borders of the Everland, Tarsa sang and laughed and wept anew, mourning the pain of the past and singing into life the dawning world, adrift within the endless ebb and flow of the *wyr*.

❧❧❧❧❧❧

When, deep in the night, Tarsa emerged naked from the tunnel and walked slowly past the waterfall, Unahi and the other members of the Wielders' Circle stood among the benches waiting for her, soft torches sending flickering light across their smiling faces. With Unahi were eight other Kyn Wielders, including the venerable Braek the Older, the eldest of the gathering, and the militantly traditional Sinovian, little older than Tarsa, who barely contained his contempt for the shining grandeur of Sheynadwiin. Biggiabba was the eldest representative of the Gvaergs within the Circle, and she held the trust of her people. She and a trio of shorter deep-rock Gvaergs, two male and one female, stood wrapped from head to foot in their wyrweave cloaks. Tarsa's eyes widened when she was introduced to Athkashnuk, the serpentine and antlered Wyrm whose great multicoloured bulk spread out like a molten rainbow of fire far beyond the confines of the waterfall. More figures stepped forward to meet her: four Tetawi Wielders, the mushroom-shaped Oakman Grugg and his shy daughter Mim, and assorted Ferals–including the famed Uru Three-Claw, one of the bear-faced folk who inhabited the rocky narrows of the Kraagens; the standing-fox Ryggin; and Ixis, the aerie-mystic of the reclusive eagle-bodied Harpies.

The Tetawi healer Jynni Thistledown stepped forward to congratulate the new Wielder, and beside her was Tobhi, his shapeless brown hat in his hands, a proud smile brightening his face. Unahi held a long, trailing cloak of white swan feathers and red wyrwood leaves sewn cunningly together, and this she draped over her niece's wet and shivering form. It would be Tarsa's cloak of passage; she'd seen the Tree's true form, felt the sacred fire and knew at last the Heartwood of the People. Her voice would be for understanding, whether in war or peace, and the good of the Folk would stay upmost in her thoughts.

Tarsa's body still glowed with the light of the Tree, and, while this would fade with the dawn, the new azure sigils on the young she-Kyn's flesh would remain a sign of her true face and matured Awakening–two rows of small dark circles on each temple and down both arms and legs, three blue claw marks that stretched across each cheek, and an angled slash beside a bright ring between her brows–the same symbol that now shone on the foreheads of all of the Wielders, and which Tobhi and Tarsa had once seen on the Governor's seal one night a lifetime ago in Nine Oaks Town.

Unahi draped the cloak around Tarsa's bare shoulders, and old Biggiabba gently placed a garland of juniper berries and green aspen leaves in Tarsa's hair. They turned with the reborn she-Kyn between them and offered her to the People. A shout of applause rang out from Tobhi and the gathered wyr-workers, who rushed forward to embrace Tarsa and welcome her to the Council. They presented her with new wyrweave clothing, bracers, and other gifts and led her to the great longhouse, where a rich feast awaited them.

It was a joyous night, for a Redthorn Wielder had come to Sheynadwiin.

CHAPTER 12

GATHERINGS

Market day was generally the high point of every sevenday for Quill, but lately little lifted the pall from Spindletop. The Dolltender pulled her thick shawl tighter around her shoulders to drive out the cold of the morning mist. The deep-bone chill of autumn often clutched at the woods these days; it hardly seemed like high summer at all. She shifted her river-cane basket on her hip to balance the weight of the small honey crocks inside. On the path ahead stood a couple of other she-Tetawi—*firra*—who waited patiently for her.

"*Shoya*," Quill mumbled in greeting. Her cousins smiled. Gishki, whose short black hair glistened even in the dull and misty morning, carried a long sheaf of high-marsh tobacco, dried and wrapped in thick paper. Medalla, a quiet firra who stood a head taller than the others, held a long, curved stick in one hand, from which hung three dozen small ears of red corn, tied together in thick bunches with brightly-coloured ribbons. Both were bundled up for the cold, but neither fussed as much as the Dolltender.

"What a wretched morning," Quill held out her hand to show a couple of swollen red bumps on her palm. "Even the bees are unnerved by this weather. Summer, indeed."

Gishki chuckled. "You can't very well squeeze the honey out of 'em, Quill."

The Dolltender swatted Gishki's arm playfully, but her mood went sour again, and she sighed. "Do you think we'll hear anything today?"

Medalla shrugged. "Maybe. Things are changing awfully fast these days. I just hope it's good news this time."

They continued walking in silence. The news from beyond had been troubling for much too long. Settlements burned to the south, travellers ambushed, boneyards looted, trade disrupted. *Fahr*, both elder males and striplings, had gathered together to patrol the roads in the four-settlement district, and, although they had thus far encountered nothing more dangerous than an orphaned bear cub, they continued their walks day and night. Everyone felt the tension. Something unwelcome lingered on Spindletop's borders. Sometimes the hair on Quill's arms would stand up in alarm, like the tingle in the air preceding a storm, or she would wake in her deep-root bed, gasping and quivering with fear, and watch the shadows scatter in the darkness outside her window.

The moundhouse cabins of Spindletop were thinly spread throughout the wind-swept Terrapin Hills and, in some places, even among the sparser reaches of the Edgewood itself. Quill's family home was on the eastern edge of the settlement, beside a gnarled oak that stretched its heavy bulk around her squat little cabin, but even there she was only a brief, brisk walk to the nearest neighbour. Gishki and Medalla lived with their husbands, brothers, sisters-by-marriage, and father—Quill's maternal uncle—in some of the adjoining cabins; they were the core of Spider Clan in the region. This was the common way of Tetawi settlements: families lived with one another or close by. It was a bit unusual that Quill didn't share her home with anyone, but it wasn't unprecedented, especially for a wyr-worker; if she'd lived completely apart from her Clan, however, she'd have been considered eccentric, or worse.

The well-worn path to the trade centre and ceremonial mound of Spindletop meandered through the tall, tree-scattered hills that dotted the southwestern reaches of the Everland. The trail wended its way across the marshy bottoms beneath the hills, and it wasn't uncommon to see deer and the occasional sage-hungry hill antelope grazing on the thick grasses that grew in the rich earth of the bottom lands. Grouse, turkeys, rabbits, and well-fed foxes made their homes among the trees, but the firra were the only creatures on the path this morning.

At least, that was their assumption before a massive shape darkened the fog in front of them.

Medalla saw it first and held out her hands to either side, abruptly stopping the other two. Quill opened her mouth to protest until she, too, saw the shadow move through the thickness, and she swallowed her retort. The morning light was in their favour; they hadn't been seen. Gishki glanced nervously to her left and led them toward a tight thicket of willows off the trail, taking care to walk as swiftly and silently as possible. The grass was wet and the air was heavy, so their movements were veiled, but all nervously watched the mist for any sign of pursuit. Quill's heart throbbed painfully–she wondered how the shadow could possibly fail to hear the raging beat, as the noise was nearly deafening to her own ears. She'd seen that silhouette before, and it was unforgettably etched upon her memory. It was the shape that crouched outside her moundhouse in the darkness, watching and waiting. It was young Bird's killer, the creature in her vision that had torn out the youngling's heart.

The three firra crouched in the thicket, hands clasped together, their fearful breath held as much as they dared, as they watched the murderer's silhouette move closer. It was huge and Man-shaped, at least three times Medalla's height, but thin and gangly. Its movements were awkward, jerky, with a strange, choppy hop, like a buzzard stranded aground. And the noise it made was hideous. Quill nearly cried out as a bubbling, deep-throated gurgle echoed eerily in the mist.

Medalla squeezed Quill's hand tightly, almost painfully. The Dolltender looked up. The haze was lifting in the warming sunlight, and it was lifting too quickly for them to escape to safety unseen. The shadow still stood on the road, its head bobbing carefully. It was searching for them.

The *firra* glanced fearfully at one another. If only I'd brought my dolls with me, Quill thought desperately. Then she remembered–old Pinch-face, one of her granny's dolls, had tried to talk to her shortly before she left, but the Dolltender had been in too much of a hurry to meet up with Medalla and Gishki to pay much attention to the query. She gritted her teeth. *It's a little late to be worrying about what I should've done. I've just got to figure out a way to…*

A beam of sunlight cut through the gray veil, followed by others.

The fog's breaking up! Quill could barely hold down the scream. She couldn't see the creature's features yet, but it wouldn't be too long.

There was a crackle of frost-rimed grass by the trail: the monster had seen the willow thicket. It was heading toward them.

Then, muffled in the haze but still distinct, came the low sound of Tetawi voices in the distance. Panic clawed at Quill's throat. She wanted to scream, to call out to the *fahr*, but all she could see was the dark figure moving closer, its gibbering growl shifting toward intelligible, almost familiar speech. Her mind raced to make sense of the burbling noise as a flash of sunlight shot into her eyes, dazzling her before it disappeared again into the mist. The Dolltender bit her tongue until the salty tang of blood bubbled up in her mouth. Her head spun.

A hand stretched out from the fog. The fingers were long and moist, almost translucent, each as long as Quill's forearm. The blue-black veins under the flesh pulsed with an irregular rhythm. It was nothing like a heartbeat, but its movement captivated the young firra in spite of the terror that drove through her belly like an icy spike. Dirt-caked fingernails twitched as they moved ever closer towards the thicket. The world went silent. Even Quill's heart seemed to stop beating. All she could see were those grasping fingers stretching out, reaching for her.

The voices grew louder. The shadow hesitated, uncertain. It splashed through the boggy growth near the thicket, then stopped and listened. Quill thought she had the briefest glimpse of pale white flesh through the fog, but then strong Tetawa hands wrapped around her arm and dragged the Dolltender to her feet.

"Run!" Medalla hissed as she pulled Quill behind her down the road. There was no attempt at silence now as the shape erupted into pursuit. Medalla slipped onto one knee, the fall jarring the stick from her hand, but she was up again in a moment, dragging Quill with her. Gishki ran ahead of them, her voice calling for aid. A heavy, slavering grunt filled the air. Quill wanted to look back, to fully see this creature that rushed through mud and reedy pools, but she could only run until her sides burned like fire and each breath tore agony from her lungs. The fiend wasn't just hunting at random: it sought something that had evaded it before.

The Dolltender had little doubt what it was after. It wanted her.

Gishki led the way, calling out to the voices. A half-dozen well-armed *fahr* emerged from the vapour, wide-eyed but at the ready, spears and strung bows in hand. "Behind us," Gishki gasped, grabbing a farming sickle from one of the younger *fahr*. Medalla peered through the dwindling murk, her sharp eyes taking in every strange shape that rose up through the mist. Quill looked around in terror, clutching her basket tightly to her chest.

They stood together, tense and unmoving, until the fog vanished in the sunlight. The stalker was gone. Quill told them of her vision, and the others muttered amongst themselves.

"We should tell the Clan mothers," Medalla said at last. "We'll all have to arm ourselves now."

Perwit, one of the elder *fahr* in the group, handed her a short bow and fringed quiver. "No one should walk alone. Keep friends and family close, 'specially you." He pointed to Quill, who nodded hesitantly. "We'll come back and look for its tracks; it won't get away for long."

"C'mon," Gishki said. "You can stay in the cabin with us for a while."

Quill was quiet all the way back to Spindletop as the warning spread throughout the settlement. Medalla and a couple of their older cousins stood waiting outside the Dolltender's moundhouse while Gishki helped her pack, even though they weren't going more than a few hundred steps. As they wrapped the dolls in cloth and placed them gently into a stout lidded basket, Gishki asked, "What aren't you telling us?"

"What do you mean?"

"C'mon, Quill. You've never been one for silence."

The Dolltender wiped the back of her hand across her eyes. "It's just…I don't often get lonely, even with Granny and my folks gone, but I've been feeling it a lot lately. I wish…well…"

Quill

"You wish Tobhi was here, don't you?"

Quill swallowed against the lump in her throat, but it remained lodged firmly in place. "Yes. He'd know just what to do. Nothing scares him. He grew up in the deep woods, and he's faced pretty much every kind of danger there is. He makes me feel like nothing could possibly go wrong in the world when he's near me."

The older firra shook her head, bemused. "You know, Quill, sometimes I'm amazed at you. Not long ago you followed your dolls into the Spirit World and drove that creature away before it did more killing, and you didn't so much as shiver. But now you're behaving like a kitten mewling at shadows. You can't expect your love-addled *fahr* to make you strong, Quill. You've got to do that yourself." Seeing the stricken look on the young Dolltender's face, Gishki sighed. "Do you know when Tobhi's supposed to be back from the Council?" She frowned at Puckerlips, a sweet, down-haired doll whose dried apple lips were tightly squeezed into a perpetual kiss, as she handed it to Quill.

"No," the Dolltender shrugged. "Whenever it's over, I guess. But I do wish he'd hurry. I'm tired of being so scared all the time, and he's not afraid of anything. I don't care what you say, Gishki: he'd make everything better."

<hr />

"To be honest, I en't never been so nervous in m' life," Tobhi whispered to Tarsa as the delegates to the Sevenfold Council filed together into the soaring Gallery of Song, its great walls melded seamlessly into the massive trunks of the ancient wyrwood trees that made the seven cardinal points of the structure. The Wielder nodded, her face pale. The leaf-and-feather cloak lay light upon her shoulders, but, as the significance of the gathering became clearer, it took on a heavy weight. They were witnesses to a momentous event; in a very real way their future, and that of the Everland, depended on what happened here.

Tarsa had never seen such a grand structure before; its spacious expanse was crafted of the finest Wielded materials and was thus pleasing to the senses in ways that gouged and wounded wood and stone could never be. Hundreds of cushioned benches stretched from the floor of the amphitheatre to the rainbow-paned windows near the top, with fine, bold-patterned carpets lining the walkways between them. The seashell half-dome remained folded back to allow free passage to starlight and fresh air, but brawny young he-Gvaergs sat ready at the winches to pull it closed when necessary. Everlights were scattered along the walls in carved sconces to drive away the shadows, sending out no heat or smoke to bring discomfort to the gathering.

The only open flame in the Gallery came from a large stone-lined pit in front of the Wielders' seats. Seven kinds of wood burned in the fire, their cleansing smoke curling over the twenty-eight wyr-workers and their closest allies. Many more Wielders should have been among them, but death and misfortune had followed the messengers from Sheynadwiin, and few had survived to share their news with the remaining Wielders. This knowledge cast a heavy pall over the Circle. All those who'd celebrated Tarsa's remaking ceremony were present, along with a few others who were newly arrived. Some of the Wielders were not of the Eld Folk–including the Oak-folk, the Wyrm Athkashnuk, and Kidarri, a Jaaga root-worker–and had no official representation within the Sevenfold Council, but their voices joined those of the other followers of the Old Ways, and they watched the proceedings with as much concern as their Eld kindred.

The Shields sat directly opposite the Wielders. In contrast to the green vines and bright blossoms that adorned the seats of the Wielders' Circle, a gauzy, silver-coloured curtain fell across this wing of the Gallery, veiling those behind it from the prying eyes of others but enabling them to observe the events without difficulty. Tarsa had watched many of the Shields before they disappeared behind their curtain, which was held aloft by tall silver poles that lined the wing. Whereas Wielders dressed for comfort, wearing few unnecessary adornments, the Shields left little flesh untouched by silver or silk, although it was unclear to Tarsa whether pride or humility dictated such coverings. Most wore long white robes with tight, lacy cuffs that shimmered in the warm glow of the everlights, fabric that caught the light and sent it dancing in prismatic brilliance, and they draped their arms and throats with silver bangles, bracers, rings, and collars. Few Shields allowed their hair or sensory stalks to fall free in the way of the Wielders; instead, they pulled both into ornate caps, often molded to resemble the rough outline of a crescent moon, or they bound them tightly into star-shaped arrangements with their stalks wrapped deeply into the hair. The Shield of Red Cedar Town had followed some of these practices, but his style seemed quite simple in comparison with his brethren in Sheynadwiin.

The central seats of the Gallery belonged to the scores of lower-level delegates of the First Folk. Most of the Seven Sisters were represented here, all but the Ubbetuk, who were expected at any moment. Even the rare and beautiful Wyrnach spider-folk had come to the Sevenfold Council. They stood taller than the massive Gvaergs, but were slender and graceful, with six long-limbed arms beneath their ornate blue, gold, and black robes. Others, such as the Strangeling Jaaga-folk of the open prairie-lands–descended long ago from intermarried Kyn and Men, and now a distinctive people in their own right–and a few trusted Human friends, had no official spokespeople but were welcomed along with the others. Scattered throughout the various wings of the Gallery were scribes and translators, including Tobhi, who had received his auntie Jynni's permission to assist Tarsa during the Council. Jynni, though a healer and wyr-worker, sat among the delegates in the central section. Here she was acting as the elder speaker of Bristlecone Hollow, one of four small Tetawi communities in the Terrapin Hills.

At the northern end of the Gallery stood the empty Speaker's seat, a striking synthesis of sweeping stone and wood formed into the shape of a butterfly in flight, flanked by two giant doors that led into the chambers of the Governor of the Kyn Nation. A massive table, smoothed and shaped from the trunk of a fallen wyrwood tree, sat in the wide space between the Speaker's chair and the assembly seats: this would be the council table of the leaders of the Folk, and this would be where most of the debate would take place. No one sat there now. The Council members were finishing their last discussions with their assorted parties before entering the Gallery.

"I've never seen so many Folk in one place before, Tobhi," Tarsa whispered in awe. "I suddenly feel very small."

He nodded. "I know what ye mean. But don't forget that this en't exactly common for anyone here. After all, this is only the fourth such Council since the Meldin', so we're in good company." He looked around. The dark, time-worn wood of the Gallery gleamed in the everlight glow, and all along the rafters he saw birds of every size and variety crowding and preening in the light, their bright eyes fixed on the proceedings below. More flew in through the narrow windows with each passing moment. Between the delegates in the chamber, all along the benches and aisles, gathered all manner of beasts–from bumblebees and wasps, whispering moths and buzzing mosquitoes, to the tiniest shrews and mice, squirrels and toads, up to the largest of creatures, including proud moose and grumbling bears. None expressed any fear or scorn for the others here; even traditional enemies in the beast world honoured the sacred law of peace that held sway in the Gallery. And it wasn't only the four-footed and winged creatures that gave their attention to the proceedings–the tall trees and small plants that grew untrimmed within the Gallery's walls also seemed to tremble in anticipation. Tobhi's eyes misted over. All the Everland stood assembled this night.

The Tetawa started to speak again, but he stopped when the doors flanking the Speaker's seat swung open to herald the beginning of the Sevenfold Council. A group of Redthorn warriors sitting together beside the seats of the Wielders' Circle struck a large upright drum, accompanied by two Tetawi shell-shakers and a chorus of Gvaerg chanters. The union of songs rolled together through the Gallery. It was a song of sadness, a song of defiance, a reminder of the ageless strength and endurance that had travelled with the Eld Folk through devastation and back again. Now was the time to sing again, to remind all gathered here just what their survival meant. The music grew louder as voices throughout the Gallery took up the chant; rattles materialized from travelling packs, joined by flutes, string-drums, fiddles, and all manner of improvised instruments. Even the great Wyrm Athkashnuk entered the song, hir undulating red-gold scales scratching in rhythmic time with the shake of the turtle-shell rattles.

First to enter were the eldest of the Folk, the Wyrnach spider-Folk of old, four blue-cloaked, six-armed siblings who had watched so many of their kindred fall to the ravages of the Melding. They stood beside their chairs, tall and gaunt, with glossy black hair that fell in silken pools to the floor, while the rest of the delegates entered. As with the Kyn, Wyrnach eyes had no pupils or whites, but whereas those of the Kyn shone in many hues, the four eyes that shone out of the Wyrnachs' delicate round features were deep red, like old rubies. They wore their old grief like threadbare garments, but their faces still held a spark of love for the world and its peoples.

Four giant beasts followed the Wyrnach elders, and their leader sent a ripple of admiration through the Gallery. He was Myrkash the Unbroken, a bearded bull elk of extraordinary size. While his great height and proud demeanour commanded attention, most eyes lingered on the two wide-branching racks of antlers that stretched out from the great bull's temples, each rack polished until it gleamed; the end of each tine was capped in delicately carved bronze from which hung long crimson tassels. Unlike most of his kind, whose antlers fell in the spring, Myrkash held his proud spread throughout the year, a symbol of his authority. All the beast-people with him—an aged and scarred grizzly bear, an enormous, black-scaled rattlesnake, and a grinning mountain lion—were strong with wild musk, and Myrkash pawed at the floor and let out a long, shrill bugle upon his arrival into the chamber. The beast-people in the crowd raised their voices proudly to welcome the great beast-chief and his companions.

The third group of Council members waited until the shell-like roof was raised to blot out the starlight to make their appearance. Three she-Gvaergs emerged from the shadows, their protective wyrweave body wrappings now cast aside to reveal helmets with golden spikes rising from their temples, craggy gray features, and wide, solid bodies in gleaming armour that flowed with the unsmithed grace of Wielded ore. The brutal smith's hammer and anvil were abominations to the Gvaergs; only the soft caress of a sanctified Wielder–a Hand of Kunkattar–was permitted to draw the shape of armour and axe from the Everland's precious metals, which the Gvaergs knew to be the sacred blood of their fallen ancestors.

But it was the figure that followed the she-Gvaergs who was truly a surprise to most who'd gathered in the Gallery. Tobhi's astonished gasp joined those of others as Guaandak, the Emperor Triumphant of the Marble House of Kunkattar, entered the chamber, his beard of living flame burning bright against the smoky gray of his flesh. The only items of clothing he wore were a cap and scale kilt made of flowing stone and streaked with precious ores: the blood of Kunkattar, first father of the Gvaergs. He held a golden spear in his ring-encrusted hand, and this he stood beside his seat as he waited for the other Council members. Biggiabba bowed low at his entrance, and he bent his head in response.

Tobhi leaned over to Tarsa. "He almost didn't come. Gvaergs don't generally care much for us *rijjik* unbelievers." A low grumble from Biggiabba, who sat behind Unahi, caused the old Kyn to turn a disapproving eye at the Leafspeaker. "Sorry," he whispered, blushing. Tarsa nudged Tobhi in the ribs and turned her attention back to the floor.

Four Tetawi followed the Gvaergs, among them Molli Rose, the brown-haired Spirit-talker of Victory Peak, who would be the primary voice of the Tetawi in the Sevenfold Council, and Tobhi beamed with unabashed pride as she stepped into the Gallery. Though little over three feet tall and far more humbly dressed than the others, the famed seer, in her simple green homespun dress and brown shawl, was known and loved by many Folk across the Everland for her unbreakable devotion to her people and her unrelenting opposition to the rare but always destructive corruption among some self-serving Folk. She spoke plainly and without concern for diplomatic niceties; her concern was for truth and good sense, two things sadly rare in the world these days. Her presence brought deep joy to the Wielders; if anyone truly had the best interests of the Everland at heart and understood the links of spirit, law, and land, it was Molli Rose.

The Brood Mother of the North Wind Aerie, Kishkaxi, flapped gracefully to her perch at the table. Three massive golden eagles, each as large as Molli Rose, preened themselves beside the bare-breasted Harpy, whose wrinkled Woman's face scanned the crowd and nodded, ever so briefly, to Ixis, her brood-sister among the Wielders. Kishkaxi wore a circlet of shells, pearls, and beads on her stringy-haired crown and a tinkling abalone shell necklace around her thin neck.

"I've never seen such an unhappy face on any living creature in my life," Tarsa whispered to Tobhi. She almost wept when the Harpy's gaze passed over her. Such a depth of sorrow in those dark eyes. A cold chill crept over Tarsa's skin. It was said that the Harpies could sometimes see the future. If this was true, what did those sad old eyes see for this gathering?

The young Wielder's thoughts shifted back to the door as the harsh clang of a gong broke through the drumming. From the darkness emerged the Ubbetuk contingent, dozens of small, pale gray figures marching with practiced precision into the central aisles of the Gallery. Utterly hairless, with sharp-toothed grins and luminous eyes that seemed much too big for their round skulls, each wore a long-tasselled cap that marked his or her social rank according to colour and fashion: Goldcap merchants, Redcap soldiers, Greencap mechanists, and the like. The Ubbetuk were the most removed from the Eld Green of all the Folk. They'd long ago surrendered their attachment to the *wyr* in favour of their hidden airborne cities and the earthbound lands of Humanity. Iron held no fear for them; indeed, over the last thousand years the Ubbetuk had become the most accomplished inventors and industrialists in either the Everland or the Reach of Men beyond. Steam engines, cloud-galleons, mechanical lifts and automatons, and all manner of exotic weaponry had emerged from the smoking Ubbetuk factories, and these creations had enhanced their reputation across the two lands. They'd also increased suspicions among both Folk and Humans alike that the Ubbetuk Swarm posed a powerful and growing threat. The name given to them by Men–Goblins, for a race of mythical creatures who'd supposedly inhabited the Human lands before the Melding–seemed fitting to many, as it held a heavy note of disgust in its thick-tongued brevity.

It didn't matter that there were none who could rival the Ubbetuk in stately grace, social etiquette, and genteel manners, or that Ubbetuk had held little tolerance for greed, selfishness, or undue violence. The Swarm had no equal in the world of diplomacy or military strategy; many were the wars that had been lost because an Ubbetuk councillor's suggestions went unheeded, or the desperate battles won through Ubbetuk design. Yet common knowledge held that there was one unbreakable rule among the Ubbetuk, one that cast a shadow over their otherwise unblemished reputation: "The Swarm Above All." No one knew if or when that precept would be called into service, but many looked at the indispensable Ubbetuk councillors, strategists, advisors, and scholars in every corner of power throughout the Reach and the Everland, only to shake their heads in foreboding. Dark glances followed the brightly-capped representatives as they threaded their way through the Gallery to take seats, blushing and apologizing in sweetly musical voices for the disruption.

The last of the Ubbetuk to enter was the undisputed head of the Swarm, the Goblin Chancellor, Blackwick, one of the most feared and respected political leaders in the known world. He wore robes of the purest white that outshone even the luminous glow of the Celestial Shields. Around his neck stretched a broad white collar, like a ridged sunburst, and on his bald head sat a white cap inlaid with golden thread. He wore a single blue pearl on a long silver chain around his neck. His only other accessory was a long, wasp-headed walking stick carved from a single length of unknown black wood. His eyes, though surrounded by innumerable wrinkles, were clear and unclouded by age or infirmity. The Chancellor smiled serenely, revealing a mouth full of dagger-sharp teeth, and stepped to his own chair at the table with three Whitecaps of the Swarm's Ruling Council at his side.

The last to enter the Gallery were the Kyn representatives, and Tarsa's eyes widened when a familiar figure stepped up to the Speaker's chair. Three other Kyn, including a copper-haired she-Kyn Shield, joined the others at the massive table, while a fourth, the Speaker's zhe-Kyn consort, sat on a cushion beside hir lover's great butterfly seat. The young Wielder stared at the silver-haired Speaker as the realization sunk in fully. *The Pine Branch elder at the waterfall, the one who pointed me to the Tree, is the Governor of the Kyn Nation and the Speaker of the Sevenfold Council. Oh, Mother, if only you could be here with me now! The Old Ways are still strong in our people.* "There's nothing to fear now," she whispered softly.

Yet the slightest tingle of discomfort clutched at her sensory stalks, for the Wielders belonged at that table, rather than having been relegated to the audience where they were separate from the doings of the Council. That the Shields had a representative at the main table was more troubling than she wanted to admit.

Garyn Mendiir lifted his hands into the air and the drumming slowed to a halt. Everyone in the hall stood and faced the Speaker. For a moment all was silent, and then Garyn lifted up his voice, a deep, ageless timbre that echoed through the Gallery of Song.

"*Hanahé*, my kith—the deepest welcome and wishes for good health to you all from myself and all the Kyn Nation. May our gathering this night, and over the six nights to come, be filled with the spirit of peace and good judgment, and may the decisions we make bring benefit and peace to the generations that follow. *Hanahé!*"

The Gallery erupted in applause and shouts of "*Hanahé*" in response. Garyn waited a few moments for the noise to subside before motioning for everyone to take their seats.

That night was devoted to introductions and the first giving of gifts from the Kyn to the other members of the Council, to be followed by a similar ceremony each night of the assembly from the representatives of one of the other Folk. Tarsa noticed that each gifting brought a glower of disapproval from the Shield at the Council table, who had been introduced as Neranda Ak'Shaar, one of the leading Lawmakers of the Kyn Nation. It didn't make much sense to the young Wielder that Neranda would be present, but Tarsa wanted to trust in Garyn's wisdom, and she knew too well that the complexities of this world of politics were still outside her experience. *He must have a good reason for including her among the Kyn delegates*, she told herself, and she tried to push the whisper of doubt from her thoughts.

When the first gifting had finished, Garyn turned to the Council members. "It is time to begin the Sevenfold Council. Remember, even in these changing times, that the old rules of council still stand strong: harmony above all, consensus at the end. Those who do not agree with the collective voice may do so without rebuke and without obligation, but they must stand outside the circle of rights, protections, and responsibilities at that time. Once consensus has been reached, after deliberation and discussion with those gathered here, the decision is made. If there is no consensus, the Council fails."

His shoulders sagged slightly, and a shadow of pain flitted across his face. "My kith, my friends, my people–this is our dilemma. We are faced with a decision unlike any other since the Melding, and this choice, like that ancient catastrophe, has been forced upon us by the greed of Men. We have been commanded to abandon the Everland."

A great uproar shook the Gallery as those gathered cried out their rage and anguish in response to Garyn's words; even the aching groan of leafy trees joined the throng. Tarsa's voice rose with the others, and Tobhi called out a battle trill. At the table, only pale Neranda and the Ubbetuk Chancellor remained composed.

Garyn raised his hands again, and the noise dimmed. "These are dangerous times in the Everland. The recognition of our autonomy, which once kept our lands safe, is no longer honoured by the nations of Men, particularly the Iron Fist of Eromar, Lojar Vald, to whom we sent food and medicinals during the plague years. He has forgotten that kindness, or has chosen to repay it by threatening to steal our homes. Whatever his reasons, we have been given a choice: to surrender our ancient homeland in exchange for a territory to the far west, toward the setting suns, and some measure of gold and trade goods to re-establish ourselves in the new land, or to face the wrath of Eromar and its Dreydmaster. Vald's foundries are belching out black soot in preparation for an invasion. Our scouts tell us that even the farmers of Vald's land have surrendered their plows for iron swords and armour." His maroon skin paled slightly, but his eyes burned like gray fire.

The cloak on Tarsa's shoulders seemed to grow heavier as Garyn spoke. There was no outcry in the Gallery now. All sat in silence as the full weight of the Speaker's words descended.

"If any doubt the sincerity of Dreydmaster Vald's demand, look upon this." He nodded to a she-Kyn Redthorn warrior who stood beside the antechamber door. She exited and returned with a large covered basket that she placed on the table. Garyn reached down and pulled the cloth away to reveal three bloody Kyn heads, each branded with a jagged, three-tined mark on the forehead, the symbol of the House of Vald. A wave of shock shot through the Gallery. The Kyn gasped as their sensory stalks recoiled in agony; a few fainted from the swift and unexpected pain.

The Speaker breathed heavily, his jaw clenched, but continued. "These were three of our wisest elders, all of whom were part of the diplomatic delegation to Eromar City. Of the fourteen ambassadors who left for Gorthac Hall not quite a year past, only five remained two tendays ago, and I greatly fear that none of them will return. This is a reminder, delivered to us on the eve of the Council by unknown hands, to make clear what Vald believes to be our choice: removal, or death.

"You have been called to this place during these seven nights to decide, as the gathered Nations of the Everland, on our response to Dreydmaster Vald and his people. Will we surrender our homeland, or will we resist? Pain and darkness rule either path, but it is a choice we must make. This is the matter before the Sevenfold Council. This is the matter we decide."

CHAPTER 13

THE FOLK CONSIDER

Debate raged in the common trade tongue through that night and would, after a few hours' respite, continue through the nights to follow. Though she often had to rely on Tobhi to translate some of the more esoteric terms, Tarsa was generally able to follow most of the discussion. That first night was largely devoted to a lengthy discussion of the increased conflict on the borders of the Everland; Myrkash, the beast chieftain, told of small bands of Humans who had even reached the inner Kraagens on slaving raids. A pack of wolves and bears had devastated those bands and freed their hostages, but some of the slavers had escaped, and rumours crept into the forests and valleys of larger groups armed with weapons far more deadly than mere iron. Tobhi, Tarsa, and Unahi exchanged knowing glances at this news.

Blackwick, the Ubbetuk Chancellor, told of increased intolerance in towns and cities throughout the Reach, a hostility that increasingly ended in the death or mutilation of Ubbetuk diplomats and merchants. It had become something of a favourite hobby for young Human thugs to kidnap an Ubbetuk and pierce one of his bulging eyes with a thin iron skewer. Blackwick recounted these horrors with stoic calm, but the air crackled when he spoke, and none doubted his outrage.

Debate of Vald's demand, which the Dreydmaster had euphemistically titled "The Oath of Western Sanctuary," followed the gruesome list of towns and settlements razed, Folk butchered and violated, kidnappings, land theft, and torments almost beyond telling. The Shields, and a small but vocal group of Celestial Kyn delegates, stood firm on the side of accepting Dreydmaster Vald's conditions and migrating to the western lands as the most sensible choice for survival. Even the Wyrnach, the firstborn of the Folk, leaned toward that choice. They were few, with no new younglings in many years, and their hearts were heavy with loss. They wanted no part in war or bloodshed; they wanted merely to withdraw and remember times when they walked freely through leaf and shadow. The most eloquent speaker for the Shields and their allies, Tarsa soon learned, was the lovely blue-skinned Lawmaker who rivalled even Garyn in her speaking skills and who, like the Governor, was fluent in many languages, including the shared trade-tongue used at the Council.

"We cannot pretend that rejection of this treaty will aid our survival in any way; if anything, it will merely strengthen Vald's resolve to remove us by force. This is, to him, a purely domestic issue: our resistance is an uprising of subject peoples, not the independent assertion of liberty by self-governing nations. My Celestial kindred and I understand the ways of Men, and we know the internal politics of both Eromar and the larger Reach better than anyone here. As we have already heard with heartbreaking clarity, the Humans are growing bolder with each passing day, and more of our people are falling prey to the violence. How many more must we sacrifice before we face the grim certainty of our present situation?"

Molli Rose stood up, her dark eyes narrow. "Maybe ye understand Men a bit too much t' keep your judgment unclouded. What makes ye think that this Man will even honour his promises? Seems to me we'd be givin' up an awful lot on the word of a thief and a murderer."

Neranda nodded. "Yes, it is a risk, but what is the alternative?"

Myrkash, the elk chieftain, snorted in his deep, hollow voice. "We can fight. That's a good alternative, eh? Would you have us give up our homelands without spilling the blood of the kith-killers?" A few wolverines, bears, and eagles in the main chamber cried out in agreement.

Neranda turned a cold eye on the great bull elk. "Are we then creatures without any thought of the consequences of our actions?" A number of beasts growled, but she continued. "We can fight, certainly, but there are far more Men than you can possibly realize. I have travelled beyond the Everland and seen the menace that the Humans pose. They breed like plague-year rodents, overwhelming the land, consuming all until the rivers go dry and the skies are choked with ash. They have four younglings to each one born among the Folk, and all are raised to hunger beyond need. There is no end to their growing numbers, no end to their greed, no end to their desire. Beasts who once roamed free in Human lands have learned to flee or die, and sometimes even flight is not enough to ensure survival."

The elk snorted in anger, but it was the Harpy Kishkaxi who responded, in a voice like sand on stone. "Thou art not the only one well-travelled, blood-hair. We have seen much cruelty in the hearts of Men, and much treachery. Surrender promises naught but prolonged death and destruction." She settled back on her perch, her feathers puffed up in agitation, and cocked her head at Neranda. "T'would be best to strike while yet the fire burns in our hearts and leave no doubt of our resolve."

"Perhaps." The Ubbetuk Chancellor leaned forward. "And perhaps not. We should not dismiss the suggestion without considering its merits. What are the features of this land to which Dreydmaster Vald would have us move? Is it a territory that would be more defensible than the one we hold now?"

"*We?*" roared Guaandak, the Emperor of the Gvaergs. "Your kind are hardly a consideration. You've surrendered your right to any voice in this matter. You hide in your hidden cities and deign to join us only when it suits your advantage. Only those who've not abandoned the first teachings to embrace the unclean ways of Men should have a place at this table. *Rijjik* do not belong here." His eyes shot to both Blackwick and Neranda, who returned his gaze without flinching. Guaandak's beard burned white hot, scorching the table. The Whitecaps with Blackwick shifted uneasily in their seats, but the Chancellor waved away their concern and the sulfurous smoke.

"My Gvaerg kinsman, we are not enemies. I am not advocating removal, nor am I advocating resistance. I merely believe that we should be fully aware of our options before making a decision that will affect everything we hold dear. And though it is true that the Ubbetuk have long travelled to other lands outside the Everland, this will always be our first home, and we hold nothing but love and respect for it. Please forgive me if my words offend; such was not my intention."

Guaandak glared at the Chancellor but, seemingly pacified, leaned back in his stone seat. Molli Rose turned back to Neranda. "There's a lot to think 'bout here," she said softly. "One thing we haven't talked 'bout is heavy on m' mind. Have ye never thought 'bout what the move will do to the Old Ways? They come from our kinship with the land, after all. What happens if we break faith with our most ancient home?"

The she-Kyn shrugged slightly. "That is hardly a matter of importance to this Council."

Molli Rose laughed. "Of course it is! What could possibly be more important?"

The tension in the Gallery thickened instantly. The old Kyn conflicts between Greenwalkers and Shields had often bled into the affairs of the other Folk, and their current situation was no different. All eyes were upon Neranda. For only the shadow of an instant, a flash of unease crossed her powdered face, but it disappeared just as quickly, leaving those who saw the expression unsure of their eyes in the soft glow of the everlights.

"Luran will guide us, no matter where we go," Neranda responded with a smile.

"Really?" Tarsa called out from her seat, unable to restrain herself any further. She'd listened to the Shield with growing impatience and chafed at the cold she-Kyn's condescending tone toward the plain-speaking Tetawa. The Council members turned to the Wielders. Most seemed unconcerned by the breach of protocol, but Neranda's face flushed with anger. "And what of those who aren't Celestials? Luran speaks only to the Shields, not to those Kyn of the Deep Green, nor to the other Folk. What do you say to us?" The young Wielder stood tall, her dark hair cascading down her back, eyes burning like winter lightning. Tobhi grinned. He was always up for a fight, and nothing would please him more than to see Tarsa batting the strutting Shield around the table. It didn't look likely to happen, but it was a pleasant thought.

Neranda turned to Garyn. "With respect, Governor, please bring order to this situation. It is not the place of observers to interrupt these proceedings."

Garyn waved away her objection. "As the Shields are proudly represented at Council, it would be irresponsible to deny the Wielders the same right to represent the Kyn. She may speak."

Neranda nodded in acquiescence, but her lips tightened.

"Again I ask, what of those who do not follow Luran's way?" Tarsa asked.

All was silent in the Gallery. Neranda looked hard at the young Wielder. She hesitated for a moment longer, then said, "The differing paths of the Celestials and the Greenwalkers have too long divided the Kyn; in truth, each party must choose the path it wishes to walk. Yet, as you note, it would be both unfair and unwise to allow the unfortunate divisions among the Kyn to determine the fate of all Folk. Vald does not draw such fine distinctions; the danger of Eromar is hardly discriminating. The survival of everyone must hold precedence over the particular beliefs of any given Kyn. Such questions will do nothing but distract us from the true importance of the issue before us."

A number of Folk in the crowd nodded in agreement, but Tarsa shook her head. "If you honestly believe that, you don't know anything about the Everland, or about what's at stake. There's nothing more important than this question." She addressed the entire Gallery. "We belong to this land; its heartblood pulses through us, giving us strength and life." For the first time, she understood how deeply her encounter with the Eternity Tree had changed her. There was no longer any room for doubt or fear. She spoke with the strength of a Redthorn warrior, and with the understanding of a Tree-touched Wielder. "The bones of our ancestors are buried here; the Eternity Tree blooms in its soil. Our words and stories flow in its winds and waters. Our strength abides in the Everland."

Her voice rose through the Gallery. "Our lives are bound to this world, and its survival is bound to us. We belong to one another–life to life. If we abandon our responsibilities to our homeland, it will weaken, as will we.

And we know what happens when Humans perceive weakness. You Shields may be deaf to the bloodsong, but you're still connected to the *wyr*. This is our home. This is our inheritance, our legacy. What could possibly matter more?"

The Gallery erupted in applause, from all but the silver-curtained wing where icy silence reigned. Unahi nodded approvingly to her niece. Even some of the Council members joined their voices in support of Tarsa's words. Garyn motioned to the drummers and they pounded loudly on the drum to quiet the raucous crowd. Neranda sat back in her seat, face pale as the Greatmoon, her burning eyes fixed firmly on the Redthorn Wielder.

As the applause rolled through the Gallery, one of the golden eagles perched beside Kishkaxi erupted into flight and shot like a burning spear into the rafters, toward a black shadow that fluttered toward the partially-open roof. Before anyone could stop her, the eagle extended her talons and slashed out in bloody fury. A collective gasp echoed through the Gallery of Song at this violation of one of the peace-city's most ancient laws, but the shock became anger as the shadow fell to the ground, changing from a twisting mass of raven feathers to a jumble of tattered black shreds of cloth covering a spindly, pale body no larger than a Tetawi cub.

"Witchery!" Tobhi whispered as the creature stood and turned, with hunched back, to glare upon the silent crowd. It looked like a wizened Human infant, utterly hairless, with seeping black holes gaping wide where once had been soft eyes. Dozens of tiny sharp teeth jutted out of a mouth too large for the head, and long, black-nailed claws glimmered in the light. The horrified Folk looked upon a Not-Raven, malevolent ghost of the Human world, brought to its shadow life by unnatural means for the sole purpose of unraveling secrets to share with its unknown master.

For a moment it seemed that the Not-Raven would speak, but the eagle dropped from above, talons extended, and smashed into the ghost-creature again. A burst of raven feathers scattered in the air. The eagle flapped upward, joined now by her two aerie sisters, and they circled around the wounded, fluttering ball of feathers and twitching flesh as the Not-Raven tried in vain to re-establish its shape. Again and again the eagles tore into the ghost, driving it farther back with each attack, until, with a furious simultaneous assault, they pushed it into the Wielders' fire-pit. The fire flashed a noxious yellow. A long wail of anguish erupted from the sickly flames and pierced the shocked silence of the Gallery, but it lasted for only a moment, fading with the stink of burning flesh in the cleansing scent of the seven woods.

Garyn nodded at Kishkaxi and her eagle companions. "Our words have not remained unheard this night, but that is of little true concern, for there are no secrets in the Sevenfold Council. What we say is given to all; the honest do not fear our words." A rush of murmuring rippled through the crowd.

The Governor held his hands out to the Gallery. "Dawn approaches," he called out when the chamber grew quiet again. "We will continue this debate later, when our minds are firmly focused on the matter before us, and when the taint of witchery is no longer upon this hall. All delegates are released until dusk, when we will convene again." Garyn turned to his consort and whispered to the zhe-Kyn before following the Council members back through the doors to his inner chambers.

Most of the members of the Wielders' Circle departed together. Tarsa joined them while Tobhi gathered up his pencils and bark-paper. A shadow drifted over him as he stuffed his writing tools into his big satchel. Looking up, the Leafspeaker recognized the dark-haired zhe-Kyn who'd sat at Garyn's side that night. Tobhi hadn't seen many zhe-Folk; the only such Tetawa he'd heard about was a much-loved healer who lived not far from his home settlement. Neither male nor female, nor truly separate from either, the zhe-Folk walked between the worlds; they had strength unmatched by other Folk and were honoured for it, at least among those who followed the Old Ways. Celestials tended to dislike the zhe-Kyn and other zhe-Folk, but their whisperings hadn't yet erased the place of the zhe in the Everland, though they'd done much to make the zhe-Folk less welcome in Sheynadwiin. This young stranger wore dark, finely-woven wyrweave breeches and a knee-length jacket of midnight blue tied with a green sash. Hir dark knee-length hair was draped over one arm as zhe bowed low.

"Greetings," the zhe-Kyn said. Hir voice was deep and gentle, like spring water over smooth stones. "I am Averyn of Thorn Branch, a healer of Sheynadwiin and consort to Garyn Mendiir. You are Tobhi, the nephew of Jynni of Bristlecone Hollow?"

The Tetawa nodded and extended his hand, palm forward, in greeting. "Ye've helped m' auntie a few times with her medicinals. Glad we finally got to meet. Can I help ye?"

The zhe-Kyn held out a small cloth bundle tied tightly with a blue cord. "You are the one who has been teaching the ways of Sheynadwiin to the Redthorn Wielder?"

Tobhi nodded again, his eyes narrowing slightly. "That's me."

The zhe-Kyn smiled. "Molli Rose was right—you are most certainly the one we seek. I will look forward to speaking with you again soon. *Hanahé*." Zhe held hir fist to hir chest and left the Gallery.

Tobhi opened the bundle and pulled out a piece of birchbark paper. Holding it up to the light, he read the message, and his face went pale. He didn't move until the throbbing of his heart eased slightly, then he slid the paper into a belt pouch, swept up his satchel, shoved his hat down on his head, and rushed up the stairs and out of the Gallery, his dark hair blowing behind him. He gasped in alarm as a hand landed on his shoulder. He swung around to face Tarsa, who regarded him with concern.

"Sorry," he said, as he gathered his fallen satchel. "I guess I'm just a bit skittish after all them doin's in there."

"I understand." The young Wielder pointed toward a small crowd that was walking up toward the waterfall and the Eternity Tree. "We're gathering for breakfast soon; will you join us?"

The Tetawa shook his head. "I don't think I can." He showed her the package Averyn had given him.

She pulled out the folded paper, but handed it to Tobhi after a glance.

"What does it say?" As fluent as she was becoming in new languages, she still hadn't learned to read.

Tobhi swallowed thickly. "I'm goin' away, Tarsa. Garyn is sendin' a group to Eromar, to protect the last of the ambassadors before the Council's vote. I been asked to help bring 'em home."

CHAPTER 14

CHOICES

"Why would ye want *me*?"

Tarsa and Tobhi sat on plush raised platforms on the floor of Garyn's rooms at the Gallery House, clay mugs of honey-sweetened sassafras tea in their hands. The curtains were drawn. A few stone bowls smouldered with burning cedar branches, and the soft smoke curled through the large, wood-panelled room. Although Redthorn warriors stood watch outside, Garyn didn't want to risk another uninvited guest like the Not-Raven, and the cleansing scent of cedar was a sensible precaution.

Garyn and his consort Averyn sat next to the she-Kyn and Tetawa, but they weren't alone. Unahi, the Greenwalker Sinovian and his sister Jitani, Tobhi's aunt Jynni, and Molli Rose completed the circle. All were grimly quiet, but none more so than Tarsa, who'd been under a deep pall since Tobhi's announcement.

Garyn turned to the Tetawa. "Our people in Eromar are in danger, Tobhi. While officially the guests of Dreydmaster Vald, they are little more than prisoners, playthings that he destroys at whim. As yet, he still maintains the veneer of diplomatic courtesy–he claims that the dead ambassadors were assassinated by brigands on the road back to the Everland, branded with his sigil only to ensure their 'safe' return home. 'Collectors' would think twice before laying claim to the head of a Kyn thus marked. This is apparently his idea of diplomatic charity."

Sinovian barely managed to stifle a snarl. Tarsa looked at him. His hair was shaved in the old fashion, with only a long braided topknot remaining between his twitching stalks; intricate honour markings emblazoned his face, arms, and bare chest. Great copper hoops hung from his stretched ear lobes; copper armbands, similar to Tarsa's own, wrapped around his upper arms. Sinovian wore an etched-shell gorget around his neck, another sign of his bravery and leadership skills. He was handsome, but a rage that bordered on hatred coarsened his features, making him more sullen than sensual.

His sister was a different matter entirely. She was a striking she-Kyn, with dark bronze skin, pine-green hair, and golden eyes that caught the dancing firelight. She wore well-travelled trade-leathers and high brown boots, and a loose-fitting blouse that left little to the imagination. A stout scabbard hung low on her wide-buckled belt. But while her body was memorable, her uncovered head was even more so: where four sensory stalks should have been were only two, wrapped tightly in copper bands. Jagged scars were all that remained of the others. Few Kyn survived a stalk-slashing; few would want to. The sensory world was rendered intelligible by their stalks, and the thought of such a loss was sometimes enough to kill a captive Kyn. But this she-Kyn didn't seem tortured by her loss, for she smiled at the young Wielder and lowered her eyes shyly, almost playfully.

Tarsa caught her breath. Jitani's nearness was intoxicating. The sweet scent of the she-Kyn mingling with the cedar smoke made Tarsa's head spin, almost as much as did Jitani's lingering golden gaze.

Garyn's words brought Tarsa's blushing attention back to the discussion. "Yes, it is all pretense. Vald is toying with us, while at the same time abiding by the letter of the laws of the Reach, which hold him accountable for the fair treatment of all ambassadors who visit his home. But that pretense will not last much longer. If the Council takes a stand against Eromar, nothing will hold back Vald's fury, and those Kyn who remain at Gorthac Hall will die."

He reached out and touched Tobhi's shoulder. "Vald is watching, waiting, preparing. The Not-Raven is surely not the only spy sent to observe the proceedings of the Sevenfold Council, and such Darkening-brood are only one threat. The hearts of some in Council, and in the Gallery at large, have turned in Eromar's favour. Though I do not believe that they will sway the entire Council, I fear a deep schism. Without a near-unanimous vote, we will find consensus nearly impossible, and the Sevenfold Council will have gathered for nothing.

"We have six days remaining before the Council votes on Vald's demand–six days for a small and trusted group of delegates to travel the vast distance to Eromar, meet with our people there, and return to the Everland with them and all of the information that they have gathered from months of close observation. They have done their job admirably; now, it is time to bring them home."

Tobhi nodded. "They're spies, then?"

Garyn shook his head. "Not entirely. We have other allies, other ways of observing our enemies without putting our diplomatic envoys fully in harm's way. The ambassadors' first duty was to serve as the diplomatic voice of Sheynadwiin, but yes, they were also charged with learning as much about Gorthac Hall and the inner ways of Eromar as possible, in the hope that such knowledge could protect us when the Iron Fist closed. I had not thought that Vald would move so soon. But such is the way of Man's world."

"But I still en't sure why ye want me t' go," Tobhi said. "I en't a diplomat."

"No, you are not. But you are wise in the ways of the Folk, you speak the Reach-language of Men, and you are calm and brave in a crisis. We need someone there who will not draw suspicion; Sinovian is sending a follower of the Old Ways to keep attention focused away from the others in the party, someone who will be an overt symbol of our resistance." He pointed his chin towards Jitani, who nodded her head in assent. Tarsa's chest tightened.

"The time for trained politicians is past, Tobhi. We have already sent wise ambassadors–mostly Kyn, but some Tetawi and Ubbetuk as well–to the various ruling houses throughout the Reach: Eromar, Harudin Holt, even great Chalimor itself, and all that they have found has been rejection, if not worse. The hearts of Men have turned against us, even among many whom we believed to be our friends. What we need now is someone who is devoted to the Everland, not to the promises made by Men, whose words have no more strength than dust. You have clearly demonstrated those qualities through your work with the young Wielder here." Garyn smiled at Tarsa, who weakly returned the motion. "Yet it must be someone subtle, someone who might be overlooked as he goes about his business. There are none better suited to this task. And you come with the highest recommendation."

Unahi and Molli Rose both nodded, their faces grim. All knew too well the dangers would Tobhi face, but they also knew the risks for the Folk if the last ambassadors died without sharing what they'd learned in their many months at Eromar. There was no certainty that anything of value would be found, but the possibility was worth it. It was a thin hope, but it was something.

"I cannot command you to go," Garyn said. "Nor would I wish to do so. As all the Eld Folk are born into life with freedom, so too must we exercise our freedom throughout the days and seasons that follow. The power given to the Firstkyn is not the power of coercion; only the strength of my convictions and, with hope, some measure of wisdom. I do not command this, but I ask you: will you go to Eromar?"

Tobhi looked at Tarsa, then to the others in the circle. Unahi's eyes were downcast. Molli Rose and Jynni smiled sadly at the young Tetawa. Sinovian and Jitani stepped away to a shadowed corner of the room to allow them some privacy.

"I'd talk with m' Clan mothers," Tobhi said. Garyn nodded, and the three Tetawi withdrew to another corner.

The Governor and his consort stood. "We will leave you to discuss this together," Averyn said, and they joined Sinovian and his golden-eyed sister. Tarsa moved to sit beside her aunt, who reached for the younger she-Kyn's hand.

"Do you think he's really going to go?" Tarsa asked.

Unahi nodded. "I do."

"He can't leave," Tarsa whispered. "He's the only one who has any time for me here."

Unahi's expression grew hard. "The world won't stop because we wish it. Your time will come, but it's not now. Tobhi will do what's best, and so will you. Sometimes we've simply got to let life take its course. The Governor is right: Tobhi has the strength and the training to succeed where others can't. The knowledge these ambassadors hold could be Eromar's undoing, so we need them back home."

A sudden thought struck Tarsa. "I want to go with him. I want to help."

"No, I don't think so. It's much too dangerous." The firmness in Unahi's voice indicated that the discussion was over.

"I'm a Wielder, as much as you. Why shouldn't I go?" Tarsa asked, not trying to mask her anger.

"Enough!" the elder Wielder snapped. The others glanced over, and Unahi leaned in towards her niece. "This isn't a youngling's game, Tarsa. This is a matter of enormous importance to the survival of the Everland, and frankly, you're not ready for something like that. Leave it be."

"But…"

"I said, *leave it be.*"

Tarsa pulled away from Unahi, her face flushed with fury and humiliation. Bitter words pushed at her lips, but she knew better than to set them free here; she didn't want to add public disrespect of an honoured elder to her embarrassment. Swallowing her anger, she turned to see how Tobhi was faring. Molli Rose and Jynni had gathered Tobhi into their arms, and all three wept.

He might not survive, the Redthorn Wielder thought suddenly, a hard knot of fear clawing at her stomach. *Even if he returns with the diplomats, there's no guarantee that they'll be able to do anything to stop the invasion. This might be the last time that he'll ever see any of us. They all know it, and they're afraid for him.* Her eyes darted to Jitani, who stood calmly beside her brother. *They could die in Eromar, far from the Everland.* Her own words at the Council echoed again in her mind. "*Our strength abides in the Everland.*" *What will happen if they don't go? The remaining ambassadors will die, far from home, their spirits lost in the world of Men, their knowledge–perhaps our only real hope–lost to us.*

Tobhi wiped his eyes with the sleeve of his tan shirt and walked over to Garyn. "I'll go. When do I leave?"

Tarsa went numb at the words; she couldn't speak. She didn't understand why she was so attached to the Tetawa; she'd only known him for a few weeks. But he was one of the few dependable features in her life. He was the only one who listened to her with any real interest. He shared his stories with her; his family embraced her with a warmth she'd rarely known among her own kith. He was, she suddenly realized, the only real friend she now had. Unahi was family and generally kind, but she treated Tarsa as a youngling, not as a full-grown she-Kyn who'd proven her mettle both in battle and in her encounter with the Eternity Tree.

No, Tarsa couldn't let him go to Eromar without her. She still had such need of a friend.

A second arrow whistled through the air, followed by many others; the surrounding trees popped and cracked like sap-rich logs in a fire. Vergis Thane hugged the ground as another missile smashed into the branches above. He trusted his weather-stained cloak and hat to make him nearly invisible in the undergrowth, and they seemed to be working well so far, but it was only a temporary measure–the damned Deermen knew he was there. But Thane had survived much more dangerous situations than this. Besides, they weren't likely to strike too carelessly for fear of injuring their spirit-weaver.

The Unhuman Deerman struggled against the Seeker's grasp. Thane drove his knee sharply into his prisoner's belly in response, and the trussed creature went limp. It knew well enough to refrain from crying out. Thane didn't believe in waste, but he wouldn't hesitate to kill the creature if it made itself a nuisance or threatened his own escape.

Thane listened carefully. There were at least a dozen armed Deermen in the trees, probably more, and certainly others on the way. Though little over four feet tall from hoof to antler, with the furred torsos of savage Men, mixed by some strange Unhuman witchcraft with the heads and lower parts of black-tailed deer, the creatures were fiercely defensive of their home grounds and of their kind. If Thane planned on getting away, this would be the time to do it, before the odds were more difficult to manage.

He reached down and pulled the little Deerman's face towards him, yanking hard on one of the creature's long ears. «I don't know if you understand my words, but you'd better understand my tone,» he whispered, his voice no louder than a mouse's sigh. «If you cause me the slightest bit of trouble, I'll slice you from seed-sack to eyeballs and leave your guts for the buzzards. If you behave, I might consider taking that collar off you.» He squeezed the iron band around the Deerman's hairy neck. The creature gritted its teeth and whimpered as the increased pressure dug the metal deeper into the blistered flesh, but it didn't cry out. Satisfied that his intent was unmistakable, Thane turned his attention to their escape.

The Seeker and his prisoner lay crouched in a leaf-strewn hollow on the slope of a thick valley in the heart of the Everland. He'd followed the trails of at least five different Fey-witches, but most of these hunts had faded to nothingness. It was as if the creatures had simply vanished. At one location, the ruins of a town within a massive stone bowl, he'd come across dozens of shrouded Kyn bodies on scaffolds and the remnants of a recent campsite. The stink of twisted power–Fey witchcraft–was heavy in this place, especially around a ravaged stand of disfigured pines. Whatever had happened here was still fresh, but the thin trail of the powerful Unhumans he followed had been swallowed up by the massive energies of death and destruction in the town.

He'd lost that trail, but found others, a few of which had vanished like the one within the stone ring, but some remained fresh. It was one of these that had brought Thane to the small band of Deermen and their wide-antlered Fey-witch. The creature had been injured before Thane arrived—one leg was bound in a willow-branch splint, and one of its noble antlers had been snapped in half—and this made the capture that much easier. But these creatures were wily, and he'd barely managed to get his quarry out of the village before he and his prisoner were attacked by a large group of cloven-hoofed archers.

The Seeker slid slowly upright, like a patient rattler preparing to strike, until his single ice-blue eye was clear enough of the undergrowth to scrutinize the terrain around him. Most of the stone-headed arrows had come from upslope, towards the creatures' village. Escape downhill was the most direct route, but also the most dangerous, as Thane would be at a disadvantage and a clear target. He scanned the ridge again, and a thin smile creased his features. He might be a target, but he wouldn't be alone.

The sharp blat of a horn echoed upslope through the trees, followed by others on the left and right, quickening downward to cut off escape. This was the moment he'd been waiting for. Thane rolled over and spun his captive onto his back, then jumped up and raced downhill, the terrified witch acting as a living shield from behind. The Seeker held the creature over his left shoulder by its bound legs, while in his right hand he held his long knife. A few arrows smashed into the ground around his feet, but most of the archers restrained themselves, hesitant to strike at the Man for fear of hurting their kinsman.

A hairy shape rose out of the undergrowth before Thane with a heavy oak cudgel in its hands, but the Seeker drove onward, his blade shining like silver fire in the mid-morning light. The club swept down, and Thane twirled around, shifting his weight slightly for balance as the cudgel smashed into his bellowing captive. He completed the spin to drive his knife into his stunned attacker's throat, slicing viciously to the side until it stopped short against bone. Kicking the blood-spurting body to the forest floor, Thane rushed down the slope. The Fey-witch cried out in pain and horror, and they were surrounded again by armed Deermen, spears and clubs swinging through the air. Thane never missed a step. As each weapon flew toward him, he turned his captive toward the threat, while sending blood splattering across the trees with his own knife. The creatures quickly fell away from the Seeker, and he was moving again, this time without pursuit. The battered Fey-beast over his shoulder shook with deep sobs.

Thane ran until he was certain that the hunt had ended, if only briefly, and dropped his prisoner to the ground. The Fey-witch groaned. Its face was battered and bloody; there were fresh wounds on its chest and a nasty gash on its upper thigh. Pulling some leaves and a flask of water from his pack, Thane chewed the leaves and washed the wounds, layered them with the leaves, and wrapped the most serious of them with coarse linen strips. He gave some of the water to the Deerman, finishing the flask himself.

«I don't have either the time or interest to carry you. Remember what I said before: if you disobey me, you die. Now,» he cut the bindings on the Fey-witch's hoofed legs, «you're going to walk. I'll give you a little time to prepare yourself, and then we're moving on. Understand?» The spirit-weaver nodded, breathing heavily, and struggled to its feet.

«Good.» The hillside rang with loud wails and cries. For a moment, the little witch-creature looked as though it might answer, but a glance from Thane sent the prisoner into pained silence.

«Let's go. It's better for you and your friends if we leave quickly.» The Deerman nodded and stumbled desperately into the trees following the one-eyed Man with the brutal blades.

✼✼✼✼✼✼

Jitani looked at the young Wielder in astonishment. "You want to what?" She'd been pleased and surprised when Tarsa followed her out of the Governor's chambers, but this was far from what she expected to hear.

"I want to take your place among the diplomats to Eromar."

The golden-eyed she-Kyn shook her head. "That's impossible. It's not my decision, anyway–Sinovian is the war-leader, and it's his responsibility to decide these matters. He needed someone he knows, someone he trusts. And I've already given my word. I..."

Tarsa's lips trembled. "Please," she whispered, taking Jitani's rough hands in her own. "This is something I need to do."

The touch of Tarsa's flesh was like fire, but Jitani couldn't bring herself to pull away. "Why?" she asked softly. "Why does this matter so much to you?"

"He's my..." She struggled for a word. This wasn't anything like a romantic attachment, but it was more than simple friendship. He was kith and family to her now, generous beyond acquaintanceship.

She smiled. "He's my brother." Such a simple word, but it was thick with feeling. Jitani suddenly understood some of the deep, aching loneliness that radiated from the young Wielder. She'd heard stories about Tarsa from Sinovian and Unahi, but it wasn't until now that she understood just how isolated the Redthorn Wielder had been in her life. Jitani had always had family and friends; some had given their lives in her defense. Standing here, holding Tarsa's hands in her own and looking into her wounded, hopeful eyes, Jitani knew that what she took for granted was, in large part, alien to the Wielder. True family was rare for Tarsa, and thus precious.

It was crazy, foolish, and dangerous. It put Jitani firmly against her brother's wishes, and, although he couldn't challenge her choice, as all Kyn were acknowledged to have the right to decide their actions for themselves, he could certainly be unpleasant about it, and he was well-trained in surliness and long-harbored grudges. Still, she couldn't do otherwise. She might not have the same sensitivity she'd had when all four of her sensory stalks were whole, but she didn't need them to understand Tarsa's desperation.

She pulled one hand away and held her fist against her chest. Reaching down, she handed Tarsa a long wyrwood knife, straight and leaf-bladed, from a scabbard around her calf. "Your heart is strong, Redthorn Wielder, though I'm not entirely sure about your mind," she said with a weak smile. "We'll fight boldly here, never fear. Fly quickly, and care for your Tetawa

220

brother. And when you finish, return safely to us."

Tarsa slipped the knife into her belt and brought her fist to her chest, her eyes brimming. "Wait," she said as Jitani turned away. "Tell Unahi that I didn't mean to... No. Just tell her that I had to do this. I'm sure she'll understand."

Jitani nodded, but she wasn't as optimistic. If what she'd seen of Unahi was any indication, the grumpy she-Kyn would likely take the news worse than Sinovian, if that was possible. As the young Wielder rushed back to her rooms to gather her travelling gear, Jitani walked back to speak with her brother and Unahi, dreading each step along the way. It was Tarsa's gratitude and burning touch that gave her the courage to face their anger. She just hoped it would be enough.

CHAPTER 15
THE DECISION

Although he'd seen many wondrous things in his travels across the Everland and through areas of the Reach, Tobhi had never imagined anything quite as fabulous as this Stormbringer, the Ubbetuk cloud-galleon that descended from the sky above Sheynadwiin to take them to the border of Eromar. He'd wondered how they would travel the many miles to Eromar City in such a short time, especially as they only had six days remaining until the Council's final response to Vald's demands.

The Tetawa stood with four Kyn and all of their travelling trunks on a wide wooden platform that hung over a rocky outcropping on the western edge of the Sheynadwiin grotto. The only member of their party still missing was Jitani, and she'd be arriving soon. He was surprised and a bit disappointed that Tarsa hadn't stayed around to say goodbye to him, but her unhappiness was clear when she left the Governor's rooms, so he tried to not be too hurt by her absence. All people dealt with their grief in different ways; perhaps this was easiest for Tarsa.

Tobhi turned his attention to a last check of his own gear. He never left anywhere without his well-worn hat, but his beaded belt and richly-woven vest were new, as were his fringed leather boots, all gifts from his aunt Jynni. Aside from a few changes of clothing, some rope, minor medicinals, and a week's worth of dried fruit and yam cakes, he was travelling light this trip. He had his lore-leaf pouch hidden under his oiled overcoat, and his satchel—containing quills, ink, pencils, bark-paper, a long-stemmed pipe, and a pouch of smoking tobacco—was slung comfortably over one shoulder. His stone-headed hatchet lay tied by its travel thong across his back.

The Kyn councillors were an unremarkable bunch. They stood a bit apart from Tobhi and talked quietly among themselves. Two were elders, and two were a little younger than Tarsa. All wore gray satin jackets, and the two she-Kyn were regal in their long-flowing dresses. Tobhi frowned. They didn't look at all like the battle-hardened veterans he'd been expecting; indeed, the younger two looked to be little more than bored cubs. Tobhi returned his attention to the far more interesting spectacle of the black clouds and cracking blue lightning that moved toward to the platform.

Blackwick spoke quietly with Garyn and Molli Rose nearby as flashes of the Stormbringer came into view. The Ubbetuk airships were said to be all gears and steam and bulging gas-balloons, translucent sacks that deflated and inflated in rhythm with the grinding of machinery deep inside their bulbous frames. On occasion, Tobhi thought he could see the sails of this one among the clouds, along with glimpses of what looked like a strange, insect-like hull, with metallic oars that hung like legs over the side. But glimpses were the most he could have, for the airships were mysterious, and their appearance changed depending upon the viewer. Humans saw great misshapen monsters in the air, and they drew from their most fearful legends to name them "Dragons"; many Folk perceived the Ubbetuk wonders as nameless mechanical abominations that resembled nothing of either the green or mythic worlds. All agreed on one reality about the airships: the fierce black storm clouds that surrounded the galleons and gave them their honoured name among the Ubbetuk–"Stormbringers."

The clouds twisted and boiled around the airship, obscuring most of the structure from view and adding to its strangeness. More unnerving was the crackling blue fire that skittered across the length and breadth of the craft, occasionally streaking to earth, and giving an otherworldly aura to the already imposing experience. It was said that a flight of Stormbringers could upset the natural weather and cause catastrophic changes in the lands around them; Tobhi had overheard a group of Human hunters in a Béashaad border tavern speculate that if a full flight of Dragons ever took to the clouds, they would likely blast a hole in the sky to rival the Melding.

The first spatters of rain struck Tobhi's upturned face, and with them came a sudden fierce wind. Above those sounds, the air was alive with a buzzing hum and the sharp smell of a spring storm. He had to turn his face away from the sight, for between the rain, wind, and lightning, he couldn't keep his eyes open long enough to make out the dim shapes on the deck of the ship. He was glad that Smudge was back with the roaming deer herd in Sheynadwiin, for the Stormbringer would have driven the little beast into a panic. It was now no surprise to the Leafspeaker that the Ubbetuk were treated with some measure of suspicion; the cloud-shrouded shape did nothing to welcome closer observation. Was it a cloud-skimming galleon that moved closer, or some gigantic creature out of nightmare?

As the Stormbringer descended and the rains increased, the rolling taint of iron crushed down upon Tobhi and the others, and he felt himself wilting as it approached. The Tetawa's skin burned. "How re we s'posed to travel up there surrounded by all that iron?" he called out to Molli Rose. "We'll never make it to Eromar like this."

Head bowed in the rain, Molli walked over to him. "Ye don't think I'd let ye go without a bit of help, do ye?" she shouted through the rising winds. "Well, here ye go, one for you, and one for Jitani when she arrives. The others already have their own." She reached into her jacket pocket and pulled out a bracelet and a matching choker of alternating rows of white and black glass beads—the choker, set with a blood-red stone, for Jitani, and the thick bracelet with a glimmering blue-green pearl for Tobhi. "They're iron-wards, and powerful ones at that. They'll keep the worst of the poison from bringin' ye low. Ye may find that they'll be a far sight more useful in Man-lands than even on that Ubbetuk contraption." Tobhi slipped the band over his wrist and felt the burning tug under his skin fade. His stomach still rolled awkwardly, but it at least now it didn't threaten to overwhelm him. He smiled with gratitude at the Tetawa matron, for iron-wards this powerful were precious.

"Now," Molli Rose took his hand and smiled, "I've got to be gettin' back down the hill; there's lots to do, as it's the Tetawi who'll be hostin' the giveaway tonight." Her eyes grew soft. "Take care, cub, and know that our prayers are with ye all. Ye've already proven yeself more than able to handle some difficult times, so just do what ye can and then get back to us." He nodded and embraced her, and she headed through the rain down the path towards the grotto.

The Chancellor and Garyn walked toward the group. Two blue-capped attendants held a large rain-parasol to shield the Chancellor, but Garyn contented himself with an oiled longcoat and a wide-brimmed hat. "Where is Sinovian's emissary?" Blackwick asked. "There is little time remaining."

"I'm here!" Tarsa called out as she ran up the hill toward the dock, her arms heavy with a hurriedly-gathered pack of supplies. Tobhi stared at her in surprise.

Garyn frowned. "Where is Jitani?"

Tarsa stuck out her chin defiantly in spite of the rain and nearly-overwhelming taint of iron around her. "I'm taking her place. She's going to stay and continue to help the Sevenfold Council. I'm here to help my brother."

Tobhi's lips quivered, but he smiled. Brother. The word had a nice sound, as much for its truth as its purpose. He nodded his acceptance, and she met his grin with one every bit as wide.

"The airship is nearly ready to depart," the Governor said, his voice sharp. "Sinovian chose Jitani as his representative, not you. This is no time for such nonsense, Tarsa'deshae."

"It en't nonsense," said Tobhi decisively as he handed the other iron-ward to Tarsa. "She's a Redthorn warrior, too, and a Wielder of no mean skill. That could come in pretty handy."

"That's not the issue here…" Garyn began, but he stopped as another group of figures came over the hill to walk toward the dock: Unahi, Jitani, and a visibly furious Sinovian, all thoroughly drenched by the sudden rains.

"Wielder," Garyn called to Unahi. "Please, we are running short of time."

Unahi nodded and looked hard at Tarsa. "Is it true what she told me?"
Tarsa glanced at Jitani and nodded. "Yes."

"I see." Unahi's lips tightened into a thin line. Tarsa would have almost
preferred to see fury and burning rage in Unahi's eyes instead of this cold
disappointment. "Very well. She's made the choice, as have you. There's
nothing more to be said." Sinovian glared at the young Wielder with
almost murderous rage, but Jitani's golden eyes were warm. Tarsa looked
away.

Blackwick cleared his throat. "So be it. The cloud-galleon will take you
as far as Lake Ithiak, which is a little over a day's journey to the east of
Eromar City. I have provided a coach and four rather special ponies, along
with an Ubbetuk groom, to take you the rest of the way. May your feet
find you swiftly on the road home." Without another word, he and his
attendants followed the path taken by Molli Rose.

Lightning crackled around the platform, and the ground shook as
thunder rumbled through the grotto. Garyn's face was worn with worry
and indecision. His piercing eyes assessed the young Wielder for a long
time. At last he sighed and handed a fist-sized copper ball to Tobhi while
addressing all of the travellers. "When you are ready to return, break this
in the darkness of the moon- or starshine, and the nightwasp will
summon the Stormbringer again to bring you home. We will look for you
within the week. Be wary, my kindred. Lojar Vald is a cunning Man, and a
cruel one. He has no love of justice or the Eld Folk, but he will not likely
challenge you openly—not for a while, at least. 'Accidents' abound for Folk
who enter Gorthac Hall. The sooner you are free of Eromar City, the safer
you will be."

He looked at the other Kyn diplomats and slid in close to Tobhi, his
voice low, nearly drowned out in the noise from the Stormbringer. "The
travellers I had originally chosen for this journey have fallen ill and are
unable to accompany you. Apparently, Tarsa is not the only unexpected
change in our plans. I have my suspicions of the reasons for their 'illness,'
but, until they have recovered, I cannot say for certain. These four are not

trained as warriors; they are traders and minor dignitaries, but all are dependable, if uninspiring. If we had more time…"

His eyes followed the other Kyn as they moved toward the loading platform. *Dependable, but also expendable*, the Governor thought darkly. *These truly are unhappy, desperate times.*

"All that they know is that they are to finish trade negotiations and help to escort the remaining diplomats home again. They will do their job efficiently and effectively; you need not worry about them endangering your true purpose. I would send you alone, but that would arouse Vald's suspicions too much, and we cannot risk it. It is a heavier burden that I am placing on you, Tobhi, and I am sorry for it. But it cannot be helped."

The Leafspeaker held his fist against his chest. "We'll be strong, I promise ye that. And I en't alone, so don't ye worry 'bout us."

Garyn's eyes flickered toward Tarsa, but he nodded. Turning back to larger group, he said, "Hurry back to us, all of you. We will have much need of your wisdom upon your return." They all bowed low, gathered their travel packs, and walked to the edge of the platform, where a single rope ladder descended from the dark clouds. Tobhi walked ahead of Tarsa, his eyes wide and neck straining to discern the shape of their strange transport.

As Tarsa stepped beside the Tetawa, Unahi called to her. "Niece, wait!" The younger she-Kyn turned, preparing for a firm lecture or Garyn's refusal. Instead, the elder Wielder held up her wyrwood staff, its golden surface still etched with the marks of thorns from Tarsa's battle against the Human grave-robbers.

Unahi wiped a strand of silver hair away from her drenched face. "Take this with you. It served you well before; perhaps it'll continue to do so on your present travels." Tarsa tried to protest, but Unahi bristled. "Don't argue. You'll have more need of this than I will, and if you won't heed my warnings, you should at least be prepared for the dangers to come." Her voice softened, but her lips were still drawn and disapproving. "Don't make too much of this—it's only a small thing."

A wave of love rushed through the Redthorn Wielder, and Tarsa swept the bent old she-Kyn into her tattooed arms. "It's not such a small thing to me, Auntie. Tsodoka."

Unahi stiffened and pulled herself free. "You've got a long, darkening road ahead of you–it's a road you've chosen freely, though I tried to spare you. Take care of yourself, and of Tobhi. He's kith to you now, and that brings responsibility. Don't fail him. Come home as quickly as you can. May Zhaia bless and keep you safe in her leafy bower." She lightly touched the azure Wielder's mark on her niece's forehead, and then the old she-Kyn was gone, lost in the screaming wind and rain.

Tobhi glanced around and waited for Tarsa to slip over the railing before following to his own seat. As their transport rose upward, he turned back to peer over the edge. For a moment something caught his eye beside the receding platform, but it was just a flash of colour in the storm-shadowed trees below, not enough to really tell if something was truly there.

"That bit o' witchery last night is spookin' me," Tobhi mumbled to himself as he craned his head back towards the site, trying fruitlessly to catch another glimpse before black clouds and blue fire obscured his vision completely. Something nagged at his memory, a troubling thought just out of reach.

Tarsa's hand on his arm broke his reverie, and he promptly forgot about the movement on the ground below as the she-Kyn pointed in awe at the strange whirring gears and machinery. He was too lost in excitement to remember where he'd seen before that brief glimmer of burnished copper tresses, that momentary gleam of violet eyes that now gazed upward through the rain as the Stormbringer disappeared from sight.

"Our options are fading quickly, Captain," Neranda whispered to the he-Kyn beside her. It was the seventh and final night of the Sevenfold Council; six days had passed since the Redthorn Wielder's outburst and subsequent departure. Pradu Styke, whose minion Myyrd had not long ago been thoroughly rebuffed by the Lawmaker, now sat beside Neranda at the table, having arrived in the afternoon at her request to watch with growing alarm as debate slowly gave way to consensus. The beast-tribes, Tetawi, Gvaergs, and Ferals were unanimous in their opposition to the Dreydmaster's Oath of Western Sanctuary, and their counsel seemed to be swaying the Wyrnach. The Kyn were still divided, but, even with Styke's recent arrival, the Celestials were losing ground.

Neranda looked over at the Ubbetuk Chancellor, who sat with this hands folded beneath his chin, his eyes narrowed in concentration. He would be the key. The bonds between Ubbetuk and Humans–through trade, politics, and culture–were stronger in many ways than those between Ubbetuk and the rest of the Folk. Blackwick wasn't likely to alienate one of the growing powers in the Reach, certainly not for a group of wayward forest-dwellers who refused to face the inevitable.

The Ubbetuk were Neranda's greatest hope. They were everyone else's greatest fear.

Blackwick suddenly looked up and caught her gaze with his own. His face was inscrutably distant. Then, almost imperceptibly, he nodded at her. His eyes closed again in thought. The Lawmaker leaned back in her own seat, heart throbbing wildly. For the first time in days, she had a spark of hope.

Though the debate might have raged for weeks more until a consensus emerged, with those few opposed eventually withdrawing from the issue, all now gathered in the Gallery of Song felt the heavy press of time upon them, a new and unwelcome pressure largely unknown before the arrival of Men. There was very little time remaining. By dawn, they would have to reach a decision, and it would determine the future of the Everland–perhaps even the very future of the Folk.

When a brief silence descended, Neranda stood and addressed the Council. "My kith, older sisters and younger brothers, I have heard many good words, many brave words about standing against Eromar and its demands. I do not doubt your hearts, nor your courage, but you speak from the safety of your mountain valleys and deep forests, your caves and aeries. Listen to one who understands the ways of Men, one who has travelled among them, learned their speech, given himself to the study of their minds and passions. Before we close this Council, before the coming of the dawn, listen to Captain Pradu Styke, guardian of the western border."

Garyn nodded, his face haggard with exhaustion and the creeping shadow of the future. Some of the Council members shuffled uncomfortably in their seats, and Molli Rose exchanged a knowing, suspicious glance with the Gvaerg Emperor Guaandak, but all were silent as Styke stood to address everyone in the Gallery. Even now Neranda didn't trust him, and his earlier attempt to coerce her vote still burned in her righteous heart, but her allies and friends were fading, and she needed the Captain more than she cared to admit.

Styke brought his fist to his chest in salute and turned to the Gallery. He was a proud Celestial warrior, dressed in a long, split-backed black jacket of the Human fashion so common in the borderlands. His stalks were bound and wrapped in tight blue cloth around his head, his thick hair was cut at the shoulder, and his green leather boots were buckled and brightly polished. Yet he was still Kyn, still marked with honour tattoos and scarred from many battles over the last thirty years of protecting the western edge of the Everland. Captain Styke was arrogant and opportunistic, but he'd long since proven his qualities as a warrior.

"Men are hungry creatures," he began. His was the voice of a born orator: deep, smooth, and convincing. The Folk listened, and even those who knew his intent found themselves drawn to his words. "Men feed wherever they can find sustenance, and when that's gone, they feed on one another. They don't know balance. They poison themselves with everything

Neranda

they consume, and even then they can't stop themselves. Hunger and life–these are the same things to Men. I've seen what they can do. I've seen more than one town fall to this unending hunger, and I've seen Folk torn to pieces by the ravenous will of Men. Don't try to fool yourselves into thinking that this will end, because it won't. They'll keep coming, slowly now, but eventually more and more, wave after wave to smash against us, scatter us on the storm while they feed on what little remains."

He walked slowly around the great table, pulling all eyes towards him. "Sunflower Hill was a small Tetawi town not far from my well-guarded Kyn town of Defiance. We used to trade with the Tetawi–they brought us river-reeds and honeycomb, and we gave them wild rice and meadow deer, having long ago given up the prohibition against eating animal flesh." The beast-lord Myrkash snorted. "We even celebrated a few marriages between the towns, and raised our voices in joy when younglings were born to our people, Kyn or Tetawi by the blood of their mothers. I danced and sang with the Folk of Sunflower Hill. I was proud to call them my kith.

"And then, one morning, when I stepped from my cabin and looked out over the western ridge, I saw thick smoke climbing into the sky above Sunflower Hill. We gathered about twenty well-armed warriors and rode as fast as we could to help our friends. But we were too late. The village was gone, destroyed in the night by Men hungry for blood."

The Captain stopped. His eyes were locked on the etched stone floor, and he was quiet for a long time. When he spoke again, his voice was pierced by remembered hurt.

"We walked through the town, hoping against reason that some had survived. A few still lived, but the Men had done terrible things to them, especially the she-cubs; few were ever able to walk again, let alone look on the world without haunted eyes. Younglings, elders, those between the rich bounties of youth and adulthood–all were dead, or worse. I've never seen such horror, and I've been a warrior since I could hold a hatchet. The Humans didn't stop with driving people from their homes, or with raiding the storehouses. No, their hunger went deeper. They wanted pain. They fed on it, needed it like parched tongues need water. And the blood…it flowed in steaming streams that morning.

"Two warriors ran for reinforcements to come to the village, and the rest of us went after the Men. We found them soon enough; there were only nine of them, and they were laughing and celebrating their easy raid. They still stank of death.

"I don't remember much of the battle that followed, but it was short. We butchered them, crushed their bones to dust, ground them into the dirt and burned even their ashes until nothing remained, not even their memory. They didn't even have time to scream." He looked up, and tears streamed unchecked down the sides of his face. There was no deception in his face, only deep, scarring pain. "I remember only one thing clearly. A Man was tying something to the saddle of his horse when we attacked, and, after he was dead, I looked at the saddle. Hanging from the saddle horn, tied delicately together with long ropes of bloody black hair, were the tender, secret parts of nineteen Tetawi–male, female, and the between-worlders, both young and old–carried away as a memento of the attack."

The Gallery of Song was silent except for the scattered sounds of weeping. "Do not doubt, my kith, that the Men will come again, because their hunger grows every day, and they have no love of the Folk. We can leave our homeland now, while we still live, or we can stay and wait to share the fate of Sunflower Hill. We can't withstand this tide forever. We can bend like the willow, or break like the oak. We must withdraw. We have no other choice."

"Before your courage fails you, listen to what I have to say." Sinovian, the young Greenwalker, stepped down from the Gallery, where he and others had been watching the proceedings with increasing anger. The consensus of the Council had started to unravel after Styke's passionate speech. It had been easy to dismiss the Celestials as selfish or cowardly before, but the testimony of one who had lived and fought against Men for years was difficult to ignore.

Cutting off Neranda's objections, Garyn waved Sinovian forward. It was past midnight. Dawn would bring either consensus or collapse, and time and hope for all sides were diminishing. Tobhi and his companions hadn't returned as the Governor had desperately hoped; there would be no reprieve, no timely information from the surviving ambassadors. All would depend on the eloquence of those present.

The young warrior turned to the Wielders' Circle and brought his fist to his chest in greeting as he stepped to the Council table. The gray eyes that gazed on the Council were filled with deep anger, but love and anguish lay there too, and it was these qualities that now drove his words.

"The words of my he-Kyn elder have some wisdom. He speaks the truth about these Men that he's encountered, for I've seen the same cruelty to the north, where my home once lay. I don't disagree with anything Pradu Styke says about the ways of Men. But it's for this reason that we must fight Lojar Vald and his demands."

Styke stood up. "Did you hear nothing I said? We can't fight Vald–it's hopeless pride to claim otherwise."

Sinovian turned a harsh eye on the Captain, but Garyn intervened. "You have had your opportunity to speak, Captain Styke."

"What more has to be said?" Styke persisted. He glared around the table. "We can continue debating this issue until the next Melding, but it's not going to change a thing. We'll never have another opportunity like this one. We can take these terms and move someplace safe, someplace where we'll be free of Humans once and for all."

"And where would this be, Captain?" Sinovian said, his voice suddenly soft, the shift in tone breaking the spell of Styke's words. "If, as you seem to believe, we're all destined to die anyway, what does it matter if we die now or later? If we can't possibly fight these Men, and if they're never going to stop trying to take what's ours, why should we leave?"

Styke glared at the young warrior, but Sinovian persisted. "Have you ever thought that running might be the very worst thing that we could do? If we give up our homelands now, the most precious bond we have to the Old Ways and the Ancestrals, if we deny the trust that we've shared with the land for all these ages, how can we possibly imagine that we'll be able cling to anything we have in the future? Maybe by surrendering we'll actually be abandoning ourselves to a false fate. If we make a stand here, and lose, we'll at least know that we've done the very best we could to hold fast to those things that are most important to us. What's more, these ravenous Men and their kind will know it too. But if we give up now, if we abandon our homes, the bones of those who came before, and the covenant of the Tree with the expectation that Men will treat us fairly in the future when there's less at stake, we're setting ourselves on a path to certain destruction."

No sound came from the Gallery. A weight of exhaustion and creeping fear now settled over the gathered assembly. Neranda stood angrily and turned to Garyn. "I implore you, Uncle, to put an end to this charade. Think of the dignity of this Council. This…Greenwalker has made his point quite clear."

The Speaker nodded. "You are right, Neranda, and thank you for reminding me—it is time to finish this." He looked at the delegates of the Sevenfold Council. "We have deliberated for seven nights, and heard voices in support of Eromar and others in opposition. What say you, my kith? Do we stay in our homeland, or do we surrender?"

Neranda's face went pale and her mouth hung open in shock. It was too soon. "Uncle, wait. There's still more time. We must not rush–" she cried, but Garyn slashed his hand down angrily, cutting her off. She wanted to remind the wavering Council members about the wisdom of accepting Vald's terms, to end the discussion with the understanding that survival depended on surrendering this land that tied them to the savagery and ignorance of the past. But the situation was now beyond her control.

The Speakers of each of the Folk Nations gathered with their councillors for long, tense moments. Neranda remained at the table as the other Kyn representatives gathered beside Garyn's seat of office. She had little hope that her voice would make much difference in their negotiations, but Pradu Styke met with them in a last effort to sway their thoughts. His words this night carried a great deal of weight; he might open ears that were now deaf to her. The only other leaders at the table were the Ubbetuk Chancellor and the Emperor of the Gvaergs, as their sole decisions would guide their people.

Do not fail me, Chancellor. Do not fail the Seven Sisters of the Folk. Neranda's nails dug into the arm of her chair. Blackwick looked up again, as if reading her thoughts, and nodded to her again. Exhilaration raced through the Lawmaker's body. She was dizzy with fear and anticipation.

Molli Rose and the Tetawi representatives returned to the great table. "For the Tetawi people, and for the Everland, we reject the Oath of Western Sanctuary. We won't surrender our home." Her hands trembled, but her voice was firm. Neranda barely heard the Tetawa's words; there had been little doubt that the small Folk would refuse to sign the treaty—they were a stubborn, ignorant people anyway, and certainly not worthy of the admiration Garyn seemed to have for them.

Kishkaxi, the Brood Mother of the Harpies, ruffled her feathers and hissed in her dry voice, "The Feral-Folk will remain in our aeries and villages. There will be no alliance with Men. We will continue as of old." The golden eagles called out in agreement, answered by a chorus of birds and beasts from the windows and rafters of the Gallery.

"No Human will desecrate the caverns of the Gvaerg Empire," growled Guaandak, the Emperor Triumphant, as he struck his golden spear on the ground. "The Gvaergs are now and have always been a free people; that will not change. Let Men do their worst—we will drive them from the mountains with forge-fire and stone. We join with all true Folk in the defense of our 'Holt. I reject Eromar and its *rijjik* Dreydmaster. They will find nothing but death in the Everland." A low, proud chant rose up from the Gvaergs in the Gallery in praise of their leader and his righteous decision. Guaandak sat back and smiled righteously.

Myrkash the Unbroken, the chieftain of the beasts, smashed his hoof on the floor in agreement. "Our blood may fall, but we'll take many Men with us. We're not leaving our mountains."

The four Wyrnach representatives returned to the table. Neranda shifted slightly. They might shift the balance; if the Wyrnach and the Ubbetuk expressed reservations at this point, consensus would be impossible and the work of the Sevenfold Council would collapse.

Sethis Du'lorr, the serene speaker of the graceful Spider-Folk, bowed low to the Gallery. In a hollow voice that seemed to come from the deepest shadows of the Eld Green, the ancient creature whispered, "Though my heart is filled with fear, and though darkness crouches on the horizon, we shall stand beside our younger siblings in defense of the Everland. If we fade, we will fall with the fury of all our lost kindred in our hearts. The Wyrnach reject the Oath."

Styke stomped back to his seat beside the copper-haired Lawmaker. Garyn's voice was stronger than it had ever been. Now, at last, he spoke the words that had long been on his heart. "I have long consulted with my people, and I have heard their voices. Though some may disagree with this decision, there is no doubt that the vast majority of the Kyn do not wish to leave the Everland. As Governor of the Kyn Nation, bound by duty to serve my people and their interests, and with the blessing of the Assembly, I reject Eromar's demands."

All eyes turned to the Ubbetuk Chancellor, who sat unmoving, his hands curled over the handle of his wasp-headed walking stick. All depended on the Ubbetuk. Would they add their voice to the consensus, or would they step away? If they exercised their right of dissent, would the rest of the Sevenfold Council be able to withstand the inevitable assault?

Neranda could barely breathe. All her work, for all these years, came to this moment.

Blackwick looked at the Council and out at the Gallery beyond. His smooth voice was heavy but calm. "It is a dangerous road we travel, my friends. We have been given two terrible choices, and, although there are doubtless other options, they have thus far eluded all our collected wisdom." He turned his penetrating gaze to Neranda, who sat trembling in her seat. "The Ubbetuk do not eagerly wage war, and we do not seek conflict with anyone, either Men or Folk."

Neranda's violet eyes brimmed with grateful tears. Her legacy was assured.

"And yet," Blackwick continued, his eyes still focused on the copper-haired she-Kyn, "we do not turn away when injustice falls upon us—or upon our kith, no matter how distant. The Sevenfold Council will have consensus: the Swarm stands with the Folk."

There was a moment's pause before the Gallery erupted in thunderous applause. Guaandak burst out laughing and grinned at the Chancellor, who merely nodded in return. The golden eagles who guarded Kishkaxi lifted themselves into the air and cried out as they raced through the Gallery of Song, the joy of those assembled lifting their wings higher.

Molli Rose walked to Garyn and took his hand in her own small brown fingers. He watched, his heart heavy, as Neranda strode swiftly from the Gallery, her face ablaze with anger and shame, Pradu Styke and the gathered Celestials following behind her. He shook his head. "I fear, Molli, that we have made more enemies than Eromar this night. And with the Kyn divided, our future is still uncertain."

The Tetawa didn't respond. Garyn was right: the real struggle was just beginning. She gave Garyn what she hoped was a comforting smile, but she stopped abruptly. "Where is he?" she asked, looking around the crowded Gallery.

"Who?" the Governor asked, exhaustion heavy on his shoulders.

"Blackwick. The Chancellor is gone."

The night was cold in the shadows near the platform. Neranda's ceremonial robes would not have kept her warm in the darkness before dawn, but her body burned with fury, and she felt only the slightest chill. Her business wouldn't take long; she would have time enough to gather more suitable clothing for the journey to come.

Everything had started well, but the unravelling had begun with Garyn's pet Wielder and her speech from the audience that first night. It was a flagrant breach of protocol, but Garyn's decision had already been made; by allowing the young she-Kyn's outburst, the Governor had surrendered the integrity he'd once had as a leader.

Neranda had thought that the unexpected departure of this so-called "Redthorn Wielder" would have minimized the damage of those inappropriate words; the Shield had stood in the shadows and watched with no small satisfaction as the Ubbetuk Stormbringer departed with the tattooed warrior and her Tetawi lapdog. Yet Tarsa'deshae had had a strange effect over the Council, and though gone for the subsequent six nights of discussion, her spirit remained powerful in the Gallery of Song.

The Shield's lips curled in bitter scorn. This young Wielder represented all that was blind and unnatural about the Wild ways of the Deep Green. Those who walked the Celestial Path these days were still a sizeable group, but there should have been far more, especially given the recent chaos. Their ranks should be swelling with Kyn and other Folk looking to benevolent Luran for guidance; there were sadly too few who were willing to give themselves to the pain and sacrifice necessary for true seekers of wisdom. It didn't help that the barbaric rituals of old were no longer hidden in furtive darkness. Even Garyn Mendiir, the leader of the Nation and Speaker of the newly-announced Sevenfold Council, had given himself back to their embrace. Irresponsible and foolish, he would lead them all to misery; of that Neranda had little doubt.

These are dangerous times, Uncle, she thought darkly, *and though you are unwilling to make the necessary choices to ensure our survival, there are others who are most certainly prepared to do so.*

Neranda closed her eyes, forcing a calming reason through her rage.

NAMES AND OTHER STORIES

A

- AIRSHIPS. The primary military and mercantile transportation craft of the Ubbetuk Nation. These galleons draw elemental energies from the air for lift, causing dramatic atmospheric disruptions and great lightning storms that can be seen for many miles. Called Dragons by Humans; the preferred colloquial Ubbetuk name is Stormbringers.
- AKJAADIT. "The Hummingbird's Granddaughter." The Dragonfly in Tetawi teachings.
- ALCHAEMY. The twin Human sciences of physical change, both bodily healing and elemental transmutation.
- THE ALLIED WILDERLANDS. A southern province of the Reach. It is a loose confederation of independent townships inhabited by rugged and self-reliant Humans who often trade with and marry among the Folk.
- THE ANCESTRALS. The first of the Kyn to emerge from the Upper Place to the Eld Green; the primeval ancestors and progenitors of the Kyn Nation.
- ANDAAKA. A southwestern province of the Reach best known as the home of Bashonak, the heart of Dreyd-worship in the Republic.
- THE ASSEMBLY OF LAW. The governing council of the unified Kyn Nation, which replaced the Gathering, an earlier council-meet of the autonomous Kyn towns.
- ATHKASHNUK. Wyrm Wielder present at the Sevenfold Council.
- AVERYN. Zhe-Kyn healer; consort and advisor to Garyn Mendiir.
- AVIALLE. The River-Mother; a spirit-being of the Eld Green.
- AWAKENING. The first emergence of *wyr*-powers in the life of a young Wielder, generally around the time of puberty. It is often a physically traumatic experience; if a Wielder is unguided in the transformation, the uncontrolled *wyr* can lead to madness and/or death.

B

- BASHONAK. The capital city of the Dreydcaste in the Reach. It is a massive

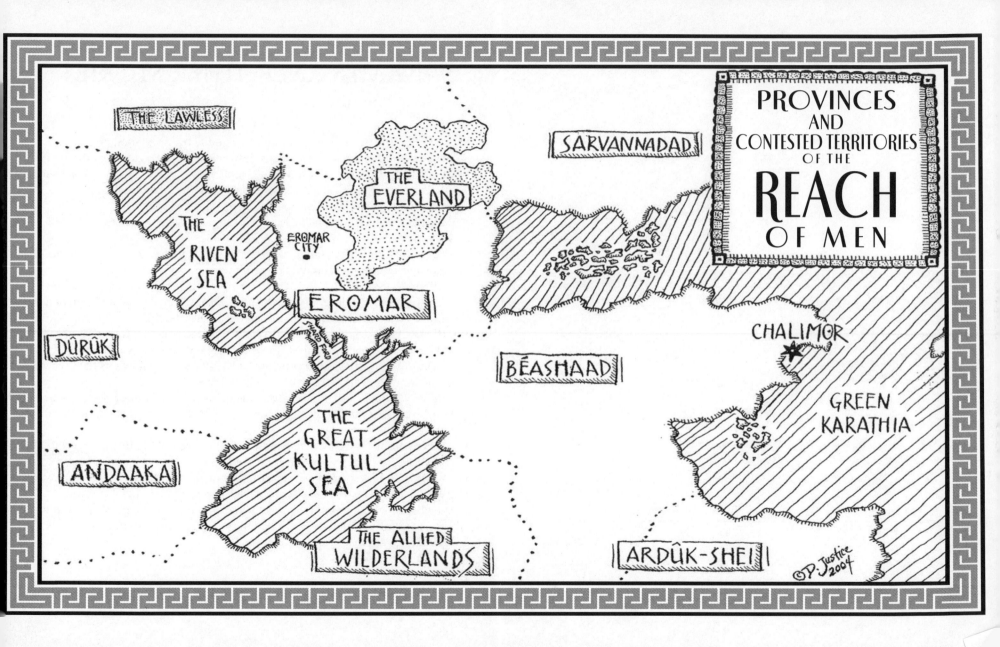

stone fortress at the edge of the Tuskwood, known as much for its rigidly authoritarian creeds as for the skilled military training of its adherents.

- BÉASHAAD. The capital province of the Reach, located on the eastern edge of the continent. Its inland region is a temperate mix of hills, farmlands, and wide prairies, while its coastal waters teem with marine life. The great metropolis of Chalimor is built on the eastern shores of Béashaad.
- BEAST-TRIBES. The various communities of animals, birds, and beasts who call the Everland home. Each group has its own chosen leaders, and those leaders often meet in council.
- BETWEEN-WORLDERS. Folk who share characteristics of multiple genders.
- BIGGIABBA. Gvaerg Matron and Wielder.
- BINDER. The second rank among the Dreydcaste. They draw the essence of spirits caught by Seekers into their snaring-tomes for use by Reavers.
- BIRCHBARK HOLLOW. A rugged valley in the Everland, at the eastern edge of the Meshiwiik Forest; home of the Brown Lodge and the Igwimish Mound, the central council house and ceremonial grounds of the western Tetawi.
- BIRD. A young Moth Clan he-Tetawa of Spindletop.
- BLACKFLY FEN. A dense and fetid swamp at the southern tip of the Everland.
- BLACKWICK. The aged Chancellor of the Ubbetuk Swarm.
- BRANCH. One of the seven clans of the Kyn. Each Branch is named for an ancestral tree-spirit and is known for its gifts in particular spheres of Kyn life: Willow, trade and diplomacy; Oak, leadership and philosophy; Ash, healing; Thorn, defense; Cedar, lore and the arts; Apple, horticulture; and Pine, mysticism and dream-guidance.
- BRAEK THE YOUNGER. A he-Kyn Lawmaker of the Celestial Path; estranged son of Braek the Older.
- BRAEK THE OLDER. A he-Kyn Wielder and Greenwalker; father of Braek the Younger.
- BROWNIES. A slightly pejorative but widespread Human term for Tetawi.
- BUBORRU. The Badger-spirit and wisdom-keeper of Tetawi teachings.
- THE BURNING MOUTH. An iron-veined pit on the outskirts of Red Cedar Town used to imprison Wielders during the Purging.

C

- THE CANOPY VEIL. The barrier between the Eld Green and the mortal world of

Humanity.

- THE CELESTIAL PATH. The philosophical principles of Luran-worship, descended from Dreyd teachings brought by the Proselytors who accompanied the first Human traders into the Everland. The Path is characterized by a denial of the flesh and an emphasis on the power of the purified mind, a commitment to hierarchy and obedience, a rejection of the *wyr* and the relational values of the Way of Deep Green, and an embrace of the individualistic and commercial values of Humanity.
- CHAADA. A young Moth Clan she-Tetawa of Spindletop.
- CHALIMOR. The capital city of the Reach of Men, named for its location between the white shores of Chal Bay and the rugged slopes of Mount Imor; political, artistic, and cultural center of Humanity; home to the Hall of Kings and the Reachwarden.
- CHANGELING. A Tetawa with the ability to shapeshift into the form of her Clan animal. The shape-changing Tetawi witches–Skeegers–are related to Changelings but without the calming Clan influence.
- CHANTING SASH. A woven or braided belt, generally of wyrweave or sturdy linen, into which a Wielder sews or beads some of her more powerful prayers, stories, and medicinal formulas. The sash serves as a calming memory aid to help balance the Wielder's mind and emotions as she does her work.
- CLAN. The primary social and political foundation of Tetawi life, with each being matrilineal in authority and descent. All Clans are named for an animal, which is deeply honored by all members of that Clan. The most powerful are the Four Mother Clans: Raccoon, Spider, Kingfisher, and Trout.
- CLOUD-GALLEON. See AIRSHIP.
- CRAFTING. The Human use of occult ritual and elemental alchaemy to shape the fabric of reality.

D

- DALADIR TRE'SHEIN. Celestial he-Kyn diplomat for the Everland; stationed in Eromar City.
- DARDATH VALE. The ancient valley home of the Kyn city of Sheynadwiin in the heart of the Kraagen Mountains.
- DARKENING. A pocket of Decay within the mortal world.

- DECAY. A chaotic elemental force that destroys all mortal things.
- THE DEEP GREEN. The ancient ceremonial and kinship traditions of the Eld Green; maintained by the Wielders. Also known as the Old Ways.
- DEERMEN. Deer-headed Ferals of the Kraagen Mountains.
- DELVHOLME. The great underground capital of the Gvaerg Nation.
- DESHA'AL MYYRD. Minor Celestial dignitary in the service of Pradu Styke.
- DOLLTENDER. A Tetawa wyr-worker who draws on hand-made dolls–usually with dried-apple heads and corn-cob bodies–for spiritual guidance.
- DOWNBRIAR TOWN. A Stoneskin-ravaged Kyn town in the southern Everland.
- DRAGON. The Human name given to a mechanized Ubbetuk airship.
- THE DREYD. An order of now-immortal Human priests and sorcerers who overthrew the old Immortals of Men and assumed their place, thus causing the cataclysmic Melding.
- THE DREYDCASTE. The rigidly authoritarian and Human-supremacist followers of the Dreyd. Their holy city and seat of power is Bashonak.
- DREYDMASTER. A leader of the Dreydcaste. There are generally no more than three Dreydmasters in the world at any single time, though the Dreydmaster of Bashonak is widely regarded to be the authoritative voice among them.
- DROHODU. "Grandfather of the Mosses." Spirit-being; green-skinned consort to Zhaia and father of the Kyn.
- DURUK. The westernmost province of the Reach, characterized by broken and blasted lands at its eastern border, wind-swept prairies in the center, and stormy coasts in the west. Its largest settlement–aside from the tent-cities of the Jaaga-Folk–is the notorious Harudin Holt.

E

- EATERS OF OLD. The collective name for an ancient group of grotesque, carnivorous beings best known for their uncontrollable hunger. The Stoneskins are among the most powerful of the Eaters.
- THE EDGEWOOD. A dense pine and scrub oak forest to the south of the Everland and within the territories of the Spindetop Hollow Tetawi.
- THE ELD GREEN. The lush, ancient world of the Folk before the arrival of Men.
- THE ELDARVIAN WOODS. The largest forest in the Everland. Deep and shadow-filled, this dense woodland is the home of the largest population of wyrwood trees in the Reach and is thus vigorously protected by the Folk.

- EROMAR. A heavily industrialized and militaristic province that abuts the Everland on the north, east, and south. Eromar is the primary political antagonist of the Folk.
- EROMAR CITY. The capital city of Eromar, built on a bluff overlooking the Orm River. It is the location of Gorthac Hall, the home of the Dreydmaster Lojar Vald.
- THE ETERNITY TREE. The physical manifestation of Zhaia, the first mother of the Kyn, the source of the wyr in the Everland, and the living covenant between the Folk and the land.
- EVERLIGHTS. Perpetual Wielder-shaped balls of soft-glowing wyr-fire.

F

- FA'ALIK. The zhe-Kyn lore-keeper of the Redthorns of Red Cedar Town.
- FAHR. In the Tetawi tongue, the word for a male.
- FEAR-TAKES-THE-FIRE. A he-Kyn ambassador to Eromar who dies under mysterious circumstances.
- FEASTER. See EATERS OF OLD.
- FERALS. Folk whose bodies resemble a union of Humans and beasts, such as the birdlike Harpies, the antlered and hoofed Deermen, and the sly and furred Fox-Folk.
- FEY-FOLK. A slightly pejorative term among Humans for the Folk. "Fey" designates mystery or strangeness at best, evil difference at worst.
- FEY-WITCH. The common Dreyd term for Wielders and other wyr-workers.
- FIRRA. In the Tetawi tongue, the word for a female.
- FIRSTKYN. Town chieftains among the Kyn before the separate towns were unified.
- THE FOLK. The collective term for those peoples and nations originating from the Eld Green, including the Kyn, Tetawi, Gvaergs, Ferals, Beast-tribes, Wyrnach, Ubbetuk, and the Jaagas, among others. While such an encapsulating term acknowledges the shared post-Melding history of such peoples, it can also erase their significant cultural, geographic, ceremonial, and physical distinctiveness.

G

- THE GALLERY HOUSE. The home of the Kyn Governor in Sheynadwiin; located

at the back of the Gallery of Song.
- THE GALLERY OF SONG. The central gathering chamber of the Kyn Assembly of Law and the Sevenfold Council.
- GARYN MENDIIR. Pine Branch he-Kyn Governor of the Kyn Nation and Speaker of the Sevenfold Council.
- THE GATHERING. The ancient council-meet of the autonomous Kyn towns before unification. Replaced by the Assembly of Law.
- GETH. Cedar Branch she-Kyn of Red Cedar Town and aunt of Tarsa'deshae.
- GISHKI. Spider Clan she-Tetawa of Spindletop and cousin of Quill Meadowgood.
- THE GOBLIN CHANCELLOR. See BLACKWICK.
- GOBLINS. The common term used by Humans for the Ubbetuk; often perceived by Ubbetuk as an insult, as it associates them with a mythological race of monsters common in Human folktales before the Melding.
- GORTHAC HALL. The sprawling, many-gabled estate of Lojar Vald in Eromar City.
- GOVERNOR. The political leader of the unified Kyn Nation.
- GRANNY TURTLE. Spirit-being and creator of the first Tetawi people.
- THE GREAT ASCENSION. The Human name for the Melding; refers to the rise of the Dreyd over the Old Immortals of Men.
- THE GREATMOON. See PEARL-IN-DARKNESS.
- GREATWYRM. Also known as Wyrm. A dragon-like serpent with poison saliva, deer-like antlers, and panther-like legs, which makes its home in subterranean tunnels and deep swamps. Greatwyrms cannot fly, but they can run swiftly and swim well.
- GREENWALKER. An adherent of the Way of Deep Green.
- GRUGG. An elder Wielder of the Oak-Folk.
- GUAANDAK. The Emperor Triumphant of the Marble House of Kunkattar of the Gvaerg Nation.
- THE GVAERG NATION. One of the Seven Sister Folk nations, the Gvaergs are rough-featured, hairless giants who live in vast cave cities beneath the earth. Their link to the *wyr* is through earth-borne spirits. Gvaerg society is rigidly divided into proud and pious Houses under the ancestral authority of aged patriarchs. The suns are deadly, as their light turns he-Gvaergs to dead stone, but wyrweave wrappings can defend against that fate.

H

- HARPIES. The most powerful of the Feral peoples with the heads of wizened old Women and the bodies of massive eagles.
- HARUDIN HOLT. The western-most city of the Reach, second in size and influence only to Chalimor. It is a tiered and sprawling city built on the lime stone cliffs of the storm-shattered Reaving Coast, and is best known as a haven for pirates, mercenaries, criminals, and fortune-hunters. Though it is managed in the name of the Lord Mayor, the Three Guilds are the true power of Harudin Holt.
- THE HEARTWOOD. The *wyr* essence of the Eternity Tree.
- HICKORY. A sour-faced apple-head doll belonging to Quill Meadowgood.
- HIGH MARCHING TOWN. A Stoneskin-ravaged Kyn town in the southern Everland.
- THE HIGH TIMBER. The thinning pine and aspen trees near timberline in the Kraagen Mountains.
- 'HOLD. See THRESHOLD.
- HUMANS. The collective term for those peoples and nations originating from the lands beyond the Eld Green, including such diverse populations as the theocratic Dreyd of Andaaka, the fiercely independent miners and foresters of the Allied Wilderlands, the republican aristocrats of Béashaad, and the defiant tribespeople and merchants of Sarvannadad. While such an encapsulating term acknowledges the shared post-Melding history of such peoples, it can also erase their significant cultural, political, and physical differences.

I

- IRON. Deadly poison to all Folk but Ubbetuk and Gvaergs. This virulent quality is well known to many Humans, and they use it to their advantage against many of the Folk, particularly the Kyn.
- IRON-WARD. Amulets created by the Gvaergs for their Folk kith to protect the latter from the toxic effects of iron.
- ISEYA. She-Kyn maidservant to Neranda Ak'Shaar.
- IVIDA. Cedar Branch she-Kyn of Red Cedar Town and aunt of Tarsa'deshae.
- IXIS. Harpy Mystic and Wielder.

J

- THE JAAGA-FOLK. One of the Folk peoples, descended from the Strangeling unions of Kyn and Humans. Though not one of the Seven Sister nations, the Jaagas consider themselves and are generally considered by other Folk to be kith of the Seven Sisters. They are a musical, largely nomadic, patrilineal people who inhabit the northwestern wilds of the Everland, as well as the sweeping grasslands of the Reach province of Duruk.
- JEKOBI. Raven Clan he-Tetawa of Birchbark Hollow, Leafspeaker, and father of Tobhi Burrows.
- JENNA. See GRANNY TURTLE.
- JITANI ALD'AAR. She-Kyn warrior and mercenary; sister of Sinovian.
- JYNNI THISTLEDOWN. Badger Clan she-Tetawa of Birchbark Hollow, healer, and maternal aunt of Tobhi Burrows.

K

- KAANTOR. The Human Blood King of Karkur and treacherous instigator of the Melding.
- KEI'SHAAD MENDIIR. Pine Branch she-Kyn of Thornholt Town and mother of Garyn Mendiir.
- KIDARRI. She-Jaaga root-worker.
- KISHKAXI. Harpy Brood Mother of the North Wind Aerie.
- KITH. Family, relations. Depending on context, the term refers to either immediate, extended, or distant relationship through blood or adoption.
- KIYDA. Cedar Branch she-Kyn of Red Cedar Town and deceased aunt of Tarsa'deshae.
- THE KRAAGEN MOUNTAINS. A massive mountain range bisecting the Everland from north to south.
- KUNKATTAR. Spirit-being of stone; father of the Gvaerg peoples. Each Emperor Triumphant is considered by the pious Gvaergs to be the reincarnated embodiment of Kunkattar.
- THE KYN NATION. The most numerous and widely-dispersed of the Seven Sister nations. The *wyr* of the Kyn is drawn from the green growing world and elemental forces of nature, although a growing number of Kyn follow the Celestial Path and ways separated from the *wyr*. Kyn have a heightened sensitivity to the spirits of nature through their serpentine sensory stalks. Their

matrilineal branches are descended from the seven sacred trees of the Everland. Sheynadwiin, the great peace city of the Everland, is their political and cultural capital.

L

- LAN'DELAR LAST-BORN. Cedar Branch she-Kyn of Red Cedar Town and deceased mother of Tarsa'deshae.
- THE LAWLESS. The rugged, snow-swept region at the margin of the Reachwarden's influence. It is without a central government, although there are numerous small settlements scattered throughout the area that maintain their own laws and order. While home to many brigands, outlaws, and petty despots, it is also home to many fiercely independent people–Folk, Human, and beast–who settle their own grievances and avoid conflict unless it is forced upon them.
- LEAFSPEAKER. A Tetawi wyr-worker who interprets the patterns of wyr-shaped leaves to communicate with the Spirit World and to preserve stories and teachings. The leaf-reading skills are the Tetawi expression of Kyn teachings, thus highlighting some of the co-operative links between the two peoples.
- LEITH FYNON. He-Kyn Celestial messenger in the service of the Sevenfold Council.
- LOJAR VALD. "The Iron Fist." Prefect of the state of Eromar and ambitious Dreydmaster.
- LORE-LEAVES. Wyr-working tools used by Tetawi Leafspeakers.
- THE LOWER PLACE. One of the three primary worlds of existence in the Eld Green and, to a lesser extent, the Melded world. It is a realm of chaos and shadow, though not evil.
- LURAN. Moon-maiden. The Celestial manifestation of the Human Dreyd entity Meynanine; revealer of the Celestial Path to the Kyn Shields. For most Folk, the Greatmoon of the Everland, Pearl-in-Darkness, is male; the virginal female representation is drawn from Human cosmology.

M

- THE MAKERS. Ancient predecessors of the Wielders who first learned to harness the *wyr* currents of the Eld Green. Though powerful, the Makers became selfish and tyrannical, and they were overthrown by the Folk; those who survived taught their Wielding descendants to be humble, and to use their powers in service to the People. The Shields drew upon the old memories of the rebellion against the Makers in their instigation of the Purging.

- MANDRA. She-Kyn maidservant of Neranda Ak'Shaar.
- MEDALLA. Spider Clan she-Tetawa of Spindletop and cousin of Quill Meadowgood.
- MEDICINALS. The herbs, roots, plants, bones, insect stingers, animal glands, and diverse other pharmacopoeia used by the Folk for healing.
- MEERDA. A Moth Clan she-Tetawa of Spindletop; mother of Bird and Chaada.
- THE MELDING. The catastrophic union of the Eld Green and the mortal world of Humanity a thousand years past.
- MERRIMYN HURLBUCK. Young Human Binder and fugitive from Eromar City.
- MIM. Shy daughter of the Oak-Folk Wielder, Grugg.
- MOLLI ROSE. Tetawa Clanmother, Spirit-talker, and leader of the confederated Tetawi settlements of the Everland.
- MOTHER MALLUK. The great Boar spirit of Tetawi teachings.
- MOUNDHOUSE. Stout Tetawi cabin with sharp eaves, cedar-tiled arched roof, interior and exterior carved support posts, and deep-set hearth. Moundhouses generally surround a ceremonial mound at the center of the settlement.
- MYRKASH THE UNBROKEN. The great elk chieftain of the Everland beast-tribes.

N

- NAMSHÉKÉ. "Storm-in-Her-Eyes." The youngling name of Tarsa'deshae.
- NERANDA AK'SHAAR. "Violet Eyes, Daughter of the House of Shaar." Celestial she-Kyn of Pine Branch. Legislator and Shield.
- NINE OAKS TOWN. A Stoneskin-ravaged Kyn town in the southern Everland.
- NOT-RAVEN. A malevolent ghost and flesh-eating spy of the Human world.

O

- OAK-FOLK. A small and furtive people of the Everland. They are spirit-bonded to ancient trees and spend their lives tending their home groves. Though shy, Oak-Folk can be fierce opponents when treated with disrespect.
- THE OATH OF WESTERN SANCTUARY. The name given by Lojar Vald to the writ of expulsion presented to the Everland Folk.

- ODA'HEA. She-Kyn leader of the Red Cedar Town Redthorns.
- THE OLD IMMORTALS (OF MEN). The gods of Humanity who were overthrown by the Dreyd during the catastrophic Melding. Though displaced, it is rumoured that the Old Immortals did not die and have long plotted their return to ascendancy.
- THE ONE MOON PATH. A euphemism for the Celestial Path, which holds a single moon as the supreme representation of Luran's remote beauty and purity.
- THE OLD WAYS. The teachings and traditions of the Eld Green that predominated among the Kyn before the rise of the Shields.

P

- PEACE-CITY. A site of sanctuary, where violence and physical conflict are forbidden, and where all given refuge. The Kyn capital of Sheynadwiin is the oldest peace-city in the Everland.
- PEARL-IN-DARKNESS. The Greatmoon of the Everland. He is sole survivor of a trio of celestial night-spirits of the Eld Green; his brothers were shattered in the Melding, but their broken bodies remain in the form of a sparkling silver ring that surrounds the world in both night and day. Pearl-in-Darkness emerges from his grief to show his face to the Everland every thirty days; for most of that time, he is in various stages of mourning for his lost brothers.
- PEREDIR. The mortal world of Men before the Melding.
- PERWIT. He-Tetawa captain of the Spindletop militia.
- POX. A blistering, feverish illness that originated in Human lands and has caused successive waves of death among the Folk, especially the Kyn. Death from the pox is slow and excruciating.
- PRADU STYKE. He-Kyn Celestial captain and opportunist.
- PUCKERLIPS. Apple-headed doll belonging to Quill Meadowgood.
- THE PURGING. The decimation of the Wielders by fear-maddened Kyn during the last great pox epidemic. Up to two-thirds of Wielders were killed during the three-year campaign of terror, during which time the Shields rose to power.

Q

- QUALLA'AM KAER. The fifth and current Human Reachwarden.
- QUILL MEADOWGOOD. Tetawa of Spider Clan. Dolltender and wyr-worker.

R

- RAMYD THALSSON. Human merchant and father of Garyn Mendiir.
- THE REACH (OF MEN). Also known as the Reach Republic. The primary political and economic power in the Melded world, dominated by Humans and their ambitions.
- REACH-TONGUE. The common Mannish tongue in the Reach.
- REACHWARDEN. The elected leader of the Reach Republic, chosen for a five year term by a majority of parliamentary representatives.
- REAVER. The highest rank among the Dreydcaste. Reavers use alchaemical formulae and crafting to control the spirits captured by Binders.
- THE REALIGNMENT. According to Celestial doctrine, the final cleansing of the Melded world of all corruption and impurity. Only rigid adherence to the ways of the Celestial Path will provide safety during this tumultuous future event.
- RED CEDAR TOWN. A Kyn town in the southern Everland; home to Tarsa'deshae.
- REDTHORN WARRIOR. Greenwalking warriors dedicated to the Old Ways and the vigorous defense of the Folk.
- RYN. A Tetawa scout in the employ of Sylas Gwydd.
- RYGGIN. A Wielder of the Fox-Folk Ferals.

S

- SATHI'IN. Cedar Branch she-Kyn of Red Cedar Town and aunt of Tarsa'deshae.
- SEEKER. The lower rank of the Dreydcaste. Seekers wander through the Reach in search of Folk Wielders and Human witches, whom they bring to Dreydholds for the use of Binders and Reavers.
- SENSORY STALKS. Fleshy head-tendrils that give the Kyn a deeper sensitivity to the elemental and emotional world around them. He-Kyn have one on each temple; she-Kyn have two on each side; zhe-Kyn generally have three, with two on one side, one on the other.
- SETHARIAN KILLS-TWO-MEN. Oak Branch he-Kyn of Red Cedar Town; father of Tarsa'deshae.
- SETTLEMENTS. Tetawi community sites.
- THE SEVENFOLD COUNCIL. A political assembly of Folk leaders, called only at times of great importance to all the Folk.

- THE SEVEN SISTER NATIONS. The Kyn, Tetawi, Gvaergs, Ubbetuk, Wyrnach, Ferals, and beast-tribes, representing most of the Everland Folk.
- SHEYNADWIIN. The ancient peace-city and capital of the Kyn Nation, nestled at the heart of Dardath Vale among the Kraagen Mountains.
- SHIELD. The spiritual, political, and economic leaders of the Celestial Path.
- SHOBBOK. The Winter Witch; a spirit-being of the Eld Green.
- SINOVIAN. He-Kyn Redthorn warrior and resistance fighter; brother of Jitani Al'Daar.
- THE SISTER SUNS. The two celestial spirits of the daytime: Goldmantle, the bronze elder sister, is calmer and larger than Bright-Eyes, who burns white-hot with the fires of youth.
- SKEEGER. Cannibalistic Tetawi changeling.
- SMUDGE. Ill-tempered mule deer mount of Tobhi Burrows.
- SNAKE-HEAD. An insulting term used to refer to the Kyn. It refers to their thick, vaguely serpentine sensory stalks.
- SPINDLETOP. A small Tetawi settlement in the Terrapin Hills of the southern Everland.
- SPIRIT-WEAVER. Human term for Wielders.
- THE SPIRIT WORLD. The hidden realm of elemental beings, the dead, and spirits of the Green world.
- STONESKIN. A fierce carnivorous creature with an unquenchable appetite. Named for the layer of protective stones embedded in its flesh.
- STORMBRINGER. The preferred Ubbetuk term for their airships, named for the storms that surround each airship when in flight.
- STORMDRAKE. A massive winged and lightning-spitting serpent that inhabits the upper sky.
- STORY LEAVES. See LORE-LEAVES.
- STRANGELING. A descendant of a he-Kyn/female Human union. If born into a Branch, the descendant is understood as a Kyn; if born out of a Branch (thus, if the youngling's father is non-Kyn), the descendant is generally defined as a Strangeling. The Jaagas are a distinct people born of Strangeling unions and now known by their own name for themselves.
- STRIVIX. "The Unseen." The great and fearsome Owl of Tetawi teachings.
- THE SWARM. The collective Ubbetuk Nation.
- SYLAS GWYDD. A respected Human trader who lives in Sheynadwiin.

T

- TANGLETOP FOREST. A dense wood at the southeastern edge of the Everland.
- TARSA'DESHAE. "The Spear, She Breaks It," or "She-Breaks-the-Spear." She-Kyn of Cedar Branch. Redthorn Warrior and Wielder. Niece of Unahi.
- THE TERRAPIN HILLS. The rocky hill country around Spindletop at the eastern rim of the Edgewood.
- THE TETAWI NATION. One of the Seven Sister nations, the Tetawi are an honest and forthright people, short and brown-skinned. Their social and political lives are centered in their matrilineal Clans, each of which is descended from a spirit animal of the Eld Green. They make their homes in squat moundhouses, generally in rough hill country or in forested areas. Their connection to the *wyr* is through empathy with the beast-folk; due to this, Tetawi are the greatest healers amongst the Folk.
- THISTLEWOOD. A small pine forest in the southeastern Everland.
- THORNHOLT. The second-largest Kyn city in the Everland, located in the southern Eldarvian Woods.
- THRESHOLD. A pocket of the Eld Green that survived the Melding. The Everland is the largest 'Hold in the Reach.
- TOBHI (ETOBHI) BURROWS. Tetawa of Badger Clan. Leafspeaker, scribe, and lore-keeper.
- TOWNS. Kyn community sites.
- TRADE-TONGUE. The shared economic and political language of the Folk.
- TREE-BORN. See KYN NATION.
- TRUMP-THE-PEG. A strategy game popular among Humans, played with multi coloured pegs on a long wooden board.
- TSIJEHU. An ancient cedar tree that once stood in the center of Red Cedar Town.

U

- THE UBBETUK NATION: Of all the Seven Sister nations, the Ubbetuk are the most estranged from the *wyr* and most comfortable among Humans, and one of the few Folk who can withstand the poison of iron. Small and hairless, with huge eyes and wide, sharp-toothed mouths, their appearance belies their soft-spoken gentility and sophistication. Led by Blackwick, the Chancellor of the Swarm, the Ubbetuk are renowned (and feared) as the most technologically accomplished and politically adept among the Folk. They inhabit hidden cloud cities far from the prying eyes of Humans and other Folk, though they are actively engaged in trade across the Reach through their fleet of Stormbringer airships.

- UNAHI SAM'SHEYDA. Cedar Branch elder she-Kyn Wielder of Thistlewood. Aunt of Tarsa'deshae.
- UNHUMANS. The pejorative term used by Humans for the Folk.
- THE UPPER PLACE. One of the three primary worlds of existence in the Eld Green and, to a lesser extent, the Melded world. It is a realm of order and light, though not necessarily good.
- URU THREE-CLAW. A Wielder of the bear-faced Ferals of the Kraagen Mountains.

V

- VANSAAYA. Cedar Branch she-Kyn of Red Cedar Town and eldest aunt of Tarsa'deshae.
- THE VEIL. See THE CANOPY VEIL.
- VERGIS THANE. Unassuming one-eyed Seeker of the Dreydcaste.
- VICTORY PEAK. A mountain considered sacred by the Tetawi of Birchbark Hollow; home to Molli Rose.

W

- THE WAY OF DEEP GREEN. See DEEP GREEN.
- WEARS-STONES-FOR-SKIN. Stoneskin that ravaged the Kyn towns of Downbriar, High Marching, and Nine Oaks.
- WHITECAPS. Members of the Ruling Council of the Ubbetuk Swarm.
- WIELDER. Greenwalkers and wyr-workers of the Kyn.
- THE WIELDERS' CIRCLE. The Grand Council of Folk wyr-workers in Sheynadwiin.
- THE WILDWATER. Large, raging river that flows through the Kraagen Mountains.
- WILD ONE. A pejorative Celestial term for a Greenwalker.
- WITCHERY. The use of *wyr* or other skills toward selfish and generally destructive aims.
- THE WYR. The life source of the Everland, formed from the living voices and

embodied memories of the ancestors, the spirits of the Eld Green, and the life-spark of the Folk themselves. It is the elemental life-song of creation, drawing on and giving sustenance to all remnants of the Eld Green, strengthened by attentive care and weakened by neglect. Its embodied manifestation is the Eternity Tree.

- WYRM. See GREATWYRM.
- WYRNACH. The eldest of the Seven Sister Nations, the Wyrnach are also known as the "Spider-Folk" for their eight limbs and multiple eyes. They are a rare and reclusive people, standing well over eight feet high, and are well known among the Folk for their wyr-fed powers of divination.
- WYRWOOD. A type of tree that grows only in 'Holds, the wyrwood is a vital resource to the Folk. Its leaves and naturally-shed outer bark, when stripped and pounded into flexible fibres, can be used for durable wyrweave fabric, clothing, and armour; its red roots and fallen branches can be shaped by Wielders into both armour and weapons, as can its rarely-accessed heartwood; and its golden sap is both nourishing and medicinal. The tree roots of living wyrwood draw poisons out of the surrounding soil, thus purifying both earth and water. Its lofty canopy provides housing for many Folk, as do the massive trunks of the more ancient trees. In many ways, the wyrwood tree provides the daily link between the Folk and the wyr-currents of their homeland.
- WYR-WARD. A device of Human Crafting that addles the mind and blocks the access of Wielders to the *wyr*, thus leaving them vulnerable and confused.
- WYR-WORKER. Those Folk gifted with the strength and talent to draw upon and guide the *wyr* toward particular aims or goals.
- WYRWEAVE. Fabric made of the inner fibres of the wyrwood tree.

Z

- ZHAIA. Tree-Mother. The ancient spirit of the green world from whom the seven Kyn Branches are descended.
- ZHE-KYN. A third gender among the Kyn that shares some of the qualities of both the she-Kyn and he-Kyn. Zhe-Kyn are border crossers, and they often excel at healing, which requires sensitivity to the different challenges of these often distinct social worlds. See BETWEEN-WORLDERS.

WYRWOOD

The Way of Thorn & Thunder

Book Two

The Sevenfold Council stands firm against Dreydmaster Vald's treaty terms—they will not surrender the Everland. Their will is strong, but there is a traitor in their midst, and Vald intends to win this struggle...by any means necessary.

The young Redthorn Wielder, Tarsa'deshae, and the Tetawa Leafspeaker, Tobhi Burrows, have gone to Eromar City, the center of Vald's influence, in hopes of rescuing the diplomats who have long languished in the shadows of Gorthac Hall. But only one remains alive, and he knows all too well the price for fighting the Dreydmaster's will. It will take all their strength, courage, and good fortune to escape with their lives.

Whether they have a home to return to is another matter entirely....

CHAPTER 1

Another burst of jagged white sky-fire exploded in the air,
followed within the space of a breath by a blast of thunder so loud
that it rocked the Stormbringer. The freezing rain smashed against
them with blistering force, and nothing seemed to keep its chill from
clawing into their muscles and bones. The galleon twisted around in
the air again as another spear of lightning flashed across the deck to
fill the air with a bitter, metallic tang.

Tarsa was bent nearly double, holding her head between her
knees,
trying to find a wyr-fed place of calm from the terror and motion
sickness that pounded her mind. She and Tobhi were firmly tethered
to a stout oaken mast; they wouldn't be lost overboard in the
upheaval of the storm, but the constant spinning and slamming of
the ship had bruised them badly, and the constant drenching of cold
rain did nothing to help their discomfort.

She'd long since given up any attempt at maintaining her poise;
she simply sat curled in a tight ball in the failing hope that this
nightmare would finally come to an end. The iron-ward had kept
the poisoning at bay but not the sickness, and the Wielder had
vomited more than she could imagine had ever been in her stomach.
She, Tobhi, and the other diplomats had earlier tried to enter the
Stormbringer's inner hold, but the intensity of being surrounded by
so much of the toxic metal was too much for their protective
talismans, so all the non-Ubbetuk aboard found makeshift seats on
the upper deck, where the open air gave some small bit of relief.

Tarsa almost regretted that decision now, for her thoughts were
jumbled and tangled with dizziness and fear. Her senses had gone

wild when the galleon entered the perpetual black storm that lay on the northwestern edge of the Everland. It was past these brutal clouds, where lightning and thunder ruled supreme, that the lands of the Folk ended and the world of Men began. This was an elemental borderland unlike any other in the Melded world, and Tarsa's growing awareness of the *wyr* seemed to make her more vulnerable to the flood of sensations and atmospheric phenomena than the others.

For his part, though drenched by icy rain, bruised by the chaotic movement of the airship, and more than a little sick himself, Tobhi found the journey fascinating, though not very pleasant. While not much of an inventor himself, Tobhi had always liked strange and unusual things—he was a lore-keeper, after all, with a particular love of weird tales—and this was by far one of the most unusual experiences of his life. The rumors of Ubbetuk airships were creative, but they fell far short of the brutal, visceral reality of sky-fire, ice, and wind. He spent most of his time watching the bulging gas-sacks and whirring machinery on deck, or catching occasional glimpses through the lightning and darkness of the silver-skinned storm drakes who flashed past the ship, their massive fanged mouths open in roars of defiance against the puny land-walkers who dared take to the skies in their iron-wrapped abomination. This world was so unlike the heavy earthiness of the great forests below, and though his heart lurched from time to time as the galleon jolted away from another arc of lightning, Tobhi felt as much exhilaration as fear.

They'd left Sheynadwiin in the early afternoon and traveled through the night before reaching the storm. Now, hours later, the wind grew louder, more intense, becoming a desperate wail of anguish and grief. This time Tobhi and Tarsa both bowed their heads and clung tightly to one another as the burn of rain on flesh cut into them mercilessly. They couldn't breathe, could barely think, as the air itself seemed to push down against them, forcing them against the deck, smashing their bodies into the wood, the breath from their lungs, the very heat from their bodies, with unrelenting fury. Their hands squeezed tighter, and this connection was soon the only reality either could focus on. The wind and rain and ice and thunder and suffocating pressure grew fiercer, more brutal, and still they held tightly to one another, groaning in pain and defiance.

And then, without warning, it was over. As though a door slammed shut behind them, the Stormbringer slipped from the rain-choked darkness of the storm and into bright sunlight. The air at this frigid height was little warmer now than it had been before, but the thin light of a single sun and blue sky were welcome to those who had been buffeted around for hours in the stinging rain. Some of the Ubbetuk whispered amongst themselves about the surprising violence of the storm on this particular journey; it was almost as if the dark clouds had been targeting the galleon for their full force of rage and anger. Yet now, as the wall of roiling gloom receded in the distance, it became a shadowed memory in the brilliant light of a new day. All on the deck lifted their squinting eyes to the sky, and more than a few shed grateful tears.

But Tarsa was not among them. Her face was hollow with something more than pain.

"What is it?" Tobhi asked, wiping his eyes with the back of his hand, as the she-Kyn unwrapped her sensory stalks and pulled her hair away to let them move, unhindered, in the sunlight.

Her voice was ragged. "I didn't know this would happen. It's worse than I could have imagined."

"What are ye talkin' 'bout?" His eyes were fixed on the sensory stalks. They nearly always danced and curled with a rhythm all their own, as though each had a heartbeat of its own. But now they all hung limply down the sides of Tarsa's head.

"The *wyr*, Tobhi. It's almost unreachable here...I can barely feel it. What are we going to do? I can't be a Wielder without the *wyr*."

✤✤✤✤✤✤

The Way of Thorn & Thunder continues.
Look for Book Two *WYRWOOD* from Kegedonce Press.

Daniel Heath Justice is an enrolled citizen of the Cherokee Nation, and was raised on the eastern edge of the Rocky Mountains in that part of the Mouache Ute territory now known as Victor, Colorado. Daniel has recently received his permanent Canadian resident status and teaches Indigenous North American literatures and Aboriginal studies at the University of Toronto. *Kynship* is the first volume of the Way of Thorn and Thunder trilogy, all volumes to be published by Kegedonce Press. He is also the author of *Our Fire Survives the Storm: A Cherokee Literary History*, forthcoming from University of Minnesota Press in December 2005.